APPEARANCES

T. H. FOREST

Other books by T.H. Forest

Adult
Twinkies & Beefcake

Young Adult
Kelly's Folly

For my cousin Tom Holdorf,
who nearly thirty years ago worried
I would think his photo project was
pornographic (it wasn't btw).

I miss you every day.

CONTENTS

PART TWO

ENDURANCE

PART THREE

EVENTING

PART ONE

STEEPLECHASE

———

1

———

Awakenings

2014

MATT LOOKED FOR HIS NAME among the placards held by chauffeurs as he left the baggage claim at Heathrow, and strode toward the man holding the 'M. Dion' sign.

"Welcome to London, sir."

Matt followed him to the black Range Rover, his eyes scanning the crowd out of habit, and took his navy Brioni suit coat off before getting into the backseat. He turned his attention to his laptop, taking two phone calls in between reading contracts as they made their way to Oxford. As CEO of the company he founded, Matt's days were long and busy and he was determined to finish what he couldn't on the plane, so he could focus on enjoying the weekend with his closest friend.

It was a rainy June day, but as the car sped northwest the sun began to fight its way through the clouds, and Matt felt his spirits lift. He ran his hand distractedly through his short, wavy black hair, thinking he needed a haircut, as he looked out the window. He read the highway signs and texted Finn that he was close, smiling at her celebration emojis.

The driver opened Matt's door and he stood, putting on his coat and gathering up his folio case as he saw Finn appear in the street-level door of her flat.

"Chuckleberry Finn!" Matt beamed, using the nickname he gave her when she was in middle school. He hugged her tightly, kissing her as they pulled apart. He scanned his eyes over her and smiled at her magnetic beauty, feeling as drawn to her as he had all those years ago.

Matt turned to the driver who was eyeing Finn appreciatively and shook his hand, pressing a generous tip into his palm. "I'll see you Sunday."

"Thank you, sir, enjoy the weekend."

"I'm so happy you finally made it." Finn smiled and led him into her flat. "How was the flight?"

"Fine. Got a lot done. Thanks for the ticket, but I can afford my own first-class now." He winked.

"I know. But I made you come, and I'm so glad you did."

Matt looked at her from the side of his eye. "So, Chuck, show me around your new flat." Matt put his arm around her. "I like the look of it already, pretty street," he added as he followed her down a short, narrow hallway, wheeling his suitcase beside him. He lifted it up the two steps into the room and scanned the large, open space, seeing a bedroom and bathroom to the right, and the door to Finn's suite to the left of the modest kitchen. He put his things in the guest room and praised her flat.

"I thought we could meet some friends of mine for dinner at the pub up the street. I really want you to meet Ollie, the guy I've been telling you about," Finn said with a smile she was trying hard to keep in check.

Matt looked at her with a sigh. "I've been here five minutes." He shook his head. "What is this new pet passion of yours, playing matchmaker?"

Finn tilted her head. "I'm telling you, he's spectacular, you're really gonna like him. You're out of the Navy now, can't you relax a bit?" she said gently and looked around. "You're so regimented, and frankly, angry sometimes. I can't help but think it's because of what you deny yourself. What you deny *about* yourself." She shrugged. "I love you. I just want to see you happy. You know that."

"Jesus, Chuck, you getting your PhD in ancient Mesopotamia or fucking psychology?"

Matt shook his head and opened the fridge distractedly. He closed the door without taking anything and went past Finn to the guest room to change into his running gear, keeping his mind blank. He strode back into the living room while strapping his phone onto his arm and studiously ignored Finn's penetrating gaze.

Finn shook her head with a sigh, scanning his long muscular legs. "I'm sure you remember the route along the river, just go to the end of the road toward the universities, past my old flat, and you'll eventually come to it beyond the parks. Don't be long though, I told people we would be there at six."

He kissed her cheek and took the key she gave him, tucking it into his sock.

Matt found his way to the river, looking at the sights and dodging around pedestrians on the sidewalks. He followed the familiar path along the water, eyeing whichever college of Oxford was on one side, and the greens on the other. He thought about work, and the companies he planned to contact while he was there, and he thought about Finn, and the nonsense she had planned.

They'd known each other since the day his little sister, Lisa, brought her home after school, when he was fourteen and she was eleven. He grinned with the memory of how she stared at him, wide-eyed and giggly, when he walked into the kitchen from swim practice. He had worried that he had something on his face or that his damp hair was sticking up, such was her reaction to the sight of him, but quickly realized that she was just that way, particularly around him.

Thus her nickname was born, and Matt found himself gravitating toward her when she was over, and she was over *all the time*. She was a magnet, even then, and he wasn't the only one she pulled into her orbit. The older she got, as she matured from a pretty little girl into a stunning, intelligent woman, more and more people fell under her spell.

Finn was precious, and Matt was fiercely protective of her. He'd taken it upon himself to make sure that not one unworthy man got close. He chased countless scores of them away from her (many of whom she never knew he scared away), but unavoidably there were a few who slipped past his guard. Those guys he would study for flaws (or manufacture them), and then casually pointed them out to her ('Chad-the-gonad likes to touch himself when he thinks he says something profound;' 'Rick-the-dick laughs at his own jokes;' 'Chasten's real name is Jason, and I'm pretty sure I saw him in a dress downtown'). He knew once he said something, she would be helpless against seeing it for herself.

He loved her and trusted her with his innermost secret-self. Her pedestal was sky-high and he guarded it carefully, whether she appreciated it or not.

Matt turned his thoughts to the evening ahead and felt a percolating in his stomach, not unlike the feeling he had on his first mission as an officer in the Navy SEALs. Finn had wanted to send him pictures of this *Ollie* person, but Matt was adamant; he didn't want to see him, much less meet him. He wished he could get out of the evening all together and thought about making up a work excuse. He crossed the river to reverse direction back to Finn's flat with that dream on his tongue, but knew she'd never believe him.

Matt owed so much to Finn: her championing of his ideas for his company, her financial backing of the venture, and his condo in the North End of Boston that she helped him buy, made him all but beholden to her. So, one dinner out with a guy he could *easily* ignore was the least he could do. He'd been ignoring men for years; he wasn't going to stop now. No way the guy could turn his head. He'd have to be straight to do that because he didn't find overtly gay men appealing, in fact, they made him uncomfortable. He had tried to tell Finn that, but she insisted.

"Matt, Ollie is not like that, I promise. He's just a gorgeous, wonderful man, and very private about his sexuality," Finn said.

"Chuck, I'm straight, really. I have been my whole life. I have a girlfriend. I shouldn't have said anything to you. That was just high school me, being confused," Matt said stiffly, uttering the words like a mantra.

"Just come visit me anyway. We'll have dinner as a group, I won't say a word to him, and if you don't like him, forget I said anything. But please come. I miss you," she begged.

Matt showered when he got back to Finn's flat, and changed into jeans that were just shy of tight and a white button-down shirt open at the collar. He ran his hands through his hair a few times, leaving it stylishly messy, and slipped on his Italian leather shoes. He fought the urge to pace as he waited for Finn in the living room. She finally appeared, wearing skinny jeans, a cropped sweater and sparkly chandelier earrings.

Finn swept her eyes over Matt. "Fuck, you look hot," she declared and led Matt out the door with excited chatter.

They made it to the pub just before six. Matt scanned the restaurant (and corners) as Finn waved to three people seated at a table near the back. He followed her as she weaved her way to them, eyes in the restaurant tracking them both.

Matt checked out the guy they were walking toward and inwardly cringed. He had a mop of curly hair and ears that stuck out ever so slightly. He was wearing some sort of sports team jersey and had pale, plump arms that were covered in dark hair. Matt stopped next to Finn and kept his face carefully blank as the two women and the sports fan looked up at him.

"Hey, everyone!" Finn exclaimed. "This is Matt. Matt, this is Sophie, James, and Vicki."

Matt exhaled with relief that James wasn't the fabled Ollie, and shook hands with everyone before taking a seat next to Finn.

"God, you two make a beautiful couple," Sophie praised with a smile.

"Thank you, Sophie. But we're not a couple," Matt replied flirtatiously, wondering how close she and Finn were in case he needed a hook up to get out of the evening.

Finn squeezed his leg, distracting him from his 'Plan B.' "Don't try to make me jealous." She looked back at the empty chair next to Vicki. "Where's Ollie?"

James rolled his eyes. "That boy is never on time. Probably obsessing over his hair or something."

Matt looked around the table as everyone laughed and felt a new surge of worry that Finn was trying to set him up with a femboy, and not just that, but one who violated his primary rule: punctuality. He frowned lightly at Finn's profile, and suddenly wanted to be anywhere but there. *Even Afghanistan was sounding pretty good.*

The server took food and drink orders, looking down at Matt expectantly as he was lost in thought. "I'll have a martini, dry," Matt said, hoping to calm his sudden nerves.

"There he is," Vicki announced twenty minutes later, as a tall man entered the pub, turning heads.

The first thing Matt noticed, as Ollie smiled broadly and crossed the room, was how his golden hair shimmered with streaks of white and dark honey. He wore it long on top and short on the sides and looked as though he took quite a bit of time making it perfect, just as everyone had teased. The second thing he noticed was Ollie's firm body and how his clothing skimmed his muscular frame in a way that somehow left nothing to the imagination, or rather, Matt couldn't help but imagine the bare skin beneath. His stomach did a small flip, and he swallowed reflexively, sitting back in his chair as though he were pushed, something inexplicably tight in his chest.

Matt stood (of course he stood, it felt as though an electrical current had jolted him from his chair) and met eyes the color of the Mediterranean Sea. He watched as Finn kissed the most perfectly balanced mouth he'd ever seen, and supposed it felt as amazing as it looked.

"Ollie, this is my friend Matt, from Boston. Matt, this is Ollie," Finn said with a smile, bringing Matt back into the moment.

Matt shook Ollie's hand, feeling a tiny zip at the contact. He smiled his practiced smile that was seasoned with denial.

"Nice to meet you, Ollie. Is that short for Oliver?" Matt asked casually, grasping for something to say.

"It's not short for Jonathan. Nice to meet you," Ollie replied with a friendly grin, his voice deep and pleasant with the crisp accent of a Duke.

Ollie held Matt's eye briefly before taking a seat opposite him, next to Vicki. He ordered a pint, and didn't apologize for being late. Matt watched as Ollie turned immediately into some conversation about sports with James, and felt dismissed. He knew it wasn't a 'set-up' but that Ollie had taken no interest in him at all hit Matt unexpectedly hard.

Matt took a large swallow of his gin and tuned out the conversation as he looked around the pub. He felt Ollie's eyes on him, and fought the urge to meet his gaze, confused with the attention. He felt out of sorts all of a sudden and looked at Sophie with her white blonde hair and dark roots. She had a neediness about her that Matt would've normally pounced on.

Matt smiled, needing a distracting conversation to tune out Ollie's unexpected magnetism. "You study history too?"

Sophie's pretty face lit up from the attention. "No, communications and media studies. My father thinks I watch programs and study celebrities all day." She chuckled appealingly. "He's not wrong."

Matt laughed, and caught Ollie's head turn from the corner of his eye. "Sounds like a class a friend of mine used to teach at Boston University. Something about pop culture, I can't remember the title, but their homework was watching reality TV. Personally, I'd rather stab my eyes out."

"God, I love that shite!" Sophie exclaimed with a laugh. "I think there is some truly fascinating psychological study in that. I mean, what kind of person opens their lives to the camera and the world?"

Matt nodded his head in agreement. "Yeah, I've only one person who knows anything about me, and she's sitting right here." He gestured to Finn. "Any more than that, no thanks." He looked across the table at Ollie who was laughing with James but half-listening to them.

"I could never, either," Ollie interjected. "Not just because I agree with you about privacy, but also those bloody contracts they make you sign, positively exploitative and wholly without rights for the individual."

"Oh, I don't know," James chimed in. "Aren't we all on display for the world?" He swept his hand toward the security cameras behind the bar and on the door. "Has anyone asked our permission to be filmed? There are cameras everywhere. That footage can end up in the hands of the police, or on social media, and you might never know that people all around the world are laughing at you tripping on the way to the loo."

Ollie tilted his head back and laughed. Matt eyes flew to Ollie's strong and defined throat and took a breath at the sight of it, smooth and muscular with a gorgeously defined Adam's Apple. He wondered what it would feel like under his tongue.

Ollie looked at James. "That was hilarious! And it should've ended up on the internet." His eyes sparkled mischievously at Matt. "James was completely pissed and tripped his way to the bathroom. It was like watching a drunken ballet. If I hadn't been laughing so hard, I would've gotten my phone out and filmed it for posterity."

"Yeah, yeah, have a laugh." James shook his head. "I remember a certain someone tumbling down a hill and nearly into the river."

Ollie raised his eyebrows with a smile. "Didn't spill a drop of my pint though." He winked at Matt. Matt's breath hitched in response, feeling as though he were the only person in the room with Ollie and that smile. Matt forced his eyes away and waved at the waiter for another round before excusing himself.

The bathroom was well-lit and Matt blinked to adjust from the contrast of the dim pub, and then blinked again as he looked at himself in the mirror. He saw what he always saw, a face like his dad's with olive skin, straight nose, angry brow, hollow cheeks, and blue eyes that hid so much. He turned from the sinks with a stiffness that was second nature and walked to the end urinal, unzipping his fly as the bathroom door opened. Ollie appeared, nonchalant and gorgeous.

The sound of the pub disappeared as the door shut, and Matt was suddenly aware of how alone they were, and the intimacy of the moment. Ollie stopped at the at the only other urinal and looked at Matt with a smile.

"No cameras in here," he said in his smooth voice, his accent like a caress around Matt's ear.

Matt chuckled politely as Ollie turned his focus away and unzipped his pants. *Don't look, don't look,* he thought (futilely) as he couldn't help himself to some side eye. *Oh, Jesus,* he breathed, and wasn't sure if he said it, or if Ollie had, or if it had just been an unspoken thought bubble, but when he looked up, he met Ollie's eyes, and they were… well, appreciative. Matt stopped, suddenly short of breath, and zipped up, giving Ollie a wide berth on his way to the sinks and then fled the bathroom, his shoulders stiff.

Matt kept his eyes on Finn when Ollie rejoined the table a moment later, focusing instead on whatever it was she was saying. If Ollie felt awkward, he hid it well. James continued with his list of all the reasons why Liverpool was the best team in the League, which, based on Ollie's vehement contradictions (and the glint in James' eye), was designed solely to rile Ollie up.

"That is such shite! United is the better team and you fucking know it." Ollie shook his head.

"Right. Who won in March?" James pursed his lips and tilted his head. "Shut out no less."

"Ahhkkh," Ollie scoffed. "You wankers got lucky. We'll get you in December, I promise."

"Care to put some money on it?" James raised his eyebrows.

Matt held his breath. There was another rule of his hanging in the balance.

"If I were a gambling man I would, but all you'll get from me is my certainty." Ollie finished his pint with a smile.

Matt exhaled and hid his pleased grin in his drink. *What are you so pleased about, Lieutenant? It's not like you can have him,* he chastised himself and looked away from Ollie's shining face.

He stared down into his beer, watching the last of the foam bubbles disappearing from the surface as he pondered the evening, and Ollie specifically. Would his stomach be flipping in the way that it was every time he looked at him, would his breath be stolen with every laugh from Ollie's throat, if Finn hadn't told him Ollie was gay? If she'd never planted the seed? Would he be obsessing over every detail of Ollie (his perfect hair, the hollow of his throat behind his silver necklace, that beautiful part of him he glimpsed in the bathroom) if hadn't known?

Matt glanced at Finn, watching her profile as she smiled at something Vicki was saying, and wondered why he let her bring him here. He felt a flash of anger (and an awakening of something deeply buried) and took a long swallow of beer. He was short of breath, and sharply anxious, and his emotions were on an unwelcome rollercoaster.

Get a hold of yourself, Lieutenant, he thought with a clench of his jaw and his fist.

Matt looked at his Submariner Rolex and saw that it was past ten. He signaled for the check and gave the server cash, eager to end the evening, worried he couldn't keep his eyes off Ollie any longer. He needed to strengthen his protective wall, and definitely stop drinking.

"Whoa, thank you, Matt!" Sophie said with an appreciative smile and put her hand on his arm, as everyone else chimed in their thanks, putting away their wallets.

"Yeah, thanks, Matt." Ollie smiled and ran his hand through his hair, the underside of his muscular bicep flexing under the tight sleeve of his cashmere sweater.

Matt watched, mesmerized, before tearing his eyes away and standing abruptly. It was an innocent gesture that felt so scandalous to witness. He was suddenly overcome with the urge to feel Ollie's hair between his own fingers (he bet it was as soft as silk) and felt another flash of anger at himself for it. He pulled out Finn's chair, desperate for a distraction, a task.

Ollie watched him with open admiration, scanning his eyes up and down Matt's body, his gaze like a caress, and Matt felt another zip at the intimacy of it before turning away. The group followed him outside like a well-trained platoon, and stopped when he stopped, the sky dark around them. He hugged Sophie and Vicki chastely and shook James' hand before turning to Ollie with his hand extended.

"Nice to meet you."

Ollie's palm was warm and dry and transmitted a whole litany of promises and need.

"Really great to meet you too, Matt. I hope to see you again soon. You here all weekend?"

Matt nodded, holding Ollie's gaze. "Yeah, Chuck and I are just hanging around. I'm sure she'll drag me sightseeing somewhere," he added politely, his protective wall solid and his emotions in check.

"Great, see you around," Ollie replied somewhat breathlessly, his eyes on Matt's mouth.

"Bye, Ollie." Finn kissed him.

Matt followed Finn into her flat and locked the door behind them. Finn waited with her eyebrows raised expectantly as he came up the two steps. "Well?"

"Well, what?"

Finn punched his shoulder with a laugh. "Answer me."

"He's very handsome, and really funny. He looks so much like you, same hair color, same eyes, but just a bit more of a square jaw than your heart-shaped face." He squeezed her chin gently between his thumb and forefinger, and sighed. "But, Chuck. I'm not gonna do anything about it."

Finn frowned. "Why not? Ollie's amazing, and I could tell he was into you."

Matt shrugged. "I'm not gay. Night, babe." He kissed her and went to brush his teeth.

She was gone from the living room when he finished, and with a sigh of relief, he went into his bedroom. He leaned against the closed door and shut his eyes with an exhale, feeling the buzz of alcohol finally washing over him. He imagined he could still smell Ollie's heady scent, feel that strong, warm hand in his, feel the embrace of that accent that made every word sound *infinitely* more interesting.

There was something about Ollie, in the way there was something about Finn, but the difference was he had never been sexually attracted to Finn. The magnetism was intense, entirely new, and *not at all* welcome. Matt opened his eyes and looked down at the evidence of Ollie's effect on his body and groaned. He scowled, angry at himself, his lack of discipline, the cracks he felt forming in his wall. He undressed with frustration, folding his clothes over the back of the chair, and climbed between the sheets. He slipped his hand into his underwear, thinking of Ollie, but wishing he weren't.

* * *

Matt worked through the weekend, taking breaks every so often to let Finn drag him from place to place, showing him the sights. They bumped into Ollie and some of his football teammates late in the afternoon on Saturday, celebrating their win at another pub near the colleges and joined them for a couple of drinks.

Matt felt awkward about having fantasized about Ollie the night before, and yet couldn't take his eyes off him. Ollie's short-sleeved uniform shirt skimmed his trim frame, and his shorts, while baggy, stopped at mid-thigh, leaving everything else naked and exposed. His arms were golden, defined and firm, and his bare legs were solid muscle and still pale from the lack of warm sunny days. Matt felt his mouth go dry at the thought of running his hands over those legs, laying *between* those legs.

Matt turned away with a silent curse and took a long sip of his beer, fighting the emotion, fighting the urge, and looked at Finn, flirting lightly with one of the players. He loved her but, in that moment, he was furious with her.

Why'd you do this to me? Why did I let you?

Matt smelled Ollie's heady, sweaty scent a moment before he appeared at his elbow, and took a deep breath through his nose as he turned to look at him.

"Hey, Matt. Glad we bumped into you." Ollie clinked his glass to Matt's, his accent curling around Matt's name like a hug. "How's your day been? Finn take you to any of her dusty, musty libraries?" he teased.

Matt smiled tightly. "No, but not for want of trying," he replied, his eyes looking anywhere but at Ollie's naked limbs. "You haunt libraries too?"

"I do." Ollie grinned. "But not quite so ancient as the ones Finn prefers."

Matt made a small sound, and swept his eyes over Ollie's body, before catching himself with slight panic and scrambled for an excuse as he looked around and away. "Is James on your team?"

"No, he doesn't play." Ollie rolled his eyes. "He's the worst kind of fan, no real-world experience. That's why he likes Liverpool," Ollie added dramatically, as if that would mean something to Matt.

"You play for Oxford, or is it a club league?" Matt nodded at Ollie's white, number 7 jersey.

"I played for Oxford during undergrad, but now it's a club league, we play more in the summer than during school."

"You must really love the game," Matt said admiringly. "Congrats on the win today. You score any of those goals?"

"I did. Two, and an assist," he answered humbly.

Matt clinked his pint glass to Ollie's. "Well done."

Ollie quirked his eyebrow at the huskiness of Matt's voice. "Thanks," he answered in a low voice.

They stood in silence, something heavy suddenly hanging between them. Matt felt a little lightheaded and cleared his throat. He took another long swallow, finishing his beer with Ollie's eyes on him. Ollie licked his lips, his eyes locked on Matt's throat, the tantalizing tip of his pink tongue was visible for the briefest of moments. It was too obvious, too disconcerting, too arousing. If Ollie were a woman Matt would have reacted with a flirty smile and a touch of his fingertips on her arm, maybe her hip. Instead, he turned breathlessly, slamming his empty glass on the bar harder than he meant, and touched Finn's elbow.

"Come on, Chuck, we gotta run. I've got that . . . conference call." He barely trusted himself to look at Ollie again but forced himself to, keeping his face carefully blank. "Nice to see you again, Ollie."

Ollie took Matt's extended hand firmly in his and shook, lingering ever so slightly before releasing it. "Great to see you too, Matt," he replied with a disconcerted smile.

2

Slumbering Giant

MATT CALLED SAM when he got back to Boston the next day. "Let's have dinner. I'll pick you up at six."

"Okay," Sam said in a happy voice. "See you then."

Samantha, Matt's on-again, off-again girlfriend, was waiting on her front steps in a bright blue and white patterned wrap dress that hugged her athletic, small-breasted frame. Her long brown hair fell in a shining cascade down her back. She climbed into Matt's Audi S5 and kissed him as he leaned over expectantly.

"You look gorgeous, Sam. I got us a reservation at Josephine's."

"Great." She smiled. "You look amazing as usual, Matt."

She put her hand on his thigh as he pulled away from the curb and scanned her eyes appreciatively over his black pants, and lavender striped Brooks Brothers button-down shirt, open at the neck. Both, like all his dress clothes, were tailored to fit him like a glove.

Matt tuned out most of Sam's chatter during dinner, thinking about work, and more pervasively, Ollie. The more he thought about Ollie (his hair, his throat, his body) the more he wanted dinner to be done so he could bury himself in Sam and be free of the torment, the memory of his time in Ollie's company.

He looked around the dining room as Sam kept talking. He thought about their relationship, how he had toyed with the possibility of a life with her. She would be the ideal wife in many ways, particularly the ways that mattered. She never pried or asked probing questions, she was beautiful (the perfect arm candy for all the events he was expected to attend), and most importantly, she was eager to please without all the post-coital chatter that so many other women craved and required. He spent more time making sure she enjoyed herself as a reward for being quiet, and always made sure she came first. He had never made it a priority with any of the other women he slept with, though most did anyway, or he assumed they did from the noises they made. If a woman couldn't speak up for herself and demand an orgasm, choosing to fake one instead, that wasn't on him.

He looked at Sam, nodded at whatever she said, and took another bite of his food. He had ultimately broken it off with her after a few months (only calling her now to erase Ollie from his memory) because the one glaring thing he couldn't stomach, was her complete and utter, *boring* submissiveness. She was too passive, too quick to apologize, and had no sense of humor (not that he spent a lot of time laughing himself). The thought of spending the rest of his life with Sam had made him cringe when he *actually* considered it.

Now he looked at her and wondered if he could have his cake and eat it too. Sam would be far too timid to question him if he were bold enough to take Ollie as a secret lover. It would make her flaws tolerable if he could pull that off. The scandalous thought of it made him stir. He shifted in his seat and flagged the waiter for the check.

After dinner they went back to his sprawling condo in the North End. Sam pressed herself against him in the elevator, nearly six feet in her stilettos. He closed his eyes and kissed her, sweeping his tongue through her mouth as he cupped her bottom in his large hands, bringing her tight against his body. Sam moaned against his lips and wrapped her arms around his neck. He returned her kisses until the elevator slid open and then followed her to his door.

Once inside, she untied the bow of her wrap dress and peeled it off, letting it drop to the floor as she stepped out of her heels. Matt ran his eyes over her naked body before guiding her into the bedroom, kissing her as he undressed himself with her help. His hands roamed over her skin as he kissed her neck, and then her jaw, and then her small, soft mouth. He was horny, but not for her, and he tried to find his focus.

He slipped a finger between her legs, and while she was more than ready (slippery and sighing into his mouth as he stroked her) he was still barely at half-mast. She pushed his underwear down and took him in her small hand, her grip firm and familiar. He pressed on her shoulders lightly as he broke the kiss, encouraging her to take a seat on the bed and pressed his hips forward as he stepped out of his pants. Sam took him in her mouth and happily began working to make him hard.

Matt closed his eyes and moaned at the thought of Ollie's perfect mouth on him. *I bet he knows his way around a dick*, Matt thought as all the blood rushed to his groin. He imagined it was Ollie's tongue circling the tip, Ollie's mouth taking him deep. He pressed Sam back on the bed when she pulled away after her second gag, and kissed her deeply before rolling her onto her stomach. He ran his hands over her back and bottom and slid his fingers between her cheeks with a small sound of appreciation.

"Your body is so beautiful," he praised, uncertain whether he was speaking to the body on his bed or the specter of the male one in his head.

He reached for the side table drawer, took out a condom and tore the wrapper open with his teeth, rolling it quickly on as he spread her legs and lifted her bottom up to meet him, entering her slowly with his eyes closed. He saw Ollie's legs, imagined his smooth, muscular ass under his hands as he moved slowly inside Sam, listening to her soft moans. He lifted her to her knees and then up, to press her back against his chest, wishing her back was as broad as Ollie's to help with his fantasy.

Kissing her neck, he ran his hands over her breasts, pinching her nipples gently before moving down her torso to slip his fingers between her legs again, stroking her as he wondered what it would feel like if it were Ollie's dick in his hand instead. He increased his pace with Sam's breathing, sensing her impending orgasm and his own. He waited until he felt her tighten and cry out before moaning through his own release, careful not to say Ollie's name.

He let her spend the night, but eased her out after morning sex that was not as fulfilling in the light of day.

"I'm not traveling this week," Sam said as she leaned against him in the doorway. "Call me."

Matt kissed her lightly. "Sure," he replied non-committedly and watched her walk to the elevator.

3

Static Cling

FINN RETURNED TO BOSTON for the Fourth of July, catching the fireworks from Matt's roof on the third, and then spent the following day on a boat he rented, with Naomi, Finn's roommate from college, and Erica, Naomi's roommate in Brookline. The day started out sunny, but gradually clouded over, so Matt kept his eye on the weather app. He followed the USS Constitution doing her annual turnaround and twenty-one-gun salute in Boston Harbor, before steering away from the crowd of boats to drop anchor near one of the harbor islands.

They swam to the beach, the water cool and refreshing, but didn't linger among the sparse crowd. Matt hung back to float and contemplate the sky as he listened to Finn and her friends climb into the boat, ignoring their calls to him. The water was soothing, and he always felt safer when he was immersed in it.

Matt had discovered his affinity with the waves when they would visit his father's parents on the coast of Italy in the summers, and quickly became obsessed with swimming. He joined a club team in a town not far from where he grew up, and swam competitively throughout his youth. He would've made the national team (maybe even the Olympic

21

one) but his family couldn't afford the travel and training. He graduated high school and the Naval Academy as captain of both varsity teams, and it was at the Academy that he had been encouraged by more than one of the higher-ups, to try for the SEALs.

Matt straightened and tread water, thinking of his time in the Navy, the friendships he formed, the missions he'd led, the harrowing experiences he'd survived. He hadn't been retired very long, but was already distancing himself from everything SEAL-related. His service was something he was proud of but didn't dwell on, many of the memories just too dark to contemplate, so he pushed them back into their metaphorical box and slammed the lid as he swam to the boat.

He saw Finn and Erica watching him, Erica with appreciation in her eyes as she tilted her head and said something he couldn't hear. He guessed she was asking Finn if he was single, or asking why she and Matt 'broke-up.' According to Finn, those were the two questions she was most frequently asked in regards to their relationship, and he knew her answer to the latter was always the same: 'Matt has a wandering eye, and we're better as friends.'

Matt dove under the surface as he contemplated their charade. Finn, ever his steadfast friend, had agreed to a fake engagement when his macho, unyielding father was dying. His father had been obsessed with seeing his only son with a woman on his arm (especially after that last summer in Italy), and Matt felt compelled to have him believe that he was headed to the altar. His father had been thrilled at the match. Finn was American royalty, insanely wealthy, and everything he dreamed of for his first-generation son. They called off the 'engagement' not long after his father died, and Matt resumed his playboy ways. Finn wasn't wrong about his wandering eye, but it wandered because he never wanted anyone close; he kept everyone but Finn at arm's length.

He looked over his shoulder and smiled at all the fish gathered behind him before surfacing silently at the back of the boat.

"Boo!" he said softly when he was less than a foot from Naomi sunning herself on the diving platform.

"Jesus, Matt!" Naomi jumped with a laugh. "You're like a ninja."

He pulled himself out of the water in one fluid motion and grinned as he swept his hands back and forth across his scalp, shaking the water from his hair.

"Sorry. I forget how complacent civilians can be."

He winked and thought of how much she looked like Gwyneth Paltrow as he scanned his eyes over her bikini-clad body. She was a beauty, but he would never screw around with any of Finn's friends (too messy), and Naomi was one of Finn's closest and most trusted friends.

Naomi chuckled and sat up, sweeping her eyes over Matt's wet body before shifting her gaze to the boat. "Erica has the hots for you. Just to warn you, not that you need warning."

Matt exhaled a laugh. "She seems nice, but you know my rule."

"I do." Naomi smiled and stood as Matt came to his feet.

He gestured for her to go ahead of him and looked at the clouds looming overhead as he grabbed his towel and crossed to the steering wheel. He started the engine, lifted the anchor, and followed the buoys back into the harbor. He dropped anchor again and they changed out of their suits under big beach towels, all elbows, and glimpses of pale bare skin. Finn served up a quick meal and they spilt a bottle of wine as they chatted about summer plans.

Matt felt Erica's eyes on him, heard the promise in her words, but continued to keep her at bay as he met Finn's amused gaze from time to time. After putting everything back in the cooler. Matt divided a second bottle of wine between their four glasses and sat in the front of the boat, holding his arm up as Finn tucked herself under. He squeezed her to his side and looked at the city, so beautiful from the water, despite the gray skies. He smiled wistfully, thinking of a certain Brit (again) and turned his attention to what Finn was saying.

"You know, it would be so fun to have Ollie here. He would love this," she said quietly, reading his mind. "He's so funny, and fun to be around, as you said yourself."

Matt scoffed a laugh. "Look, Naomi's taking our picture," he said and smiled for the camera before standing and starting the engine in dismissal.

"You have to rent a boat again next year, that was so much fun," Finn said later, lying next to him in bed and scrolling through the pictures she took. Matt's second bedroom was his home office, and didn't have a spare bed.

"I'd rather buy a boat, but since that's not happening for a few years, sure, if I'm in town on the fourth, I'll rent a boat, that was fun."

"Whose necklace is this?" Finn asked as she rolled over to put her phone on the side table.

"Sam's," Matt answered with a sigh.

Finn turned back to look at him. "You seeing her again? I thought you ended things because she was getting too attached. Now she's leaving jewelry here? Uh oh. It's a slippery slope."

"I know, but a man has needs." He grinned lewdly.

"Agreed, and Ollie's the perfect person to fulfill those needs. It is the twenty-first century you know."

"Good night, Chuck."

He put up his 'wall' and rolled away from her.

"You can shut everyone else out, but not me," Finn whispered after the space of several breaths. "I won't push you. I just want you to be happy."

Matt grunted and then stared silently at the wall, the light from the city outside fighting its way into the darkness.

The next morning Finn slid her feet into her wedge sandals and kissed Matt. "Can I use your visitor spot again tonight?"

"Sure, I'll put my car there to save it for you. Just move it to the garage when you get here," he replied, going into the kitchen to pour more coffee. "You got a hot date or something?"

"Bye!" she called, closing the door behind her.

4

She's Not Me

SAM WAS LOOKING at the pictures on the mantle in Matt's smaller living room while waiting for him to finish with a last-minute conference call. She sighed with a small smile as she stared at a picture of him with a few of his SEAL teammates, gorgeous in his desert fatigues and body armor, his eyes hidden behind his Ray Bans. She slid her eyes to the next silver frame, a photo taken at his graduation from the Naval Academy. His father, a few inches shorter, but otherwise an older version of Matt, on one side of him, and his mother, whose head barely reached Matt's shoulder, on the other, with two women next to her; one dark-haired, clearly one of Matt's sisters, and the other with honey blonde hair and a beautiful smile.

Sam was looking at the next picture of Matt, in his dress uniform, ribbons and medals on his chest, with the same blonde woman, when she heard a key in the door. She had just enough time to take in the rest of the details of the photo before glancing between the office and the door with shock. *Who else has a key to Matt's condo?* The blonde in the picture was wearing a white, halter evening gown that hugged her perfect body, and her hair and make-up were flawless. Matt had his arm around her, hand low and possessive on her hip, his Naval cap tucked under his other arm, while she had her left hand on his chest, showing off a sizable engagement ring.

The door swung open, and Sam found herself face to face with the beautiful blonde. She was wearing a white, spaghetti-strapped summer dress with a fitted bodice and a flowy skirt that came to mid-thigh, showing off her long, tanned legs, and white, Jimmy Choo wedge sandals. Her tall elegance made Sam feel short and frumpy in her flat Jack Rogers and billowy maxi-dress.

Sam shifted her shoulder with a frown, and twitched her head as the blonde took the key out of the door and closed it behind her.

"Hi." The blonde pulled up at the sight of Sam standing next to the photos, and looked at the necklace around Sam's neck. "You must be Sam." She stepped forward with her hand extended and a smile on her face. "I'm Finn."

Sam shook her hand, stunned and unnerved in a way that made her unsteady, like she was drunk. She found her voice. "Hi."

Matt appeared in the doorway of his office, a smile on his face and crossed the room to kiss Finn's cheek.

"Hey, Chuck. You look beautiful. I was expecting you earlier." He looked at Sam. "You've been introduced?"

Sam nodded mutely, her insides a blur.

Finn handed Matt a small packet of loose photos tucked in a folded piece of cream-colored paper. "I didn't think you'd be here, sorry to interrupt. I thought you said you were going out, and assumed you walked." She crossed to the key rack next to the door and took Matt's Audi key down. "I'm just gonna move your car."

Sam took a breath at Finn's audacity. Matt was so guarded about *everything*, the thought of anyone touching what was his with such a cavalier attitude, never mind driving his car, was incomprehensible.

Matt followed her. "Not necessary, Chuck. Sam and I are going out and taking the car, I'll move it." He paused skimming his eyes over her outfit. "You got a guy waiting downstairs? You want me to let your boyfriend park in my visitor's spot?" he asked narrowing his eyes.

Sam watched in horror as Finn rolled her eyes at Matt.

"I swear to god if you cause a scene, I will never speak to you again."

Matt shrugged. "Fine. Can I meet him?" He glanced at Sam. "We could all go out to dinner together."

Finn laughed. "No fucking way, Matt. In fact, I'm telling him to circle the block until you leave." She pulled out her phone and sent a quick text.

"Come on, Sam, let's go." Matt put the photos on the counter without looking at them, pocketed his phone and plucked the car key from Finn's fingers with a shrug of his eyebrows.

Sam followed Matt and Finn dazedly into the hallway. He had never mentioned Finn to her, and the pictures on the mantle hadn't been there the last time she and Matt had been dating. Her mind was spinning and she wondered how deep his feelings went for his ex-fiancée.

"So, is this a new guy?" Matt asked casually.

Finn sighed. "Sam, tell me about yourself. Where are you from?"

Sam slid a glance at Matt. "Upstate New York."

"What brought you to Boston?"

"College. I went to Tufts," Sam replied with pride.

"Oh, good school."

The elevator doors opened and they stepped out. Sam watched Matt stride ahead, perhaps in hopes of catching Finn's date double parked outside and heard Finn's irritated sigh.

There were no idling cars nearby and Matt scoffed, looking back at Finn walking with Sam. "Where you guys going?"

Finn laughed. "You're an idiot if you think I'm going to answer that question."

Matt shrugged and raised his eyebrows. "I have spies everywhere. You're clearly eating in the North End. Maybe we'll join you for dessert."

Sam met Finn's glance, and willed her to say no.

"You will do no such thing. Sam wants a romantic night out with you, go enjoy yourselves." She turned to shake Sam's hand and gave Matt a small hug. "Run along now." She pushed him lightly.

"Where does Finn live, if she needs your parking space?" Sam asked in a forced casual tone once they were seated at Douzo.

"She's from Wellesley but lives in the UK. She's getting her PhD at Oxford," he added proudly.

"Oh," Sam replied, a look of relief crossing her features. "You two were engaged?"

Matt signaled for the waiter without answering her question. He put up his wall, the one he knew she would never dare breach, and ordered sushi and cocktails for them, not interested in or willing to discuss Finn with Sam.

Later that evening, back at the condo, Sam pounced on him, stripping him naked and performing with gusto, her firm breasts bouncing as she moved vigorously up and down on top of him, likely in hopes of driving Finn from Matt's mind. If she only knew that he would *never* think about Finn in bed, and that he was actually picturing Ollie, imagining what his chest looked like underneath his shirt (smooth and muscular), what his armpits would look like when his hands were folded behind his head (lightly furred and perfectly sinewy), she would have known that no amount of performance would ever be enough. He closed his eyes and ran his hands over her firm thighs, feeling the muscles flex under his hands and groaned his release.

He disposed of the condom and put his underwear back on. Sam cuddled up against his side and he waited until she fell asleep before gently nudging her back to her side of the bed, as he did every time she spent the night.

* * *

Sam woke early, while Matt was still out for his run, and pulled on her underwear. She walked quickly into the kitchen, the photos Finn had given Matt burning in her mind. With a quick look at the door, she opened the folded paper and read the note.

Thank you again for an amazing day.
I love you forever. –C

Sam's heart clenched with jealousy at the note and the five photos inside. They were all clearly taken on the fourth in the harbor, a day she had hoped to spend with him, but he never responded to her texts. The first picture was of Matt, large and gorgeous in a pair of sexy short swim trunks that accentuated his long tan legs and lightly outlined his manhood (sizable even when asleep). He had a bikini-clad woman under each arm, one with long, pale blonde hair, and one with curly black hair.

The next was of Finn with her hair in a bun, wearing a tiny, white string bikini. Her body was smooth and fit, her perfect breasts, slim waist, and flat stomach on full display. She was at the wheel of the boat with Matt behind her, his hands on her hands as they drove, the wake of the boat white and foamy behind them. His chest was pressed against her back and his SEAL tattoo, of an eagle holding an anchor with a gun and trident crossed in front, shone prominently on his flexed bicep. They were smiling happily in their matching Ray Bans, and Sam fervently wished she had been there so she could've thrown Finn overboard.

There were two scenery shots, and the last photo was of Finn and Matt in the front of the boat at dusk. Finn wore a long strapless sundress and was tucked under Matt's arm. Her hair was loose and tousled over her shoulders, and her feet were hidden as she curled up next to him in his track pants and an unzipped hoodie over his bare chest. His face was relaxed and utterly beautiful, with a broad smile for the photographer. He had his feet up, ankles crossed on the bench across from him, and Finn's arm was resting on the naked skin of his flat stomach, the stomach only Sam should be touching.

Sam heard the elevator ding and hurriedly put the photos back as they were and ran to bed, tears behind her eyes.

Matt appeared in the bedroom doorway wiping the sweat from his tanned chest with his t-shirt and looked down at her.

"I'm going to my mom's for brunch, I'll drop you at your place on the way," he stated as he walked around the bed and into the bathroom, closing the door behind him.

Sam heard the shower turn on and wondered disgruntledly if he was going to see Finn while he was in Wellesley.

5

Flesh for Fantasy

MATT TRIED TO LOSE HIMSELF in work, as he usually did. Work, and traveling for work, was so demanding he rarely had time for anything else, including Sam, or his family, but he found thoughts of Ollie impinging on his focus. The air thinned around him as he thought of how easily Ollie had breached his protective wall. He worried over his weakness. *Why after so many years was he suddenly unable to control his thoughts, his urges, his desire?*

He shook his head, and called Finn, the source of his angst (his ire). "Hey, Chuck, I've got some meetings set up in London later this week."

"Fantastic! What day? I'll have the mints on the pillow."

"I'll email you my flight info and let you know when I'll be in Oxford." He looked out his office window. "Is Ollie around?" he asked casually.

He felt Finn's smile through the phone. "I'm pretty sure. He does go home from time to time, in fact I went with him for dinner just last week, but I can see if he's around."

"Okay, but please don't say that I asked."

31

"Of course not, I wouldn't. But I have to say, he asks about you every time I see him. He was very smitten with you. Thinks you're the most beautiful man he's ever seen. Said he was bummed that you're straight."

Matt closed his eyes with a smile. "I'll see you in less than a week."

Matt filled every free moment between that phone call and his flight with work, working out, and swimming laps at L.A. Sports Club. He took Sam out one night, but she was acting weird, so two days later he was back to his wandering ways and went to a hotel on Battery Wharf. When in Boston, he preferred hooking up with women from out of town, so there were no complications locally. He had sex with a beautiful woman he met at the bar, blowing her mind in her hotel room (while his was filled with thoughts of Ollie) and leaving with a temporary sense of satiation.

* * *

Less than a week later he was back in London, meeting a driver with a sign like last time. He gazed blankly out the window as the trees and cars rushed by, wholly unable to focus on work, or anything, as his mind raced with too many thoughts to track (most of them revolving around a certain gorgeous, hilarious Brit).

Was Ollie as beautiful as he remembered, or had he built him up impossibly in his mind? (No way his accent was as smooth as Lake Waban at dawn. No way he smelled like sunshine over the ocean. No way his hands were as large and as strong as his own). Matt shook his head with a wince as the car glided to a stop in front of Finn's.

Matt went for a long run after letting himself into her empty flat. He followed the river and thought about himself, about Ollie, about the future. He wished there was a solution to his dilemma, wished again that he wasn't feeling the feelings he was feeling. Wished he felt complete with a woman, while knowing he *never* would. He wished he could accept himself for who he was, but there were too many reasons why he never could. Between his father, the deeply conservative Roman

Catholic church they attended weekly, and his time in the Navy, he had learned that his true sexuality was a sin and something to deny at all costs.

His father had wanted him to join his construction business, but Matt had no aptitude for it. So, he tried to please his father another way, figuring that joining the Navy SEALs, America's most elite fighting force, the pinnacle of 'manhood,' would appease him, and he was right. His father was *so* proud. He had no idea of the secret Matt was hiding. No idea that what got Matt through Annapolis and his time in the military, was his anger and shame about the urges he was feeling. He had internalized his denial so effectively that he became quite adept at ignoring it altogether (until now).

He dodged around a woman with a stroller and continued along the riverway, shifting his thoughts back to Ollie. Ollie, an unexpected disruption to his orderly and regimented system. Ollie was perfection. That body, that smile, that charm. How was Ollie still single?

And why can't I stop thinking about getting him naked?

Matt felt the gravel crunching under his feet as he ran, thinking of the type of man he found attractive. Back in high school, in the locker rooms, his eyes always (cautiously) sought out the blondes with the sinewy muscle, with strong shoulders and taut abdomens, with waists built for gripping. As he aged, his desires had only become more specific: a flat expanse around the navel, a curve—like the letter C—of the buttock, and an indent in a smooth bottom as the muscle flexed in motion. Matt blew out a shaky breath and crossed the bridge over the river as he imagined just how perfectly Ollie fit all those ideals.

The one time he had acted on his urges, had been with someone who had none of those things. He had been lean and dark-haired, but he had offered himself in such a way that Matt didn't care enough to be picky. He was seventeen, and horny, and reckless, and a world away from Wellesley. Each encounter with that Italian boy had been, for the most part, furtive and brief, and intoxicatingly thrilling. Until his father caught a look exchanged between them, read Matt's nervous behavior, and Matt's fantasies and actions were brought to a grinding halt. His father's suspicion had been terrifying enough that Matt hadn't looked at another man sexually since.

Reflecting on it as he ran, he was astounded that he had lasted as long as he had. Sex with a woman was fine, but nothing compared to the memories of sex with that boy that he clung to from all those years ago, thinking of them in order to get off on occasion. He would conjure those memories as though he were watching someone else, and they always managed to be enough. But not anymore. . . .

He sighed and clenched his teeth, increasing his speed as he turned onto Finn's street, no less confused about himself than he had been when he started his run.

They all met again for dinner at the same pub. This time, Ollie arrived early and sat next to him. Matt's stomach flipped and he fought to keep the pleasure off his face at Ollie's proximity, his almost unbearable closeness. Ollie's cologne, or styling gel, or soap, smelled so delicious (it *was* like sunshine on the ocean) that Matt had to fight the urge to close his eyes and breathe deeply in ecstasy. Ollie's thigh was in reach, and their shoulders only barely avoided contact on several occasions.

What if...?

"How are things in America, Matt? The weather good?" Ollie interrupted Matt's thoughts with an accent that was smoother than *any* lake at dawn.

Ollie's face was calm but with something trembling underneath.

"Yeah, we've had great weather. Makes me wish I had a beach house." He smiled, holding Ollie's gaze.

Ollie returned the smile. "Don't we all?" He took a swallow of beer. "You seeing anyone? Someone you'd be bringing to your imaginary beach house?"

His question caught Matt off-guard, and he worried that he was being too free with his glances at Ollie, too free with his deep, appreciative breaths, too transparent with his '*what if*' thoughts.

"Yeah, as matter of fact I got a girlfriend," he answered nonchalantly, his voice a mixture of machismo and regret, noticing a brief flash of disappointment cross Ollie's face. "How 'bout you, you seeing anyone?"

"No, not for a while now."

Matt couldn't help the small smile that appeared on his face before he covered it by taking a sip of his drink, blowing out the breath he didn't know he was holding.

"Why're you smiling?" Ollie asked quietly.

Matt ignored the question and remarked on Ollie's tan to change the subject.

"Yeah, been playing quite a bit of football, some tennis. You're quite dark yourself. You've got some Mediterranean blood?"

"Both my parents were off the boat from Italy when they were single digits," Matt answered with a smile at Ollie's appreciative tone. "They met in Boston, in high school, where they grew up a few blocks from each other. I bought a place not far from where both sets of grandparents lived."

Ollie made a thoughtful sound. "Dion's not a very Italian last name."

"My father shortened it from Diontangelo when he was eighteen. He was determined to assimilate and blend in with the Anglos. We were raised in the one of the Waspiest towns in Massachusetts."

"You speak Italian?"

"*Ovviamente*," Matt answered, managing, just barely, to keep his grin from being flirty. "Though it's pretty rusty."

Ollie looked at Matt's mouth and made an appreciative sound. "Doesn't sound rusty," he said quietly and brought his eyes back to Matt's.

Matt watched him for a beat and slid his glance away, scalded by the heat in Ollie's eyes. He took a small bite of his food, choking it down as a distraction, suddenly feeling as though the air was charged with electricity and if he looked at Ollie again, he would be jolted by it.

He looked at his watch and then at Finn, who caught his look. Matt waved the server over for the check and paid cash.

"Well, guys," Finn said, looking at the table. "I've got a big day planned for Matt tomorrow, we're going to Bath, so it's time for us to say goodnight."

"You're going to love Bath," Ollie said to Matt, stopping him from standing with a hand on his arm. "Very Roman. You'll feel right at home. It's gorgeous, like you," he added in a near whisper.

Matt smiled, Ollie's hand warm and kinetic on his arm, hiding his pleasure at Ollie's words behind his uptight façade. "I appreciate the compliment, Ollie. Are the women there beautiful as well?" He stood not waiting for an answer, Ollie's hand sliding slowly off his forearm. He said his goodbyes and left following Finn, feeling Ollie's eyes on his back.

6

One Step Forward Three Steps back

MATT CALLED SAM AGAIN when he got home (knowing that she'd been properly chastised by the weeks apart). He took her to dinner and then back to his condo for sex, waking her again in the night when persistent thoughts of Ollie woke him. The memory of Ollie's face, the tenor of his voice, the heat in his eyes as he so openly flirted with him at that dinner was too arousing for his brain. The fantasies only seemed to be increasing in their urgency, but Matt was determined to overcome them.

Ha.

He began to imagine scenarios where he and Ollie were alone, how he would touch him, and Ollie would let him. He imagined the two of them in a bathroom stall (Ollie facing the wall Matt panting in his ear), in his room at Finn's (Ollie begging for mercy on his knees, not a stitch of clothing between them), on a vacant beach (the moon high above them as Matt buried himself inside Ollie). In each scenario, Ollie would moan. Moans that sounded suspiciously like Sam's, which would bring him back to reality, causing him to stutter before finding his release.

* * *

Sam was ecstatic with the attention. She was head over heels in love with Matt, and hoped his sudden, demanding attention meant he felt the same. Especially after the confusion about his relationship with Finn. She had been furious with herself after his weeks-long radio silence, furious that she'd made her insecurities known. She knew he hated clinginess and pouting, and vowed to be more nonchalant, like he was.

Sam remembered the first time she laid eyes on him at a charity dinner. A chance meeting at an event Sam almost hadn't attended. She had broken up with Wes, the guy she had been seeing after graduation, but he needed a date, and she agreed, hoping to network at the event. She had her hair and makeup professionally done, and wore an ocean blue, backless gown with spaghetti straps that hugged her trim body.

When they got to the Plaza, she and Wes went in separate directions, Wes also eager to network. Sam quickly found her eyes drawn again and again to Matt as he worked the room, first with a statuesque blonde clad in a slinky black dress on his arm, then later alone when the model seemingly got bored. Sam followed him to the bar after dinner, and nearly fainted when he turned his devastating smile on her.

"You enjoying yourself?" he asked with that smile, his eyes sweeping over her body admiringly.

Sam felt her stomach flutter wildly under his gaze. "Sure. You?" she replied, shocked she could find words under his sinful gaze.

His smile turned knowingly lopsided, and he stepped up to the bar. "What are you having?"

"Pinot Grigio, please."

Matt turned to the bartender. "And a bourbon on the rocks." Sam studied him as he ordered his drink and felt her knees want to buckle. She told her friends about it later and they had laughed at her, but they didn't know, they weren't there. He was tall, easily six-three, as broad as a quarterback, and as gorgeous as a movie star. He exuded confidence like pheromones as he stood there in his expensive tuxedo that fit him like a glove. Matt had looked at her expectantly as he passed her the wine and clinked his glass to hers.

"Cheers."

"Cheers," Sam replied and followed Matt like a fish on a line as he stepped away from the bar. They chatted and exchanged names, Sam giving him her business card which he pocketed discreetly. They flirted with increasing intensity until his date reappeared and pressed herself possessively against Matt's side, their eyes level in her heels.

She said something to Matt in another language, her voice sultry and exotic, and put her hand possessively on his flat stomach.

Sam watched something flicker behind his eye before he replied in the same language. His date frowned and then pouted, speaking again with a glance at Sam.

Matt shrugged and spoke in a quiet but commanding tone. The blonde pushed away from him and said something angrily before striding away as though she were on the runway at fashion week, heads turning as she passed.

Matt turned his gaze back to Sam and smiled. "Wanna go back to my place?"

Sam hesitated, not wanting to seem easy, but as his eyes detached from hers and scanned the room, looking as if he was going to ditch her, she agreed.

She closed her eyes with a smile, as she felt Matt reach for her again and remembered that passionate night, where she discovered just how phenomenal he was in bed. Then remembered how he had called her a week later and took her to dinner beginning their few months of dating, everything fantastic until he stopped calling her a few months later, breaking things off because he said he was too busy with work.

That he was calling her again, and letting her spend the weekend, wanting sex multiple times in a night, and showering her with compliments about her body, made her heart sing. She was so happy she had taken up CrossFit which had tightened her body into a solid mass of lean muscle, because Matt clearly loved it.

She looked up at him as he gazed down at her, brought back into the present, and moaned softly as he pressed into her, filling her almost painfully. She never complained, though she always left sore. So many of her girlfriends would be jealous if they knew how big he was (he was massive), or how skilled he was, with his fingers and his tongue. She hugged him to her, kissing his neck, his breath warm in her hair as he panted with effort. He rolled her onto her stomach and ran his hand down her back before entering her again, squeezing her bottom tightly.

She let her mind wander briefly as he moved inside her. She loved being with him, being seen with him, and most importantly, being seen by him. She wasn't bothered that he didn't talk much, that he spent a lot of the weekends working, and that he never opened up to her about what he was thinking. Her father had been the same way, and he was a good man, a good father. She knew Matt had been through a lot, serving overseas, and she never wanted to pry, for fear of upsetting him. Sometimes he was moody, angry, but never directed his anger toward her, so she didn't worry, she just loved.

Matt was everything she wanted in a man, though she disliked how much he traveled for work, how much time he spent in the UK in particular, but she knew he was building his business, and she wanted him to be successful. She dared to imagine getting married, imagined being the wife of a future *billionaire* and felt herself on the verge of an orgasm. She touched herself as he thrust, crying out her release as he slowed and then stopped with a quiet groan as he came.

Sam smiled as she felt him collapse against her back, satisfied with bringing him to orgasm. She pushed aside her jealousy at the discovery of the two pictures from the boat now propped on the mantle, and at the thought of Matt visiting Finn when he was overseas. She was determined to make him see all the ways in which she was better for him than that dismissive bitch.

7

Questions, So Many Questions

OLLIE WENT TO FINN'S for movie night, where she always made fresh popcorn and had his favorite beer. They had begun to make a weekly ritual of it during the long breaks between terms last year, and kept it up over the summer. Their bond was solidified within moments of meeting when they discovered their mutual love of eighties and nineties cinema, particularly Scorsese, Kubrick, and Coppola. They were working their way through Scorsese's catalog and were halfway through *Good Fellas* when Finn paused the movie for a bathroom break.

Ollie reflected on their friendship as he waited for her to come back. Their comradery was instantaneous, and though he had only known her about a year, he felt like he had known her forever. Unlike other women who paid attention to him, she hadn't been flirtatious or questioning, she just had a way about her that felt easy and trusting. Ollie found himself confiding in her the second or third time they met (far sooner than he had with anyone else) and remembered how something had flared in her eyes, like excitement. He shook his head.

Why had she reacted to my sexuality like that? he wondered then and now.

Finn returned and sat down with an exhale. "Ready."

Ollie turned the remote over and over in his hands as he contemplated her. "Your friend Matt, he's *really* beautiful. I mean, how is it that someone can be that beautiful?" he asked rhetorically with a chuckle.

Finn smiled and nodded in agreement. "He is gorgeous, and such a love. I've known him forever."

Ollie smiled and made a friendly sound as he chose his words carefully. "He's straight? He said he has a girlfriend, but . . ." Ollie hesitated. "I only ask, because sometimes I feel him looking at me. *God,* it's thrilling. Am I just indulging my fantasy or. . . ." He raised his eyebrows and held his breath.

"Matt is the greatest guy, Ollie. He's very driven, super disciplined, and very private." She held Ollie's gaze with a smile before taking the remote from him.

Ollie frowned slightly at her evasive response and turned his face to the TV as Finn pushed play. His mind was elsewhere as he obsessed over what Finn didn't say about Matt (that beautiful enigma). Matt was unquestionably straight (right?) and flirted openly with Sophie and Finn. But then Ollie would catch Matt staring at him, with something behind his eyes that Ollie recognized from the men he'd dated. His stomach flipped again at the memory of Matt's strong, veined forearm under his hand, the way Matt had leaned ever so slightly toward him at the touch before pulling away with a grim determination. He didn't dare hope that there was something more.

* * *

Matt was a mess at work; one minute focused on the deals that were streaming in, and the next sitting in a trance, like the ebb and flow of the tide. Being with Sam, and the other women, wasn't helping in the way that he had hoped. He found himself daydreaming about Ollie at work (endless, dirty scenarios), so lost in his thoughts that when his assistant, Stacey, buzzed his office phone he would nearly jump out of his skin, instantly panicked that she knew what he was thinking. It wasn't just Ollie's body or his gorgeous face, it was his wild laugh, the way his accent smoothed the edges of words (polishing them in his mouth). And it was his wit, his intellect, but most of all, it was his heady scent.

Matt sighed and took out his phone. "Hey, Chuck. How's the world of languages that no one speaks anymore?"

Finn laughed, a pleasing trill that felt like home. "You're an asshole. Why am I friends with you again? All you do is mock me, and chase guys away."

"You're friends with me because I make you cool by association. Otherwise, you are the biggest nerd to walk the planet. Hopeless. And I chase the unworthy away. Trust me I'm doing you a favor."

He took a breath. "I'm not actually calling just to mock you. I'm letting you know that I have a couple of follow-up meetings in London this week and would love to see you."

Finn made a happy sound. "Excellent! I'd love to see you too, babe. August is so dead here. I wish I had stayed home longer. Send me your flight info and let me know when you arrive."

"Will do," Matt replied and looked out his window. "How dead is dead, Chuck? Is *everyone* gone?"

He felt Finn's smile in her pause. "Not everyone."

"Good. See you in a few days." He hung up and looked out his office window, thinking of Ollie's mouth.

8

Paper and Glue

MATT ARRIVED AT HEATHROW on Monday morning and had back-to-back meetings, spending the first night in London. Arriving at Finn's the following morning, he dove right back into work with conference calls, first with his sales team, and then his tech team. He and Finn went out Tuesday night with Sophie and Ollie, Sophie sitting next to him and Ollie across. Matt tried not to stare at Ollie's bare arms (beautiful, muscular arms that disappeared into the tight sleeves of his Burberry t-shirt). He found his eyes drawn again and again to the thin necklace shining so brightly at the base of Ollie's throat, nestled above his collarbone. He wondered what it would feel like to have that collarbone under his lips, what it would taste like, and turned to Sophie in a near panic at the direction of his thoughts.

Sophie flirted madly with him and Matt turned on the charm in response. Matt finished his beer and flagged the waiter for another as he sat back and put his arm behind Sophie on her chair. He caught Ollie's eye, as he had on-and-off all night, and forced himself to look away, wishing vehemently that he didn't have to. He wished he could be flirting with Ollie instead, his arm on Ollie's chair, or *shoulder*. The thought alone made him dizzy and nervous like an amateur, and he frowned inwardly at himself.

"What do you do for work, Matt?" Ollie asked when Sophie left for the bathroom, drawing Matt back to the conversation. The sight of them flirting with each other, Matt's arm practically around Sophie, filled Ollie with a strange sense of jealousy.

Pay attention to me, straight boy.

"I own a cybersecurity company. I guess it's still considered a start-up, though we're in year three and business is really picking up," Matt replied, holding Ollie's gaze for the first time that evening, and Ollie swore he saw flames instead of pupils.

Ollie made a sound of appreciation, suddenly unnerved and strangely awakened by Matt's unwavering gaze. "What's the name of your company?"

"SharkFinn," he answered with a smile and held up his glass to Finn. "She's my business partner."

Ollie raised his eyebrows. "Whoa, that's fantastic." He squeezed Finn's thigh under the table. "Look at you Miss Business Mogul. And here I thought you just haunted libraries."

Finn laughed and laid her head on his shoulder. "I'm full of sur-prises, Ollie darling." She looked at Matt. "So is he," she said meaning-fully with a grin.

Matt shook his head at her with a pointed look.

Ollie looked between the two of them and held Matt's gaze, his stomach fluttering at what she was insinuating, what she was confirming.

"Is that so?" He looked up as Sophie rejoined them, drawing Matt's eye away and extinguishing the flame.

Ollie bristled with irritation at the interruption, especially after what he had most *definitely* seen in Matt's eyes. He no longer believed he was imagining things, and the knowledge made him breathless.

9

It's a Trap!

"I'M GOING TO LORD ARCHER'S. I'll be home before dinner on Friday," Finn declared the following afternoon, emerging from her room with an overnight bag, her hair tied back into a ponytail.

Matt looked up from the sofa, his hands hovering over the keyboard of his laptop.

"What? Why? Is there an emergency cuneiform situation?" he asked mockingly with a smile.

"You're hilarious." Finn put her hand on her hip. "Actually, it's because this is your third visit to Oxford. You ask to see Ollie every time you come, and now you've been here for three days, you look at him like he's a dessert you can't wait to eat, and yet you've done nothing about it," she said, her green eyes twinkling. "I've invited him for dinner tonight, he's bringing Indian." She picked up her bag and shifted her body saucily. "Bye!"

Matt put his laptop aside and stood abruptly. "What?! He's coming here? *Alone?*" he cried, his body jolting with a flash of panic (and something else).

"Don't sound so scared, Matt. You were a SEAL for fuck's sake. I told you, he thinks you're gorgeous. You'll do fine. Don't deny yourself," she added, kissing him and stepping back.

"So, you've graduated from matchmaker to pimp now, huh?" Matt frowned with a sigh and looked away, his stomach flipping madly, a burn forming behind his ribcage. "It's been a lifetime. I don't think it's a good idea. I like admiring him from afar.

"I mean, could he keep my secret?" He looked back at her with a face full of worry and a chest full of hope.

She smiled gently at him, and nodded. "Yes. Ollie's a private person. Not many people know about him either. You deserve this. He's an amazing guy. Do it for me. He'll be here at six. Love you!" she called with a laugh as she hurried out the door.

The buzzer rang at six and Matt nearly jumped out of his skin. He had showered after a long run, then put on jeans and a white button-down, before pacing the flat barefoot for almost an hour. He went down the two steps and took a deep breath trying to calm his pulse. He opened the door with false bravado.

Ollie was on the stoop wearing salmon-colored flat-front chino shorts, a soft white and blue striped, crewneck shirt with the sleeves pushed up, and pristine white sneakers. He was holding a large paper bag and smiled when he saw it was Matt. Matt took a deep breath, taking in Ollie's appearance; his impossibly styled and perfect hair, his bright blue-green eyes, smooth-shaven face, muscular legs, and heavenly lips.

"Hello, Matt, I've got curry takeaway," Ollie said, giving Matt's bare feet the side-eye as Matt stepped aside to let him in.

Matt found his voice. "That sounds great, thanks."

His eyes followed Ollie as he crossed the space and put the bag of food on the dining table. He blew out the breath he wasn't aware he was holding as he allowed his gaze to linger on the perfect C-curve of Ollie's ass.

What if . . . ?

"Where's Finn?" Ollie asked looking around, interrupting Matt's train of thought.

"She . . . went to Lord Archer's. You know, Ned, her mentor. Until Friday," Matt answered slowly, with a shrug.

Ollie looked at him for a moment and then away. "Oh." He pulled out his phone and looked at the blank screen before looking back at Matt, his eyes scanning him boldly. "Okay."

Matt swallowed nervously as he held Ollie's knowing gaze for a beat. He fled to the kitchen to get plates, napkins and utensils, busying himself to calm his nerves. He glanced back and saw Ollie unpacking the food with a small smile on his face and felt a thrill course through his body at the promise in that smile.

Not for you, Lieutenant.

Matt clenched his jaw against the intrusive thought and joined Ollie at the table. His eyes seeking out Ollie's bare skin as fervently as they had ignored it every other time. He worked hard to fight his body's response to Ollie's proximity, his knowing and flirtatious smile, and grew frustrated with himself.

"That's a posh accent you have, Ollie. Where in England are you from?"

"Kensington," Ollie replied, his mouth curving into a bow that just begged to be kissed. "It's a small neighborhood in London."

"Ah, Princess Di, Kensington Palace. Let me guess you went to Eton too, right?" Unable to soften the edge in his tone, feeling momentarily small and poor. "You play polo?"

Ollie chuckled awkwardly. "You're making me out to sound like a snob."

Matt shrugged. "Are you?"

Ollie shook his head defensively. "Christ, no."

Matt exhaled and looked away from Ollie's wounded expression. "I don't think you're a snob, Ollie. I'm just giving you a hard time. I like your accent," he replied, angry at himself for being mean, for feeling inadequate, and most of all, for feeling like an amateur.

Ollie nodded brusquely, and Matt panicked, before Ollie's face softened amicably again.

"So, Finn said that you recently retired from the Navy SEALs." Ollie put his elbows on the table as Matt nodded. "What rank? Just curious."

"Lieutenant. It was a medical discharge this past winter due to an injury."

Ollie raised his eyebrows. "What kind of injury?"

"Work related," Matt answered vaguely with a grin, tracing circles on the tabletop with his finger, imagining it was Ollie's chest.

Ollie laughed. "What was it like, being around all that American testosterone?"

Matt laughed lightly and looked away. He sat back in his chair, laced his fingers on top of his head and spread his legs wide, his body responding like muscle memory.

"At times unbearable." He looked back at Ollie, feeling the weight of the question, the weight of the room. "Other times. . . ." He shrugged.

Ollie rubbed his bottom lip with the tip of his thumb. Matt watched the suggestive motion for a moment, mesmerized, the tension suddenly as heavy as his limbs. He cleared his throat and stood, unfolding his arms and legs, taking their plates into the kitchen.

Ollie watched Matt cross to the sink with a slight frown. *What the fuck just happened to the mood?* He sealed up the leftovers and put them in the fridge. He took a breath (and a chance) and turned to Matt who was rinsing their dishes without actually running any water over them. Ollie touched Matt's arm as he closed the distance between them, running his fingers from the bottom of Matt's cuffed sleeve to his wrist.

"Why do you keep running away from me?" Ollie asked softly.

Matt turned. "What are you doing?"

Ollie pulled his hand away as though burned and took a step back.

"Oh fuck! I'm *so* sorry. I should've known from the bare feet." He held up his hands defensively, his eyes wide, his heart in his throat. "Did I misinterpret the way you were looking at me, and," he looked down at the front of Matt's jeans, the tip of his tongue appearing briefly between his lips, "that." He looked back up at Matt.

Matt's eyelids flickered and he shook his head slowly. "No," he breathed.

Ollie's stomach unclenched with a large flutter. "Oh, thank god," he said with a relieved exhale. "The disappointment I just felt was *crushing*."

He cupped the back of Matt's neck in his large palm and pulled his mouth down, kissing him gently, resting his other hand on Matt's waist as he leaned in. Matt gripped the counter behind him, his knuckles slowly turning white, and returned the kiss. Ollie savored Matt's mouth, the buttery taste of his tongue, and made a low sound, feeling that kiss all the way to his toes. Matt pressed himself against Ollie in response.

"You can touch me you know," Ollie murmured against Matt's mouth. "In fact, I'd *really* like it if you did," he added breathlessly.

Matt pulled back from Ollie's mouth. "Ollie. It's been a long, long time since I've been with a man." He gazed at him longingly. "I don't want to hurt you."

"Christ, that's hot," Ollie said in a low voice. "I'm a big boy, you won't hurt me."

"Would you let me?"

Ollie furrowed his brow slightly. "Are you into that?"

Matt shrugged lightly. "Not really."

Ollie looked away. *What does that mean?* "That's not an answer."

Ollie decided to ignore it and pried Matt's hand off the counter and put it on the back of his pants, sighing against Matt's mouth as Matt squeezed his bottom. He felt Matt's fingers trace the seam between his pockets before pressing possessively.

Matt pulled him in tighter, Ollie's arousal unmistakable and eager against his own, and kissed him with abandon, letting passion override his brain as he felt himself unspool. He carded his fingers through Ollie's soft hair and a moan escaped from between his lips (it *did* feel like silk). He ran his fingers past the strands to the shaved bottom part which was fuzzy and foreign feeling under his sensitive fingertips. He cradled Ollie's head gently as he filled his mouth with his tongue, humming low in his throat when Ollie met his tongue with equal passion.

Matt's lips sought out the smooth hollow where Ollie's neck met his shoulder, he nibbled on Ollie's perfect earlobe, and tasted the sensitive spot just behind Ollie's ear. He moaned softly at the sound of Ollie's short, audible gasps that increased in their vigor as the minutes passed.

Matt's body was like a tightly strung instrument under Ollie's beautiful and capable hands. Hands that were spanning his shoulders, smoothing over his chest, ducking around his waist and gripping his ass. He felt Ollie untuck the back of his shirt, and then his warm hand (full of electricity) on his skin. Matt closed his eyes and allowed himself to revel in the sensations, his body feeling right again after so many years of wrong.

But then, as he swept his tongue around Ollie's, an unwelcome, disdainful voice popped into his head (suspiciously similar to his dad's voice) and Matt pulled back at the same time he pushed Ollie away.

"I, I can't do this," he stammered breathlessly. "It's not you, Ollie. God, you are so. . . ." He shook his head with a sorrow he felt to his core. "I just can't. You should go."

Ollie looked at him with a disappointed frown on his impossibly beautiful face, his kiss-plumped lips parted. "What is it then? You shouldn't deny yourself. I can feel how much you want this." He palmed the front of Matt's jeans and squeezed gently. "I want you just as badly. It's okay," he whispered with a flare in his eyes.

Matt closed his eyes against that enticing flare and swallowed, the sensation of Ollie's hand on him nearly buckling his knees. It would be so easy to just let him peel his zipper down and work his magic (no question Ollie knew some magic), but Matt just couldn't risk it. He grabbed Ollie's wrist firmly, resisting the angry urge to press the sensitive flesh between the bones, and pushed it away.

"I have to deny myself. It can't be any other way. You have to go."

Ollie left with reluctance and a sad expression, leaving his number with Matt. "Call me if you change your mind."

Matt slept a few hours, tossing and turning the rest of the night. He finally got out of bed before dawn and went for a long run, playing scenarios through his mind. He felt tears behind his eyes, which only infuriated him. He couldn't stop thinking about Ollie. The taste of him, the feeling of his mouth, Ollie's lips fitting against his own like a missing puzzle piece. He thought of his firm ass, most assuredly as beautiful as he pictured, as beautiful as it felt, and knew it would be heaven to bury himself inside. He knew that Ollie would have let him, would maybe even have begged him to. He pushed aside that erotic image with a grimace, and increased his pace.

He returned to the flat and after a shower and focusing on work for a while, he finally picked up his phone, looking at the number Ollie wrote on a torn piece of paper. He ran his thumb over it lightly as if it were Ollie's smooth skin.

"Stacey, please change my flight to tonight, if possible, if not, then first thing tomorrow," he said when she answered on the first ring, closing his eyes and gritting his teeth.

* * *

"Matt. What happened?" Finn asked when he answered his phone the following day, her voice full of concern.

"Nothing. I had to leave. Something came up with work." Matt looked at the ceiling of his condo. "Sorry I dashed without saying goodbye."

There was a long pause. "I don't believe you."

"Well, I can't help that, Chuck."

"Did something happen with Ollie?"

"No. Did he say something?" Matt asked cautiously.

"No, Matt. I told you, he's private," she answered with an edge to her tone. "He said you guys had dinner and then he left."

Matt closed his eyes with relief. "See, like I said, nothing happened, and now I gotta go. I've got a work call I have to take. Bye." He pressed end and put his phone down by his side on the bed, feeling miserable.

10

Only Fools

OLLIE MANEUVERED THE BALL down the field, his body focused on getting around the other team's defense while his mind focused on Matt (it hadn't been focused on anything but Matt since that incredible, and depressing, night two weeks prior). He feigned left and took the ball right, kicking powerfully up and over the goalie's head and into the net.

He was instantly swarmed by his teammates. "You're on fire, Ollie!"

Ollie wiped the sweat from his face and ran to the sideline to get his water bottle, drinking deeply before running back to center field. He had played football for as long as he could remember, and played it well, but this week, he knew it was his pent-up sexual frustration that was driving his skill. His mind was utterly consumed with thoughts of Matt and his beautiful body, the taste of his mouth, the scent of his skin. He'd stupidly checked his phone every ten minutes for the first week, even though Finn had told him Matt left early and without saying goodbye.

He's never going to call you. He's . . . well, I don't know what he is, but he's definitely in denial.

Ollie sighed and thought of the moment he laid eyes on Matt in the pub that first night.

Matt was facing the door and when their eyes met, it was like a cheesy romance novel. Ollie had to temper his smile and shift his gaze so he wouldn't trip over himself in his haste to be closer to that god of a man. Matt's dark and confident beauty, his piercing eyes, his gravelly voice, hit Ollie in all the right places and he would have remained speechless if not for Matt seeming just as affected.

Ollie was so overwhelmed by his body's response that he had to focus on James to distract himself, to keep himself from drooling. Two pints later he had the courage to follow Matt to the men's room, strangely desperate for a moment alone. Once there he was treated to something from his wildest dreams.

Ollie blushed as he remembered saying something like, 'holy, Jesus,' under his breath at the uncut vision in Matt's hand. He then worried Matt had heard him from how quickly he zipped up and left.

Ollie was hooked, like a teenager with a new crush. Whenever Finn texted to say Matt was in town, Ollie took extra care with his appearance, and for the first time in his life arrived on time. Anxious to see Matt and his five o'clock shadow, to hear his sexy American accent in that deep, gravelly voice of his (as though he'd shouted commands at soldiers for years).

The man was walking sex appeal, and Ollie lusted after him with abandon. So, when he arrived at Finn's flat, and found Matt there alone, watching him hungrily, he couldn't help but look around for his fairy godmother.

It had been dizzying trying to decipher the mixed signals that were flying Ollie's way. He was like a bully in one breath, and then contrite with the next, but something about him begged for Ollie to stay, to understand. So, Ollie took a gamble, and the reward, however (frustratingly) brief it was, was worth it.

He could still feel Matt's perfect mouth against his own, feel the strength in his lower back, the ridges of Matt's washboard abs under his fingertips. He remembered the feeling of his sizable hardness under his hand (so much bigger hard than when he glimpsed it in the pub bathroom).

When Matt pushed him away, he had nearly cried. Ollie's body had been on fire, and he tossed and turned all night back at his flat before finally taking matters into his own hands, literally.

Ollie was brought out of his musings when a teammate called to him. He caught the ball between his feet and passed it to Ivan, his best friend and roommate (friends since year nine at Eton) and then dodged around the defensive player in front of him. Ivan dribbled the ball straight at the goalie and kicked it over to where Ollie was waiting to score with a hard kick that billowed the net out with the impact. Ollie beamed and gripped Ivan tightly, pushing thoughts of Matt away as the rest of the team raced to them both.

After the game the team went to the pub around the corner to celebrate and review each play with excited abandon. Ollie was on his second pint when he felt eyes on him, the hairs on his neck standing up as the room shimmered slightly. His stomach flipped at the sight of Matt staring at him from next to the bar.

Matt's eyes, locked on Ollie, were dark and fathomless in the low light. He looked like a model in navy-blue linen pants and a light blue linen shirt, the sleeves cuffed as usual, exposing forearms that were corded with veins. There was something beckoning in Matt's posture that Ollie couldn't resist.

Ollie blew out a nervous breath and ran his hand through his hair self-consciously, suddenly desperate for a shower. His sweaty clothes were stuck to him and his legs were covered in grass stains, like everyone else at his table, but none of the guys had a god staring at them. His body stood of its own accord and made its way to Matt, as if being swept out to sea, helpless to alter course. Matt watched him approach, heat behind his eyes, and tore his glance away, before looking back at Ollie, his eyes skimming over Ollie's bare legs.

"Hey," Ollie said with a smile as the din of the bar around them receded, leaving him alone with Matt in a bubble of longing.

Matt clinked his glass to Ollie's pint with a smile, seemingly speechless. Ollie held out his hand and Matt took it firmly, his eyes fluttering slightly from the contact.

"Ollie!" Finn cried happily from behind Matt as she turned, breaking the spell, the noise of the pub returning deafeningly. "We followed the sounds of celebration all the way here from my flat. I take it you guys won again." She laughed.

Ollie kissed her cheeks. "Yup. Five aught."

"How many were yours?" Matt asked, his deep gravelly voice drawing Ollie's eyes and sending a shiver down his spine.

Oh, how I'd missed the sound of that voice.

"All of them," Ollie replied with a grin, melting under Matt's gaze.

Matt's eyebrows went up and he made a sound of appreciation before taking a long swallow of his drink.

"What are you having?" Ollie nodded at Matt's glass.

"Gin and tonic. When in Rome." Matt shrugged with a grin; his face nonchalant but his body coiled.

Matt knew he was lost, teetering on the precipice of no return. First, it was the sight of Ollie sitting amongst his teammates, a light illuminating him seemingly from within. And then it was the scent of him when he stopped within reach, sweaty and musky. Matt had felt his legs want to sway and had to lock his knees.

"Ollie!" one of his teammates called, interrupting them. "Get back over here and settle this dispute. And bring your bird."

Ollie nodded at the table and looked back at Matt. "Want to join us?"

Matt looked between Ollie and his table of friends. "Sure. Chuck?"

She smiled. "If Stuart can keep his hands to himself this time."

Matt put his arm around her shoulder. "I'll break them if he doesn't," he promised firmly.

Matt bought the table a round, and sat back, listening to the team banter while watching Ollie surreptitiously. He was clearly the star of the team and they treated him as such, with a mixture of admiration and light teasing. Ollie brushed it all off, color in his cheeks as he met Matt's eyes. It was a humble blush that did all kinds of things to Matt's insides, and he had to look away.

Ollie caught the tension in Matt's shoulders and kept his eyes averted. He didn't want anyone to speculate about Matt, well, any more than he himself was. Was Matt a closet case, or in denial, or a reluctant 'baby-bi?' Whatever he was, Ollie couldn't help the thrill remembering Matt's mouth on his, his soft tongue, his strong hands, the treasure just behind Matt's zipper. He couldn't help but glance at Matt's mouth, then at his large hand gripping his nearly empty glass, before looking away.

He was distracted from his musings at the sight of Finn lifting her phone as she stood. His stomach plummeted with disappointment when Matt stood with her.

"Congrats on the win guys," Finn said as her eyes scanned the table. "We've gotta run."

Ollie stood to kiss Finn and shake Matt's hand, hungry to touch him one last time before letting him go.

"Sorry to see you leave."

"See you around," Matt said so casually Ollie wondered if everything had just been one-sided between them.

Ollie watched him leave, and smiled when Matt looked back for one last glimpse when he reached the door. *Maybe not so one-sided after all.*

11

Master and Servant

Finn kissed Matt goodbye when her car arrived in the morning to take her to Lord Archer's estate and vast library.

"I hope you don't plan on hiding here while I'm gone," she said pointedly.

"Bye, Chuck. Say hello to Ned for me."

He watched the car pull away and opened his laptop, trying to lose himself in emails but was unable to focus. He pressed his fingers to his eyes briefly and picked up his phone. He typed in Ollie's number, caressing the piece of paper with his fingertips, and hit send before he could chicken out, *again*.

"Hello, this is Oliver."

Matt closed his eyes at the way Ollie's name rolled off that beautiful tongue of his. "Hey Ollie, it's Matt."

"Oh, hi!" Ollie said, a surprised smile in his voice.

"Yeah. So, listen . . . I," Matt stammered and stopped himself, opening his eyes with resolve. "Wanna come over later?"

"I'd love to. Are you sure?" Ollie asked cautiously.

"Yes, Ollie, I am. Be here at three."

The buzzer rang at three, startling him again, his nerves frayed. He answered the door in his bare feet, feeling déjà vu. Though this time he was wearing a pink button-down, the top two buttons undone, and jeans. Ollie was wearing black flat-front chino shorts that stopped mid-thigh and a white button-down, sleeves cuffed like Matt's.

Ollie stepped through the door, glancing briefly at Matt with a shy smile, and closed it behind him. As Ollie made to walk past him into the flat, Matt put his arm across the hallway, his palm on the wall, barring Ollie's passage. Ollie turned his head and exhaled heatedly at the look in Matt's eyes.

Matt pulled Ollie to him without saying a word and kissed him. His fingers gripped the back of Ollie's neck like a lifeline as he opened his mouth to Ollie's tongue. He tried to keep their teeth from clashing, but Ollie was as hungry as he was and even less afraid. He gripped Ollie's firm bottom with his other hand and squeezed, taking Ollie's breath.

They stood, nearly as one in that dim, windowless hallway, their hands roaming as they fought to catch their breath. Matt felt light-headed as he lost himself in the minty taste of Ollie's mouth, and then his impossibly smooth jaw as he trailed kisses to Ollie's ear and back to his waiting mouth.

Matt felt the heat of Ollie's breath on his lips, on his tongue, as he panted in sync with his racing heartbeat. He felt Ollie's shaky fingers on the buttons of his shirt, his tentative fingertips on his chest, as though afraid he would be stopped. Matt moaned, the sound escaping him as Ollie pressed his palms against his chest.

No way he would stop him again.

"Oh, Ollie." Matt felt his nipples harden and tingle under Ollie's fingertips.

Ollie sighed against his neck as he teased them. "Your body is fantastic, and you taste so good," Ollie breathed and then ran his soft tongue up the column of Matt's throat.

Matt smoothed his hands slowly over Ollie's body, memorizing the contours, feeling Ollie's heart pounding under his palms. He studied Ollie's face as they kissed. Admired his long lashes (the color of Cape

Cod sand), his nose, so perfect and straight. Matt kissed the tip of it gently and smiled when Ollie's eyes fluttered open.

"You are so beautiful. You haunt my dreams," Matt whispered as he cupped Ollie's face in his hands and tilted his head back, exposing Ollie's throat to his tongue and nibbling teeth. Ollie murmured something unintelligible into Matt's mouth as he rolled his hips into Ollie's, searching for relief that only Ollie could provide.

Ollie's large smooth hands on his skin felt so foreign, so unquestionably male and utterly, overwhelmingly, arousing, it made him dizzy. He leaned back against the wall to steady himself.

"I could kiss you for hours, Ollie. The taste of you, your mouth, so perfect," he murmured against Ollie's lips. "I can't wait to see what else it can do," he added brazenly, *expectantly*.

Ollie's lips curled up in a sexy grin. "I can't wait to show you."

Matt hummed low in his throat and kissed Ollie's neck, his lips finding the sensitive spot behind Ollie's ear that made him moan. He felt Ollie tug his belt open, and then his nimble fingers on his button and zipper before lowering to his knees. He brushed kisses over Matt's nipples and stomach, his tongue teasing his bellybutton.

Ollie made a low sound of appreciation as he freed Matt from his underwear. "Christ, your cock is *magnificent*."

Matt held his breath as he watched Ollie run his tongue around the tip, as Ollie kissed his way down the shaft, and then as he ran his soft tongue back up and across the top, pressing inside briefly before taking the whole thing deep in his warm, wet mouth. Matt felt a zing through his entire body as though he'd touched a wet finger to an outlet. Ollie's eyes were closed (perhaps in ecstasy) as he worked Matt over, twisting his head slightly each time he reached the tip, one hand joining his mouth and the other stroking and tugging gently on his balls.

Ollie opened his eyes and looked up at Matt, his pupils so big his eyes looked black. He pulled off and jacked Matt slowly as he caught his breath.

"You taste amazing," Ollie declared and licked the clear drip from the slit of Matt's dick.

"Jesus, Ollie," Matt exhaled and rolled his head back against the wall, marveling at the sensations of Ollie's mouth, his hands, so much better than Sam, than anyone.

Magic.

Ollie's tongue was everywhere. He felt it in the crease where his thigh met his groin, he felt it up one side of his dick and down the other, he felt it on his balls, just before they disappeared one at a time into Ollie's hot mouth.

"JesusfuckingChristOllie." The words were a rush, and then followed by a string of Italian expressing a similar sentiment.

Ollie smiled and took Matt back in his mouth, one hand stroking Matt's shaft and the other on Matt's hip. Matt ran his hands through Ollie's thick hair, holding his head as he thrust, his eyes locked with Ollie's. After months of fantasizing about this very moment, this very thing, with his eyes closed, he had no intention of ever closing his eyes again.

Ollie moved his hand out of the way and onto Matt's other hip as Matt inched deeper and deeper, over, and over. Matt's breath came in short gasps as he lost himself in the rhythm, only slowing when he felt saliva on his balls and noticed Ollie's eyes watering.

"Mmnf, nnn," Ollie made a sound of disagreement and shook his head once. He slid his hands around Matt's hips to dig his fingers into his ass cheeks, urging Matt on as he bobbed his head and gagged. His throat closed tightly over the head of Matt's cock and that was it.

"Oh god, Ollie. I'm gonna come," Matt groaned as the pressure in his spine became a heaviness between his legs.

Matt surrendered to the building starburst, his body tensing then loosening like the bursting of a seam as he cried out.

Matt felt Ollie's tongue slowly roll around his cock as he swallowed every drop, gasping as the air returned to his lungs.

"Holy shit," Matt added when the waves subsided, his breathing heavy and his heart pounding as though he'd just sprinted uphill in full gear.

"Oh my, Lieutenant. What a welcome," Ollie exclaimed breathlessly, swallowing as he rocked back on his haunches and wiped his eyes and chin on his sleeve.

Matt leaned his head back briefly against the wall, pulled up the front of his jeans and took Ollie's hand, helping him to his feet. Matt kissed him deeply, tasting the saltiness of himself on Ollie's tongue with a smile. He wanted to touch Ollie, but not yet, not in the hall. One more kiss with a swipe of a tongue across Ollie's bottom lip, and a gripping of fingers, Matt led Ollie to the bedroom.

Matt closed the door behind them and unlaced his fingers from Ollie's. With a glance and the flash of a smile, Matt opened the top drawer of the dresser. He took out a strip of condoms and a small bottle of Swiss Navy and put them on the bedside table as Ollie watched with smoky eyes. Matt scanned his eyes over Ollie, pausing on the glint of his silver chain above the dip where Ollie's neck met his shoulder, and blew out a slow breath.

"Take your clothes off. I want to look at you," Matt commanded softly.

Ollie let out a little moan, and began unbuttoning his shirt, holding Matt's gaze. "Just to look at me?" he asked with a cheeky grin, his clothes dropping to the floor around and beneath him.

Matt stripped off his shirt with a low chuckle and draped it on the back of the desk chair behind him. "No, Ollie." He shook his head. "I'm gonna do such things to you. I've just got to decide which, of all the things I've fantasized about doing, I'm going to do first."

He stared hungrily at Ollie's smooth and muscular chest and let out an appreciative breath as he continued to scan lower. Ollie's skin was a golden hue with the exception of a white outline of tiny swim trunks. He had a neatly trimmed patch of hair just above his glorious erection, the sight of which made Matt's stomach do a little flip. This gorgeous man was naked and aroused because of him. Matt was both afraid and desperate to touch him.

"God, your body is outstanding. Even more amazing than I imagined. And I've been imagining it a lot. Lie down," Matt ordered, as he stepped out of his jeans and folded them on the back of the chair. He stepped out of his Tom Ford trunks and laid them neatly on top of his jeans.

"You are bloody beautiful, Lieutenant. Even more beautiful than I imagined, and I have been fantasizing about you nonstop. God, your tattoos," Ollie murmured from the bed, running his eyes over Matt's chiseled body, the tattoo on his bicep, and the long, silver trident tattoo over his heart. Ollie sighed. "Your body. Christ, your cock."

Matt lowered himself to the bed and pulled Ollie against him, kissing him deeply, tasting the dip of his neck, teasing his lips over Ollie's collarbone. He licked the underside of Ollie's jaw and pressed his thighs against Ollie's as Ollie ran his hands up Matt's back. Matt closed his eyes and inhaled, Ollie's delicious scent filling his nose as it coated his skin. He felt more alive in that moment than he had in more than a decade. His skin tingled everywhere it touched Ollie's warm, almost fevered, skin, and he wanted every inch of him on his body.

He pulled Ollie astride him, smiling inwardly at the feeling of Ollie's strong thighs on either side of his hips, Ollie's erection hard and warm on his stomach. Ollie kissed him gently as Matt ran his blunt fingertips up and down Ollie's back, deepening the kiss and squeezing Ollie's bottom tightly.

"This is nothing like I remembered," Matt said quietly, more to himself than Ollie. "You can't tell anyone, Ollie. I mean it," he whispered firmly against Ollie's mouth. "If you can't be quiet this ends now."

"I won't say a word," Ollie said softly. "No one would believe it. I can't believe it," he added with a small smile, a tiny dimple appearing in his cheek.

Matt kissed him again, for his promise, for his *everything*. "Good, because your body, your mouth," he whispered against Ollie's neck and ear, shaking his head slightly in wonder as he buried his fingers in Ollie's soft hair, "I don't think I could actually stop myself."

He swept his tongue slowly around Ollie's and ran his hands over Ollie's smooth, white bottom, his fingers teasing the cleft of his cheeks. Feeling bold, Matt slipped a finger into his mouth and ran his tongue over it, holding Ollie's gaze before returning his hand to Ollie's crease.

Matt couldn't help the moan, any more than Ollie could as he pressed back onto Matt's finger. Ollie's lips on his neck, the motion in his hips sharpened Matt's senses and wakened his body. Ollie fucked himself on Matt's fingers with increasing urgency as he sighed with need in his ear.

Matt rolled Ollie onto his back and reached for the side table. He stared down at Ollie's gorgeous face, unable to look anywhere else as he paused what he was doing.

You're really gonna do this? There's no turning back if you do, Matt thought as he looked away.

Ollie sat up on his elbow at Matt's hesitation and gripped Matt's ass, pulling his hips in. He reached for the small bottle and popped the lid.

"Why don't you get your fingers back inside me and then tell me you want to change your mind," Ollie challenged with a quirk of his eyebrow. He ran his fingertips over the trident tattoo and Matt's nipple before laying back and taking Matt's hard length in his hand.

Matt let out a husky laugh and took the bottle from Ollie. "Bossy boy."

"Only because I want you so badly, and I do so hate to be kept waiting," Ollie whispered and stroked himself, using just his thumb and two fingers, drawing Matt's eye. "Be sure you use extra lube and go slow. *Seabiscuit,*" he added with a small grin.

Matt's chuckle turned into a growl. "I'll be the one giving the orders."

He bit Ollie's neck lightly, and with a tear of the packaging, and a snap of the lid he was between Ollie's thighs. His eyes locked on Ollie's face, his arm cradled Ollie's head, his lips a hair's breadth from Ollie's as he pulled his fingers away and eased in.

"God, you're so tight," Matt breathed.

"Christ, you're so *big,*" Ollie panted with a hint of amusement and a look of concentration on his face that matched Matt's as he bore down lightly to help Matt in.

It took several breaths until he was finally buried inside, and Matt lowered himself onto his elbows with a moan. He held his breath as he waited for Ollie adjust. Ollie nodded after a moment and Matt began moving slowly in long teasing strokes, his breath coming in short puffs as he sped up, until Ollie pushed gently on his chest.

"You keep rubbing your washboard over my cock and I'm gonna come as fast as you did in the hallway," Ollie gasped with small laugh. "I doubt even you, Lieutenant, can come again so fast, so give me a little space."

Matt lifted up to look at Ollie as a thrill pulsed through his body. He kissed Ollie gently, holding himself away and still.

"The thought of watching you come, *making you come*, will get me there in no time," he whispered against Ollie's lips.

Ollie moaned and Matt smiled as he raised up on one fist and held Ollie's thigh open with his other hand. He thrust in earnest; his eyes locked on Ollie's face as the sound of bodies slapping filled the room. Matt rolled his hips, changing his angle of attack and felt his balls tighten in response to the drawn-out moan that slipped from Ollie's throat.

"Oh god, Matt," Ollie panted. "That is the opposite of what I asked for. You're gonna make me come."

Matt let go of Ollie's thigh and began stroking him, his eyes focused on what his hand was doing. Ollie was so smooth and warm and hard in his hand; he almost didn't want it to end. *Almost.* He held his breath and clenched his jaw, waiting for the show, his own orgasm hovering in the wings, as he moved his hips in short deep strokes.

"Oh . . . oh, god," Ollie cried out, and there it was, like a fireworks display. Splatters of thick white cum painted Ollie's chest and hit the pillow next to his head.

Oh my, Matt thought, his last clear thought before surrendering to an explosive orgasm of his own. He collapsed onto Ollie's chest, his body still quivering.

"Holy fuck." Matt pressed his ear to Ollie's neck and heard his pulse pounding just as wildly as his own.

Perfection, he thought as he kissed Ollie's neck, his ear, his jaw, and hugged him tightly, savoring the moment before clean-up.

Ollie was loose in his arms, as though he couldn't move, or do anything but lock his hands behind Matt's back.

"That was amazing."

Matt waited with a pleased smile for Ollie to stop gasping and panting, and then rolled away to dispose of the condom and get the towel he had tucked into the side table.

"I think I got most of it, but you'll have to flip the pillow." Matt grinned as he mopped Ollie's stomach and then his own.

Ollie ducked his head and rubbed his eye shyly. "I'm not usually that, *emphatic*." He rolled onto his side as Matt stretched out on his back.

Matt tucked Ollie under his arm, lost in the sensations that were still coursing through his blood. So pleased with Ollie's response, the chemistry they had. He waited for the shame and uncertainty to wash over him (the taste of Ollie's skin in his mouth, the scent of him in his nose) and raised his eyes to the ceiling with a smile at the lack of anything other than pure contentment.

He felt Ollie's fingers like a whisper over the raised, two-inch, jagged pink mess of a scar just above his right hip. "What happened?" Ollie asked softly.

"I was shot," Matt answered quietly, reluctant to talk about it.

"Christ. How?" Ollie came up on one elbow with a frown.

"By a gun," Matt answered with a chuckle, warm from Ollie's concern.

Ollie let out a small laugh but with a continued frown and raised his eyebrows expectantly when Matt didn't elaborate.

Matt sighed and pressed his head back in the pillow, furrowing his brow, lost in the intimacy of the moment. "We were in Afghanistan, looking for someone." He slid his eyes to Ollie's and then away. "It was dark, I had planned for everything. We had intel, eyes in the sky. One of my guys didn't clear the corner, place was a mess, hard to see. He died. I didn't. Obviously. I got the fucker though. Shot him in the leg, and stabbed him in the neck." Matt closed his eyes, seeing the event clear in his mind, feeling the flash of anger and helplessness.

"Jesus Christ," Ollie breathed and laid back in Matt's arm with a slight frown, the violent image sudden and unwelcome.

"I would've been dead too, if I hadn't had my appendix out as a kid."

Ollie made a sympathetic sound, and shuddered lightly trying to envision himself in Matt's shoes, and was wholly unable to.

"What did you mean about my bare feet?" Matt asked quietly after several moments of silence.

Ollie paused trying to remember what he was talking about and then chuckled, relieved at the change of subject. "No gay man I know would ever answer the door barefoot. Especially if company was expected." He shrugged. "It's a very 'straight' thing to do. But it's okay, you have beautiful feet. In fact, everything about you is beautiful." He kissed Matt's nipple.

Matt made a sound like a short laugh. "Apparently the men in the Navy think casual footwear and slippers are a gay thing too. Broke me of the habit at Annapolis freshman year with one comment: 'what are you gay, Dion?' I honestly didn't even know that was a thing. I grew up with sisters. The only acceptable casual footwear among all those cadets and soldiers was flip flops in the showers. They made me wear flip flops, Ollie," he said in mock horror.

Ollie snickered and snuggled into Matt's side, feeling small (though he wasn't) next to Matt's tall and solid body. He outweighed Ollie by at least three stone and was solid muscle. Ollie had just begun to hum *Your Body is a Wonderland* when he felt Matt's fingers under his chin. He sat up at the expression in Matt's eyes, and kissed him softly, then deeply as Matt rolled him onto his back with a full body sigh.

Ollie pressed his head into the pillow and wondered if he were dreaming. How could this be the uptight and guarded Matt Dion he met months ago? The man whose hands he had to pry off the counter and beg for his touch. This Matt, was nothing like that man, and that wasn't a complaint.

Ollie rapidly lost track of everything Matt was doing with his hands and mouth and yet was fully aware. A mouth on his nipple, then the other nipple, a hand on his shoulder, on his thigh, cupping his calf as he kissed his way down Ollie's leg. His big toe in Matt's warm mouth, a kiss on the back of his bent thigh, a whisper of breath just behind his balls before being rolled over.

Ollie felt Matt's hands on his bottom, his fingers smoothing themselves in the cleft between his cheeks, then heard the pop of a lid and the tear of a package. He marveled over Matt's stamina before moaning with pleasure as he felt, first Matt's fingers, then his cock pressing inside him. Matt's other hand slipped between the mattress and Ollie's body to stroke him.

Wonderous and attentive top, Ollie thought as he closed his eyes with a sigh and lifted his hips.

Matt sought Ollie's mouth, forcing Ollie to turn his head over his shoulder to meet Matt's tongue, and need. Matt was slow at first, but then rolled Ollie onto his side and gripped him under his arms, one hand cupping the back of his neck half-nelson style, and increased his pace, his urgency.

"More . . . harder . . . yesss," Ollie moaned, his pleasure overriding the burn as his senses were lost to him.

Matt collapsed against Ollie's shoulder. "Holy fuck."

Matt nibbled his way from Ollie's neck to his shoulder. He kissed Ollie's back, licking the sweat he found there, before releasing Ollie's raised knee and rolling away. Ollie flopped onto his back, his body still humming with desire and lust, and ran his fingers over his erection.

Matt looked over his shoulder and scanned his eyes down Ollie's body, catching sight of Ollie's hand on himself. Impulsively he leaned forward and kissed Ollie's stomach.

"We're not done yet," he said as he took Ollie in his mouth, stroking him with his tongue, just like Ollie had done in the hall.

Ollie moaned and pressed his hips up encouragingly, so Matt pressed his fingers inside him, wondering if the prostate was like a G-spot like with some women. Judging from Ollie's response, the answer was a resounding yes, and Matt bent his fingers into a beckoning gesture as he slid them in and out.

Matt closed his eyes at the audacity of what he was doing, the thrill of Ollie's body tensing and writhing under him. Never had he considered putting his mouth on a man. The thought had always made him uneasy. But everything about that afternoon felt new, and earth-shattering, and Ollie's smooth hardness inside his mouth felt so perfect, so right, so *normal*.

Before he could worry about whether or not he was doing it right, Ollie groaned loudly, bent his knees, and slid his fingers into Matt's hair as he lifted his hips off the bed. Matt considered pulling off, *you're gonna let a guy come in your mouth, Lieutenant?* But the taste of Ollie was too sweet, and he swallowed reflexively as he pushed the thought aside.

Matt kissed the inside of Ollie's thigh and looked up to find Ollie watching him with a satisfied smile. He dragged himself up Ollie's body and kissed him.

"Did I hurt you?" he asked quietly as he held Ollie's gaze. Matt couldn't remember a time when he'd ever bothered to ask a woman that question.

"No. That blow job was incredible." Ollie blushed.

"I didn't mean that. But thanks." Matt grinned and brought Ollie's hand up to kiss the tips of his fingers. "I meant the sex."

"Oh." Ollie slid his glance away. "A little," he breathed after a moment. "But, it's okay. It felt amazing. You're . . . so big. I see why people use poppers." He laughed lightly and ran the palm of his hand lightly down Matt's chest and over the ridges of his abdomen. "I hope I get to get used to it," he whispered.

Matt looked at him for a few beats as he pondered letting Ollie get used to him. He grinned and kissed him softly, feeling as though he could lose himself in Ollie's kisses for an eternity.

"What are poppers?"

"Oh, it's something you sniff to relax your muscles, and it's a pretty big, but short-lived rush. Lots of gay guys use them," Ollie replied. "Tops and bottoms."

"Have you?" Matt asked with dismay.

"No, not me, I've never needed to." He laughed lightly. "I'm quite boring really."

"I don't think you're boring at all," Matt said quietly. "But I don't want you using poppers or any drugs."

"I don't, and I won't," he replied, holding Matt's gaze.

Matt smiled and kissed Ollie again, teasing with his tongue. "I'm starving. I ordered pizza earlier; it should be here in about fifteen minutes."

They took a short break to eat and talk and laugh about nothing. Ollie barely finished a slice in the time it took Matt to eat the entire thing and then he was on his feet, dragging Ollie into the shower with a laugh. Matt took his time lathering Ollie's body with soap, savoring the slippery feeling of their limbs twining around each other as they fought for the stream of hot water.

Ollie was so easy to rile, and had the easiest-to-find tickle spots he'd ever encountered, not to mention the most delicious laugh. Matt had to restrain himself from full-on torture. He managed until the very end, when he finally let Ollie have the water, only to turn it ice cold before dodging out of the stream.

"You fucking bell end!" Ollie shouted and pushed past Matt, his laugh echoing off the tiles.

Matt's sides hurt with laughter as he shut off the water and grabbed a towel. "What's a bell end?" He ran his eyes over Ollie as he toweled off.

"You," Ollie replied earnestly with a grin.

Matt straightened and began twirling his towel with his eyebrows raised.

Ollie took a step back. "You wouldn't."

Matt fought his grin and tilted his head. "I don't know. What's a bell end, Oliver?"

Ollie shrieked and ran from the bathroom, his towel dropping to the floor in his haste to get away.

Matt tackled him on the bed, catching Ollie's laughter in his mouth as he tickled him mercilessly.

"Stop! Stop! I can't breathe!" Ollie cried as he writhed, his abdomen taut with laughter.

Matt rested his hands on Ollie's hips and gazed down into his face, so flushed and beautiful. His eyes danced as he caught his breath and stared up at Matt.

"Where did you come from? Am I dreaming?"

Ollie melted into Matt's hands. "I could say the same."

Matt lowered his head and kissed the smile from Ollie's mouth. He eased his body half on the bed, half on Ollie, and ran his hands over Ollie's damp skin.

"You have the most beautiful legs," Matt exhaled. He squeezed Ollie's knee and then swept his hand back up between his thighs, cupping Ollie's balls in his hand. He captured Ollie's moan against his lips as he stroked upward, and felt the goosebumps he raised on Ollie's beautiful body.

Ollie was giddy with awareness, and almost giggled, especially with how quickly things turned serious. He wondered, as Matt's mouth and hands roamed his body, if Matt was expecting more sex. He couldn't help his body's response (everything about the man turned him on), but he was hoping penetration was done for the night, and, more importantly, that he didn't have to say that out loud. He wasn't a timid lover, by any stretch of the imagination, but something about Matt made him tentative.

When Matt reached for the lube and not the condom, Ollie leaned forward. When Matt dribbled some of it into his hand and over Ollie's cock, Ollie relaxed into the mattress. And when Matt took them both in his large hand, moving his hips in sync with his grip, Ollie moaned and pulled Matt by his shoulders into a deep kiss.

Matt covered Ollie's body as he caught his breath, and then rolled to his side, pulling Ollie against him after he wiped their stomachs with the hand towel. "That was . . . something I've never done before."

"Really?" Ollie marveled, his blood still roaring in his ears. "Well, I hope it felt as amazing for you as it did for me."

"More than amazing." Matt kissed the tip of Ollie's nose. "Especially because of you. I love the sounds you make. Your face when you come."

Ollie felt his skin flush as he ducked his head into Matt's armpit. "That's embarrassing."

Matt nudged his tickle spot with his strong fingers, chuckling as Ollie squirmed away.

"Sexy. Irresistible. And anything but embarrassing," Matt whispered against the side of Ollie's head.

Ollie tightened his arms around Matt's body and took a deep breath through his nose, committing Matt's intoxicating scent to memory. He closed his eyes briefly and felt the haze of sleep wash over him. He made to pull out of Matt's arms, thinking about the walk home.

"Where are you going?"

"It's getting late, I should go."

"No." Matt tightened his arms. "I want you to stay."

Ollie relaxed back into the bed, a flutter in his stomach at the command. "Okay, but I didn't bring anything with me."

"Chuck has extra toothbrushes and things in the bathroom drawer. She always keeps packaged stuff like that."

"Great. I'll just go brush my teeth then. Back in a flash." He felt Matt's eyes on his body as he left the room without bothering to dress.

Matt brushed his teeth as well and then spooned himself around Ollie when he came back to bed. It was cool in the bedroom, despite the summer night, and Ollie fell asleep immediately, cocooned in Matt's arms.

12

The Good with the Bad

MATT WOKE IN THE MORNING at five thirty like clockwork and the world came back to him after a moment of disorientation. He pulled himself slowly away, careful not to wake Ollie as he disentangled his body from his, and looked at him, naked on his side facing the curtained window. Blonde, beautiful and golden skinned, his back smooth and muscular like an Italian Renaissance painting of a god, Ollie was a vision and Matt blinked to be sure he wasn't hallucinating.

Matt had woken up surrounded by men countless times, but never to one naked in his bed and while he was marveling over Ollie, he still felt a brief flash of anxiety before remembering that they were alone in the safety of Finn's flat. It was just then that Ollie sighed sensuously, rolled onto his back, and smiled in his sleep, causing a visceral response Matt felt like a zap to his groin. He looked away, confused but content, and closed his eyes briefly before getting out of bed to dress for his morning run.

Matt found a small piece of paper on the desk and jotted a quick note, leaving it on the pillow for Ollie, not knowing what time Ollie usually woke. He tied his sneakers thinking about just how little he

73

actually knew of Ollie, but what he did know about him he liked, *a lot.* Matt put his phone in his armband holster and quietly left the flat.

The run along the river was peaceful, Matt encountering only a handful of other runners out enjoying the silence. His mind was fully focused on Ollie and all the incredible things they had done. A night with more than a few firsts for him, all of them far exceeding his expectations and memories.

Incredible? More like depraved and disgusting, his father's voice interrupted.

His elation crumbled with the intrusive thought. If his father were still alive, he would *never* have acted on his feelings. Hell, he would never have flown to the UK to begin with, he would have shut Finn and her stories about Ollie down before she could even pique his interest.

"But *you're not alive, Papa,*" he whispered with an angry frown and pushed aside his shame, focusing instead on Ollie, perfect, happy-in-his-skin Ollie.

Matt's heart felt light for the first time since he was a small child (before he knew anything about judgement) and he stopped running, suddenly overcome with the unfamiliar sensation. He wondered briefly if he was having a heart attack, but he was wholly without pain, in fact it was the opposite, and so foreign that he experienced a flash of anger. If this was what happiness felt like, *true* happiness, then why had he gone so long without feeling it?

Fuck you, Papa. And then instantly felt guilty for the thought.

Matt shook his head and began running again, focusing on the positive. He knew he wanted more of Ollie, he needed more of Ollie. He had thought, *like an idiot,* that having sex with Ollie would cure him of his obsession, but it had only opened the floodgates.

Ollie was unlike *anyone* else, and felt so incredible to be with, to be inside of, to taste, that the teenage memories of that boy in Italy he clung to so desperately were pathetic in comparison. Like the difference between a dry, tasteless, mass-produced, store-bought peach, and a lush, juicy, delicious one grown in his grandparents' orchard in Italy (or Kensington in this case).

Matt laughed to himself. It was life in technicolor after decades of black and white. He increased his speed as he ran back to Finn's flat. He wasn't going to change his lifestyle, but he wasn't going to let Ollie go either.

Ollie woke earlier than usual. He was not a morning person by any account and rarely woke before ten during the summer. He found a note on the pillow next to him, the handwriting neat and strong, and smiled.

GONE FOR A RUN, BACK BY 7 – M

He laid back on the pillow and sighed happily, reliving the intoxicating events of the previous day and night. Matt was a god, and insatiable. He had never been with anyone so gorgeous, or so well-endowed, or who fucked so well. He felt a twinge thinking about Matt's moves, the spine-tingling sounds he made, the positions he had put him in. He pressed his face into Matt's pillow and breathed in his heady scent, a mixture of clean soap and pure sex, with undertones of the salty ocean and sun-kissed sand. Ollie thought of the way Matt tasted, sweet and indescribable, then of the way he moved, spare and thorough, and then of all the things he'd said, dirty or otherwise.

Ollie was hooked.

He pulled the covers up and remembered how he nearly fell out of his bed when Matt called him yesterday. He barely remembered the conversation, and had spent the rest of the day watching the clock tick out the minutes until three. Time passed excruciatingly slowly, and he'd been filled with doubt about Matt's intentions. He had played over and over the sound of Matt's voice.

What coded message was hidden in his brief invitation? Did he just want to talk? Did he want to make sure Ollie hadn't gotten the wrong idea from their kiss? Were they just going to chat and eat before Matt kicked him out again, frustrated?

Ollie had paced his flat, and then the block, and then spent nearly an hour getting ready (showering thoroughly, shaving carefully), until finally it was time to leave. When he arrived at Finn's with a stomach filled with butterflies, he nearly swooned at the way Matt barred his entry, the heat in Matt's eyes, the desire vibrating in him. Ollie blew out a breath heatedly with the memory, and smiled, thrilled that Matt didn't keep him wondering all night about his intentions. It was clear Matt couldn't have waited another second either.

He flung back to sheets and pulled on his underwear, feeling sore but happily so. He couldn't get enough of Matt's body and how amazing it felt to be with him, it was worth the pain. For the first time in his life, he understood the blurring of the two sensations.

No, he had never experienced anything like that before and he wanted more, he *needed* more.

Ollie didn't have any clothes other than the ones he arrived in so he opened the dresser drawer, shaking his head that Matt would bother to unpack for a long weekend, and took one of Matt's neatly folded t-shirts. It said 'Navy' on it and was a size too big, but smelled deliciously of him. Ollie held the shirt to his nose, breathing deeply, before putting it on and opening the bedroom door.

Matt was in the living room, shirtless in his running shorts, doing wide-armed push-ups, music playing on low volume. Ollie stopped short to watch, his mouth dropping open appreciatively as Matt's muscles flexed with each one. Matt moved his hands closer, under his chest, and began again, utterly focused. Ollie counted to a hundred when Matt stopped and lowered himself to his forearms, holding a plank position for five minutes.

Just as Ollie was beginning to think about pulling up a chair, Matt pushed himself to his knuckles and then into a standing position. Dripping sweat, he looked up and caught Ollie standing there. Matt smiled, breathing heavy and wiped his face with his t-shirt.

Ollie shook his head and raised his eyebrows. "Bloody hell, Lieutenant. Are you an android?"

Matt smiled in response and went into the kitchen to fill his water bottle. He drank, watching Ollie carefully, running his eyes over Ollie's body, his eyes hot as he slowed over Ollie's bare legs. He filled his bottle again and drank half.

"I like my shirt on you." He walked past Ollie. "Get the stuff off the side table and join me in the shower in two minutes." He turned into the bathroom without waiting for a response and shut the door.

Ollie stared at the closed door with a look of surprise on his face, looked down at his tented underwear and with a shrug went to do as Matt ordered.

Matt emerged from the bedroom tying his tie, a Brioni suit coat draped over his arm, and looked at Ollie sitting on the couch scrolling through his phone.

"I'm headed back to London for meetings, including a dinner. I'm sure you have things you have to do today, or you can hang here, I don't care, I just expect you here when I get back," he said as he pulled on his coat, and pocketed his phone. He picked up his laptop and put it in the leather zip folio case.

"What if I have plans?" he asked rebelliously, tilting his head.

"Cancel them."

Ollie frowned slightly at Matt's tone. "And if I don't?"

Matt looked at him, narrowing his eyes imperceptibly. "You're a grown man, and can make your own decisions," he answered with a shrug. He reached into his pocket and tossed a box to Ollie that he caught against his chest. "Give those to Chuck." He put on his Ray Bans and walked out the door without a backward glance, looking like a model.

Ollie turned the box of ear plugs over in his hand and stood to look out the window. He watched as Matt got into the back seat of a black Range Rover, the driver holding the door open for him. Matt looked up at Finn's living room window and smiled as he climbed into the back seat. There's no way he could see into the room from the glare of the sun, but he did it anyway, as though he knew Ollie was watching. Ollie closed his eyes with a shuddering breath, something about Matt, a *je ne sais quoi*, overrode the warning bells in his head.

13

Understand Me

FINN AND OLLIE LOOKED UP from the couch as they heard the door open. Finn paused *Cape Fear* as Matt came through the narrow hallway in the dim light, his tie loosened and top shirt button undone. He gave Ollie a secret smile when he came in.

Smart choice, Matt thought.

"Hey, babe." She sat up from Ollie's shoulder. "How was London?"

"British," Matt responded with a grin. "I got two contracts to review and wined and dined a third that I feel confident about closing in the next couple of weeks. I'll be busy tomorrow reviewing them."

"I could help you," Ollie offered.

Matt smiled. "I have lawyers to do that for me, but thank you."

"Matt, you should let Ollie have a look at them. He is a lawyer, and he's top of his class. He's the smartest person I've met at Oxford," she added and looked at Ollie with a broad grin.

Matt looked at Ollie. *Well, well. Will wonders never cease?* he thought with a pleased smile. Finn never exaggerated and he believed her opinion to be above reproach.

"Is that so? I just assumed you were a history major like Chuck. Why didn't you say something?"

"You never asked." Ollie shrugged.

"You know contract law?"

Ollie grinned and nodded. "I have my Bachelors in UK and EU law, and I've just graduated with my Masters in law and finance. I did all my electives in contract law, and mergers and acquisitions." Ollie paused. "I start my MBA in October."

"I told you," Finn said smugly and leaned back lacing her fingers on top of her head.

Matt scanned his eyes over Ollie, catching the glint in Ollie's eye. "Great. Now I'm in an even more celebratory mood." He put down his folio and walked to the breakfront that Finn had converted into a bar. He took down a glass and went to the kitchen for ice.

Finn appeared at his elbow. "I'm glad everything went well today." She kissed his cheek. "And yesterday. . . . " She grinned.

Matt felt a nervous flutter and looked at the back of Ollie's head. "Did he say something?"

"No, not a word," Finn shook her head and leaned in close. "But jeezus, it's on both your faces, and he practically began vibrating when you walked through the door.

"I'm going to bed, and I'll have my music on. Oh, and the earplugs I found on my pillow in my ears." She laughed and then looked at him solemnly. "You deserve to be happy. I love you so much, and I really hope this works out, because I love Ollie too."

He pulled her up against him, and kissed her forehead. "Whatever I did to deserve a glance and a giggle from you all those years ago, I am forever grateful. I owe you everything." He furrowed his brow seriously and then kissed her lightly on the lips. "Now go to bed." He waggled his eyebrows salaciously at her.

Ollie said goodnight to Finn and watched Matt walk back to the bar and pour himself two fingers of whisky. He took a swallow and returned Ollie's gaze with a quiet expression on his face.

Matt sat in the chair next to the sofa. "You made the right decision," he said softly, looking at the ice in his glass. "Don't jerk me around." He looked back up at Ollie. "I didn't care for your 'what ifs' today."

Ollie frowned slightly, rebellion welling. "Well, I didn't care for the order that you gave me. I have a life you know."

Matt studied him carefully. "I meant what I said. You're a grown man, and can make your own decisions. I would never force you to do something you didn't want to. Nor expect you to." He waved his hand. "If you hadn't come back, I would have understood your decision. I wouldn't have liked it or agreed with it, but as I said, you are free to decide, just don't play games." He paused and held Ollie's gaze. "I've just thrown away a decade of discipline, I'm taking an awful risk with you. I don't say that for any reason other than to make you understand my position. I can't be carefree, but, Ollie, you make me want to be."

Ollie looked away briefly. He hadn't considered their relationship (if it could be called that yet) from Matt's perspective and had sudden clarity that this man, who had been living such a repressed life, might not actually know how to deal with what he was feeling. The thought that Matt was risking so much to be with him, that he wanted to be 'carefree' because of him, made Ollie tingle and he felt his body begin to warm.

He understood in that instant, that Matt was a man who was used to giving orders, and having those orders followed, and that perhaps with Ollie, he didn't yet comprehend how else to be. Ollie blew out a slow breath as he held Matt's gaze.

I'll teach him.

Matt quirked his eyebrow and finished his whisky. Ollie watched as he unfolded his body and crossed to the bedroom, closing the door behind him. He stood, feeling Matt like a gravitational pull, and stepped through the door quietly. He leaned back against it in a near swoon at the sight of Matt undressing. He had his coat and shoes off and was unbuckling his belt. His clothes were so perfectly tailored to his body, Ollie couldn't decide if he wanted him to continue or stop.

"Come here, Ollie," Matt said quietly, his hand stilling. "I want to undress you and look at your beautiful body. You've tormented my thoughts all day. *Again.*"

Ollie's stomach flipped and he pushed himself away from the door. "And I want you to leave your clothes on," he said, reaching for Matt's zipper. "God, you're magnificent."

* * *

Finn left in the morning for tennis with Sophie, and Matt had pounced on Ollie immediately after the door closed, to Ollie's great delight. They'd been up late, and Matt had been for a run, but he still had the energy to fuck Ollie into the mattress.

"How'd you get rid of all your hair?" Matt asked when he came back to bed after their morning marathon session, running his fingers between Ollie's legs.

Ollie flashed seductive smile. "Nair for my bollocks, wax for my crack."

Matt chuckled with a wince. "Doesn't that hurt?"

"Yes, but it's so worth it." He swirled his tongue around Matt's. "You like it don't you?"

Matt growled appreciatively and rolled Ollie onto his back. "I love it."

"Here you go." Ollie appeared in the living room before dinner in a pair of shorts, and handed Matt the two contracts he had reviewed. "I made quite a few revisions and suggestions."

Matt put his laptop next to him on the couch and flipped lightly through the pages, noticing that nearly every page had some form of edit or commentary. He looked up at Ollie.

"Thorough, in and outside the bedroom," he said with a grin and a happy flutter in his stomach. "I like it."

Ollie smiled happily.

"I'll give my legal team clean copies and see how their work compares." He paused. "When do you finish your MBA?"

"Next summer, after my internship," he answered sitting down in the chair next to the couch.

Matt studied him silently. "I leave tomorrow."

Ollie shifted his beautiful blue-green eyes away. "I know."

"Come to Boston, I'll buy you a ticket," Matt said impulsively.

Ollie looked at Matt with his eyebrows raised. "I've never been," he said with a smile.

"I assume you have a passport?" He closed his laptop, put the papers on top and set it on the coffee table.

"Of course."

"Send me a picture of it, and I'll get the tickets for the week after next," Matt said and patted his lap. "How long could you stay?"

Ollie straddled Matt with a kiss. Matt pressed his tongue into Ollie's mouth, hungry for the taste of him.

"I have to look at my calendar, but I'd say probably a week or so."

"Good," Matt sighed happily and ran his hands up Ollie's naked back, kissing him again, his five o'clock shadow causing Ollie to shrug his shoulder reflexively.

Matt maneuvered him fluidly onto his back, his muscles flexing with the effort, and covered his body with a contented sigh.

* * *

"Thank you for the tickets. I can't wait to see you in a week," Ollie said with one eye on his computer screen.

"You're welcome," Matt replied with a smile in his voice. "I can't wait to have you in my bed."

Ollie smiled and leaned back on his bed with a flutter in his stomach. "I have something to confess, Lieutenant," Ollie whispered, holding the phone close to his mouth, mindful of his flatmate on the other side of the wall.

"Oh yeah, what's that?"

"I stole a pair of your underwear," Ollie breathed as he looked down at himself. "And I'm wearing them right now."

Ollie could hear Matt's breathing as the silence stretched. "Is that right?"

Ollie made a sound of agreement.

"I too have something to confess," Matt said quietly. "I found your underwear at the bottom of my suitcase when I got home, and not only do I sleep with them, I'm wearing them right now too."

"Oh, is that so?" Ollie closed his eyes at the visual and ran his finger over his erection, the material already damp at the tip.

"Yup. Though I have to say they're more like panties, Oliver," he said with a small laugh.

"Well, on you I suppose they would look like panties. Your magnificent cock must feel quite constrained. You should free it, Lieutenant," he whispered, slipping his hand beneath the waistband of Matt's underwear, wishing he was finding Matt's hard cock instead of his own.

"Oh, it's not only been freed, it's in my hand right now."

"Jesus Christ."

14

Coming to America

OLLIE BOARDED THE PLANE, a thrill in his belly with the first-class seat and with the thought of what was waiting for him in Boston.

The past week had dragged and he was desperate to see Matt again, smell Matt again, touch Matt again. He smiled to himself and looked out the window, happy that the seat between him and it was unoccupied.

"Champagne?" the flight attendant asked, holding a tray of glass flutes filled with sparkling wine, the bubbles coursing up the sides ecstatically.

"Yes, please. *Slainte*." He took one and raised his glass before taking a sip. The attendant watched him appreciatively and then turned to the woman behind him.

The woman across the aisle smiled and raised her glass. "Cheers!" she said in an American accent.

Ollie smiled. "Cheers."

She looked at him carefully. "Are you on *Sons of Anarchy*? I don't mean to be an annoying fan."

"No," Ollie replied with a smile. "I've never heard of that one. I take it that's an American show?"

"Yes, but one of the leads is British, Charlie Hunnam. You look like a younger, clean-cut version of him, and I thought maybe like most actors the hair and beard were just for the role." She smiled.

"I know him. He's done quite a bit here, and at university I had a flatmate who said I looked like him."

"Oh, well it's a compliment," she said flirtatiously.

"Is the show any good? What's it about?" Ollie asked, taking another sip.

"It's really good. It's about a motorcycle gang in California, but of course so much more than that." She laughed lightly. "You should check it out."

Ollie shrugged. "Okay."

They chatted intermittently throughout the flight, the woman flirting openly. Ollie found out her name was Heather, she worked in marketing for a large global company, and made the trip to London several times a year. The last detail she added suggestively.

Ollie was pleased with the attention, smiling to himself that she thought he was a celebrity, and that she didn't know he was gay. He wasn't in the closet, but he valued his privacy, and his sexuality certainly wasn't the business of strangers. Matt took it a step, or twenty, further: denying his sexuality entirely to the world, to himself truly, with the exception of Finn. Before he left he was very clear about the subject.

"I won't ever touch you in public, other than a handshake or a bro hug," Matt *said, while Ollie watched his profile. He turned his head on the pillow to look at Ollie. "No one can ever know about me, Ollie. No one does know, except Chuck and you, and the teenager that I was with when I was seventeen." He paused. "We won't have romantic dinners out, no holding hands in the park, no kissing you for the world to see." He rubbed his lips together. "I say this, so you know what to expect, especially in Boston. I need to know now that this is something you can agree to."*

Ollie bit his lower lip thoughtfully. "I'm not a fan of PDA to begin with. I don't care for people snogging in the park or over dinner. I'm not in hiding, but I am private. It will be difficult to keep my hands to myself though, you are so bloody gorgeous, and feel so good in them." He smiled and leaned in for a kiss.

Ollie looked up as the flight attendant returned again. "We'll be landing soon," he said with a smile and walked away.

"Logan airport, and Boston, are notoriously confusing," Heather said. "Let me know if you need any help finding the baggage carousel, or your accommodations," she added with an inviting grin.

"Thanks," Ollie said noncommittally with a smile.

Heather ended up shadowing him to the baggage carousel and through customs. They exited the double doors into a crowd of people waiting for their loved ones. Ollie scanned the crowd and saw Matt, looking impossibly handsome in linen, hanging back close to the exit, standing a head taller than most of the people around him. Ollie smiled broadly meeting his eye, as a warm pressure built behind his ribcage. His heart thudded when Matt flashed him a lazy smile in return.

"There's my friend. Nice talking with you."

She followed his gaze, and widened her eyes appreciatively. She reached into her pocket and pulled out a business card. "Call or text if you need a tour guide."

Ollie took the card and looked back at Matt, who was watching with an amused expression on his face.

She gave him a long look before walking away, slowing down slightly as she passed Matt. He smiled and inclined his head at her as she went by.

"Hey, Ollie, how was the flight?" Matt asked dryly, shaking his hand and giving him a one-armed bro hug with the other. Ollie took a deep breath through his nose and closed his eyes briefly at Matt's intoxicating scent.

"Uneventful."

"Is that so?" Matt smirked, taking Ollie's bags and leading the way out the glass doors to the parking garage, putting Ollie's luggage in the trunk and then opening the passenger door.

"Nice car, Lieutenant," Ollie said appreciatively, admiring the immaculate interior.

Matt pushed the start button and the engine roared to life. He squeezed Ollie's thigh briefly. "I missed you," he said quietly, staring at him.

Ollie lowered his eyes to Matt's crotch, suddenly on fire at the thought of straddling that lap. "Just drive, for fuck's sake. I want to wash the stench of the airplane off of me, and then lick you from head to toe. It's all I've thought about."

Matt chuckled, a low, warm sound that traveled directly to Ollie's groin. He put the car into first and pulled smoothly out of the parking spot. It was a short drive to his condo in the North End, and an endless ride up the elevator from the garage. Matt forbade him from standing near him because of the cameras. The tension built as the bell pinged each floor, punctuating the rising of their desire.

Christ, is this lift powered by hamsters? Ollie thought as he studied the bulge in Matt's pants.

Matt shot him a glance when they finally reached the fifth floor and stepped off the elevator. Ollie barely noticed the brick hallways as he followed Matt inside his condo, which was a masculine mixture of more brick, wood beams, and white walls. Hardwood floors were decorated with a smattering of richly colored oriental rugs, and furniture was spare but expensive-looking. Ollie managed to get a quick glance around before locking eyes with Matt as he closed the door behind them.

Matt dropped Ollie's bags and grabbed him, pushing him against the wall and kissing him deeply. Matt's hungry and gripping hands were like fire on his skin as he swirled his tongue around Ollie's ecstatic one. Ollie had been nervous that Matt would revert back to his guarded self, especially after the prudish elevator ride, but if anything, Matt was even more of a fiend than he'd been back in Oxford.

Ollie hurriedly undid the buttons of Matt's shirt, kissing Matt's neck and licking his throat, his lips never breaking contact with Matt's body. He didn't want any sudden change of heart, and began rethinking his need to shower. Matt groped him over his jeans, his hand on the front as insistent as the one pressing low in the crack of his ass.

"Nice place, Lieutenant," Ollie said breathlessly through kisses.

Matt pulled back to look at him with smoky eyes. "You have five minutes to shower. I'll give you the tour later."

Ollie followed Matt through the bedroom and into the bathroom, his fingers tightly gripped in Matt's large hand. He stripped quickly and stepped under the warm water, careful not to get his hair wet. The shower was big enough for two, but Matt just stood in the doorway and looked between his watch and Ollie expectantly. Ollie grabbed a washcloth from the shelf at the end of the stall and ran it under the water as he watched Matt grab the pull-up bar above his head in the doorway. Matt lifted himself off the ground in one fluid motion and began doing chin-ups with his knuckles facing out, and then some more with his knuckles facing in.

Ollie fumbled with the body wash and swabbed vigorously between his legs. He might have washed his armpits, probably soaped the rest of his body as well, but he couldn't have testified to that in a court of law to save his life. All the blood had fled his head and gone straight for his cock. He rinsed the soap from his body with his eyes locked on Matt.

Matt dropped to his feet and stripped off his clothes when Ollie shut off the water. Ollie took the towel Matt handed him and admired Matt's glorious cock. *Yes, it is as beautiful and perfect as I remembered.*

"I meant to ask in Oxford, where're your tan lines?" Ollie whispered and raised his eyes to meet Matt's.

"I'm on the top floor, I have two decks, roof access, with plenty of privacy. You're gonna lose your tan lines too. Though I do love this smooth white ass of yours." He smacked Ollie's bottom with a satisfyingly sharp crack and smiled at the flare in Ollie's eyes.

Ollie followed Matt into the bedroom with a stinging ass cheek and ran his hands over Matt's back as he pulled the covers back on the bed. Matt turned and kissed Ollie with barely contained urgency.

"I missed you," Matt murmured into Ollie's neck, kissing his way along the column of Ollie's throat. "So many nights spent remembering, dreaming, plotting . . . I'm gonna take you apart piece by piece, and maybe put you back together."

Matt bit Ollie's neck and then whispered something in Italian as he ran his hands over the smooth ridges of Ollie's body. He guided him onto the bed, stretching out atop Ollie so every bit of their skin was touching. The stubble on Matt's jaw burned tantalizingly against his throat and then on his chest drawing a moan from Ollie's mouth. He couldn't wait to feel it on his stomach, on his thighs, but the rate they were going, this wouldn't progress that far.

Matt felt Ollie's moan in every nerve of his body. He kissed all of Ollie's sensitive spots, licked his nipples, and then rolled him over.

"I missed this," Matt said before spreading Ollie's cheeks and diving in with his tongue.

Ollie was the first man he'd done this to and just like the blow job, Matt had no idea how much he would love it. Going down on a woman was fine, but it had never turned him on like when he had his tongue buried in Ollie's ass.

"God, I missed you," Ollie murmured when Matt rolled him back over and covered his body with a moan. "You and your tongue."

"We are gonna have a great week," Matt replied, reaching between their bodies to take Ollie in his hand with a grin and a groan.

"Your mouth is not only beautiful, it does beautiful things," Matt praised, tracing Ollie's lips with the tip of his index finger before kissing him softly.

Ollie trailed his hand lightly down Matt's chest at a loss for words, his contentment overwhelming him as the room and the world came back to him.

"You must be hungry, I know I am," Matt murmured against Ollie's mouth, and rolled away, tossing Ollie the towel. "Get dressed, we're going to the restaurant across the street. We'll sit at the bar, and maybe buy a drink or two for some pretty women."

Ollie frowned at Matt's back as he wiped his chest. "Why would we do that?"

Matt looked back at him as he pulled on his clothes. "Appearances, Ollie. We might not have to, I'm a regular there. I'm just reminding you about how it has to be here, while you're here."

Ollie nodded and stood from the bed. "Fine with me." He left the room to get his luggage, uneasy with the extra subterfuge. *Why bother?*

Matt ordered food and drinks without asking Ollie what he wanted, but Ollie smiled to himself, not caring, because Matt somehow knew exactly what he liked. Everything Matt ordered was perfect and what Ollie would have ordered for himself. Ollie wondered how he knew, and felt a flare of desire from the attention. It took all his self-restraint to not rub the back of Matt's neck, or thigh, as he would have with any other lover, and clenched his fists instead and took a sip of his beer.

"This looks like a really nice little neighborhood. It's the Italian section of Boston?"

"Yeah, my mother's parents lived two blocks that way until they died, and my father's parents lived a block and a half that way until they moved back to Italy. They only stayed until my father graduated high school," Matt answered, gesturing the directions with his hands as he spoke.

"Your father didn't want to move back with them?"

Matt shook his head. "He had met my mother at that point, and had a good job working construction. He loved America. His parents never learned the language, and never felt at home here. We visited them back in Italy almost every year until I graduated high school." Matt looked out the window, a flash of something crossed his face and was gone before Ollie could name the emotion.

The waiter brought their food, whisking each course away as soon as they finished. Fresh oysters, fresh pasta, and incredibly fresh seafood had Ollie's taste buds tingling with pleasure. Ollie smiled to himself as he watched Matt, so confident and in his element, and then remembered what they'd been doing just thirty minutes prior. He looked away with a quiet gasp as his body tingled along with his taste buds.

The conversation was casual, but the looks Matt gave him smoldered. And were gone as fast as they appeared. Ollie kept his own heated gaze in check as he sat back with his last bite, taking in the ambiance, noticing the restaurant filling up around them. Jetlag pounced on him and he yawned behind his fist for the second time.

Matt signaled the bartender for the check. "Don't fall asleep on me just yet," Matt said under his breath as his eyes scanned the room.

Matt paid the bill and they walked back to his building, separated by the holy ghost. Once inside Matt's condo they reached for each other, the time out in public short, but vexing.

15

All My Love

The next few days were a whirlwind of sexual satisfaction, interspersed with Matt working all hours of the day, and Ollie reviewing whatever documents Matt gave him. It was a dream for Matt to have Ollie in his condo, where he could do all the things he imagined and fantasized about doing to him in the privacy of his own home, free from judgement and prying eyes. Ollie was a willing and enthusiastic partner, with incredible skill and imagination of his own, rousing feelings in Matt he never knew he had, especially on day two, when he took a break from work to make Ollie quiver and moan, and found himself quivering and moaning instead.

"You're finally off that dreadful phone, or are we on speaker, Lieutenant?" Ollie asked coyly as he looked up from the bed, holding his book open with a splayed hand. He was clad only in his tiny briefs, looking freshly showered and entirely lickable.

Matt grinned, loving how Ollie pronounced it 'leff-tenant' the British way, like a secret nickname only he could use. "I have about thirty minutes, what do you got for me?"

Ollie slipped his bookmark into his book and tossed it onto the nightstand. It landed in the same spot where Sam's necklace had been not so far in the past, but it may as well have been a lifetime ago.

"I have your greatest desires." Ollie smiled softly as Matt climbed across the bed toward him.

Matt kissed each of Ollie's impish dimples and then his waiting mouth, losing himself in Ollie's soft lips, his soft tongue, as though he'd been doing it forever and not just a few dozen times. He let Ollie peel his shirt off.

"That sounds like a tall order, Oliver. You ready to fulfill that promise?"

"Oh, I always keep my promises," Ollie breathed and rolled Matt onto his back.

Matt pressed his head into Ollie's warm pillow as Ollie kissed and nibbled his way down his body. When Ollie reached his bellybutton, he pressed his tongue into the shallow divot with a sexy smile that Matt met with a smoldering gaze, waiting eagerly for Ollie's mouth to go even further south.

Ollie kissed him over his underwear and then licked a swath up Matt's cock after peeling them off. He smiled at Matt's resulting moans, taking him deep and then pulling off to tease Matt's balls with his tongue. He moved lower, jacking Matt slowly with his hand as he swept his tongue over Matt's sensitive taint. Matt lifted his hips encouragingly, his gravelly groan making Ollie grind his hips into the mattress.

"It feels good, doesn't it?" Ollie raised up to meet Matt's hooded gaze. Matt nodded, his Adam's Apple bobbing as he swallowed roughly. "Just you wait." Ollie smiled and sucked his finger suggestively.

Ollie wasn't entirely sure if Matt had ever experimented with anything anal on himself, but was guessing he hadn't (though he was more than obsessed with Ollie's ass). After a brief hesitation, hoping it wasn't too soon, Ollie held his breath and circled Matt's hole with his wet finger. He licked the underside of Matt's balls at the same time that he pressed gently into Matt.

Ollie pulled up on his elbow when Matt clenched and lifted his shoulders off the bed to glare at him.

"What are you doing? Mine's exit only." Matt frowned with hooded eyes.

"You've never been introduced to your prostate?" Ollie raised his eyebrows, his hand stopping mid stroke as his finger paused.

"No," Matt answered hesitantly.

"Oh, babe, you're in for a treat!" Ollie beamed and grabbed the lube. "Why do you think I howl so much when you fuck me?"

"Because you love my dick? And I fuck you like a god. Your words, not mine." Matt grinned cockily.

"I do, and you do, but there's more. Trust me."

Matt looked at Ollie with a furrowed brow and fell back onto his pillow in acquiescence. Ollie covered his fingers in lube, and worked with focus, determined to make Matt light up like a Christmas tree. He had to tell Matt to relax more than once until he'd finally got past Matt's uptight clench.

"God, you're so hot, and tight. I'm gonna make you feel so good. As good as you make me feel," Ollie promised, stroking Matt's cock back to attention when it flagged.

Ollie knew he hit the spot when Matt's hips shot off the bed. Matt gasped and then opened to Ollie like a flower. Ollie shifted up to take Matt's cock into his mouth and before long Matt was pressing against Ollie's finger, rolling his hips up until Ollie gagged and then back down into the palm of Ollie's hand over and over until his moan became a scream and Ollie's mouth was flooded.

"Jesus Christ, Merlin!" Matt gasped as he unclenched his fists from the sheets and ran his fingers through Ollie's hair. "You are a sorcerer."

"Did you see stars?" Ollie grinned as he wiped his mouth and climbed over Matt's body.

"I saw the whole solar system, Ollie," Matt breathed before kissing Ollie, his tongue rolling slowly around Ollie's as though he was trying to merge them.

"I popped your cherry!" Ollie beamed and then squealed when Matt poked him in his side.

"I was gonna make you breathless another way, but this might be more fun." Matt grinned mischievously.

Ollie struggled to get away. "No. Stop! That's mean. I'm horny!" he cried and writhed, gasping, as Matt pressed his fingers into Ollie's sides as though he were playing the trumpet.

Matt rolled on top of Ollie and kissed his laughing mouth. "Well, I better do something about that," he said as he stared down into Ollie's handsome face and kissed him again, folding one of Ollie's arms behind him on his pillow so he could admire and then kiss Ollie's armpit.

*　*　*

When they weren't destroying the bed (or the couch, or Matt's office chair), Matt couldn't keep his eyes off Ollie, following his every move, admiring the way his legs flexed, the tilt of his head when he turned to the sun, his beautiful armpit when he ran his hand through his wavy hair. Matt loved to bury his nose in the smooth spot where Ollie's neck met his shoulder and breathe in, Ollie's incredible scent like a crisp fall morning with undertones of sandalwood and sex. Ollie was everything and more than he had ever hoped for: confident (but fully obedient), adventurous (especially in bed), and hilarious (he'd never laughed so much in his life). The more time he spent with Ollie, the more he felt like a whole person, finally. His heart was full but so light he worried it would escape from its cage.

Ollie was in heaven, and enjoying himself far more than he imagined he would. He wasn't sure what to expect (especially after Matt's strict list of dos and don'ts for when they were in public) but it certainly wasn't constant, unbridled passion and sex. He chuckled to himself with the absurdity of their behavior, sniffing each other like dogs in heat, touching every moment that Matt wasn't working (and sometimes when he was), eyes following each other's every move. Ollie was amazed that he ever believed Matt was straight, amazed how Matt had hidden it for so long.

Ollie loved the way Matt's hand always left a burning a trail over his body, the way his hot eyes scorched his skin, almost reaching a fevered pitch as they slowed over his legs. Ollie felt so powerful, so needed, and so absolutely stunned that he (of all men) had been the one to break Matt's rigid resolve. Stunned too by how new to intimacy Matt seemed, and he wondered why. Surely Matt had had relationships, been cherished, or cherished another? He was too skilled a lover not to have, and yet, it all seemed unfamiliar to him. Matt's inexperience only spurred Ollie to want to do more.

His only goal for the week was to please Matt however and whenever he could. He was happy to follow Matt's orders (bend this, touch me here, come for me), and when Matt was working, Ollie did what he could to torment him: walking naked past the office door, dropping things just to bend over and then taking his time picking them up, stretching shirtless in his sightline when Matt was on the phone. All done so that Matt's eyes would follow him, knowing that when Matt hung up, he would come looking for Ollie, press himself inside him with a passionate sigh, touch him with his strong hands, use his glorious tongue.

* * *

On Ollie's third day in Boston the buzzer rang, startling him as he reviewed a contract on the couch. Matt jumped up from his computer and went to the speaker. He pressed a button and opened the condo door after a moment, greeting whoever it was in rapid Italian.

A short, balding man wearing a white button-down shirt and black chinos with a portable rolling rack of suits appeared wheeling his wares beside him, the wheels squeaking in chorus with each other.

"Oliver." Matt gestured with his head for him to come over. Ollie stood and crossed the room to shake the man's hand. "This is Tony, he's my tailor. Tony, this is my new UK lawyer, Oliver. He's fresh out of school and needs a few decent suits," he said looking at Ollie, and then back at Tony. "I'll leave you to it then. *Grazie.*" He strode to his office, closing the door with one last look at Ollie.

Tony sized Ollie up as Ollie frowned at the door Matt closed behind him.

"Matteo got your measurements perfectly it seems. Let's start with this one," he said with a thick Italian accent, and pulled a navy-blue Tom Ford suit off the hanger. "Take off your shorts."

You sound like Matt, Ollie thought to himself, feeling like a doll. He scowled rebelliously as he slipped off his athletic shorts and stepped out of them, wondering how much ribbing his friends would give him if they knew his boyfriend (was Matt his boyfriend?) was dressing him.

Forty-five minutes later Ollie was fitted for three suits, and several shirts. Matt came out to say goodbye to Tony as he left with the rolling rack, pressing some cash into his hand and speaking more Italian, Tony laughing at whatever it was that Matt said.

He looked at Ollie once the door was closed. Ollie shook his head. "You're not seriously buying me those, *Matteo*. They look quite expensive."

Matt nodded. "You're a smart, beautiful man who is destined for great things. I will not sit back and let you wear mid-grade suits off the rack." He took Ollie's hand, a warm zing passing between them as usual. "You caught things in those contracts that my legal team didn't, netting me far more money and peace of mind. You earned those suits. If your internship can be done here in the states next summer, I want you working for me. I'll find you a place to live, pay you handsomely, and tack on all kinds of fringe benefits," Matt added with a grin and suggestive flick of his eyebrows grabbing Ollie around the waist.

Ollie smiled against Matt's mouth, pleased with the praise, and wrapped his arms around Matt's neck. "I like the sound of that. You mean like my own coffeemaker?"

Matt chuckled and kissed Ollie's neck, his lips dancing over Ollie's light stubble. "Yes, I will make you coffee every morning."

Ollie rolled his head back and then looked at Matt contemplatively. "What about casual Fridays? And your American 'Hump Day' celebrations?" he asked mischievously.

"Every day will be hump day for you, Ollie." Matt licked Ollie's bottom lip with slow deliberation. "And Fridays will be so causal you'll work from home naked."

Ollie laughed his rich, deep laugh, and kissed Matt, touching his tongue to his. "As long as naked Friday takes place here with you, then I accept the offer."

"Of course," Matt replied with a hum. "It's company policy that naked Friday for British interns be supervised by the CEO."

Ollie held Matt's gaze and made a thoughtful sound. "Supervised? Do naked Fridays get out of hand?"

"There hasn't been one yet, but my recent experience with a certain Brit, tells me that close supervision will be required." Matt raised one brow and grinned.

Ollie pressed his nose to the hollow of Matt's throat before licking a path to his ear and nibbling on the lobe. "And knowing this American CEO, I'm certain there's a *strict* list of dos and don'ts. I wonder, how will those rules be enforced?"

"Oh." Matt laughed low in his throat and spanked Ollie sharply, savoring the flare in Ollie's eyes as the sound echoed. "Quite painstakingly, I can promise you that. I doubt any American would dare defy the rules, but I'm guessing that one particularly cheeky upstart from Kensington, might test his boundaries. In fact, I strongly encourage him to. Find out firsthand what the US military worked so hard to train me to do. I know more than a hundred ways to enforce *all* the rules."

"Oh my, Lieutenant. That got someone's attention. Dare I say two someone's attention?" Ollie looked down between them, and then back up at Matt with a saucy expression.

Matt made a low sound and pulled Ollie tight against his body.

16

Shaken not Stirred

"YOU SHOULD CALL that Heather chick from the plane," Matt said offhandedly, loading the breakfast dishes into the dishwasher the following morning. "I'm flat out today and don't want you bored another day here."

"You want me to go on a date?" Ollie frowned. "With a woman?"

"I sure as shit don't mean with a man, Ollie." Matt looked at him carefully.

Ollie rolled his eyes to cover the pleasure he felt in his stomach at Matt's tone, and wondered again why he liked it so much.

"Did you just roll your eyes at me?" Matt asked narrowing his eyes.

"Did you just suggest I go on a date with a woman? While I'm here, fucking you." He pulled a face and spread his hands.

Matt looked at him for several moments. "I didn't mean a date, I just meant go see the city, with a woman who had offered to show you around. I don't want you to feel as though you came all this way to stare at these four walls.

"I'm still building my company and have to spend a lot of time on work, but I want you here, and I begrudgingly recognize how selfish that is. If you're with a woman, then I don't need to worry."

Ollie returned his gaze. "Worry? I could be out with a man; it makes no difference. I only want to be with you."

Matt's eyes burned as he flicked a glance at the clock on the stove and touched the front of his underwear. "I'm glad we're on the same page. Come here."

Ollie decided against contacting Heather and walked the streets of Boston, doing touristy things by himself, and enjoying every minute of it. He wandered through Faneuil Hall, Boston Common, and walked the Freedom Trail with all the other summer tourists. It was hot but glorious, and he found that he loved the city, so small, and yet so like home. He ended up at the Black Rose for a pint, listening to the talented live performer playing acoustic and electric guitar, singing everything from Prince to Deep Purple. His phone buzzed as he was about to order another pint.

> **Be home in 10,**
> **we're going out**

Ollie left some money on the bar and walked back to Matt's.

"Where have you been all day?" Matt asked.

"Fucking Heather." Ollie walked into the kitchen to pour himself a glass of water.

Matt came around the other entrance to the kitchen. "What was that?"

"Yeah, I took your advice, and spent the day with a woman. Maybe you should've worried more," he added in a dramatic voice, laughing to himself.

Matt narrowed his eyes and crossed the room, put his face next to Ollie's neck, and breathed in deeply through his nose. "What did I say to you about jerking me around?" he said quietly backing up. "Are you so young, that I need to repeat myself?"

"No. Christ, I was kidding. Don't you have a sense of humor?" Ollie frowned at Matt's reaction.

"Oh, I have a sense of humor, when people are being funny, not mocking." Matt watched Ollie carefully and gripped his waist, running his fingers under the waistband of Ollie's shorts. "We have dinner plans. I've decided I do want to take you out somewhere fabulous, and watch you enjoy yourself," he said as he undid Ollie's shorts.

Ollie closed his eyes as Matt slipped his hand into his underwear and kissed the sensitive spot behind his ear, quieting the alarm bells that were ringing mutedly in his brain.

"Okay. Sounds great," Ollie breathed.

Ollie followed Matt into Mistral, noticing how Matt scanned all the corners and then the room as he entered. Then he admired how smooth he was with everyone he encountered from the *Maître D*, to the bartender, to the waitress who said, 'hi, Matt,' in a breathless voice as she passed. Her eyes sweeping over Matt's impossibly tailored Brioni pants and white button-down. The crisp white emphasized the dark color of his Italian skin, and Ollie hoped she wouldn't drop the tray she was carrying as she swooned.

Ollie looked down at the dark jeans and pale pink button-down, he was wearing, and, while he knew he looked good, he was nothing compared to Matt. He fingered the silver chain around his throat distractedly as he watched the bartender hurry over.

"What do you want to drink, Ollie, other than a pint?" Matt asked his eyebrow raised, snapping Ollie out of his reverie.

"I'll have a single malt," Ollie answered with a smile. Matt looked at Ollie's mouth briefly and turned back to the bartender to order.

They clinked glasses and a moment later Matt stood as a gorgeous woman with long dark hair, in a slinky backless summer dress, appeared and pressed herself against Matt, kissing his lips and hugging him around the neck. Matt wrapped one arm around her (his hand low on her hip, Ollie noted irritatedly) and responded in kind. Matt extricated himself from her embrace and looked at Ollie.

"Sam, this is my UK lawyer, Oliver." He introduced them with a glance at Ollie, who managed to close his mouth just in time to smile tightly at Sam.

"Pleasure," Ollie said, shaking her hand as his mind raced.

Sam smiled; her thin face radiantly beautiful. "Nice to meet you. This is Imani." She turned to introduce the sultry woman next to her. Imani had glossy black hair, and was wearing a spaghetti-strapped summer dress that draped seductively over her slim body. At any other moment Ollie might have admired her beauty, but not then. "Imani, this is Matt, and Oliver."

Imani shook their hands and ran her eyes appreciatively over Ollie.

The bartender came back with the check. "Your table is ready."

The waitress with a thing for Matt appeared at his elbow (a spot of drool on her chin) ready to show them the way. Matt threw several bills down on the bar and nodded thanks to the bartender. Ollie picked up his drink and followed them warily to a cozy table in the back corner.

Matt and Sam sat on the plush banquette leaving Ollie and Imani to sit in the upholstered chairs opposite. Ollie watched in shock as Sam rubbed Matt's thigh familiarly (her hands touching what Ollie had run his tongue over less than an hour earlier) and then as Matt stretched his arm across the back of the banquette behind her. Matt trailed his finger over Sam's bare shoulder as though it were Ollie's bottom lip. Ollie stared at him, wondering what the fuck was going on, but Matt wouldn't meet his eye.

Matt ordered a bottle of wine and a few appetizers for the table. Imani insisted on making small talk, which Ollie politely engaged in, while keeping one eye on the travesty unfolding across the table. There was something burning behind Ollie's ribcage, and it wasn't pleasant. He felt as though he were participating in an improv that was anything but funny.

They ordered dinner, Ollie pointing at something on the menu without looking and then ordered another scotch, wanting to feel a buzz instead of the jealousy burning in his stomach. He was furious that he couldn't stop Matt from touching *that woman* and irritated that he had to guard his gaze so Imani and Sam wouldn't sense anything. All he wanted to do was stand up and shout, 'what the fuck?' but he bit his tongue and looked around the room to cool his anger.

Sam stood and left the table, looking pointedly at Matt, who followed a beat later. Ollie watched them leave, a cold pit in his stomach, and then turned to Imani who was smiling at him.

"So, you go to Oxford for grad school? But you're already a lawyer?"

Ollie nodded, his insides seething. "In the UK a law degree is undergrad, but I've just got my masters in law, and am starting my MBA this October."

Imani's beautiful face lit up with a smile. "Wow, gorgeous and smart." She gave him a heated look.

Ollie returned the smile. His upbringing forbade him from behaving as anything other than a gentleman in that moment. It wasn't Imani's fault he was feeling so out of sorts. He inquired about her about life in Boston, and they chatted until Matt returned to the table.

Ollie frowned and fought a sneer. "You have lipstick on your mouth."

Matt wiped his mouth on his napkin, an air of nonchalance Ollie was hoping was just performative. Sam came back to the table a minute later, with freshly applied lipstick and a satisfied look on her face.

Ollie's stomach churned. He wanted to throw his drink in Matt's face and storm out. He wanted to hop the first flight home, and those thoughts must have been all over his face because Matt gave him a quelling look (un-*fucking*-*believable*). Ollie finished his scotch and left the table, the blood roaring in his ears.

Matt appeared in the bathroom doorway a moment later. Ollie finished and zipped up, flushing the urinal with an angry flourish. He walked past Matt to the sinks.

"What is your problem," Matt asked quietly, checking the stalls for occupants.

"What is my problem?" Ollie asked incredulously. "What in the bloody hell are you doing? What utter nonsense is taking place here tonight?"

"I'm keeping up appearances. I wanted to take you out for a fantastic meal, a *romantic* meal. And this is the only way I can do so. I am only doing to her what I wish I could do to you here," he said quietly and nodded out to the dining room. "And she expects it."

"Oh my god. Is that your *girlfriend?*" Ollie gasped with realization. "You brought me out to dinner with one of your lovers." He shook his head, his body cold. "And if I had done the same in Oxford?" He glared at Matt. "I don't think you really thought this one through."

Matt gnawed on his bottom lip. "Maybe I didn't."

Ollie scoffed in disbelief. "I'm leaving."

Matt grabbed Ollie's arm. "No, Ollie. Let's just go back to the table, finish our meals. Feel free to take your frustration out on me with Imani," Matt said over his shoulder as he opened the door and left.

Ollie stared at the door for several moments, every emotion he had ever felt running through his mind and body.

What in the actual fuck?

He tried to picture a scenario where Matt's behavior would be sanctioned and was at a loss. He looked at himself in the mirror as he washed his hands and, with an angry sigh, rejoined the table as their meals arrived. He studiously, and angrily, ignored Matt, focusing solely on Imani; flattering her for her beauty, her smooth skin, her slinky dress, and trailed his finger over her bare shoulder.

Imani scooted closer to Ollie and put her hand on his chair next to his hip, leaning in close to his ear. "Your accent is making my toes tingle."

Ollie felt Matt's eyes burning into him, and Imani's lips next to his ear. He turned to face her, their noses less than a foot apart. "Speaking of sexy accents, where are you from, Imani?"

"Barbados. I came here for high school and never left, and I'm so glad I didn't." She looked at Ollie with sultry eyes. "Has anyone ever told you how much you look like that hot guy from *Sons of Anarchy?*" She smiled seductively.

He looked back at her with an equally seductive look. "A few people. I didn't bring my motorcycle, but would you care for a *ride?*" he asked in a low deep voice and quirked his eyebrow at her, just drunk enough to consider leaving with her to spite Matt. She wouldn't be the first woman he had sex with.

Imani laughed throatily. "Oh, yes please. Come back to my place. I'm not far from here, and Sam wants to be alone with Matt."

Ollie glanced at Matt and sat up at the storm cloud on his face, before remembering that Matt was the one who put them in this position.

Matt stood and left the table as Sam watched his back worriedly, and then looked at them with a placating smile. She smoothed her hair like a timid waif.

"He gets a little moody. Don't worry, it's nothing."

Ollie ground his teeth, and nearly scoffed at her submissiveness. Matt's behavior was so much more than *nothing*, how could she just sweep it aside? He frowned and took a healthy swallow of his beer, wondering if there were truly any difference between him and Sam; both of them so eager to explain away Matt's inexplicable behavior.

Matt returned to the table, and sat down. "I have a terrible headache brewing. I hate to beg off dessert." He looked between Sam and Imani. "I've paid the bill and you can tack on whatever you want." He put a hundred on the table and smiled at Sam, squeezing her knee. "Oliver and I are leaving."

He kissed her lightly and stood, Ollie following suit. Matt strode away from the table and Ollie made a little half bow, kissing Imani's knuckles.

"Goodnight, ladies," he said with a smile, happy to be leaving, but fuming inside.

Ollie found Matt tipping the valet and getting into his car. Ollie got in the passenger side and closed the door. Matt put it in first and chirped away from the curb without looking at him.

Ollie studied his profile. "Well, that backfired spectacularly for you."

Matt shot him a look. "I said take your frustration out, not grope and eye-fuck her at the table in front of the whole restaurant," he spat.

"Oh, right," Ollie scoffed. "I should've taken her to the back hall and finger-fucked her, while grinding my cock against her hip." He shook his head disgustedly and then gasped as Matt flinched. "God, I hope you washed your hands," Ollie said angrily, his stomach burning with jealousy. "I can't believe you. What was it you said about not jerking you around? No playing games? What kind of 'do as I say not as I do' bullshit was that?"

Matt clenched his jaw.

"I don't know what kind of complacent rubbish your girlfriends give you. What *Samantha* gives you," Ollie sneered. "But I won't roll over and take your bullshit. I will be on the next plane faster than you can say 'Bob's your uncle.' And you can kiss this ass and this mouth goodbye, as if they'd never been." Ollie gritted his teeth.

Matt's jaw clenched, and Ollie imagined he could hear teeth cracking as they rode the rest of the way in silence.

Matt slammed the condo door shut behind them and Ollie stopped in his tracks. "I'm seriously hoping it's not me you're angry with," Ollie said as Matt walked to the bar and then turned away without pouring a drink. "The person who deserves your ire is in the mirror."

Matt stalked to the bedroom as Ollie crossed to the living room slider and looked at the harbor, the lights of the city reflecting on the water like flames. His stomach was cold and he wasn't sure what the coming night held. He wondered if he should cut his losses and leave like he'd threatened. Matt was even more fucked up than he imagined.

Ollie looked up, torn from his musings at the sight of Matt emerging from his bedroom, dressed in his running gear. He watched as Matt picked up his phone and crossed to the door.

"Where are you going?" Ollie called with a frown.

"I'll be back in a couple of hours," Matt said curtly, pulling the door firmly behind him.

Ollie stared at the closed door and then looked at his phone for the time. He knew he couldn't get a flight out that late, but resolved to look for one in the morning. He brushed his teeth, his body full of disappointment. He so wanted Matt to be the one, and again, he was wrong.

Ollie rinsed his toothbrush and scoffed at himself. *You're twenty-three, you have your whole life ahead of you, and Matt is just a steppingstone on your journey. A lesson to be learned.* He switched off the light and went to bed, waking a couple of hours later when Matt climbed in beside him, his skin clean and heavenly-smelling.

"What are you so afraid of?" Ollie asked quietly, turning his head to look at Matt.

Matt stared at the ceiling. "Nothing. Everything. You." He shook his head. "And, I'm angry," he said in harsh tone. "At the world, at myself. At god." He closed his eyes. "Go back to sleep, Ollie."

Ollie watched him sadly for several moments before closing his eyes and doing as he was told, thinking maybe he wouldn't leave without an explanation.

Ollie woke again in the deep dark of night to an empty bed, Matt's side cool under his hand. He listened for sound from the bathroom and hearing none got up, a slight panic in his belly. It was a moonless night and the condo was blanketed in darkness. He made his way carefully to the main living room and saw Matt outlined against the sliding glass door that led to the deck. He was naked like a Greek god, glorious and perfectly formed. He had something in his hand, and turned as Ollie approached.

"I was just coming to wake you," Matt whispered and opened the slider. The summer night air breathed warmly in, raising the hairs on Ollie's arms and legs.

Matt reached his free hand out to Ollie, beckoning. Ollie stepped into his arms and pressed his naked body against Matt's, fitting there perfectly like the missing half of something important. They kissed lingeringly in the open air of the doorway, Matt responding ardently against his hip.

Ollie put his hand on Matt's chest. "Are we going to talk about dinner?"

Matt's eyes shone in the dark. "No." He took Ollie's hand. "Come on."

He led Ollie out of the air-conditioning and up the two steps into the warm summer night. Matt's proximity, Ollie's involuntary reaction to Matt's body all overrode his brain. *We'll talk about it later,* Ollie thought as he looked around at the mostly sleeping city. They were invisible on Matt's private deck, the space contained by a waist-high wall of brick, and separated from his neighbors by a high brick wall that went up to the overhanging roof.

"I want to pretend the world can see us," Matt said quietly, slipping his hand around Ollie's front and pressing up against him.

He kissed a trail from Ollie's neck to his ear. Ollie closed his eyes and rolled his head back to Matt's shoulder, guessing this was an apology of sorts, one he was more than happy to accept.

"This will be as close as I can come to publicly acknowledging us. Can we skip the condom?" Matt's breath a whisper against Ollie's ear, raising goosebumps on his skin.

Ollie's stomach fluttered with expectation, and he nodded. "Yes."

Matt moaned low in his throat as Ollie looked out over the buildings and at the harbor beyond. He heard the snap of a lid and felt Matt's slippery fingers smooth between his cheeks and then into him. Ollie sighed passionately as he pressed back.

"Dio," Matt exhaled against Ollie's neck. He murmured something else in Italian before switching back to English. "You feel incredible. So tight, so warm. You just might be the death of me."

Ollie closed his eyes in ecstasy as Matt began moving. "Small deaths only, Lieutenant. And I'll be right there beside you."

Matt's hand closed over Ollie's throat as his lips grazed his ear. "I'm gonna fuck you senseless, but you have to be quiet." He bit Ollie's neck gently. "If I can keep it down, when you feel like this?" He thrust against Ollie with a quiet moan in emphasis. "You can be a good little church mouse."

Ollie closed his eyes and prayed for restraint, like *a good little church mouse*, he thought with a groan.

Ollie listened to Matt's heavy breathing, felt Matt's heartbeat thudding through his body as he considered what the neighbors might've heard if they were awake. Skin slapping furiously (especially towards the end), choked moans and groans, and two strangled cries of pleasure as he and Matt orgasmed one after the other.

Matt's hand pulled away from Ollie's cock with one last stroke, as the other squeezed his throat before letting go. "Christ, Ollie. That was. . . ." He stepped back, unsteady on his feet.

Ollie let go of the half wall and turned to look at Matt, his heartbeat pounding in his ears. Matt's eyes were dark, and his face was happy. Ollie felt his heart flutter and leaned forward to kiss Matt.

"Do you want me to wipe that up?" Ollie looked pointedly at the white splatter between his feet.

Matt shook his head and gave him a small smile as he inhaled through his nose. "I want to remember this. Even long after the rain washes that away, I will know it was there." He turned and went into the condo.

Ollie leaned back and turned his face to the sky with his eyes closed. He always felt at peace under the stars, the vastness of the universe reminding him that nothing really mattered as much as it seemed. He let out a deep breath and looked around the deck before turning his gaze to the empty living room.

Matt had seemingly taken a large step away from his self-torment, and that eased Ollie's worry. His feelings for Matt were growing stronger every day, and what happened at dinner had made him doubt everything. However, it was becoming quite clear that Matt was living in a prison of his own creation, and it must be hell in there. Ollie made his way inside, hoping he was making the right choice in staying.

17

Decisions, Decisions

MATT WAS GONE when he woke. The note on the pillow said he was out for a run. Ollie rubbed his eyes and went into the bathroom to brush his teeth. He poured coffee, grabbed a pint of washed blueberries and sat on the deck with his book, enjoying the morning sun on his bare chest. He had closed the browser on his flight search before shutting off his laptop. He decided to put aside his jealousy and his anger and focus on helping Matt accept himself. There were so many layers to Matt, so much repression, Ollie knew he needed to be patient and understanding.

You had better be worth it, Lieutenant.

Ollie looked up ten minutes later when the slider opened, and sweaty Matt stuck his head out with a flash of white teeth.

"Lazy bones, so sexy in the sun," he said quietly with a laugh. "One of these days I'm waking you up and you're coming with me."

Ollie pulled a face. "I run, but there's no way I could keep up with you, and I wouldn't dream of asking you to take it easy on me," he said with a suggestive smile.

Matt squinted and smiled thoughtfully at his meaning, his eyes moving over Ollie's body. He glanced at the dried spot on the deck from the night before and looked back at Ollie.

"Come inside in twenty minutes." Matt's head disappeared and the slider closed.

Ollie looked at the door and sighed. Matt was a powerhouse with an endless supply of energy. Ollie knew he was inside doing sit-ups, push-ups, and chin-ups, he did it every morning without fail. He smiled, thinking how lucky he was to be the beneficiary of the end result, that beautiful body that was all his to explore, admire and enjoy. He looked down at the front of his underwear. "Yes, we are very lucky indeed, aren't we, little Oliver."

Ollie joined Matt in the shower twenty minutes later. He washed his back until Matt turned around and kissed him, his lips seemingly every-where at once. Ollie closed his eyes and opened his mouth wider for Matt's tongue when his lips returned to his. He ran his hands over Matt's hot skin as Matt reached between them. Ollie groaned long and slow, and opened his eyes to find Matt watching him, his eyes locked on Ollie's face and body. Through the haze of passion, Ollie realized that Matt always had his eyes open.

"Why do you always have your eyes open?" he whispered against Matt's lips.

Matt pulled back with a small, sexy grin. "I closed my eyes and fantasized about you for months. I don't want to miss a second of any-thing with you."

Ollie felt his erection jump in response to the heat of Matt's tone. "Oh," he breathed.

Matt squeezed Ollie gently with one final stroke before turning him to face the shower wall. Ollie felt Matt's lips on his neck as he pressed his fingers inside him. "I'm sure I'll close my eyes someday, but not today," he sighed against Ollie's ear as he moved his fingers away and eased his hips slowly forward.

"Oh god, Lieutenant. That is so bloody hot, and you feel so fucking good," he groaned as Matt began fucking him slowly.

* * *

Ollie spent the afternoon away from the condo, clearing his head and giving Matt space to work. He spent a great deal of time between all his stops thinking about the future. *Could there be one with Matt?* Ollie's mind was more settled by the time he rode the elevator to the top floor laden with bags, but he was no closer to a decision about the coming months.

"Where have you been?" Matt asked when Ollie came through the door.

"Scouring your wonderful fish and farmer's markets." Ollie put the bags on the kitchen counter with an 'oomph.' "And I noticed you have fuck all for cooking spices and necessities, so I prowled the shops." Ollie lifted out fresh vegetables and jars and bags of spices and fresh herbs. "Your cabinets are filled with cereal, peanut butter and jam." Ollie shook his head with a laugh. "You live on breakfast and take out? I mean, you have eggs in the fridge, so I can assume you know how to scramble them."

"That's a pretty reckless assumption." Matt grinned. "I didn't even know I had eggs in there. You check the date on the carton?"

Ollie threw his head back and laughed. "You lie, Lieutenant. There's no way you don't know exactly what's in every cabinet and receptacle in this flat, and exactly how it's positioned so that you know when something's been touched."

Matt smirked. "I'll admit that you're mostly right, but when it comes to foodstuff, I know the inventory of cereal, milk, wine, now beer," he looked pointedly at Ollie, "and bread for my PB&Js, and that's it. I didn't buy those eggs, but they pre-date you, so technically you can't be jealous," he added in a rush.

Ollie looked at him and shook his head with a sigh. "How you made it this far," he said under his breath, and resumed pulling things out of the bags. "Lucky for you you're a top. I mean, have you ever heard of fiber?"

"I eat fiber," Matt replied defensively.

"Not enough to bottom." Ollie laughed. "Maybe I just pay more attention to it because I don't like to douche, fucks with my gut biomes," Ollie added with a blush.

"Oh. I never even thought about it," Matt mused and then poked Ollie's side when he scoffed. "It's a compliment. It never crossed my mind because you're so clean, so perfect. So minty and whatever else that spice is; reminds me of fall or Christmas."

"Cloves, and now we're changing the subject because I'll never get dinner made if we start talking about my bum balm and sex." Ollie pushed against Matt playfully and went back to unpacking the bags of fruits and vegetables.

Matt stepped back and continued to watch him, his muscles flexing as he lifted things out, how his hair fell forward into his eyes before he swept it back with his fingers.

Yeah, we need to change the subject, Matt thought, or I'm gonna strip you bare right here.

"You know how to cook?" he asked, keeping his hands from reaching out and grabbing Ollie.

Ollie smiled proudly. "I love to cook. I wanted to be a chef when I was little."

Matt raised his eyebrows with pleasure, thinking again just how perfect Ollie was. "What are you making?" he asked in a voice he hoped sounded more nonchalant than it was.

"Well, I hope you know how to shuck an oyster," Ollie said, pulling out a container of fresh oysters on ice.

"That I do know." Matt crossed the space to stand behind Ollie, unable to resist touching him. He wrapped his arms around Ollie's middle and kissed the sensitive spot behind his ear.

"Good, because we're having oysters with a homemade mignonette, spicy shrimp in a sizzling garlic sauce with cilantro, then seared tuna with a soy, garlic, ginger dipping sauce, noodles with veggies in a spicy Thai peanut sauce and grilled bok choy with miso butter." He nodded at the small grill on the deck. "I'm glad you have that, though it looks like it never gets used." He grinned. "I hope the tank's full."

Matt turned Ollie to face him and stared into his eyes before kissing him. "If this is a dream, I never wanna wake up."

Ollie returned the kiss with flourish before pulling out of Matt's arms. "Well, it's not. So, go shuck those oysters, prep-boy, get me some serving dishes, and then get out of my kitchen," he ordered, smacking Matt's ass.

"Jesus, Ollie, that was phenomenal." Matt wiped his mouth with his napkin and picked up his glass of white wine.

Ollie beamed happily. "Thank you, Lieutenant. I love cooking for you. I especially loved watching you devour it." He sat back in his chair with his glass, certain again in his decision to give Matt a chance. "I hope you saved room for dessert. I stopped at Modern Pastry and got a delicious looking assortment of goodies. Including something called a Boston creme cupcake. Looks divine."

"I saved room for two desserts, Oliver. One I'm going to eat here, and the other I'm going to enjoy in the bedroom later." He raised his eyebrows suggestively.

"Great minds think alike, because I did that too." Ollie looked meaningfully at his half-eaten dinner and smiled as he stood to clear the dishes.

Matt grabbed his wrist, pulling him into his lap. "I'll do KP. Clean-up," he added at Ollie's questioning look. "And, I decided I want my second dessert first, and I think I'll enjoy it out here instead of in there." He nodded with his chin toward the bedroom and helped Ollie sit astride him. "I love when you let your hair dry naturally," he said against the column of Ollie's throat, as he buried his fingers in Ollie's hair. "So sexy and wavy, and irresistible." He ran his hands down Ollie's back and squeezed his bottom as he kissed him deeply with a sigh.

18

Confessions

THE FOLLOWING NIGHT, Ollie's last in Boston, they were on the deck, enjoying the warm evening after dinner. The smell of the ocean came on the breeze, the city sounds muffled by the humid air. Ollie had a beer, and Matt a gin and tonic, the ice clinking mutedly in his glass as he drank. Ollie closed his eyes contently and leaned his head back on the chaise.

"You are breathtaking," Matt said. Ollie opened his eyes and turned to look at him. "I don't want you to leave."

Ollie's stomach fluttered. "I don't want to, either. Matt, I . . . really like you."

Matt nodded and murmured in agreement.

"I have a fairly arduous year of school ahead of me, but I hope you can visit. This could be really great for both of us in a way. I need to focus on school, and you need to focus on building your company, and you're right, I have been a distraction to you." He held up his hand at Matt's protest. "I know a bit about startups, and how much work is involved. It's not fair for me to put demands on your time."

"You have not asked anything of me, that I didn't ask for myself." Matt shook his head and then looked at the wall dividing his deck from the neighbors'. "Let's finish this inside." He left the deck without waiting.

Ollie closed the slider behind him, watching Matt's stiff and unsettled body language with curiosity.

"Sit." Matt pointed at the couch and paced away finishing his drink so he could make himself another.

"I'm not great with words. I'm not great with emotions." Matt scowled. "I've never had a *real* relationship, and definitely never one with another man." He glanced away briefly. "The women I've been with never meant anything to me. It was only physical, for the most part. It's what my dad expected, what society expects, and the fucking military." Matt grimaced. "I had become perfectly 'content,'" he made air quotes, "with focusing on work. Success has always been my end goal. It made me happy.

"I overcame my *urges* by punishing my body with grueling workouts." He looked out the slider at the night. "I spent more than a decade being angry. It's what got me through BUD/S with flying colors. That's SEAL boot camp," Matt explained at Ollie's questioning look. "That anger got me through countless missions with my team. I was disciplined. I kept my desires in check. And then you come along." He stared at Ollie for several moments. "Too perfect for words, in every way. So comfortable in your skin. I don't get it." He shook his head disbelievingly. "I may never get it, because, Ollie, I won't ever be out of the closet. I don't want to be. But what I do want, is you. You make me feel things I've never felt before." He swiped his hand over his face and took a large swallow of his drink. "I wish I could just undo nearly a lifetime of repression with the snap of my fingers, but I can't. I'm gonna fuck up again. I won't mean to, but when it comes to emotions and shit, I suck." He shrugged. "Drop me in a war zone, put me in a business negotiation and I will lock that shit down."

"Matt—"

"I'm not done." Matt held up his hand. "I'm good at planning, visualizing outcomes in situations I see as predictable, but things are cloudy to me when it comes to the heart. I wanna make this work." He gestured between them with his glass. "But you have to do it on my terms. If you agree, I will do everything in my power to make you the happiest man on the planet, as best I know how."

Ollie held Matt's earnest gaze and gathered his thoughts as his brain made a quiet but steady warning that sounded like 'Run!' He ignored the sound and crossed the room. Ollie wrapped his arms around Matt and sighed into his neck when his arms came up to squeeze him tightly.

"Matt," Ollie whispered against his neck. "I'm sorry you've been so unhappy and angry. I can't even imagine." He pulled back and looked at Matt. "Because I am *not* in the closet. My family and friends all know that I am gay. I can't change that for you, I don't want to. But I am private, and I'm willing to try to meet your terms. I won't blather about us. I told you I don't need public displays of affection. All I ask is that you treat me with respect, and don't pull any crazy shit like you did the other night." He raised his eyebrows. "If you can agree to that, then we have a deal."

Matt looked away, and then back at Ollie with a slow nod, his eyes growing dark. "I understand. Let's go to bed."

* * *

Matt felt Ollie's eyes on him as he pulled over to the curb in front of Logan Airport's international terminal.

"I had a great time," Ollie said with a small smile.

Matt nodded slowly and turned off the car. "Me too."

Matt stared at Ollie longingly, wishing he could take him in his arms, even though he had done so just ten minutes prior, and thirty minutes prior to that, he had been buried deep inside Ollie, clinging to the intimacy of that moment with the desperation of a man drinking his last swallow of water before walking into an endless desert.

He popped the trunk and got out of the car; his movements sluggish like a sullen teenager being forced to apologize. Ollie followed suit and stood stiffly as Matt passed him his carry-on and rolling suitcase.

He shook Ollie's hand with a sorrowful expression that was quickly replaced with a positive smile.

Ollie squeezed Matt's large palm. "I'll call you when I land."

Matt nodded. "Travel safely, Ollie. I'll see you."

Matt took a deep breath, hating the nonchalance of his tone, the effect of it on Ollie, and walked back to the driver's door. He watched across the roof as Ollie walked through the double doors and disappeared into the terminal. He clenched his teeth, got in the car, and pulled away from the curb.

19

Light and Shadow

MATT SPENT THE NEXT FEW WEEKs throwing himself completely into work. Any free time was spent running along the waterfront, and in the pool at the gym where he would swim endless laps. He initially looked forward to his calls with Ollie, talking and laughing about school, life, and work, calls that would inevitably end with phone sex, each stroking themselves while listening to the other's moans, and wishing for the other's hands, tongue, and skin on his body. It was thrilling, but after hanging up, Matt craved Ollie's presence, his body next to him in bed, like a drug. Feeling the need for Ollie's warm, smooth skin on his deep in his bones, he began feeling morose. He eventually told Ollie that he couldn't talk every day, blaming work, and meetings, but it was because he just felt empty, and the nights alone were the worst.

He was back to sleeping less and having the occasional nightmare. Each one wrought with anxiety and things that couldn't be helped. There was the recurring one, that revolved around his injury and his inability to save his teammate in Afghanistan, and now a new one, with Ollie, his SEAL teammates, and his father. Matt had awakened after that particularly heart-pounding one with a gasp, tangled in his sheets. His body was covered in a fine sheen of sweat as though he'd been fighting, and his breath wasn't bringing him the oxygen he needed. He then laid awake for hours, worrying about everything, but especially about his sexuality.

I'm not gay, he thought with a clenched jaw. *That label is not me.*

Bullshit, Lieutenant. There's not one person on this planet who wouldn't question your sexuality as hard as you are right now. If anyone saw what you had been up to with Ollie. . . .

Matt shut his thoughts down. His greatest fear was anyone finding out about him and Ollie. And if anyone ever saw them *together*, like in his nightmare, he knew he would deny everything, *he would have to.* Matt felt a fresh sense of panic at the thought of getting caught and rolled to his feet for a run.

*   *   *

Work was exceeding all his expectations, suddenly ramping up and taking off after a slow but steady burn. His sales departments kicked into high gear to keep up with the demand his incredible marketing team had generated, and Matt's team of developers grew as contracts were being negotiated. One of his most recent clients was the US government, and as a result everyone else was eager to buy. He got an email from the client he had wined and dined in London, asking him to return for negotiations. Matt had been avoiding Ollie's calls, only texting short replies, but he couldn't help his smile at the thought of their reunion, and closed his eyes.

He called his assistant, Stacey. "Book me first-class tomorrow or the day after, whatever's available to London. I'll need at least a week there. Also arrange for the same car service to meet me at whichever airport I'm flying into."

He hung up, and texted Ollie, his body tingling with anticipation.

I'll be in Oxford Friday

He got his suitcase out of the closet and began packing without waiting for a response.

The next day the buzzer rang, and Matt waited with a smile for Tony to get off the elevator. He had everything packed in a hanging travel bag as requested.

"I'll let you know if anything needs altering," Matt said in Italian, paying Tony cash. "But I'm sure it won't, you're the best." He shook Tony's hand with a broad smile.

20

Foreshadows

MATT SPENT THE FIRST TWO DAYS in London, closing the deal, and celebrating with the CEO. It was more cigars (which he didn't smoke), and more whisky (which he drank plenty of), and then he was in the backseat of a Range Rover at nine, headed to Finn's. He texted her, and then Ollie.

I'll be at Chuck's in 40
see you there

I'm already here

Matt closed his eyes briefly with an audible exhale, feeling himself stir. He smiled out the window, his fingertips tingling in anticipation of touching Ollie's smooth skin.

He let himself in with the key Finn had given him, and walked up the two steps into the living room carrying the suit bag with the driver following with his luggage.

"Hey, babe!" Finn said happily, getting up from the couch.

He wrapped her in his arms and kissed the side of her head. "I missed you, Chuck," he said with a smile. "You're a sight for sore eyes."

He reached into his pocket and pressed some bills into the driver's hand and watched as he closed the door behind himself.

Matt looked around the flat. "Where's Ollie?"

Finn smiled. "He's in your room, he wanted to greet you in private."

Matt nodded and swallowed, his face growing serious. "Thank you, Chuck."

She smiled softly. "I'm so happy for you both. Ollie told me he had a fantastic time in Boston. He came back all aglow." She looked in Matt's eyes, maybe seeing the hidden worry. "You deserve to be happy. It's okay. I've got my ear plugs, and then I leave for Ned's first thing tomorrow. His wife is having a party this weekend at their country house, I'll be gone until Monday."

Matt kissed her with a tight hug and rolled his luggage to the bedroom door and turned the knob, entering slowly.

Ollie was standing just inside, wearing a t-shirt and shorts, with a small smile on his handsome face. He shook his head and took a deep breath. "Christ, you look amazing. I missed looking at you."

Matt put the suit bag over the back of the chair and closed the door. He opened his arms and Ollie stepped into them, breathing deeply before kissing Matt's neck and wrinkling his nose.

"You smell like cigars."

"Yes, but I taste like whisky, so kiss me," Matt said before capturing Ollie's mouth hungrily with his own. Ollie moaned as Matt's tongue filled his mouth and began undoing Matt's belt and pants hurriedly as Matt peeled his shorts down. He ran his hands slowly over Ollie's ass and felt his worries melt away with the heat of Ollie's skin.

Their clothes came off in a rush and Matt guided Ollie to the bed covering his body briefly before rolling him over and squeezing his bottom. "Speaking of taste. I want this."

Ollie closed his eyes with a shiver as Matt kissed the sensitive hollow between his neck and shoulder, and then each knob of his spine, as he made his down Ollie's back. He felt Matt's warm skin on the backs of his calves, his tongue tracing a wet path up between his legs, bringing him back to the present.

There was a moment of breathlessness, where Ollie felt everything that Matt was doing, and then felt nothing, as though this was happening to some other lucky-as-fuck man. He closed his eyes in a long blink and moaned slowly as Matt pressed his face in his crease. Ollie let out a long moan as Matt's warm tongue teased over him as though searching for something, driving him wild in the process.

"You taste like heaven," Matt said reverently after a time and rolled Ollie back over.

* * *

They spent the weekend in bed, with the exception of meals and Matt's ritual run every morning. Matt felt light and happy, his heart singing at being reunited with Ollie, their banter filling the spaces between the touching. His anxiety about them being together, all but gone.

What we're doing, doesn't need a label, he thought.

Matt lay on his back, drawing circles on Ollie's bicep, as Ollie dozed in his spot under Matt's arm. He loved listening to the sound of Ollie's steady, even breathing. It was the balm to his soul that he didn't know he needed or craved. Ollie stirred and stretched languidly next to him as if Matt's thoughts had awakened him.

Matt got out of bed after a lingering kiss and hung the suit bag on the back of the door, unzipping it and peeling the sides back.

"I want to see you try those on," he said returning to the bed. "Go on," he added firmly when Ollie didn't move.

"I told you not to get me these." Ollie stood and touched the suits. "They're magnificent."

"Yes, and they'll look magnificent on you, so go on," Matt repeated.

Ollie smiled over his shoulder at him and began dressing.

"I love watching your body move," Matt said softly with a smile. "And it makes me sad to ask you to put clothes on it. So, hurry."

Ollie turned, wearing the navy, two-button, three pocket Tom Ford suit, with a crisp white shirt. It fit him like a glove, and he smiled, impressed. "So, this is what a tailored suit feels like." He ran his hand through his hair, and down his chest as he looked at himself in the mirror.

"That is what a suit tailored by *Tony* feels like," Matt clarified. "He worked for my mother, and he's the best, next to her. My god, Ollie, you look amazing." His eyes roamed appreciatively over his body. "There are ties, and a tie collar bar, for when you're feeling extra fancy, in there too, but you don't need to try those on. Put on the grey one."

Ollie took off the navy and pulled out the O'Connor grey pinstripe, with the narrow lapel and two-button coat. "There are more shirts in there too. I trust you can figure out which color goes with what."

"My mother is going to think I'm a kept man."

"Do you want to be?" Matt asked with a sly grin.

Ollie looked at Matt from the side of his eye. "I'll make my own money. Maybe you'll be my kept man."

Matt laughed. "Hurry up and put on the black one so I can have you naked in my bed again."

Ollie posed in the black suit for Matt's viewing pleasure, looking at himself again in the mirror, and then hung everything back up on the hangers before falling back into bed.

"Speaking of my mother," Ollie began as Matt kissed his neck and stroked his thigh, "my folks would like to meet you." He hurried over Matt's protestations. "I couldn't keep it from them, they wondered why and how I went to Boston, and they're my parents. Surely, I can tell them, Matt."

Matt frowned and felt sweat on his brow. "If you had bothered to ask me first, I would have said no, you can't. What part of 'you can't tell anyone about us' didn't you understand?"

Matt stood and pulled on his underwear and shorts and stalked out of the bedroom, his pulse racing.

Ollie watched him leave with a worried frown, his stomach in knots. He heard the bathroom door close and stood, pulling on his clothes. He went to the kitchen for a glass of water and waited for Matt to emerge. Matt stalked back into the bedroom and came out wearing his shirt and carrying his sneakers and socks.

"Fuck," Ollie muttered. "They're my parents, Matt. They're not going to tell anyone. No one here cares," Ollie said shaking his head, gesturing out the window.

"I care," Matt barked, lacing up his shoes. "My own parents don't know. My father died not knowing, in fact he died thinking I was about to marry Chuck." He looked up at Ollie. "Did you know we were engaged? Did Chuck ever tell you?"

Ollie shook his head furrowing his brow and looked away, remembering the picture on the mantle in Matt's condo but never considered that the ring on Finn's finger could have been Matt's.

"You fucked her?" he asked with a horrified tone, his stomach sinking with jealousy.

Matt scoffed tying the other sneaker. "No. Chuck is way too good for the likes of me."

"Thank you," Ollie sneered. "Thank you so much for that."

Matt looked up. "I didn't mean it like that, Ollie. I meant compared to the women I've used. Some of whom I used hard, and I say that without any sense of pride. It's astonishing what some women will let you do." He put the house key in his sock and stood with his phone. "I need a run." He left without saying goodbye.

Matt was gone for two hours. Ollie almost left, was putting on his shoes to do so, when he heard a key in the door. Matt appeared a moment later, dripping with sweat, his shirt tucked into the waistband of his shorts. He kicked off his sneakers and looked at Ollie with a guarded expression. Ollie watched him warily.

"I'll meet your parents. Next time I'm here. I promise," he said quietly as he walked past Ollie into the bathroom and shut the door.

"Ollie. Take off your clothes and get in here," Matt called after a moment.

Ollie exhaled the breath he didn't know he was holding and shook his head at the bathroom door before kicking off his shoes. He stripped, leaving his clothes in a puddle in the living room and joined Matt in the shower.

Matt was rough and forceful. His kisses demanding, his nibbles more like bites, his grip bruising rather than tight, and he never said a word, well, not in English. Ollie went from confused (almost bumbling) to burning and enflamed in the space of two breaths. He closed his eyes and just followed Matt's lead, his skin hot everywhere Matt's skin touched his, everywhere Matt's lips and teeth touched him.

Matt had one hand around Ollie's throat and one on his hip, and both were squeezing. Ollie moved the hand on his hip to his cock and moaned when Matt gripped him firmly, stroking him up and over the tip. Matt's hand loosened slightly around his throat as he shifted his focus to pounding Ollie into the wall in sync with his hand.

"Christ, you better hurry up and come," Ollie panted, bracing his hands on the tile.

Matt slowed and let out a moan and a burst of Italian, before leaning forward to bite Ollie's shoulder.

Ollie gasped lightly. *That's gonna leave a mark.*

"Mio," Matt declared again, more clearly.

Ollie's orgasm nearly swept him off his feet. The sting in his shoulder, the lightheadedness from Matt's grip around his throat, and the sounds Matt was still making, were a symphony in his head and he fell forward against the tiles.

Ollie turned after a moment to take Matt in his arms, kissing him as he pressed his body against Matt's. "God, that was amazing."

Matt nodded silently, his hands Ollie's warm skin, the water coursing over and between them. "You feel so right. So perfect." Matt kissed him again, scanning his eyes over Ollie's body. "You are so beautiful."

Matt stepped back and washed himself before leaving the shower.

Ollie watched Matt towel off as he washed himself. Matt was the perfect one, though (as his grandfather would say) he was wound as tight as an eight-day clock. Ollie turned off the water and thought about

Matt's reaction to his spilling the tea to his parents. Matt was guarded, secretive, but it never occurred to Ollie that that secretiveness would spill over to family. Ollie thought of how little Matt talked about his own family, with the exception of his mother, and wondered why. He knew Matt had sisters, that he'd been the spoiled only son, but weren't they close?

Ollie counted his blessing for his own accepting family, not only accepting, but encouraging and interested in his love life. His mother had sensed something different about him when he'd gone home for his sister Cassie's birthday in August and probed him about it.

"You're quite chipper, are you looking forward to Lyon?" his mum asked as they cleared the dessert dishes.

"Well, that's part of it," Ollie began with a smile he could barely contain. "I'll be arriving in Lyon after you though, because I'm going to Boston tomorrow."

"Boston?" She straightened from the dishwasher. "But we go to Lyon every year to see Uncle Lloyd and Aunt Clare."

"I'm sorry. I'll be just a few days behind you," Ollie placated. "I've been invited to Boston for a holiday. I'll meet you at the chateau on Wednesday instead of Sunday." Ollie scraped the food from the plates into the trash before handing them to her.

His mum took the plates, looking at Ollie between rinsing. "Who are you going with? Finn?"

Ollie beamed happily, unable to contain his euphoria. "Not quite, but it's to see a friend of Finn's. He's her best friend actually. He wants me to come visit him. He sent me a first-class ticket." He held her stunned gaze. "Mum, he's gorgeous, and so successful, and he likes me. I really like him. I hope I can introduce you to him soon." Ollie smiled shyly. "But he's so private. He said I can't tell anyone about us."

His mum furrowed her brow briefly, then smiled. "A secret boyfriend? Tell me all about him."

Ollie poured his story out, telling her how they met, how uncertain he had been, how Matt had come around (leaving out all the sex of course), and ending with his planned trip to Boston.

"You can't tell Cassie, please. He swore me to secrecy, but he couldn't have meant you and Dad in that. He has to be private." Ollie nodded solemnly. "He was soldier in the Navy, the SEALs, and he owns his own company."

"I won't say a word to Cass," his mum promised.

Ollie kissed her cheek. "Thank you, Mum, I'll go fill Dad in."

"Good. I don't want to be the one to tell him you'll be late to our Lyon trip." She patted Ollie's cheek with a chuckle and went back to loading the dishwasher.

Ollie blinked himself back to the bathroom of Finn's flat and toweled himself off hurriedly, suddenly anxious to feel Matt's skin against his again. He smoothed leave-in conditioner through his hair with his fingers and left the bathroom, his towel on the floor, and his skin and hair products all over the counter.

21

Bury It

Ollie left in the morning for a meeting with a professor on campus in preparation for the upcoming term. The flat felt dark and empty without Ollie's infectious laugh and crisp accent. Matt took a deep, unhappy breath and lost himself in work, refusing to give into the dark thoughts that had plagued him back in Boston. He spent the morning on the phone and on his laptop. Putting out work fires, tying up loose ends of contracts, approving client support staff recommendations by his project managers, and connecting with his CFO. He looked up as Finn came through the door. "Fred, I'll have to call you back."

"Hey, *Alice*," he said teasingly, standing to greet her. "How was the garden party?"

"Fun. I met a boy." She widened her eyes and laughed.

"Oh, is that right?" Matt wrinkled his nose. "Was his name Tweedle Dee or Tweedle Dum?"

"You're such a dick." Finn stuck out her tongue and shoved his shoulder. "He was neither. He was very charming, and quite hot." She quirked her eyebrow and pulled away. "More like James Bond."

Matt snorted. "Okay, was there a bowl of goodies begging you to eat them?" He tilted his head. "A bottle labeled 'drink me?' I've met Ned and his wife. I highly doubt they know anyone who could be mistaken for Bond." He raised his eyebrows skeptically and exhaled. "Questionable looks and abilities aside, would I like him, Chuck?"

Finn rolled her eyes and sighed dramatically. "I shouldn't have said anything." She walked past him to her room. "I'm sure you wouldn't like him," she called over her shoulder.

Matt smiled to himself. "No, I'm certain I wouldn't," he said under his breath. "I'm surprised you came out of Ned's musty library long enough to meet anyone to be honest." He laughed. "How is the research coming?"

"Great, honestly. He has spent so much time translating cuneiform, that it saves me from having to, so my dissertation is moving along much faster than I anticipated. I definitely have you and Ollie to thank for that, making me spend so much time at Ned's," she answered with a smile in her voice. "And we managed to spend quite a bit of the weekend speculating about the Mesopotamian myths. Ned thinks they're more truth than fiction. Especially the gods."

Matt knitted his brows and then laughed. "What? That they're *real?* That's insane, Chuck, but I'm glad you have such passion and belief in your research." He took a breath as he stared at her open door. "I have to meet Ollie's parents," he added casually.

Finn appeared in the doorway with a look of shock. "What?"

Matt shook his head and let out a deep sigh. "He told them about me. I'm delaying it 'til my next visit though."

Finn approached him and put her hand on his arm. "For what it's worth, they're wonderful people. You're going to love them. Very unassuming, very welcoming. They love Ollie, obviously, and will protect his secrets. I promise."

"I'm pissed he said anything." Matt shook his head with a scowl. "You told me he was private. You swore he would keep my secret."

"He only told his parents." Finn put her hand on his arm. "He's super close with them, his dad in particular, and as I said they won't say a word." She frowned at Matt's worried expression. "Look at me. Embrace your happiness. Let love in, and all the people that come with it."

He sighed and hugged her tightly after a moment. "I have. I love you like crazy, and I let you love me back."

"You dolt. You know that's not what I mean." She rubbed his back as she hugged him tightly.

They turned at the sound of the door closing, and Ollie appeared on the stair a breath later, having let himself in with Matt's key.

Matt put his finger under Finn's chin and kissed her lightly as he pulled away. "You always know what to say." He turned his gaze back to Ollie with a smile. "How was school?" he asked in a teasing tone. "I can't believe my boyfriend is a college student."

Finn and Ollie exchanged a look. "Did you really just say that out loud?" Finn asked with a happy expression.

Matt shot her a look. "Well, it's the only place I can say it out loud." He shrugged and grinned shyly at Ollie.

"I'll take it." Ollie beamed, stepping forward to give Matt a hug.

"Okay, let's not get crazy in front of Chuck," Matt chastised, side-stepping away. "Baby steps."

Finn rolled her eyes.

"I got some work calls to make, if you guys will let me get back to my business." He turned to his computer and picked up his phone.

"I have to go to the library, wanna come? We can grab a coffee and a snack on the way," Finn asked Ollie. "I'm meeting Vicki and James."

Matt looked up from dialing. "Ollie's staying here." He put the phone to his ear and listened, turning away. "Fred, hi, continue."

Finn giggled and rolled her eyes again. "You can keep me company while I unpack." She gestured for Ollie to follow her to her room. "God, he's so bossy."

"I don't mind." Ollie looked back at the door with a smile. "I know it's because he can't help himself. I imagine he barked a lot of orders as an officer. It must be a hard habit to break." He grinned and pulled Finn down next to him on the end of the bed. Ollie looked at their intertwined fingers for a moment. "Matt told me you two were engaged."

Finn's demeanor shifted as she shook her head slightly. "It was fake. Matt's dad had cancer, and Matt wanted him to believe in our fairytale." She shrugged lightly. "We spent so much time together everyone assumed we were dating anyway."

"Wow," Ollie breathed. "Why would you do that for him? I hope you forgive my curiosity, but. . . . "

Finn held his gaze. "I love him. I would do anything for him. Matt is the epitome of what I am looking for in a man, but I have no romantic interest in him, and neither he for me, obviously. I mean, when I first met him, I had such a crush on him." She looked at the door and back at him. "But we were always just friends, and when I was in high school, he confided in me about what he was questioning about himself. He trusted me with that. I know what that took for him.

"I just want to see him happy, and oh my god, you make him so happy I could explode. I've never, ever seen him like this." She touched his face. "I just knew it; from the minute I met you. The gods put you in my life for him. Please tread carefully. Because I would hate to have to kill you." She laughed.

Ollie laughed with relief and pulled her in for a hug. The bedroom door pushed opened, and Matt appeared. Finn grabbed Ollie's face in her hands and kissed him soundly before standing.

"Bye," she said, squeezing Matt's arm as she passed.

Matt watched her leave. "What did I just miss?"

"She told me about your engagement charade. That she would do that for you, for nothing in return." He shook his head in amazement as he stood. "She's remarkable and somewhat spellbinding."

"She is that. I think she's a faerie." He stepped forward and pulled Ollie to with a kiss. "I have about twenty-minutes, come entertain me with your magic tongue." He took Ollie by the wrist into his bedroom.

"I'll be back again later this month, before your classes officially start. I'm discovering that I can't go more than a couple of weeks without seeing you. You're under my skin," he whispered and stroked Ollie's face gently. "Maybe we can sneak over to Paris for a night or two, get adjoining rooms. I am trying to set up a meeting with a company there. You speak French?"

"*Oui, je parle français assez couramment.*"

"Okay, you will be speaking French for the rest of my stay," Matt said with a smile. "Very sexy, Oliver."

"*Je ferai ce que vous commandez,*" Ollie smiled wickedly.

Matt raised his eyebrows. "And what did you just say to me?"

"I will do as you command." Ollie licked his lip.

"Yes, you will," Matt said, his eyes turning smoky.

22

An American in Paris

MATT RETURNED TO OXFORD the week before Ollie's classes were to begin and stood over Ollie's open suitcase, clothes vomited all around it on the guest room bed.

"Ollie, it's one night, you won't need all this." Matt shook his head.

"Why are you going through my luggage?" Ollie picked up a t-shirt Matt had put aside and laid it in the bag. He sat back against the pillows.

"I saw how you packed for Boston and I'm glad I checked." Matt said as he pointedly refolded the crumpled t-shirt in the bag. "I'm gonna need to steam your suit before I repack it."

"I'm gonna wear it on the train. I need these other clothes in case we go out after dinner. And I'll need something for breakfast, and the train ride home."

Matt shook his head. "We're not going anywhere but to the hotel after dinner where you will be naked." Matt raised his eyebrows. "Everywhere else you'll be in a suit," he said firmly as he laid a white button-down shirt on the bed to fold meticulously. "You never know who you'll see, what connections can be made in transit, *all* forms of transit, so you should always be at the top of your game. You never get a second chance to make a first impression."

Ollie sat up. "I like being comfortable."

Matt put the folded shirt on top of the one already in the bag along with two rolled up ties and straightened, every muscle in his torso on display as he flexed unconsciously.

"It's not about comfort, Oliver. In fact, your uniform, your suit, should only serve to remind you of the responsibility you bear wearing it." He took a deep breath and let it out. "You want to be taken seriously? You want respect? You dress, and act like you deserve it. You want people to ignore you? Dismiss you? You dress and act like you deserve it." He waved his hand over the discarded pile of Ollie's athletic shorts and t-shirts. "Those are for the gym, for tending to your body, not for public consumption."

Ollie looked between the suitcase and his discarded comfort clothes. "I'm supposed to wear a suit to class?" he scoffed with a furrowed brow. "Been there, done that."

Matt shook his head with a small laugh. "No suits, but you should never wear sweatpants to class."

"Matt, I went to Eton. I know all about uniforms." Ollie raised his eyebrows.

Matt closed Ollie's suitcase and crawled over him on the bed. "Were you a sexy nerd in your little suit, or big man on campus?" He dropped a soft kiss on Ollie's mouth.

Ollie sighed as Matt's tongue teased his. "God. I could kiss you for days. I honestly don't remember what we were talking about."

Matt hummed and rolled his hips into Ollie. "Me neither."

They took the train to Paris, Matt reviewing with Ollie everything he needed to know for the meeting as a way to distract himself from the reality of traveling through a tunnel under the Channel. Matt was impressed with how quickly Ollie grasped concepts and ideas. It was quite obvious he had a brilliant mind, and Matt was certain he wanted Ollie working for him.

"Just so you know, most, if not all, French people can speak English, but choose not to, so, if you have any questions or comments for me during the meeting, please keep that in mind." Ollie interrupted his thoughts with a smile.

"I figured, but thank you for the reminder." He looked around the half-empty train and then back at Ollie in his pinstripe suit. "That suit looks incredible on you," he said quietly. "The shirt makes your eyes more blue than green."

Ollie smiled, his dimples begging for Matt's lips, and looked down at his light-blue shirt and navy tie. "Thank you. You look incredible yourself. I promise to be careful with my drool in the meeting," Ollie teased and swept his eyes over Matt's navy Brioni suit and then back up to his face.

"Yes, you have to be careful, but not behind closed doors." Matt grinned and looked back at his laptop to guard his own gaze.

Matt sat back for much of the meeting, listening to Ollie speak smoothly and confidently, his French impeccable and virtually accent-less. He looped Matt in from time to time if there was a question he couldn't answer, but for the most part held his own. They left the meeting quite happy with how it went, Matt certain that he would be hearing from them in the coming months, if not sooner. He held the door to the building, and followed Ollie into the back of the cab, Ollie pointing out the sights and districts as they sped past.

Ollie had made reservations at his favorite restaurant, where they sat on the small patio. Matt scanned his eyes around the pretty neighborhood and saw the Arc de Triomphe all lit up in the distance. The quiet chatter around them was occasionally interrupted by the sound of honking horns as the traffic battled around the Arc's roundabout.

"I can't read this menu," Matt said with a grin. "So, order me a martini to celebrate today, and anything but red meat."

"I know." Ollie smiled, and looked up at the waiter, ordering for them both.

"How is it that you speak French so fluently?" Matt tilted his head. "You speak it as well as I speak Italian, and that was my first language."

"Well, I studied it in school, but my Uncle Lloyd's wife, my Aunt Clare, is French and they live here. They have three kids close in age to me and Cassie. Their oldest, Guy, lives not far from here, in the eighth *arrondissement*." Ollie gestured over his shoulder with his chin. "Our families spend every August together in Lyon." Ollie paused with a grin. "And Guy is your typical Frenchman. He insists on only speaking French when we talk, and we talk all the time. We're like brothers."

"What's in Lyon?"

"My aunt and uncle's chateau. It's their second home. There's a working vineyard and the house is beautiful and massive, with a huge stone patio, and orchards. Guy and I would get into all sorts of trouble in the summers." Ollie grinned wistfully.

Matt looked away, suddenly nervous. "Does he know about us?"

Ollie shook his head earnestly. "No, only my parents. Oh, and my flatmates know I'm seeing someone, but they think you're a Brit. Actually, I'm pretty sure they think I'm fucking one of my professors," Ollie added with a salacious grin.

Matt chuckled, mostly with relief, as the server brought their drinks. "Good." He clinked his glass to Ollie's. "So, what kind of trouble did you and Guy get up to, Oliver?"

"Oh, smoking *weed*, and drinking wine on the banks of the river. Skinny dipping. Staying out all night, fooling around with the teenage girls, who just couldn't get enough of us. Guy is *very* handsome, very suave, very straight." Ollie grinned. "The girls loved him and loved me by proxy. I thought I liked girls then, but as I got older, I just went along, for appearances, as you're so fond of saying."

Matt held his gaze. "Does Guy look like you? I'm just trying to imagine the two of you unleashed upon the poor teenage girls of Lyon. Wet panties everywhere." He grinned with the thought.

Ollie smiled, a naughty glint in his eye. "Yes. My father's family gene is very strong. I look like him, he looks like his brother. Guy looks like

Uncle Lloyd, but with Aunt Clare's coloring. He's a brown-haired god, so much more handsome than I."

"I can't imagine anyone more beautiful than you," Matt whispered, running his gaze swiftly over Ollie.

Impossible actually, Matt thought.

"You were phenomenal today." Matt clinked his martini to Ollie's scotch and sat back in his chair, changing the subject for his own sanity's sake.

Ollie blushed and beamed happily. "It was easy to be, with you at my side. Supporting me."

Matt ate an olive out of his martini and chewed carefully, with a slow grin, opening his mouth to say something when they were interrupted by the server bringing their first course.

"*Bon appetit.*"

Matt followed Ollie back to their hotel, a small boutique on the Seine not far from the restaurant, lost in thought. His mind divided equally between the events of the day, and on the coming night. It felt a bit like something shifted, but he couldn't put his finger on it. They retrieved their luggage and their room keys and took the small elevator to the top floor, standing apart after Matt's nod to the ceiling.

Cameras.

He had reserved adjoining rooms, for appearances, and Ollie met him at the connecting door. Matt smiled and paused dramatically after retrieving a small bottle of lube from the side pocket of his bag. "I'm gonna fuck you in there first." He pointed over Ollie's shoulder. "Then we're gonna come in here." He pointed to the bed behind him. "And I'm gonna fuck you again, before going to sleep." He looked at Ollie with dark eyes. "Oh, and nothing but French from you tonight."

Ollie exhaled, loosening his tie. "Sounds like a solid plan, Lieutenant, with only Italian from your beautiful mouth."

He pulled Matt's face to his and kissed him, opening his mouth to Matt's tongue with a moan. Matt guided him backwards with a growl, undressing Ollie as quickly as Ollie undressed him. He peeled down the covers and laid back, pulling Ollie on top of him. It had been a long day of no contact and guarded looks so the kisses Ollie returned were bruising and sloppy.

"I want you to fuck me hard and deep, Lieutenant. Don't you dare goes easy on me," Ollie breathed, before switching to French.

Matt groaned and coated his fingers with lube. Within moments he was holding Ollie's shoulders and kissing the moans from Ollie's lips as he drove his hips up. His Italian was incoherent at best, but Ollie's French didn't sound much clearer. The room disappeared around them, and Matt lost sight of anything other than Ollie above him. The way hair flopped over his brow, the shadows that highlighted his cheekbones, and those lashes that looked like wet sand as they fluttered rapidly in sync with Matt's hips, were all burned into Matt's brain.

He flipped Ollie and then rolled him over as if he weighed nothing, pulling him onto his knees so he could hug Ollie's back against his chest as he slipped back inside Ollie with ease. He trailed bites and kisses down Ollie's neck, slowing to long drawn-out thrusts of his hips. Teasing as Ollie's French became pleading.

Ollie reached behind his head, burying his fingers in Matt's hair, and moaned. "S'il te plaît."

Matt took a deep breath and paused; his pleasure ready to break like a dam. He looked down Ollie's body, seeing and feeling everything with perfect clarity, the fantasy he had played out with Sam happening in full technicolor.

"Beg some more, Ollie. How badly do you want to come?" He trailed his fingers lightly up the shaft of Ollie's erection which jumped eagerly in response.

"So badly. Please, Matt." Ollie lifted his arms and gripped the back of Matt's neck as he rolled his hips. "Christ, you feel amazing. Light me up . . . *please.*"

Matt moaned, unable to resist Ollie's pleas and resumed his rapid pace, skin slapping in unison with Ollie's cries. He fought the urge to close his eyes in ecstasy, not wanting to miss a second of what would happen next. He wrapped one arm around Ollie's chest, teasing his nipple, and the other around Ollie's cock. Ollie cried out in French as he came all over the sheets and Matt's hand. Matt watched him with hot eyes, groaning loudly as he followed suit.

Every nerve ending in Matt's body was dancing as though he'd been electrocuted. His feet, hanging off the edge of the bed, tingled like they were on fire and he flexed his toes to make sure they weren't. He bit Ollie's neck gently (but hard enough to leave a mark) and followed him forward onto the bed. His heartbeat thundered in his chest, beating in sync with Ollie's pulse beneath his lips.

Words rose in his throat that he didn't dare speak (the same ones he suppressed just moments before) for fear of breaking the spell, fear of saying them wrong. Afraid, even in the dark of the bedroom, to say them aloud, fearing that they wouldn't be returned, fearing that it was too soon.

Matt rolled onto his back and stared up at the ceiling, dimly lit by the light cast in from the adjoining room. He was consumed with a deep and unfamiliar feeling. He was suddenly, overwhelmingly, aware of Ollie's heavy, satiated breathing, the heavenly scent of him and his semen, all around them. Emotions pooled in his stomach and pressed on his ribcage, nearly suffocating him. He sat up and, without a back-wards glance, strode toward the light, trying to catch his breath, leaving Ollie on the bed.

Matt woke later, in the deep dark of night, curled around Ollie's body, not remembering how they came to be intertwined on the bed, but knowing it had been done in silence. He supposed Ollie had been confused about what happened, and Matt wished he had been able to put into words what he was feeling, to put Ollie at ease. But he simply wasn't capable of the words. Not in English, not in Italian, because he had never learned how to express what he was feeling.

How could he when he had never felt anything like it before?

He could only imagine one way to express it, and it seemed to be the most natural way of all, because how could words, in the end, even begin to capture such a weightless and heavy, light and dark, ethereal and earthly, feeling?

He kissed Ollie's shoulder, and then his neck, and then the perfect spot behind his ear. He trailed his fingers down Ollie's arm, to his hip, to his thigh, to his knee and then back up, as Ollie stirred. Ollie's hair fell over his brow as he turned his head to look at Matt sleepily over his shoulder. He came awake at the look in Matt's eyes and rolled silently to face him, holding his gaze intently before wrapping his arms around Matt's neck and pressing his lips to Matt's with a sigh. Matt gripped him tightly, as though he would evaporate into thin air if he loosened even a bit and rolled Ollie onto his back.

23

Trustfall

"WHEN'S DINNER WITH YOUR PARENTS?" Matt asked when they were back at Finn's, the events of the previous evening hanging unspoken between them like a newly constructed bridge that was waiting, gleaming, for the mayor to cut the ribbon on. He looked at Ollie sitting on the couch. "I don't want to lose my nerve."

"How's Wednesday?" Ollie answered nonchalantly, while watching Matt carefully.

Matt looked at the ground, and then back at Ollie. Matt patted his pocket suddenly, feeling his phone buzz and nodded. "Fine. But if I'm to get any work done, you need to be naked." He walked out of the room pulling his phone out and answering it. Ollie smiled triumphantly as he pulled his shirt over his head.

* * *

The driver opened both back doors, first Ollie's and then Matt's, closing the door as Matt buttoned his coat and looked up at the house. It was a large, three-story, cream-colored stucco home set back from the road. There was a stone wall along the sidewalk, mature evergreens for privacy and sizeable yard. Ollie smiled shyly at him.

"Nice house, Ollie," Matt said quietly, experiencing a brief flashback to Finn's gigantic estate in Wellesley the first time he walked her home. "You grew up here?"

"Yeah, and Mr. Bean lived next door," he answered with a smile pointing at the left side of the house.

"Mr. Bean?" Matt looked at him distractedly, realizing that he was looking at a two-family. The knowledge made him feel slightly less intimidated, though each half was easily thirty-five hundred square feet, and could accommodate two of his childhood homes inside each. He pushed down those, mostly ancient, feelings of inadequacy and stood straighter, knowing it was Ollie, and Ollie didn't know him then.

"Yeah, Rowan Atkinson," Ollie clarified. "Mr. Bean." He shook his head. "He's a bloody superstar comedic actor, perfected the art of being a bumbling imbecile without saying a word. He's fucking hilarious."

Matt raised his eyebrows. "You find that shit funny? God, you're young."

"And you're stuffy and overdressed," Ollie scoffed, looking at Matt in his suit. "How old are you?"

Matt looked at him with a frown as they walked to the door. "I skipped the tie, and I told you, you never get a second chance to make a first impression." He scanned his eyes over Ollie's jeans and Oxford sweatshirt. "I've never done the whole meeting-the-parents thing, Oliver, and I want them to like me."

"What?" Ollie asked incredulously, his hand on the doorknob.

"I never wanted to meet any of them." He shrugged and took a breath as he looked up at the house. "I can't wait to see your childhood bedroom." He changed the subject with a grin.

Ollie exhaled a laugh. "They're going to love you," he added reassuringly and opened the front door.

"Hallo!" he called into the large foyer.

His mother, a trim, attractive blonde, with shoulder length hair, flashing blue eyes and a wide smile, came from the doorway on the left.

"Hi darling!" She pulled Ollie into a quick hug and stood on her tiptoes to kiss his cheek. She looked at Matt, admiring his Brioni suit.

"Mrs. Turner," Matt said smoothly. "Matt Dion. Wonderful to meet you." He shook her hand gently.

"Call me Maggie, please." She smiled appreciatively as Ollie's father came from the other side of the house.

Ollie's father was six feet tall, with greying brown hair, worn short over his ears, and piercing blue eyes behind rimless glasses. Ollie was right, his father's genes were very strong; he was handsome and the resemblance was unmistakable though his features weren't nearly as perfect as Ollie's. *No one's were.*

"Ollie," his dad declared with a smile, hugging Ollie briefly before looking at Matt expectantly.

"Dad, this is Matt Dion. Matt, this is my dad, David," Ollie introduced them with a tremble in his voice.

"Mr. Turner, sir." Matt shook Ollie's dad's hand firmly.

David squeezed his hand with a smile. "David, please, Matt. Pleasure to meet you."

"Likewise, David." Matt nodded, hoping his nervousness wasn't obvious. *Christ this was terrifying.*

"Follow me, I have things set up in the garden." Maggie smiled. "It's such a gorgeous fall day, we got lucky," she added over her shoulder as they all followed her out the French doors onto the patio.

Matt unbuttoned his suit coat and waited behind his chair for Maggie to be seated, wanting to make a good impression while collecting his thoughts.

"Please sit," David said to Matt, pulling out his own chair and sitting down.

Matt looked at Ollie already seated across the table from him and then at Maggie, before sitting down. He was not about to defy an order from someone whose approval he needed.

There was a bottle of red and a bottle of white on the table with four glasses, and a small charcuterie board of cheese and meat and fruit. Maggie poured what was requested, and held up her glass for a toast.

"*Slainte!*" she said exuberantly, holding out her glass, and took a sip of her white wine as she looked around the table. "We're so pleased to meet you, Matt."

Matt sipped his wine and sat back in his chair, feeling out of his element. He looked at Ollie who met his gaze encouragingly and touched his foot to Matt's under the table. Matt tore his eyes away with a deep, calming breath and turned his head to find David staring at him, sizing him up. He took another sip of his red wine and put it down on the glass dining table, recognizing David's calculating gaze. He had expected it, not that the expectation made it any less unnerving. He took another breath, to remind himself that Ollie's parents were accepting, loving, and fully in the twenty-first century.

Matt cleared his throat. "What an oasis you have here in the middle of the city." He gestured to the roses and lush greenery around them, breaking the silence. "I've never seen this side of London."

Maggie beamed. "It was fairly overgrown when we bought it, but David brought it all back to life, and cleared a space for Ollie and his football." She grinned at Ollie and then gestured to the flat expanse of lawn. "I think you can still see the dents in the fence."

Matt followed her gaze and smiled at the scuffs in the wood fence. He turned back to Ollie and raised his eyebrows at Ollie's sheepish look.

"Where are you from in America, Matt?" David interrupted, diving right in.

"Wellesley, it's a smallish town outside of Boston," Matt answered politely, breaking his gaze from Ollie's.

"Do you have any siblings?" Maggie tilted her head.

"I have four sisters. Three older, one younger. They've all scattered around the state. I'm pretty sure one or two of them have a couple of kids," he added with a laugh.

"There must have been quite a line for the bathroom." Ollie laughed. "You know I've only the one sister and she'd be in there for hours."

"You have no idea. We only had one bathroom."

"Only one bathroom?" Maggie remarked in a surprised voice.

"My dad added two more, but not until my oldest sister was in college. She lived at home though, he wouldn't let them live anywhere else until they got married." Matt laughed to himself. "I'm not sure how any of them actually ended up married, since he didn't let them date."

Ollie's parents laughed with surprise as they looked at each other.

"I couldn't wait for my two to go off and spread their wings. Especially this one. He leaves dirty dishes and his clothing everywhere." David nodded at Ollie.

Matt laughed, thinking of the puddles of clothing and the dishes on every surface at his condo.

"I do not, Dad. That's Cass," Ollie said defensively with a light blush.

Maggie snickered. "Ah yes, she won't put her dirty dishes in the dishwasher but she'll put them in your room."

"And she's always leaving her trainers and Beckham jerseys everywhere," David added with a grin.

Ollie looked at Matt with a blush and Matt felt his heart swell.

"I don't know, I don't mind it," Matt said with his eyes locked on Ollie. He cleared his throat and looked at Ollie's parents. "I'm tidy enough for the both of us."

Matt didn't dare look again at Ollie, knowing the expression on his face would only make him want to throw him up against a wall and strip him naked. He took a breath and changed the subject to Ollie's upcoming year of school, a discussion that continued until Ollie's mother jumped up and declared dinner nearly ready.

"I'm just going to show Matt my room, he wants to see it," Ollie announced after helping to clear the glasses and appetizers.

"Okay, dinner will be served in ten minutes," Maggie called.

Ollie led Matt up the stairs to the second door on the right. "Don't laugh," he said shyly as he opened the door.

"Why? Am I going to find dirty dishes in here?" Matt teased and stepped in, closing the door behind them as he looked around, taking in the trophies (of which there were quite a few), and the David Beckham posters. He pointed at the one of Beckham shirtless opposite the double bed that was pushed up against the wall. "Is he your soccer idol, or your inspiration for when you're alone?"

Ollie looked at him slyly. "Both."

Matt laughed, trying not to picture the erotic image of Ollie touching himself. "He's very handsome, but do you like all those tattoos?"

"I like your tattoos," Ollie said quietly, biting his bottom lip.

Matt felt a twinge in his pants. "You ever fooled around in here? I mean with someone other than yourself," he teased.

Ollie shook his head and swallowed roughly. "No, and we can't. My parents are downstairs waiting for us."

Matt took Ollie in his arms, and pressed his semi against Ollie's hip. "I *really* want to fuck you in that bed," he said huskily and kissed him as he squeezed Ollie's bottom tightly. "I would be quick. But I suppose we'll have to wait for your parents to go out of town. Pass me a note in class when they do." Matt swept his tongue slowly through Ollie's mouth, humming as he brought his hand to the front of Ollie's jeans and found him nearly hard.

Ollie brought his hand between them, fumbling for Matt's zipper, kissing him urgently, suddenly unconcerned with where they were. Ollie began lowering his body, kissing Matt's neck and the hollow of his throat under his Adam's Apple.

Matt took a deep breath and gripped Ollie's elbows. "You keep doing that I'm gonna get my wish, and your parents are gonna hear a lot of moaning and you crying out my name. So, stop," he said firmly and stepped back with an exhale.

Ollie looked at him with hooded eyes and lips plump from kissing. Matt looked away.

"Christ I can't even look at you, I'm gonna come in my pants like a teenager. Which I suppose would be fitting in this environment." He gestured around with a grin. "Show me where the bathroom is."

Ollie took a deep breath and shook his legs as he adjusted himself. He opened the door and pointed to the bathroom.

"See you downstairs," he said shakily and went to find his parents.

Matt followed the sound of voices to the dining room, where he found a table set like something from a magazine, and Maggie filling a plate for each of them from the side board. Ollie smiled at Matt as he took his seat across the table, and licked his upper lip while his parents had their backs turned. Matt took a deep breath, his body aflame with unspent desire as he counted the flowers on the wallpaper and studiously ignored Ollie and his perfect tongue.

They were halfway through the meal when Matt heard the sound of the front door opening and closing. A moment later a pretty young woman with strawberry blonde hair and the same wide mouth as Maggie's appeared in the dining room doorway. Matt laid his napkin down and stood, watching as she stopped short and looked at him with wide eyes.

"That's just my sister, Cassie, you don't need to stand," Ollie said with a laugh.

Matt stretched out his hand. "Pleasure to meet you, Cassie."

She shook his hand with a flirtatiously smile and looked at her mother. "I didn't know you were having company. Can I join you?" She looked at the dishes. "The fancy china, Mum? What's the occasion?" she asked as Maggie stood and pulled out another plate from the cabinet, and silverware from the chest.

"Ollie's friend, Matt, is here from America, he's our guest," Maggie answered pointedly.

Cassie filled her plate from the sideboard and sat next to Ollie. She looked at him and then at Matt. "How do you two know each other?"

"Through Finn," Ollie answered simply.

"Oh, that makes sense." Cassie smiled, and looked again at Matt. "Tell Finn I said hi."

Matt chewed his food without tasting it. He saw Ollie nodding obliviously.

Cassie took a sip of water. "So, what brings you to England? Other than maybe visiting Finn," she asked offhandedly, looking at Matt.

"Work," Matt answered simply. "And visiting Finn."

Cassie finished her mouthful. "What do you do for work?"

Matt glanced at Ollie, willing him to stop Cassie's interrogation. "Cybersecurity."

"Matt has his own company," Ollie's mom interjected with a proud smile.

"Oh yeah? What's it called?" Cassie asked interestedly.

Don't answer her, Matt implored with his eyes.

"SharkFinn," Ollie answered, without noticing Matt's discomfort.

Cassie chewed her mouthful and narrowed her eyes and suddenly straightened. "I know that company! I had to write a research paper on countries hacking other countries and SharkFinn came up repeatedly in my research." She furrowed her brow. "That's you? And you know him?" She looked skeptically at Ollie.

Matt gave her a tight smile. *Fuck.* He looked at Ollie who was finally watching him with nervous eyes. *It took you long enough,* Matt thought as he thinned his lips. Matt patted his chest, pretending to feel his phone, and opened his suit coat.

He stood, hoping his movements weren't reflecting the anxiety he was experiencing as he laid his napkin next to his plate. "Please forgive me." He looked at Ollie's parents. "This is work." He strode out of the room, desperate to get away.

Ollie watched him leave, a sinking feeling in his stomach.

"Cor, he's hot, Ollie," Cassie remarked, pulling Ollie out of his focus. "Is he single?" She paused with an intake of breath. "Or is he here with you?" She widened her eyes.

"Cassie," Maggie admonished.

"I think he's single. We don't talk about his love life," Ollie scoffed stiffly. "And no, he's not here with *me.*" He glanced at his parents with the lie and then flinched when he heard the front door close. "I better make sure everything's okay." He stood and left the room.

Ollie found Matt in the dark yard as he was pocketing his phone. "Oh shite, was it a work emergency?"

Matt looked at him silently for several moments. "No, Ollie." He wiped his hand over his face. "That was our driver. He'll be here in fifteen minutes."

"What are you talking about?" Ollie asked incredulously as his brain catalogued the past fifteen minutes. Cassie was nosy, but she didn't ask anything personal.

Matt narrowed his eyes. "Are you serious? Your sister knows about my company, she now knows me. I believe you said she knows you're gay," he said derisively. "It won't take her long to start speculating, if she isn't already." He turned his head to give him the side-eye. "She's a silly little girl who looks like she can't keep her mouth shut to save her life," he scoffed. "I knew this was a terrible idea."

Ollie bristled. "My parents won't say a word to her." He made a face. "Of course she knows I'm gay, she's my *sister*. She did ask if you were here with me, but I said no. She thinks you're hot, and asked me if you were single. I told her yes." He grimaced. "I fucking hate you for all that. If you leave, you're leaving alone." He strode away, simmering with anger and indignation.

Matt grabbed his arm and whirled him around. "Ollie."

Ollie put his hand on Matt's chest, feeling his racing heart, before pushing him away. "If you cared at all about me, you would come back inside and make nice, pretend everything is okay. Because it is. You shouldn't feel such . . . turmoil. Christ, your heart is racing," he exhaled and swallowed. "You're safe here. I love you. But now you're making me wonder why."

Matt squeezed his eyes shut and grabbed Ollie's arm again. "What did you just say?"

Ollie crumbled inside from the expression on Matt's face. "I love you, you fool. I would have told you in Paris if you hadn't gone all weird on me." He watched as Matt's eyes shone in the dark.

Matt covered his face with both hands, and then looked around the yard. "I'll go back in there, but the condition is your sister can't know, for now, for eternity." Matt waved his hand. "So, it will be the performance I'm used to." His jaw ticked as he looked at Ollie.

Ollie looked away, wishing Matt had returned the declaration, worried that he spoke too soon.

"Fine. Play it straight, Lieutenant. But you cannot come on to my sister." He looked at Matt coolly, attempting to shield his heart. "And you will make it up to me in bed tonight. Every way I want it, if I even want it." He strode to the door, questioning everything again and wishing he weren't. "Call your driver, and tell him we're gonna be a while."

They all looked up as Matt came back into the dining room, Ollie standing slightly from his chair.

"Sorry about that," Matt apologized smoothly. "Work is twenty-four seven."

"I understand," Ollie's father said. "My business is the same, though thankfully I don't have to spend as much time focusing on it as I used to. It's the benefit of building a business and then hiring the right people to run it."

Matt held his wine glass up. "Words of wisdom, David." Ollie's dad toasted him from the end of the table. "That's why I'm here, I'm trying to convince Ollie to come work for me," Matt said with a smile looking at Ollie.

Maggie turned her head sharply. "In America?"

Matt nodded. "Though I am breaking into the European market." He looked at Ollie who wouldn't meet his eye. "We haven't discussed the particulars, maybe he would prefer to be in charge of expanding my European division." Matt shifted his gaze between Ollie's parents. "Your son is extremely bright, and I would like to scoop him up before anyone else catches wind of his remarkable talents."

Cassie widened her eyes. "Well, if he doesn't want to go to America, I will. I'll have a degree in Economics from Cambridge in two years, surely I can find something to do at your company."

Matt looked at her and nodded. "Maybe," he replied while thinking, *never*.

Maggie and Ollie cleared the dishes, while Cassie helped set out the dessert, staring at Matt surreptitiously as she did.

"How is it you know Finn?" she asked with a tilt to her head. "I mean aside from the fact that all Americans know each other." She laughed.

Matt looked around the table, "Finn and I grew up around the corner from each other. I've known her forever."

Matt felt Ollie's eyes as he looked at Cassie. "They were engaged," Ollie said simply.

Matt shifted his gaze rapidly to Ollie as every turned their eyes on him. *Was he saying that to provide cover for him, or to be a shit-stirrer?*

"Wow," Cassie shook her head. "And you're still friends? Why did you break up? If you don't mind me asking."

"Cassandra, that's far too personal," Maggie scolded.

Matt looked briefly at Ollie, whose body language he couldn't read, then looked around the table, rolling his tongue uncomfortably through his mouth. "I was young and an idiot, and my time in the service seemed unending. Finn forgave me, and now we're the best of friends." He looked at Ollie and then at Cassie. "I haven't given up hope for us."

David exchanged a glance with Maggie and stood. "Join me for a scotch in the study, Matt while they clear the dishes. I'd love to hear more about your company." He held his arm out toward the door.

Matt stood immediately and looked at Ollie, feeling as though he was being called into the principal's office. He followed David into a large but cozy, bookcase-lined room with a white sofa and two leather club chairs, and a large desk at the far end. David walked to the bar cart near the door and poured two fingers of scotch in each glass. He gestured for Matt to sit in one of the leather chairs.

Matt sipped the single malt and let it sit on his tongue, watching David carefully from behind his 'wall.'

"So, tell me about your business, Matt," David looked at him and sipped his scotch. "When did you get started and what made you pick cybersecurity?"

"I started my business on the side about three years ago, while still on active duty, focusing on the development of my software," Matt replied, admiring David's tact. "I was a Special Warfare Officer in the

Navy SEALs, working in Cyberspace security, and I guess you could say I had an aptitude for it, sir."

David nodded appreciatively. "SEALs. Ollie said you also attended the Naval Academy. Were you planning a career in the Navy? What cut it short? If you don't mind me asking."

Matt nodded. "I did think that was what I wanted, sir, but Finn, she saw a better future for me, and then, as it happens, I was injured, and retired early. Finn is the one who convinced me to go into business for myself, and the one who helped make it happen financially."

David nodded thoughtfully. "How is business going?"

Matt took another sip of scotch. "Well, we're on target to hit sixty million in revenue by year-end, I'm expecting to double that by next year-end, and double it again. I'm now looking beyond getting new contracts and focused on buying promising start-ups for their R&D." He looked at David. "I expect to be running a close to billion-dollar company within the next five to seven years."

David looked at him with appreciation. "How old are you, Matt?"

"Twenty-eight, sir."

David raised his eyebrows. "You seem much older."

Matt shrugged. "The service ages you, sir. I did a lot of growing up in the Navy."

David nodded and watched Matt carefully, sipping his scotch. "I get that you're a private person, and I get why. But what I don't get, is your relationship with Finn, and your relationship with my son." He waved his hand. "I know what Ollie has told me, but what I heard tonight, about Finn, in the dining room and just now about her guiding your life, confuses me."

Matt looked down at his glass after taking a sip, feeling David come to his point like a sword to the chest. He waited several beats before swallowing. "To be honest, sir, I'm not comfortable with this conversation," he said, drawing his line in the sand before looking up at David. "I'm truly glad to have met you and your wife, tonight has been terrific. This is just entirely foreign to me. As you said I'm a very private person. I don't like to talk about my personal life." He looked away as the door opened and Ollie stepped through. Matt looked at him with relief and half stood from his chair.

Ollie smiled and then looked at his father, oblivious to the tension in the room. "Is there any scotch left for me?" He crossed to the bar cart at David's gesture.

"What questions are you assailing him with, father?" Ollie asked with a smile as he turned, raising his glass.

"Nothing I wouldn't ask of Cassie's suitor."

Ollie lowered his glass and glanced worriedly at Matt as he sat down on the sofa. "Dad, don't be ridiculous."

"It's okay, Ollie," Matt said with a shrug. "It's been perfectly civilized and everything I deserve." He looked back at David thoughtfully, Ollie's presence calming him, reminding him he needed to win David over and stonewalling wouldn't be the way to do it. "I suppose I should answer your question, sir. Finn is my best friend, and would do anything for me, as I would for her. Our engagement was for show only, for my dying father. She has been a guiding force in my life because she has vision, for herself and for those around her. She's the one who introduced us." He looked at Ollie and took a deep breath, exhaling slowly. "If I'm able to speak freely in this room, sir." He looked expectantly at David, who nodded encouragingly. "Then I will tell you that I love your son." He glanced at Ollie, who was staring at him with his mouth open, and put his empty glass down on the table beside him.

That wasn't so hard.

"I only ask that you and Maggie keep us a secret, please. From *every-one*, even Cassie." He stood as headlights appeared in the driveway, shining into the library. "Our car's here, and I want to thank your wife for a lovely evening," Matt said as David stood as well. He held out his hand, and David shook it warmly. Matt looked at Ollie and shook his head as Ollie made to stand. "You stay and finish your drink. Don't worry, I would never leave without you," he said meaningfully and left the room.

Ollie looked back at his father, and took a large swallow of scotch. *What the fuck just happened?*

"Well, that was interesting," David said bemusedly and raised his eyebrows. "He's an impressive young man, Ollie. Head and shoulders above Henry," David said after a moment. "And he clearly makes you quite happy."

"Dad, we don't have to have this awkward conversation." Ollie felt himself blush thinking of just *how* Matt made him happy.

"No, Ollie, it's not awkward. And I promise we won't have to have this conversation *every* time we see each other." David laughed lightly. "I just want to be sure that if you are actually considering moving to America, to work and, be with him, that he is as honorable as he seems. And that his thirst for privacy doesn't become a thorn in your side. It's an awful lot to keep in."

Ollie smiled. "Thank you, Dad. I'm thinking everything through, and haven't made any decisions." He stood and finished his scotch. "But I do love him. *Madly.*" He hugged his father tightly and left the room.

* * *

David watched the car pull away, and thought about the conversation he'd had with his son, and his son's boyfriend, and the events of the evening in general. He heard Cassie's bedroom door shut and went in search of his wife. Maggie was hanging the drying towel on the oven door as he walked into the kitchen.

"I would have helped you with the dishes," he said with a small smile.

Maggie straightened and looked at him. "It's fine, you were busy. What did you learn?"

David looked at the doorway behind him. "How about a couple of G&T's for bed and we continue this upstairs?"

Maggie nodded, mixed up the gin and tonics, and followed David upstairs.

"So?" she asked pointedly as she put their drinks on the side tables. "That was an interesting dinner, and what on earth?"

David began undressing for bed. "He's an impressive man, and very guarded." David put his clothes in the hamper. "He was quite adamant about us not saying a word about them to anyone, including Cassie."

Maggie paused as she pulled on her pajamas. "What? Even his own sister? After meeting her? That seems extreme."

David nodded and went into the bathroom to brush his teeth. Maggie followed. "What else did he say?"

David spit and rinsed his brush, and recounted the conversation. "Matt looks good on paper, and seems okay, so far, in person, but I worry about the constrained lifestyle he must lead, and how Ollie fits into that."

Maggie made a thoughtful sound. "It is odd, but I'm thrilled that Matt confessed his love for Ollie to you. I mean that is very unexpected, considering how private he is." She put her toothbrush down. "It was different for us, and I know nothing about gay relationships beyond what Ollie has told us. I wouldn't worry. I liked him."

"I always thought of America as more progressive than here," David said, pulling a face. "Ollie is over the moon for this man, but how will their relationship work? And he said he wants Ollie to come work for him? Was that real or just cover for Cassie's sake? How could he possibly?"

"David, you're far too practical, and you often worry over things that never come to be. I can't stand the thought of Ollie leaving London, so please let's not talk about that tonight." Maggie got into bed and looked at David.

"I know, I'm sorry, I can't help it. I only worry because judging from Ollie's behavior tonight, he would follow that man anywhere, even into a war zone."

24

Running up that Hill

MATT PRESSED A GENEROUS TIP in the driver's hand and opened the door to Finn's silent flat, waiting for Ollie to pass before locking it behind them.

He looked at Ollie's tense back and exhaled quietly as he followed him into the bedroom. "I meant what I said about social media: not only is it the end of privacy and the root of all evil currently, yours has a bit of a gay vibe. I Googled you." Matt continued their conversation from the car.

"I don't post anything, like I told you," he said defensively.

"Yeah, but you also follow *a lot* of gay celebrities and accounts." Matt looked at Ollie, standing motionless inside the doorway, as he began undressing. "Straight guys don't do that. You really need to delete everything. Twitter, Instagram, Facebook, whatever apps or sites you're on." He frowned, stopping with his shirt unbuttoned. "Why are you looking at me like that. I'm not wrong, and I won't budge on this."

Ollie shook his head slightly and closed his eyes. "First of all, I'm not straight. Secondly, I guess it's because it feels like shit just got real today. And I'm a little overwhelmed." He closed the bedroom door. "You

158

told my father, before telling me, that you love me." A wrinkle appeared between his brows. "And then in nearly the same breath, you tell me you've Googled me and you're chastising me for having an online life with my friends and family. It's uncomfortably controlling, and to delete it so permanently, feels like a leap of faith, where there's no turning back." He turned away looking at the curtained window. "I'm still so young, as you said yourself."

Ollie looked back at Matt. "Will you tell *me*, that you love me?"

Matt closed his eyes. "Come here, Ollie."

"No. You come here," Ollie challenged.

Matt narrowed his eyes and crossed the room to where Ollie waited expectantly. "I love you, Ollie," he whispered, feeling a weight lift from his chest. "You know that we have to be more than discreet, and you agreed to that this summer."

"I told you I would do my best," Ollie clarified.

Matt looked away. "Well, at any rate, it shouldn't come as any surprise that you need to get off the world wide web." He kissed Ollie. "It's best for you in the long run. Everyone Googles everyone now, and the world is still impressionable, under the *giant* thumb of the patriarchy."

"I haven't Googled you," Ollie retorted defiantly.

Matt studied for him a moment. "Well, you should have."

He resumed undressing, stepping out of his pants and folding them over the back of the desk chair before looking back at Ollie. "Why aren't you undressing?"

Ollie held Matt's gaze with an inscrutable expression. "I believe I said we would do what *I* want tonight, if I even wanted to," he replied with a shrug, and looked down at his belt and back at Matt. "You will undress me, and get on your knees."

Matt's nostrils flared as he returned Ollie's gaze with hot eyes. "You can't be serious."

"Oh, I am quite serious, *Matteo*. You will do what I want tonight, or I'm going to my flat," Ollie said in a quiet voice, holding his ground. He tilted his head ever so slightly at Matt's hesitation.

Something flared in Matt's chest as he watched Ollie's mouth in disbelief. He stopped within a breath of Ollie's body and lifted Ollie's sweatshirt over his head, keeping his distance just at the periphery of intimacy. He dropped it onto the dresser next to him before turning his attention deliberately to Ollie's belt. He undid it and the zipper slowly before stopping.

"You know, I only took orders from my father or people who whose uniforms had more stripes than mine."

Ollie studied Matt's low-lit face, all the beautiful angles highlighted by the shadows. "Well, now you can add a blonde grad student to that list, and I promise not to get drunk with power." He licked his lip.

Matt's eyes locked on Ollie's tongue as he chuckled to himself. "Oh, you won't ever get more than a sip, so enjoy it while you can."

He took Ollie's head in his hands and kissed him deeply, possessively, before bending his head and biting Ollie's nipples as he lowered to his knees.

* * *

"How long is Michaelmas term?" Matt asked Ollie the next morning across the breakfast table.

"Eight *intensive* weeks, starting next week, and finishing the first week of December, with no breaks in between."

Matt scowled. "Fuck," he said under his breath. "I don't want to go two months without seeing you, Ollie. Two weeks is bad enough." He studied him intently.

After a moment, Matt pushed his plate away and stood. Ollie watched him disappear into the bedroom, wondering if he should follow or not. Matt emerged a short while later dressed in his sweats, and sneakers.

"I gotta clear my head." He strapped his phone to his arm and left the flat.

"Matt. You already went for a run," Ollie called to no avail, and rubbed his hands over his face in frustration, feeling that he knew nothing at all about Matt's inner workings.

Matt returned more than two hours later dripping with sweat despite the cool autumn air. Ollie frowned at him from the couch. "Why do you fucking do that? We can't have a normal conversation about, I don't know, us? Figuring out when we can see each other?"

Matt kicked off his shoes in the entry and went to the kitchen to fill a glass with water. "You want me to sit here and rail at you instead? Because I could. I want to demand that you quit everything and move to Boston, right now. I want to drag you back to my condo by your beautiful hair." He looked at Ollie with a heated expression. "That's how I feel, and what I want. And I know that is petulant and selfish. So, when I feel certain urges, Ollie, I told you, I have to burn the energy and clear my head. I do it for you, as much as for me."

Ollie bit the inside of his lip and watched Matt drink, his throat swallowing rapidly.

"Well, when you put it that way. . . ." Ollie smiled with pleasure. "I get it. I can't come to Boston." He shook his head sadly. "But if you come here, I will rearrange as much as I can in my study schedule to be with you. I don't want to go two months either."

Matt searched his face. "I love you, Ollie." He put down his glass and crossed the space to the bathroom.

"Ollie," he called through the door after a moment. "I'm waiting."

Ollie stood with a smile and pulled his t-shirt over his head.

25

Giving Thanks

"LET'S HAVE THANKSGIVING IN OXFORD," Finn said to Matt two weeks later. "I'll make the whole thing, and we could have Ollie's parents here. We can do it the week before the actual holiday so you can still go to your mom's. Please say yes."

Matt closed his eyes as he cradled the phone against his chin. "You going to make your world-famous corn pudding, Chuck?"

"You know it, baby." She laughed. "I'll even make a double batch for you, if you promise you'll come. And I won't be seeing my folks this year so I would really love to see you."

Matt sighed and looked discontentedly out his office window at the building across the street. "Ollie needs to focus on school, I shouldn't come and put demands on his time. And I can't be there and not want him with me twenty-four seven."

"He's so smart and incredibly disciplined, like someone else I know," she said pointedly. "Your being here for three days will not damage his grades, I promise. And I want to see you," she added with a pleading note. "Don't forget that I love you too."

"Oh, Chuck," Matt sighed, "it is I who worries about such things. I could never, in a million years, forget about our love."

"Awesome, so you're coming and I will invite the Turners!" she exclaimed. "I love you, bye!" She hung up the phone without letting him dissent, a satisfied smile in her voice.

* * *

Matt flew in the Thursday before Thanksgiving, and took a quick shower while Finn bustled in the kitchen. She had the whole flat decorated spectacularly in autumn colors, low-lit with strings of white lights, and candles on the dining table. The kitchen smelled like heaven, the bar was crowded with wine, champagne, and scotch, and platters of appetizers were on the coffee table and the small kitchen island.

Matt answered the door in his grey Brioni suit, standing aside as Ollie came through with his parents. Matt followed them up the stairs and shook David's hand and kissed Maggie's cheek with warmth, and barely contained excitement. As soon as they turned their attention to Finn he swept his gaze over Ollie, admiring him in his white button-down and navy Tom Ford suit pants.

"Fuuuuck. You're gorgeous and I've missed you. Please tell me you're spending the night," Matt whispered as he shook Ollie's hand.

Ollie smiled and pulled Matt in for a one-armed hug, breathing deeply through his nose. "As if I could be anywhere else." He pressed his soft lips against Matt's neck before stepping back with one last hungry look.

Matt cleared his throat, thought of as many animals as he could that started with the letter A to tame the stirring in his pants, and turned to Maggie and David with a smile. "What can I get you to drink? We have champagne, red, white, or I could make a cocktail."

"Oh, I would love a glass of champagne. Darling?" Maggie looked at David.

"I'll have one too, please." David smiled at Matt.

"Coming right up," Matt answered as he picked up the bottle of champagne and popped the cork expertly, pouring five glasses. He handed them around, pulling Finn out of the kitchen. He looked at everyone's faces and smiled to himself with contentment.

"Here's to Thanksgiving, a holiday where we Americans give thanks to all that is good in our lives." He looked pointedly at Ollie and then at Finn. "Where we acknowledge that what truly matters, are the people we love in our lives, and those who love us in return." He raised his glass and clinked around the small group, and then followed Finn into the kitchen to carve the turkey.

"I've been meaning to ask, how was Paris?" David asked as he sat next to Ollie on the couch. "Did you see Guy?"

"No, it was a whirlwind trip. We were only there one night and. . . ." Ollie shrugged.

David shifted in his seat to face Ollie. "I think they'd really like each other. Guy has a sharp mind and many contacts in the EU. They should meet."

"I'd love for him to meet Guy," Ollie said tearing his eyes away from Matt's backside. "But what would I introduce him as? Matt will never let me acknowledge him as my boyfriend. The only people who know about us are in this room."

David looked at the kitchen and made a disappointed sound. "That's really too bad, Ollie. What is he going to be? Your 'friend.'" He made air quotes and shook his head. "You really think you could work for him? That no one would ever find out?"

"I think so. We got through the meeting in France with no trouble." Ollie smiled. "I can guard my gaze, and Matt, well, he's perfected the art. It's just an internship he's offered. It would be the perfect opportunity to see how I like it, like America, like him." He shrugged. "I've only ever seen him in short increments, and I miss him desperately when we're apart. I wonder if I saw him every day if I would still pine for him, or if it's just the novelty. There's only one way to find out."

"Right, that's the smart thing to do, a trial run." David smiled and stood when Finn announced that dinner was served.

After dinner Matt went to the breakfront to pour two fingers of single malt in two glasses without ice and invited David to the couch.

"This American holiday of yours is nice, I get it," David said, clinking his glass to Matt's.

"It's my favorite." Matt looked to the kitchen, his eyes scanning over Ollie's body. "And spending it with the people I love, and with new friends," he smiled at David, "is the best thing."

"I agree." David returned the smile. "I hope someday you can more freely acknowledge who you love and how much."

Matt held his gaze before forcing aside his irritation by looking away with a small shrug.

"You think you can work with my son, and not have people know or suspect?" David asked meaningfully. "How will you hide your feelings?"

Matt looked at David sharply, gauging his tone and intent. "Are you worried I would treat him poorly? As cover?"

"No, but there must be some way that you envision bringing him onboard without favoritism, explaining why you would need a young lawyer from the UK rather than the hordes of lawyers you have in your own country." "I've already thought about that, sir. Finn is my business partner; it's going to be her hiring decision. My team knows I can't tell her no and her father is Chairman of the Board." He smiled. "I'll work out the other details in the meantime. No one will find out, and everything will be just fine."

David nodded and finished his scotch silently, wondering, based on the unspoken part of Matt's declaration, what would happen if someone did.

*　*　*

Matt returned from his run the following morning and had a quick shower. He woke Ollie with kisses and lube, stroking their cocks together, and reveled in the resulting moans. It was Matt's favorite thing: to watch Ollie go from slumbering, to half-awake, to writhing underneath him like his life depended on it, in the space of minutes.

Matt cleaned himself with his damp towel while Ollie showered, and then handed Ollie the travel mug of coffee he'd made him with a kiss before he scurried out the door to get to class.

Matt worked until early afternoon and then took a break to meet Finn and Sophie in a coffee shop with views of the greens near one of the colleges (Matt didn't know which one, there were too many to keep straight). He was feeling relaxed and at ease, chatting with Finn's admiring female friends as his eyes swept the room periodically, out of habit.

He sat with his arm across the back of Sophie's chair at the long coffee house table and listened to their debates about history and politics, sipping his mediocre cappuccino happily. Finn put down a plate of assorted muffins and pastries in front of him and he looked up at her with a smile, grabbing her hand and kissing her knuckles.

"Awww," Sophie said with a smile and lingering look at Matt.

Finn smiled and wrinkled her nose happily at Matt. He grinned at her and looked out the window as Sophie got up to get napkins. The green had mostly emptied out, the bustle between lectures and meetings dwindled until all that remained were the students who didn't have to be anywhere, lazily walking the path, some sitting on benches, enjoying the cold sunshine.

Matt recognized Ollie's confident gait, as he would from a mile away, coming down the pathway with another student, chatting and laughing, his coat open. Matt smiled and sighed to himself. *God he is flawless.* His long legs, his easy way of walking and laughing, the way his clothes fit him perfectly.

Ollie ran a hand through his hair in the sexy way Matt loved, mussing and smoothing it languorously, the sunlight glinting off his head like a halo. His companion was looking at him admiringly as they stopped. Matt watched, the smile falling from his face as the guy took out his phone. Ollie spoke through a smile as the guy typed something. Matt's stomach dropped, filled with jealousy as he watched Ollie shake the man's hand and walk away, the guy rooted in his spot, watching him leave and scanning his eyes over Ollie's body with longing.

What the fuck?

Matt tore his eyes away with a frown and looked at Finn. She caught his glance and sat up at his expression, she looked out the window, but didn't see what Matt had. He stood, Finn following suit.

"No, Chuck, stay." He turned and left through the side door, eager to escape before he lost his head.

26

I'll Only Hurt You
if You Let Me

MATT IGNORED HIS PHONE and went for another run, putting himself through his grueling paces. Turning over and over in his mind what he saw, willing himself to understand that it was nothing, that he was overreacting (right?). But he kept coming back to the flirty way Ollie ran his hand through his hair, the way the guy looked at him, the phone in his hand.

Would Ollie fuck around? He shook his head as he walked back to Finn's flat and wondered why he was feeling so jealous, so possessive, feelings that were entirely foreign to him. He let himself in after dark and pulled up short at the sight of Ollie sitting with Finn at the kitchen table, their matching heads huddled together conspiratorially.

Ollie sat up as he scanned his eyes over Matt. "We were about to send a search party out for you," he said with a smile. "Did you run to London and back?"

Matt ignored him and got a glass of water from the kitchen. Finn stood after a moment and grabbed her bag.

"I forgot that I have study group tonight," she said to no one in particular. "I'll just crash at Sophie's." She left in a rush.

Ollie frowned as he watched her leave. He looked back at Matt with a growing sense of unease. "What's going on? Finn said you left the coffee shop rather abruptly. But didn't know why."

Matt drank his water and refilled the glass. He finally looked at Ollie. "You don't know why?" he asked in an accusing tone.

Ollie furrowed his brow in confusion . "No. I don't. I wasn't there, Matt."

Matt poured the rest of water down the drain and put the glass carefully on the side of the sink. He studied Ollie thoughtfully, his eyes tight. He took a deep breath and let it out.

"Sitting there with Chuck and her friends, listening to them talk about their classes, so," he shook his head, looking away, "full of enthusiasm, made me feel old. Maybe, you think I'm old." He paused looking at Ollie with a strange expression. "I know I'm not that far removed from college, but I spent six hard years in the Navy. You have no fucking idea what I have seen, what I have *done*. What I saw today, hurt me. I want you to tell me that what I saw was nothing."

Ollie looked around the room with his mind racing, feeling a knot form in his stomach. "Matthew, babe, I don't know what you're talking about. And of course I don't think you're old, that's absurd."

Matt closed his eyes and swallowed, nodding. "Good." He looked at Ollie and walked to the bathroom. "Then it was nothing."

He shut the door behind him. Ollie waited for him to call to him through the door, to tell him to get naked and join him, but there was no sound. He heard the water turn on. He pressed his fingers to his eyelids.

"What the fuck just happened?" he muttered to himself. He looked again at the closed bathroom door, and began undressing.

Matt looked up when Ollie came in and wiped the steam from the inside of the shower door to look at him, raking his eyes over Ollie's body. "You shouldn't be in here."

Ollie's stomach fluttered at Matt's tone, his voice rough and nearly unrecognizable. "Do you want me to leave?"

Matt opened the shower door, his expression inscrutable as they stood looking at each other, the water running in rivulets down Matt's body, the soap bubbles racing down his legs like a school of fish fleeing a shark. Ollie felt himself stir at the sight, and at the look in Matt's eyes. Matt stroked himself as Ollie stepped in hesitantly, confused by the anger in Matt's eyes and the erection in his hand.

Why is he turned on if he's so angry? Why am I? Ollie thought as he touched himself in response and reached out for Matt's chest, flinching as Matt grabbed his hand, squeezing the fleshy part of his palm. Matt squinted and searched Ollie's face, caressing his jaw gently before turning him against the cold tile wall of the shower.

He pushed himself up against Ollie's back, pressing his hardness against Ollie's bottom, his mouth next to Ollie's ear. "Remember our first kiss, Ollie?" he asked, his voice low and dangerous, his lips tickling Ollie's sensitive skin.

Ollie nodded, a shiver of pleasure going through his body at Matt's words, the feeling of his body behind him. He opened his mouth to Matt's fingers and sucked them at Matt's urging. Matt trailed the wet fingers down Ollie's spine and into his crease, pressing first one then another inside him.

"Do you remember what I asked you?"

Ollie whimpered softly when Matt pulled his fingers away. He tried to turn at the same time he heard Matt spit into his hand.

"I'm going to hurt you, and you're going to let me," Matt whispered as he pushed Ollie against the wall. "Okay?"

Ollie's eyes widened, and he felt his erection jump enthusiastically at Matt's tone. He thought for a moment, *hurt me how?* before nodding again, slowly. Matt kicked Ollie's stance wider with his foot.

"Say it, Ollie," Matt urged, his lips ghosting Ollie's neck.

A shiver of fear went down his spine as his brows searched for each other. "Okay," he whispered.

Matt moaned and licked Ollie's ear before entering him forcefully and without warning. Ollie cried out and bit his lip, as Matt's body pressed him against the shower wall. Matt pushed his fingers back into Ollie's mouth, and gripped his hip tightly with his other hand, bruising the flesh. Ollie closed his lips and sucked, as he shut his eyes, trying to catch his breath as Matt thrust roughly in and out of him, pausing to spit again on himself after turning Ollie out of the stream of water.

"Touch yourself," Matt panted in Ollie's ear as he bent his knees and changed his angle. "I want to see you enjoying this," he panted and gripped Ollie's hips in both hands.

The new angle lit Ollie up and he gripped himself, groaning with pleasure until he came, undone in hot spurts as Matt cried out with his own orgasm. It was hot, angry sex and Ollie was riding the wave right up until Matt sunk his teeth into his shoulder, feeling as though it were hard enough to draw blood. Ollie's eyes flew open with the sudden pain, but he didn't make a sound, certainly not any sound that could drown out the air-raid sirens in his head.

He felt Matt's heart pounding through his body as he remained pressed up against him, imprisoning him, still inside him, Ollie squeezed his eyes shut, fighting to catch his breath. He felt Matt's lips on his neck before he pulled away. Ollie turned to face him as Matt washed himself with soap, willing Matt to look at him. When his eyes finally met Ollie's, it was with a look full of desire, anger, and a glimmer of regret.

"Wash yourself," Matt said, handing the soap to Ollie and stepped out of the shower.

Ollie watched Matt grab a towel and leave the bathroom. He washed himself, his asshole throbbing with pain as he washed it gently. There didn't appear to be any blood, there or on his shoulder, but everything hurt nonetheless, especially his heart. He toweled off like a robot and searched for his clothes, donning them in the living room with a head full of confusion.

"I think I'm gonna go back to my flat tonight," Ollie said to Matt from the bedroom doorway.

Matt was on the bed, his phone in his hand, the screen blank. He was shirtless and tucked under the covers as though nothing had happened. He looked away from Ollie's intense gaze.

"You know," Ollie began, "I've just discovered that it's not at all astonishing what some people will let you do, when it's you who's doing the asking. I don't even know what the fuck I did wrong, or more likely, what it is you think I did wrong," Ollie said in a quiet voice.

"Matt, look at me. That, *whatever the fuck it was*, was humiliating." Ollie winced, gesturing with his head to the bathroom. "Maybe I wouldn't have minded quite so much if I knew what exactly it was that I was being punished for."

Matt made a quiet sound. "I just don't think I can get through the next year, knowing you're swanning around, flirting and giving your phone number out to every handsome young man that pays attention to you."

Ollie frowned in confusion. *What?* "What are you on about?"

"I saw you give your number to some guy on the green. Running your hand through your hair, looking gorgeous and so single," Matt answered, a strange note in his voice.

Ollie closed his eyes thinking. "Christ," he exclaimed opening his eyes to stare at Matt in disbelief. "You mean Calvin, the bloke from my analytics lecture?

"I suppose we were outside the coffee shop," Ollie mused softly, looking away. "I recommended a book to him. He wrote it in his phone." Ollie brought his eyes back to Matt's.

Matt narrowed his eyes. "What book?"

Ollie straightened. "What book?" He shook his head disbelievingly. "It's called, 'Matt Dion is a bloody fucking lunatic,' and now I really am leaving." He turned and walked angrily to the door, his heart burning.

"Ollie, wait," Matt called running after him. Ollie stopped in the open doorway and looked at Matt hiding behind the wall. "Don't leave."

Ollie looked at him and shook his head indignantly, stunned that the bastard was naked. *Was he thinking I would just cuddle with him like nothing happened?*

"I have study group early tomorrow," Ollie said angrily, slamming the door behind him.

Ollie walked home in a daze. His brain, body, and heart began murmuring to each other. *Fuck.* Ollie hadn't had that internal dialogue since he broke up with his first serious boyfriend ('Andy the asshole,' he and his friends called him) and he found it worrisome that it was happening again.

What in the actual fuck just happened? his brain asked angrily. Why did you let him do that?

Hey, his body said defensively, you agreed to it.

Because you responded so enthusiastically, his brain derided. I would never have said yes if I knew what he had planned for us.

He loves us, he felt we had broken his trust, his heart said quietly. I say we sleep on it and see how we feel in the morning.

I promise you my ass will still be on fire. I think I'm gonna need more time than that, his body interjected.

I promise you no amount of time is enough, his brain said loudly. I say we cut our losses now, before you two get us in so deep that we break if this ends.

Wait a minute. I said I needed an extra day or so, I didn't mean I never wanted to be with him, his body clarified. I mean it was shocking, and I'm sore, but it wasn't awful. I actually kind of enjoyed it after a bit. Especially the sounds he was making.

Yeah, the furiously muttered Italian was pretty hot, his heart agreed.

He was probably calling you all sorts of terrible names. I thought I recognized a few, his brain cried. You're okay with that?

He was angry, he thought we were flirting and giving our number to some other guy, I'd have been pissed too, his heart argued.

Oh, I see, and you would have raped him for that? his brain scoffed.

That wasn't rape! his heart and body said in unison. You consented.

I said I didn't know what he had planned! That certainly wasn't what I was expecting, wasn't what any of us were expecting, his brain responded in a shrill voice.

Ollie silenced his inner dialogue and let himself into his flat. Ivan and one of their other flatmates were sitting at the table in the kitchen drinking beer.

"Hey, Ollie. I thought you were spending the night with Professor X," Ivan said with a grin as he came in.

Ollie went to the fridge to grab a beer. "We had a fight."

"Did he give you a bad grade?" Kiaan teased and took a sip of his beer.

Ollie shook his head with a laugh and twisted the cap off his beer. "He's not a professor, and it was a stupid, shitty fight."

"Ah fuck, wanna talk about it?" Ivan looked him over.

Ollie flashed a smile, happy that they cared, knowing that not many mates would ever care to hear about each other's feelings, especially *gay* feelings.

"No, but thanks. He just thought I gave my number to another guy."

"Did you?" Kiaan asked, finishing his beer.

"No," Ollie said emphatically. "I gave a guy from class a book recommendation, but to be honest, I have a feeling he asked for it because he likes me."

"Is that going to be a problem with your jealous beau?" Ivan pondered.

"Nah, he's not from around here remember, and I'll just let the guy know I have a boyfriend if he ever asks." Ollie drank a long swallow of his beer. "I have a wicked headache. Do either of you have ibuprofen? Or do you think Ivan might?"

"No, but I've got paracetamol," Ivan said.

"I've got some." Kiaan stood.

Ollie followed him up to his room, saying good night to Ivan. "Can I have six?"

"You planning an overdose, Ol? How bad was the fight?" Kiaan teased as he handed Ollie the nearly empty bottle.

Ollie chuckled lightly. "No, I need some for now and some for tomorrow. I'll get you a new bottle after class." Ollie shook two into his palm and popped them into his mouth with a swallow of beer.

"The guys and I are going to the United game tomorrow afternoon, so you can just leave what you took on my bed. Thanks." Kiaan slapped Ollie's bicep congenially and went back downstairs.

Ollie went to his small room and closed the door, disappointed that he had given away his ticket to the game because Matt was coming to town. He really wished he hadn't, thinking he would so much rather be watching his favorite football team with his buddies than be avoiding his insanely jealous boyfriend.

What the fuck? Is there anything worth salvaging? he wondered as he stripped off his clothes, leaving them in a heap on the floor along with the other piles of clothing. He put the painkillers on his side table next to the half full bottle of water, collapsed face-down on his twin bed and fell asleep.

27

Once You Put Your Hand in the Flame

OLLIE WASN'T RESPONDING to any of Matt's texts or calls. Matt tried to read the acquisition proposals Krish, his CTO, had sent him before finally giving up. His morning run and workout did nothing to help clear his mind, and he wondered if he had misjudged Ollie's feelings for him. His heart felt funny and he couldn't catch his breath. After lunch, there was a key in the door and Matt stood expectantly as Finn emerged from the hallway. He sighed unhappily, his body sagging.

"Hey, babe," Finn said softly, scanning Matt's face. "Wanna talk about it?"

He scratched his head in embarrassment. "I got jealous and behaved like an idiot."

Finn frowned. "You? What did you imagine you saw?"

"Why do you assume I imagined something?" Matt asked irritatedly.

Finn made a face. "Because Ollie isn't like that, because Ollie loves you, and because he only has eyes for you. Those are the top three reasons, but there are a million more."

"I thought I saw him give his number to a guy yesterday."

Finn opened her mouth and rolled her eyes.

"He looked flirty, and gorgeous, and the guy was staring at him," Matt added defensively.

"*Everybody* stares at him, because he is gorgeous. They do it to you too!" She punched his bicep lightly with a laugh. "You have nothing to worry about. Unless you said or did something stupid last night." She tilted her head. "Did you?"

Matt slid his glance away. "I don't know. He's not responding." He looked back at Finn. "And, I don't even know where my boyfriend lives."

Finn smiled. "I do."

Matt waited outside Ollie's place for nearly an hour after ringing the bell and getting no answer. Finally, he saw Ollie come around the corner with his backpack slung over his left shoulder. Matt watched his step falter momentarily as their eyes met, before he continued walking with a guarded expression. Matt smiled nervously; his stomach filled with uncertainty as Ollie stopped in front of him.

"Hey. You still mad at me?" Matt asked quietly.

"I should be," Ollie scoffed. He looked over his shoulder at the door to his flat. "I have a football match in a bit. I need to get changed and eat something. Wanna come in for a minute?"

Matt hesitated.

"No one's home, nor will they be. You can stay in the living room if you'd like," Ollie added derisively as he unlocked the door.

Matt flinched at Ollie's tone and followed him into a moderately tidy living area, with a large dining table and some worn-looking couches in front of a sliding glass door that opened onto a small garden with plastic chairs. The kitchen sink was full of dirty dishes, with more on the surrounding counters and Matt fought a grimace. Ollie put his bag down in one of the dining chairs and opened the fridge, pulling out a wrapped half of a sandwich, and a sport drink. He ate and sipped from the bottle as he leaned against the counter, watching Matt.

"I should've trusted you," Matt began quietly, holding Ollie's gaze. "I was a jealous prick. It won't happen again. I told you I would fuck up. I'm really trying, Ollie. I love you," he added in a whisper.

Ollie made a thoughtful sound and kept chewing. He popped the last of the sandwich in his mouth and finished his drink. "And the shower?" He raised his eyebrows.

Matt stared at him, his eyes turning smoky. He shook his head almost imperceptibly. Ollie looked away and picked up his bag. With an inscrutable glance at Matt, he walked past him and up the stairs. Matt followed a beat later, pushing Ollie's door the rest of the way open and then paused in the doorway. Ollie had his shirt off and was digging in his dresser for his game shirt. There was a dark red bruise on his right shoulder, in the shape of Matt's teeth, and he suppressed his possessive response to the sight.

Mine.

Ollie straightened, shirt in hand, and caught Matt's intent gaze. He turned his shoulder to the mirror and examined the bruise for a moment.

"Thank you for not breaking the skin," he scoffed. "I bet you like looking at it. Your mark and all."

Matt stared at him, unable to form words. Ollie shook his head with a sigh and pulled his shirt on. He stripped off his pants and pulled on sweatpants and socks.

"Pass me my trainers." Ollie pointed to the closet next to the door. Matt picked up the sneakers and handed them to him.

"I don't dislike seeing it," Matt answered quietly, finding his voice as his dick stirred in his pants. "Or the one on your hip."

Ollie lowered the waistband of his sweatpants to look at Matt's fingerprint bruises and then raised his eyes to Matt's mouth. After a moment he stepped forward and kissed him lightly.

"You are so fucked up," Ollie whispered. Matt closed his eyes and made a small sound against Ollie's lips. Ollie pulled away just as Matt leaned in. "I have to get to the pitch."

Ollie brushed past him to the door without a backward glance. Matt watched him, uncertainty in every cell of his body, before following Ollie downstairs and out the door. Ollie stopped to fill his water bottle and grabbed his athletic bag of soccer gear.

He looked at Matt as they left the house. "You could come watch. Finn knows where it is."

Ollie turned and began a light jog down the sidewalk in the direction of the colleges. Matt watched him go until he disappeared from view.

Finn looked up from doing dishes as Matt came back in. He smiled at her worried frown.

"Fancy a football match?" he asked imitating Ollie's accent.

Finn smiled with relief. "I'd love to! Let me pack a bag and grab my picnic blanket."

The game was under way when Finn and Matt arrived at the field and spread out the blanket. Matt scanned the field for Ollie and found him at the end, near the net, leading the foray against the opposing team's goalie. He smiled at the utter focus on Ollie's face, the skill and agility he had with the ball, and how well he worked with his teammates. He and Finn cheered and groaned at the various plays, until suddenly Ollie scored, and he and Finn were on their feet in an instant, cheering like mad as Ollie's teammates surrounded him in congratulations. Matt watched as Ollie's eyes found his and saw him smile triumphantly, his face aglow at seeing Matt on his feet cheering.

The game continued, Ollie scoring again and assisting with another goal just before the whistle, winning the game three to nothing. Finn and Matt joined Ollie and his team at a pub up the street, following the sounds of their celebration down the sidewalk. They put their bag in with the pile of athletic bags in the corner and went to the small bar, which was two-deep with players. Matt held three fingers up to the bartender, commanding his attention with a folded fifty-pound note, and pointed to the middle draught pull, Ollie's favorite. The bartender nodded and began filling pint glasses. Matt passed the first glass to Finn, who was standing next to Ollie laughing at something one of his teammates said to her, and took the other two, giving the bartender the money, before handing Ollie his pint. His stomach flipped at the look in Ollie's eye as he brushed his fingers against Matt's.

"Everybody this is Matt. Matt, this is everybody!" He turned to his mates with a laugh.

The team shouted hello, some of the faces familiar, and Matt laughed along, proud of Ollie for how beloved he was by his teammates.

"Finn, please don't say this is your boyfriend," Ivan said with a mock sad note in his voice.

Finn smiled mischievously. "He's not anymore."

Matt grabbed his heart dramatically. "I find out here?" he wailed as Ollie laughed.

The team was boisterously happy and reliving the highlights of the game, smacking Ollie on the shoulder, or rubbing his head periodically. Several of Ollie's teammates flirted outrageously with Finn, and worked hard at trying to convince her to go out with them.

After a time, Matt read the room, put his empty glass down and held his hand out to Ollie. "Great game."

Ollie shook his hand and nodded. "Thanks." They held each other's eyes for a beat and then turned away.

Matt walked over to Finn and put his arm around her. "Okay, guys, in all seriousness, she's with me," he said with a smile, holding up his hand at their protestations. He retrieved Finn's bag and followed her out the door, stealing one last glance at Ollie who was watching him leave. He pulled out his phone once they were outside.

> **Please come to Chuck's**
> **when you're done celebrating.**

Ollie never responded, but there was a knock on the door just after nine thirty.

Smart choice.

Matt ran his eyes over Ollie's wool coat, jeans, and the small bag slung over his shoulder before stepping aside to let him in.

"Are you drunk?" Matt asked as he closed the door and followed Ollie into the flat.

"Maybe a tiny bit." Ollie smiled, turning to put his arms around Matt with a kiss. "I must be if I'm back here with you."

Matt made a slight sound and buried his hands in Ollie's hair, tasting the beer on his tongue, and guided him carefully into the bedroom. "I love you, Ollie. Seeing you today, your body." He squeezed Ollie's ass.

Matt undressed him slowly, feathering his body with light fingers and soft kisses, making up for the previous night. He kissed Ollie's right shoulder and then hip lingeringly before turning him to face the bed. He made to bend Ollie forward.

"NO WAY, Matt!" Ollie exclaimed angrily and tried to turn.

"Shh," Matt breathed against Ollie's ear, holding him still. "I'm gonna kiss it, make it better," he whispered and knelt down. "Your asshole is so pretty, so perfect. Just like you."

Ollie exhaled and sunk his head and shoulders into the bed, surrendering completely to the pleasurable sensation of Matt's tongue. Matt smacked his ass cheek lightly after a few minutes of listening to Ollie's moans and soft cries and nudged for him to turn around. Ollie straightened, swaying slightly on his feet as Matt took him in his mouth. He exhaled a loud moan.

"God, yes, Matt," he breathed. "Take it. Choke on my cock, you bloody bastard," he gritted out and thrust his hips forcefully, holding Matt's head as he came down his gagging throat a moment later. Ollie eventually pulled his fingers from Matt's hair and collapsed back on the bed, arms out to the sides. "Christ," he panted.

"Even your come tastes like alcohol." Matt shook his head as he wiped his face on his shirt before stripping it off. "And you got a little big for your britches there for a minute," he warned. "How much did you drink?"

Ollie lifted his head off the bed and grinned. "It doesn't taste like beer, you lie."

Matt raised his eyebrows. "Kiss me and taste for yourself."

Ollie put his head back down and laughed. "No thanks. I've had enough to drink." He hiccupped. Matt stood and got the glass of water on the nightstand, taking a swallow he passed the cup to Ollie.

"Hold your breath while you drink this in small swallows, your hiccups will go away," Matt sighed, gazing down at Ollie's beautiful body as he stepped out of his sweatpants.

Ollie sat up and did as Matt said, the hiccups disappearing. He handed the glass back to Matt. "Get over here."

Matt stretched himself out beside him on the bed, taking Ollie in his arms as he wrapped one leg over Ollie's thigh.

"I love you, Lieutenant," he said against Matt's chest. "But I mean it, you are not putting that enormous thing inside me." He looked down at Matt's erection, pressing eagerly against his stomach.

"I love you too. And don't worry, I wasn't planning on it. I know I hurt you yesterday, and part of me feels really badly about that," Matt said with a kiss. "You don't have to do anything, just lay with me. Little Matt can't help but get excited at the sight of you, the smell of you, and the taste of you." He smiled and ran his hand down Ollie's body and over his thighs.

Ollie was silent for a moment. "'Part' of you felt bad?" he asked quietly. "And the other part?"

Matt took a deep breath. "You don't want to know."

Ollie closed his eyes as Matt kissed the side of his head.

"Lay on your back."

Ollie heard the bottle snap open and felt Matt begin stroking himself next to his hip. He opened his eyes to see Matt propped on his elbow staring down at him, his eyes dark with desire.

"You are so beautiful, Ollie. And I am so thankful for you." He kissed him as his hand moved in short quick strokes. "See what you do to me. I'm so fucking close. Kiss me," he panted and straddled Ollie's body.

Ollie cupped the back of Matt's neck and kissed him, sliding his tongue along Matt's eager one as his other hand teased Matt's nipple. Matt groaned loudly against Ollie's lips as he came, painting Ollie's chest like he was Jackson Pollack. Ollie smiled to himself as Matt shuddered above him, his buzzed and dizzy brain no longer fighting him.

Matt grabbed the towel from the nightstand and tossed it to Ollie after wiping himself. Ollie watched as Matt pulled on his underwear.

"I'll be right back."

Matt reappeared a moment later with a large water bottle that he handed to Ollie.

"You're gonna wanna drink that, and take these." He held his fist over Ollie's open hand and dropped two orange pills.

Ollie washed the ibuprofen down with several swallows of water and settled back onto his pillow as Matt got back into bed. Matt spooned himself behind Ollie and peppered his neck with kisses.

"I love you. I'm the luckiest guy in the world." He rubbed his nose along the base of Ollie's skull and breathed deeply as he tightened his grip. "You smell like heaven."

Ollie snuggled back into Matt's body. He (helplessly and insanely) loved everything about Matt, from his hard body to his broody personality.

But if you were smart, you would run and never look back, he thought briefly. Because while broody was hot, pathologically closeted, and possessive was not. Trouble was, when it came to Matt, Ollie could barely think straight, and when he could, it was always to think of excuses.

He's learning. He's never been in love. I'm his first. I need to be patient. Those thoughts, and more, circled Ollie's brain until he finally fell asleep.

Ollie woke early (definitely before dawn) with a small headache; one he knew would've been far worse if not for the ibuprofen and water that Matt had fed him. He turned his head to look at the pillow next to him expecting to see a note, but found Matt sound asleep instead. He widened his eyes. It was the first time he had wakened to find Matt still in bed, and the first time he had ever seen him asleep. He studied Matt carefully, his beautiful face relaxed, peaceful, and young.

Ollie paused to wonder at the torment and violence that lived inside such a beautiful creature. *Was it a side effect of what he'd seen and done in the military, or something he carried from childhood?* Could Matt ever be freed from whatever it was? Could Ollie help free him from that torment, or would it be something he'd have to learn to live with. *Would he want to learn to live with it?*

No! his brain shouted (mutedly because of the headache). *Matt warned you he would fuck up but seriously, you really want this? What are you doing here?*

He apologized, and come on, it wasn't that bad, his body countered.

When did he apologize? his brain scoffed. *I never heard the word 'sorry.'*

There was a brief pause in the discussion as each part of Ollie replayed the conversations with Matt since the 'incident.'

I love him, look at him, his heart said in a rush, barreling past the question. *He's beautiful, and he loves you, he needs you. We can fix him. He's never let anyone close enough before—*

You're an idiot. You're all idiots, his brain derided. *Or worse, you're cliché.*

Ollie lay back on the pillow, tuning out the inner dialogue, as his mind simultaneously wandered and focused in that early-morning, hungover way. It would take time to heal Matt, a lifetime of repression couldn't just be undone in a matter of weeks or months. No, it would likely take years, and patience, and a tremendous amount of unconditional love for Matt to embrace his sexuality. *Am I up to that challenge?* Ollie wondered with a frown. *What if he never does?* Ollie closed his eyes with a wince and fell back to sleep.

The next time he woke the note was waiting for him. He smiled, feeling better, *optimistic.* Of course Matt would learn to accept himself, *particularly with my help,* and that wasn't delusional, or cliché. Matt was everything he wanted in a man: confident, handsome, loving. He'd be a fool to let him go. If the incident in the shower was the worst of Matt's dark side, then Ollie could handle that like a big boy, just as he told Matt.

But if Matt ever raised his hand, or tried to control who he could see or what he could do, then Ollie would run, without a backwards glance.

Ollie rolled over into Matt's spot and thought about the men from his past. There was his first, Kevin, in secondary. A dark-haired rugby player from a different school. They didn't last long, maybe a handful of months, but he credited Kevin with confirming his sexual identity. Then there was 'Andy the asshole,' from his first year at Oxford. Andy was a bad boy, and charming, *and* the biggest cheater on the planet. Their relationship had been passionate, and confusing, and ultimately, unfulfilling. Then there was Henry; brown-haired, gentle, *devoted* Henry. Ollie had believed they were meant to be, carted him around to all the family things, including Lyon, but after two years Ollie cut Henry loose.

And lastly, there was Grant, his boyfriend the summer between graduation and grad school. They met in Soho when Ollie was living at home, enjoying the lull between academic demands. Grant was the first 'grown-up' Ollie had dated. Grant had a real job, owned his own flat, and was nearly fifteen years older. Grant doted on him, took him to Spain, Portugal, and Morocco. He was a skilled and attentive lover, but he had quirks and annoying habits that Ollie eventually couldn't see past. As Ollie reflected, he realized that the things Grant did that irritated him, were all things he would never have noticed if there had been something more substantive about him, something intriguing, like there was with Matt.

Matt.

Ollie looked up at the ceiling and thought of Matt as he blew out a heated breath. Matt was complex and intense, and so were the feelings Ollie had for him. He craved that man with his whole being, in a way he never had before, like an addiction. There was nothing Matt did that Ollie could ever conceive of becoming a pet-peeve.

Except that he's a crazy person, his brain muttered.

He's intense, and passionate, Ollie's heart retorted, *we just need to teach him communication skills.*

That shouldn't be so hard, he's definitely got the oral skills down, his body chimed in lasciviously.

Ollie stifled his brain's eyeroll and pressed his face into Matt's pillow, tuning out the conversation as he breathed in Matt's scent, before throwing back the covers to get dressed and make breakfast.

Matt appeared on the steps thirty minutes later, dripping lightly from the winter drizzle.

"Something smells good."

"I made you eggs and chicken sausage." Ollie skimmed his eyes over Matt as he stripped off his hoodie and wiped his face and arms with it.

"Thanks," he said gratefully and took the plate of food and tall glass of water from Ollie with a quick kiss and sat at the table, shoveling food into his mouth.

Ollie watched him and snickered. "It's amazing how cultured and refined you *can* be, as opposed to how primitive you *are*."

Matt looked up at Ollie chewing his food, and shoveled another forkful in his mouth dramatically as Ollie wrinkled his nose and laughed.

Finn opened her bedroom door. "Something smells good. Is there any left?"

"Yes, I saved you some. Of course, I had to hide it from the caveman here." Ollie passed her a plate of eggs and sausage. "Do you want toast?"

"Yes, make me toast," Matt grunted from the table with a small grin.

Finn snickered. "I'll have a piece if you don't mind, please."

Ollie joined them after making toast with jam, and chatted with Finn between bites, as he watched Matt eat his entire plate of food, four pieces of toast, and the remaining sausages. He met Matt's eye and smiled at his wink.

"I have a paper to work on, wanna come to the library with me? It should be quiet for a Sunday," Finn asked Ollie, interrupting his exchange with Matt.

"Yeah, I've got a paper, an exam to study for, and a group project I have to stay on top of."

"Can't you work on those here?" Matt asked, looking up as they stood.

Ollie ran his eyes over Matt's body. "No, far too distracting here."

"Well, I leave today, so you can go after I'm gone." Matt stood and put his dishes in the dishwasher, refilling his glass of water.

"Oh, right I forgot this was just a short trip," Finn said sadly and hugged him tightly. He squeezed her and lifted her off her feet.

"I'll see you at Christmas, Chuck."

She smiled and nodded. "I'll say goodbye now so it's not all sad. I'll leave for the library knowing that you're still here for a few more hours. And you need time with Ollie."

"Yes, I do." Matt grinned. "I love you. See you in a couple weeks."

"Would you consider coming to Boston for Christmas, Ollie?" Matt asked as he folded another shirt into his suitcase.

Ollie looked over his shoulder at Matt. "Maybe," he answered slowly, rolling away from the book he was reading and onto his other side. He popped up on his elbow and rested his head in his hand. "What do you do for Christmas?"

Matt looked away thinking. "Go to my mom's, and to Chuck's, and then I'm guessing, this year, just lie around my condo naked thinking about you." He looked back at Ollie with a smile. "I'd much rather lie around my condo naked with you. . . ."

"So, you're saying that you would bring me home? To meet your mother, your sisters, their husbands, and then to Chuck's house, to meet her parents?" Ollie narrowed his eyes in disbelief.

Matt sighed and went back to packing. He nodded after a moment. "Maybe. Conditionally, of course."

Ollie laughed humorlessly. "I hate that word, but I'll bite. What are the conditions?"

Matt sat back on his haunches. "You stay at Chuck's Christmas Eve. I come celebrate there with you Christmas brunch, and then the three of us go to my mother's, as friends, for Christmas dinner. It will be one day of appearances, and then the rest of the time, me, loving you." He held Ollie's gaze. "Making it up to you."

"I'll think about it."

Matt narrowed his eyes and zipped his suitcase. He stood and straightened his pants before donning his suit coat and adjusting his tie with a quick glance in the mirror. He shot Ollie a look before leaving the room. Ollie stood from the bed, staring at him, *reading* him, and followed him out, thinking about how quickly he had become in tune with this mercurial man.

"Oh, I suppose you're mad because I didn't bow and scrape with a 'yes, please, milord,'" he said irritatedly. "I'm supposed to give up a holiday with my family in order to participate in some grand farce, an ocean away. Forgive me for not jumping at the opportunity."

Matt stopped short and looked at Ollie. "I told you from day one, this was how it had to be. You agreed." He held up his hand at Ollie's protest. "And don't give me the bullshit 'do your best.' You're either in, or out." He shook his head and continued walking to the door, rolling his suitcase next to him. He stopped again. "If you don't want to come because you want to be with your family, that's fine, I understand. But if you don't want to come because you can't handle *one day* of pretending, playing by my rules," he scowled, "then tell me now."

Ollie studied Matt's handsome face, and saw something like worry behind his eyes. "Fuck's sake, Matt. I am always playing by your rules, even when you seemingly make them up as you go along. And I have been discreet. *Painfully* so for me at times." He looked away. "I want to be with you. I just needed a minute to think, to let my parents know of my change of plans, and you immediately assume my delay in an answer is evidence of my not loving you as much as you love me. Well, that's bullshit," he said angrily. "Especially since I am still here after what you did to me.

"Buy me a bloody ticket, I'll fly with Chuck. I will play by your rules, and you will bend over backwards for me while I'm there."

Matt clenched his jaw, and glanced heatedly at Ollie's mouth, before looking away. "Right." He nodded. "I know I ask a lot of you, and I appreciate it, I appreciate you."

"Look at me." Ollie waited for Matt to meet his eyes. "I am solidly by your side. Now kiss me, and tell me you love me. And I will see you in Boston."

Matt let out a short breath through his nose and took Ollie's head in his hands, kissing him softly. "I love you." He closed his mouth with an intent look.

Ollie nodded. "I love you too, you fool."

28

'Tis the Season

FINN LEFT FOR BOSTON just after the term finished, but Ollie wanted to see Guy, and his parents wanted to celebrate an early Christmas, so he didn't land in Boston until the twenty-third. Matt met him at the airport, and like before they fell into bed, and stayed there for twenty-four hours, getting up only to shower and wait for Finn.

Finn let herself in, knocking and calling hello loudly as she came through the door, even though she had texted from outside the building. Ollie looked at Matt and raised his eyebrows.

"She has a key?"

Matt shrugged. "It's Chuck," he replied, as if Ollie had asked the stupidest question in the world, and rolled off the bed, fully clothed.

Ollie shook his head as Matt left to greet her. He got up with a sigh and went into the living room with his overnight bag, listening to them discuss the Christmas plans.

Finn hugged Ollie tightly. "I missed you! Should we have a quick drink, before we leave?" she suggested and then straightened with a frown. "Why do you look like a lamb for the slaughter? My parents are fantastic, and completely non-intrusive. And your guest room is on fleek." She grinned.

"Oh, god, Chuck." Matt widened his eyes and shook his head vigorously. "Never say those two words, ever again. I beg you."

She laughed and walked to the fridge with a sassy shrug of her shoulder. Matt made himself a martini while Finn opened the wine and a beer for Ollie, pouring each into a glass.

"Merry Christmas!" she cried after handing Ollie his drink and clinking their glasses. "It's gonna be a doozy, I just know it!"

* * *

Matt let himself in through the side door of Finn's parents' house on Christmas Day. He passed through the mudroom into the kitchen, carrying two bags of gifts, dressed in a navy Brioni suit and crisp white shirt with a whimsical Christmas tree tie. Kodi, the Hawthorn's black Lab, came to greet him with a woof, thumping his tail happily against Matt's knees. Matt transferred the bags to one hand and rubbed Kodi vigorously.

"Who's a good boy?" he crooned with a laugh before straightening to greet Dierdre, the Hawthorn's housekeeper and chef, with a tight hug. He pulled a small, elaborately wrapped present out of one of the bags and presented it to her with a grin.

Finn's mother, a classically glamorous, older version of Finn, wearing a fitted, red sweater dress with a wide black belt around her narrow waist and black high-heeled boots, came through from the front hall, her hair loose around her shoulders.

"Matt!" she exclaimed happily. "Merry Christmas." She hugged him and took his kiss on her cheek.

"Diana." Matt smiled against the side of her head. "Looking gorgeous as always. Bill is one lucky man."

She patted Matt's chest with a pleased smile. "Your flattery works every time, handsome. Come through, we're in the front room, have you met Finn's friend, Ollie?" she asked over her shoulder as Matt followed her through the house.

"Yeah, once or twice," he answered in a nonchalant tone, and smiled at the back of her head. He followed her through the foyer into the front living room, where there was a massive Christmas tree with a cascade of presents underneath dominating the space. Ollie stood as Matt appeared, dressed in his pinstripe suit, a white shirt, and a tie festooned with Christmas ornaments.

Matt gave him a quick smile before turning to Finn's father, a handsome man in his early sixties, with salt and pepper hair, a strong jaw and clear blue eyes. "Merry Christmas, Bill, fantastic to see you, sir." He shook his hand and gave him a hug.

"Matt, you're looking well. The company is going gangbusters, proud of you, son," Bill said with a broad smile.

"Thank you, sir." Matt smiled with pleasure. "We're beyond our target for revenue this year, and forecast predicts we will more than double that next year. But you'll hear all about it at the next board meeting."

Bill slapped Matt's arm, and looked at Finn with his eyebrows raised.

Matt hugged Finn hello and kissed her lightly on the mouth, and then shook Ollie's hand with a small wink. "Good to see you again, Ollie."

"Matt," Ollie replied nonchalantly, fully in the charade.

"Now that Matt is here, who would like a mimosa, or a Bloody Mary?" Diana asked, waving Deirdre in.

After chatting, opening presents, and brunch, Ollie went to get his bag, and Finn went to change for Matt's mother's house, while Matt had coffee in the library with Bill.

"Just make sure you continue to speculate conservatively, hang onto some of the capital you've been given, focus on development and let the contracts come to you," Bill nodded at Matt. "You are destined for greatness, Matt."

"Thank you, sir." Matt smiled happily.

Bill had been an incredible influence on him for most of his life, and his insight and acumen with business was what helped turn his software idea into a company. Matt's management style was a combination of his years of military leadership and Bill's hand's-off leadership. Bill helped Matt find and hire his top executives, poaching most of them from some of the companies that Bill's investment firm did business with. "You're the reason I'm doing so well, sir. You and Finn, I couldn't have done it without either of you."

"You took to it like the pro you are, give yourself some credit. And as far as Finn goes, I really wish things had gone better with you two." He shook his head, believing the lie Matt and Finn had created. "Everyone dallies before they get married. I see that she loves you, don't give up hope, please."

There was a light knock on the open door. "Finn sent me, we're ready," Ollie said looking between Matt and Bill. "Thank you for having me, sir, it was a real pleasure to stay here and celebrate last night and today." He shook Bill's hand as he stood.

"It was wonderful to meet you and have you for the holidays, Ollie. I hope you enjoy yourself in New York City. It's quite the place to be this time of year, just be careful on New Year's Eve," Bill added with a smile.

Ollie nodded distractedly. He waited as Matt gave Bill a hug and then followed Matt out of the room. Finn appeared on the stairs in a flowy dress with high heeled boots as Matt dug into the hall closet for their coats.

"You ready to eat more food than a Monty Python skit, Ollie?" Finn asked with a grin as she took her coat from Matt. "Matt's mom is the quintessential Italian mom. She'll be telling you that dessert is 'wafer thin' but I promise it won't be."

Matt shoved her lightly with a chuckle and looked at Ollie. "Chuck's not wrong." He shrugged and led the way out the door as he thrust his arms into his overcoat.

Matt grabbed the bags of gifts for his nieces and nephews from his trunk, passing a few to Ollie, and nodded for Finn to lead the way. It was a short walk around the corner to Matt's mother's house and Finn teased Matt the whole way.

"Be honest," Finn said, walking next to Matt. "Did you actually shop for any of these, or did you make Stacey do it?"

Matt grinned and shrugged. "I've been too busy shagging or thinking about shagging this one." He nodded his head at Ollie.

Finn threw her head back and laughed. "You dog."

Matt grinned at Ollie as they turned up the front walk of Matt's childhood home, a small, well-maintained, brick and white clapboard cape a fraction of the size of Finn's parents' house. There were two minivans in the driveway and the sound of children's voices coming from inside. Matt gave Ollie a shy smile and threw open the front door. "Merry Christmas!" he shouted.

Ollie sat back after the introductions were made, with explanations about Matt's oldest sister, Mary, spending the holiday at her in-laws in Philadelphia, and then watched as every female hovered over Matt, waiting on him and doting on him, including Finn. Even Matt's two brothers-in-law, John and Patrick, seemed in awe of him. When not fawning over Matt, his three sisters, Angela, Theresa, and Lisa, peppered Ollie with questions about his relationship with Finn. He wasn't sure if it was because they were gaga over his British accent, or if they were sussing him out as competition with Matt for Finn's affection.

Ollie was aware of Matt's eyes on him from time to time, and was careful to keep his face neutral, and resisted the urge to meet that gaze, focused on 'keeping up appearances,' as he listened to Patrick.

"It's probably nothing like soccer, excuse me, football, back home," Patrick grinned, "but it's fun, and Patriot Place is quite the experience. I have season tickets; you should come to a game the next time you're here."

"Sounds great. I'd love to check out an American team." Ollie smiled, wondering how close Matt would let him get to his brother-in-law. "Count me in."

Ollie finished his beer and excused himself, going through the kitchen to get another one from the back porch, only to find the box empty. He looked around for more before going back into the kitchen as Matt appeared in the doorway to the hall.

Ollie gave him a half smile. "Beer's out."

"There's more in the basement." Matt gestured with his head opening the door next to him and went down the stairs. Ollie followed him, closing the door quietly.

Matt pressed him up against the wall to the left of the stairs when he reached the bottom, kissing him deeply, filling Ollie's mouth with his tongue. "I've been watching you," he panted. "You are so fucking hot."

Ollie moaned, running his hands over Matt's body hungrily, stroking the front of Matt's suit pants finding him fully aroused. "Your family," Ollie whispered breathlessly against Matt's mouth.

"Your mouth is magic, I'll come fast," he said huskily and unzipped his pants. "Ollie," he moaned as Ollie knelt and took him in his mouth. Matt braced his hands on the wall above Ollie's head and pressed himself deeper, pumping his hips.

Matt was true to his word and Ollie wiped his eyes and his chin. He stood as Matt zipped his pants and grabbed another 12-pack of beer from the fridge. He gave Ollie a quick breathless kiss. "Don't rinse your mouth. You can have that beer in five minutes."

Ollie bit his lip and watched as Matt went up the stairs at a quick pace, his body a marvel.

He waited a few moments to cool off, before going up the stairs, emerging into the kitchen stealthily, turning quickly and opening the basement door again when he heard one of Matt's sisters coming from the living room.

"Oh drat, this isn't the bathroom," he said closing the door, looking at Angela.

"It's there, on the left," she answered with a smile pointing down the short hallway.

"Thank you," Ollie said with a smile and closed the door behind him. He used the toilet and washed his hands, emerging into the hallway, nearly crashing into Matt.

Matt looked at him and leaned in close, taking a deep breath through his nose. "I love smelling me on you." He closed his eyes happily. "Come into the living room, I have a cold beer waiting."

Ollie's body tingled. "How much longer are we staying? I'm so horny," he whispered.

Matt smiled and raised his eyebrows briefly. "We'll leave right after dinner." He turned and Ollie followed with a groan.

The kids opened their presents exuberantly while everyone watched, Finn sitting in Ollie's spot under Matt's arm and laughing at something he said. Ollie looked away, suppressing his jealousy, knowing he had nothing to be jealous of with them, but wishing *he* could be at Matt's side.

Lisa, Finn's pathway to Matt all those years ago, sat next to Ollie, chatting and flirting lightly. She not only had Matt's coloring, but also had the same beautiful mouth, which Ollie discovered from looking at the family pictures, they alone had inherited from their father, along with their blue eyes. Ollie found himself laughing frequently at her easy and observant humor, flirting in return, thoroughly enjoying her attention and company.

He looked up to find Matt standing over them, holding out another cold beer. "You want something, Lis?"

"Is there more red?" She held up her empty glass.

"Keep that, I'll bring the bottle."

Matt reappeared a moment later and poured her a full glass. Glancing at Ollie he walked away asking if anyone else wanted a refill.

"Matteo." His mother stood from the chair by the window. "Help me with the turkey," she said in Italian.

"Sure, Ma," he answered in English, following her into the kitchen.

He pulled the turkey out of one of the ovens, and the two lasagnas out of the other. His mother bustled around the recently renovated kitchen, pulling out platters and serving utensils. She stopped next to Matt and admired the turkey.

"Let it rest a few more minutes," she said in Italian.

"I know, Ma." He smiled, and put his arm around her.

She stood thoughtfully, wrapping her arm around his waist. "That man. He's your boyfriend. Isn't he?" she said quietly.

Matt straightened, stepping back and looking at her with a frown, before looking around the room to see if anyone was nearby. "Ma. No. What are you talking about?" he scoffed, laughing nervously, his heart racing.

"Matteo Dominic Diontangelo. Don't." She shook her head and looked at him intently.

"Ma. Seriously." Matt looked again at the doorways to the kitchen, listening to the sounds of laughter coming from the living room, and shook his head.

"*Puoi mentire al mondo, ma non a me.*"

Matt closed his eyes and winced.

"Matteo, you are my only son. I would never betray what you so obviously want to keep secret, what you *have* kept secret. I wouldn't with any of my children," she said sternly as she pulled a cutting board from the cabinet and turned back to face him. "You look happier than I have ever seen you, and I'm thrilled. You look young again." She smiled, and touched his face.

Matt studied her carefully. "Not even the girls, Ma. *Per favore,*" he begged quietly, closing his eyes.

She pulled his face down and kissed both of his cheeks. "I won't tell a soul *mi bambino.* Now carve the turkey and be sure Oliver sits next to me at dinner."

Matt sat in his father's spot at the head of the table, giving the Christmas toast, teasing his sisters, praising his mother and her cooking, before sitting and picking worriedly at his food. He kept watching his mother at the other end of the table with Ollie, worried she would say something, worried he would say something, worried someone would overhear.

He was desperate for a run, his legs jostling agitatedly under the table. Finn put her hand on his wrist, and looked at him inquisitively. He felt his eyelid jumping, and gave her a tight smile, looking around the table again. He met Ollie's concerned eyes and went weak inside, his heart racing again with the implication of his mother knowing.

He felt Finn's hand on his leg under the table, and stopped bouncing his knee. "Hey." She smiled and leaned closer. "Look at me. You're good, in fact, you're spectacular, and it's Christmas," she said quietly in a soothing tone, and squeezed gently. "Whatever is bothering you, or happened, is nothing. I, and," she nodded her head discreetly at Ollie, "love you, and if you need to kiss me now, you should."

Matt felt the weight lift off of him. He leaned over and kissed Finn, lingering like a lover would, for the audience, while his heart cramped with the weight of Ollie's gaze. "I love you, Chuck. More than you could ever know."

Matt and Ollie said goodbye to Finn and left, Matt focused on getting home and being alone with him.

"Christmas spread out between locations always makes it seem like the day never ends," Ollie said to Matt with a smile, squeezing his thigh.

Matt glanced at him and smiled in return, covering Ollie's hand with his.

"What happened at dinner, or rather before dinner, that made you so upset?" Ollie asked quietly.

Matt navigated the back roads of Wellesley toward the Mass Pike as he thought over his words. "What did you and my mother talk about at dinner?"

Ollie leaned his head back. "She was just asking me about my family, and school, and what I wanted to do with my life." He turned his head. "The usual small talk."

Matt held Ollie's gaze for a moment at the stop sign, before turning left, driving past the darkened public golf course that was blanketed in snow. "My mother asked me about you. She knows." He shrugged and turned onto the highway, shifting gears rapidly as he accelerated.

"What?" Ollie furrowed his brow with panic and lifted his head off the headrest. "How? What did she say? I promise, I never said a word."

"I know." He squeezed Ollie's knee. "I shouldn't have brought you, but I don't regret doing so. She just knew. I don't know if it's the way I looked at you, the way I didn't look at you. Or just some vibe that only mothers feel." He smiled wryly. "She won't tell my sisters, and Chuck helped me get through dinner, I hope the kiss didn't bother you."

"I know it was performance, and I'm not worried about Chuck. If she sets your mind at ease." Ollie waved his hand. "Especially when I can't do it myself." He looked out the window. "Her parents sure wish you two were still 'together.'" He looked at Matt. "Her mother gave me the third degree and they both seemed relieved that I was only staying one night. Sounds like no one she could bring home will ever compare to you. How could they?" he added with a smile.

Matt sighed. "They are the best of people. It pains me to lie to them. But, not enough to tell them the truth."

Matt exited at Atlantic Avenue, the street nearly empty, and zipped through green lights all the way to North Street.

Matt followed Ollie off the elevator, looking like a pack mule with all the gift bags and Ollie's rolling luggage while Ollie held only the key to the condo. As Ollie hung said key on the hook inside the door, Matt picked up a remote control from the table underneath and watched with a smile as strings of white Christmas lights on the beams and around the windows lit up all around the condo. He dropped the bags and smiled at Ollie's reaction.

"Whoa, Matt. Did you do all this?" Ollie looked over his shoulder at him as he walked further into the space. "Cor, the tree!"

Ollie smiled at the large, beautifully decorated Christmas tree in front of the slider, the colored lights twinkling and reflecting in the glass and presents of all sizes spilling out from underneath. Ollie grinned knowingly at the sight of a blanket on the floor in front of the fireplace and a bottle of Caymus cabernet sauvignon and two glasses on the coffee table. He shrugged out of his coat, draping it on the kitchen chair, and kicked off his shoes, astounded by the effort it must have taken.

Matt came up behind him as he loosened his tie. "You like it?" he whispered. "It took me most of the night, I couldn't sleep without you anyway. Merry Christmas, babe."

Ollie turned in his arms. "It's gorgeous, I love it. I love you," he murmured against Matt's lips.

Matt raised his head after a moment of savoring Ollie's mouth. "Those are all for you." He gestured to the presents under the tree. "Truth is I was so busy shopping for you, that I had to have my assistant do everyone else, except Chuck of course."

Ollie smiled, pleased to his core. "Be right back." He disappeared into Matt's bedroom and emerged a moment later with a medium sized bag of gifts. "These are for you."

Matt smiled and turned on the gas fireplace, pulling off his tie as he picked up the bottle of wine and made quick work of opening it. He watched Ollie touch the ornaments on the tree, some of them trinkets he'd picked up on his travels, and some of them ones his mother had passed down. Matt handed him his glass with a kiss and gestured for him to sit on the blanket, keeping his body close as he leaned his back against the raised hearth. "Cheers. Now open your presents."

Ollie opened every present until they were surrounded by clouds of crumpled wrapping paper. There were cashmere sweaters, handmade Italian loafers, cologne, a grooming kit, books, a few colorful jockstraps (which Ollie grinned over), a monogrammed zip leather folio like Matt's, and finally an Oystersteel Submariner Rolex, similar to Matt's white gold one.

"Holy shit," Ollie breathed wondrously over the watch before flipping it over at Matt's prodding. "What are these?"

"It's Sumerian. Chuck drew them for me and I took it to the engravers. It says 'you are the moon to my ocean.'"

Ollie looked at him with shining eyes and kissed him, Matt's tongue tasting of red wine. "I love it. You shouldn't have spoiled me so. Now I'm going to be insufferable."

Matt smiled and kissed him again lingeringly, his hands running over Ollie's body. "You deserve so much more."

"Your turn," Ollie said brightly, covering his pleased smile as he passed his bag of gifts to Matt. "Though after all this," he gestured to open presents all around them, "these feel more than a little underwhelming," Ollie added shyly.

Matt kissed him swiftly and set the presents out in front of him. The first small box contained a silver chain that matched Ollie's, and Matt looked at Ollie with a big smile as he put it on. The second was a platinum collar tie bar with tiny tridents on both ends, and matching cufflinks. Matt looked up at him. "Where'd you get this? I love it."

Ollie shrugged, "I had the pin made to match the cufflinks, I was very specific about the size, it had to be as understated as possible. Couldn't have you striding about with giant tridents on your neck." He smiled, pleased that Matt loved them.

Matt laughed lightly, and kissed him. The next few presents were Tom Ford boxer briefs, a tube of the styling cream Ollie used (that Matt had been stealing), and a mug that said *tastes like I need a BJ*, which made Matt throw back his head with a laugh. The last two were a bottle of Macallan 18-year sherry oak Scotch, and an Oxford University t-shirt.

"You can wear that when you miss me, and everyone will think Chuck gave it to you, but you'll know the truth," Ollie said huskily.

Matt stared at him for a moment. "It's gonna get pretty smelly, me wearing it every day that I'm not with you."

Matt pressed Ollie back until they were stretched out next to each other on the blanket, unbuttoning Ollie's shirt as he kissed him slowly, lost in the moment, the fire casting flickering shadows over their bodies. He licked Ollie's nipples, smiling when they puckered. Ollie put his hands in Matt's hair as Matt trailed kisses up to Ollie's collarbone, following the line of it to the soft dip in his shoulder.

"I love your skin, your scent," Matt murmured as he buried his nose in Ollie's neck and breathed deeply. "Makes me hard." He pressed his hard length against Ollie's hip in emphasis.

Ollie groaned and gripped Matt over his pants. Their clothes came off unhurriedly and joined the puffs of wrapping paper around them. Ollie rolled on top of Matt, straddling him, hearing a low sound of satisfaction in Matt's throat as he rubbed his cock against Matt's. He teased Matt's tongue, and kissed his neck, doing all the things that made Matt sigh, and twitch, and beg, smiling to himself when Matt squeezed his bottom tightly in response to the nibbles on his neck. Matt smacked his ass sharply when those teeth moved to his nipple. Ollie rolled his hips in response and licked the bite mark.

"Don't act like you don't love it when I do that," Ollie murmured.

"I do, which is why I responded with something you love." Matt grinned and reached under the end of the couch near his head and pulled out a small clear bottle.

"You keep one of those everywhere, don't you?" Ollie breathed against Matt's mouth, smiling with pleasure.

Matt made an amused sound and popped the lid. "With you, I have to."

29

New Year's Resolutions

THEY SPENT THE FOLLOWING WEEK exploring Boston, and each other, ever aware of the time ticking down to Ollie's departure. Ollie cooked extravagant meals that they often ate at the coffee table in front of the fireplace, sitting side-by-side on the floor, usually wearing next to nothing. Matt took him to see the massive Christmas tree in Faneuil Hall, then into the Rowes Wharf Bar to warm up and grab a drink. Ollie did his very best to keep the drool in his mouth as he sipped his scotch and imagined Matt's stubble on the inside of his thighs. Matt wasn't an exceptionally hairy man, but his five o'clock shadow always appeared just after noon.

"What're you thinking about?" Matt asked with a sly grin.

Ollie chuckled and flicked his eyebrows before looking away. He heard Matt put his glass on the low table between them and met his gaze.

"Come on," Matt said as he stood. "There's one more thing I wanna show you."

Ollie tossed back the last bit of his drink and followed Matt out the door.

It was a brisk walk back toward Faneuil Hall, their strides in sync. Matt turned onto a side street and led Ollie into a circular shaped marble and granite lobby.

"Wait here, and look up," Matt commanded before striding to the concierge desk.

Ollie looked up and couldn't help the low 'whoa' that slipped from his mouth. He heard Matt talking and laughing in Italian before returning to Ollie's side.

"What is this place?" he asked as he followed Matt to the elevator.

"It's the Custom House. It used to be on the waterfront, before this part of the harbor was filled in, and they collected duties on shipments. There's a counting room, and all sorts of history in these walls, but that's not what we're here to see."

Matt led Ollie off one elevator midway up the building and onto another one until they reached the top floor. They went through an empty game room and out onto the wraparound balcony, where the wind hit them head on.

"This is incredible," Ollie breathed.

"It's the highest outdoor observatory in Boston." Matt turned Ollie to him and kissed him briefly. "Pretty fucking gorgeous city, eh, Ollie?"

Matt smiled as they walked all around the tower hand-in-hand, enjoying the three-hundred-and-sixty-degree views from the harbor to the suburbs. He stopped when the harbor came back into view. He loved his city, so beautiful all lit up, and was pleased to see Ollie's enamored reaction.

Ollie nodded. "It's marvelous."

"Could you see yourself living here?" Matt whispered searching Ollie's face as he held his breath.

Ollie looked out at the harbor, his face shuttered and his breath billowing out in clouds of steam. He looked back at Matt and then slowly nodded. "Yes, but only with you," he paused, "and, that would be like us living in a glass closet. Matt, how could we hide us?"

Matt smiled softly, a pleased warmth in his chest. "You let me worry about that." He brushed his thumb over Ollie's bottom lip and turned to leave, Ollie following close behind.

*   *   *

"I'm having a few people for New Year's Eve if you guys can come," Finn said when Matt answered his phone. "Everyone would love to see you."

"Aren't your parents going to be home?" Matt replied, looking at the half-open bathroom door. "I think Ollie and I will hit a bar here in town and be home early for the ball drop. But thanks."

"No, they're going to the Boggs' for their annual costume dinner party. They're never home before midnight and you guys could leave right after the ball drop."

"I'll think about it and let you know," Matt answered noncommittally. "Love you."

"Who was that?" Ollie came out of the bathroom toweling off.

"Chuck, inviting us to her New Year's Eve party." Matt scanned his eyes admiringly over Ollie's naked body. *I could never get sick of looking at him.*

"Do you want to go?"

Matt shrugged. "I'll know everyone but you won't, and maybe that wouldn't be fun for you. Lies, and no contact with you." He twisted his mouth with displeasure.

"Or," Ollie said approaching him slowly, dropping the towel on the bed, "heated glances, full of longing and secrets. Brushing against you accidentally, sucking your cock in the basement." He smiled slyly. "You sucking mine."

Matt chuckled huskily. "Why don't you show me exactly what you would do to me in the basement, so I can decide if I want to go or not." He pushed his pajama pants off with a grin.

* * *

There were more than a few people at Finn's party, the parked cars lined every street in the vicinity. Matt and Ollie let themselves in through the front door, Matt taking Ollie's coat and hanging it in the closet next to the stairs. Ollie was wearing one of his new cashmere sweaters and a pair of dark wash jeans that were stylishly faded in spots. He also had on one of the new jockstraps Matt had given him and the awareness of it under his jeans made Ollie eager for later.

Matt was wearing a light pink dress shirt with a navy blue and white polka dot tie, and the trident collar pin and matching cuff links. He wanted to wear suit pants but Ollie convinced him to wear blue jeans and a sexy belt with a stylish silver buckle instead.

"Matt!" voices called happily from the living room and kitchen, as though he were a celebrity.

Soon he and Ollie were surrounded, Matt getting hugs and compliments on his outfit (grinning smugly at Ollie as he listened), and more than a few kisses. He introduced Ollie as Finn's friend from Oxford who he picked up from South Station on his way there, as Ollie listened with a hint of chagrin.

Always with the unnecessary subterfuge, his brain said quietly, *who cares?*

The party was well under way, and Matt anticipated that more than a few people would be spending the night, Finn's house large enough to accommodate all of them if necessary. He spent much of the evening with Finn tucked under his arm, holding court, while Ollie flirted politely with several of her friends, for Matt's sake. They were separated from time to time, but always managed to catch each other's eye from across the room.

Someone cranked up the music and people began dancing, clearing the living room furniture to the sides to make an impromptu dance floor. At the bar in the butler's pantry, Ollie couldn't resist brushing up against Matt, pressing his half-hard dick into his ass cheek briefly. He smiled broadly when Matt turned around in surprise.

"Please tell me there are more beers in the basement," Ollie said under his breath with an expectant look.

"There are, and unfortunately, they are in people's hands." Matt shook his head. "However, if you're up for a hot mouth on your cold cock, there's Bill's tool room in the garage," he said quietly his eyes a smoky blue. "I'll meet you there in three minutes." He walked away without waiting for an answer.

They managed to sneak separately into the garage without being seen, kissing desperately behind the door of the tool room, the smell of gasoline and oil filling their noses. Matt found a clean piece of cardboard to kneel on and Ollie pressed himself deeply into his mouth with a moan.

Matt took Ollie's beer and drank a few swallows. "Now it's a quick champagne toast and we're off, okay?"

They slipped unnoticed back into the party, the clock showing it was nearly midnight.

"Who's that handsome bloke standing with Chuck? He's been giving you the evil eye all night."

Matt turned to look at Finn and grinned. "Oh, that's some Chad or Brett that Chuck dated or hooked up with in high school. I've been fucking with him all night."

Ollie rolled his eyes, "Christ, you're getting laid tonight, you ought to let poor Chuck get some action."

"Did you just roll your eyes at me?" he asked with his eyebrows raised.

Ollie shrugged. "Just tell her to have some fun."

"Fine," Matt said with an exasperated tone.

Someone turned the big TV on in the family room and had the CNN ball drop countdown queued up for everyone to crowd around to watch.

Soon the sound of corks being popped filled the kitchen, someone was passing around plastic champagne flutes, while several other people were tasked with pouring the bubbly into everyone's glasses.

The room filled with people counting down and then shouting 'HAPPY NEW YEAR!' before immediately turning to find someone to kiss. Matt turned and kissed Finn.

"Happy New Year, Chuck! Here's to another great year. I hope you get laid tonight," he added with a wink. "Chad over there seems pretty flush."

Finn looked where he nodded, and blushed. "His name is Glenn. You've met him."

"If I really wanted to know what his name was, I could have checked his high school letter jacket in the front hall closet," he scoffed.

Finn punched his shoulder lightly. "Maybe I'm into guys who peaked in high school."

She didn't wait for an answer, and turned to kiss Naomi, and then went to kiss Glenn lingeringly.

Matt was kissed by a few other women as he scanned the room and saw Ollie getting kisses of his own. He met Ollie's eye and gestured with his chin to the front hall, pushing Ollie quickly into the coat closet, caught up in the celebratory moment.

"I thought this would be an appropriate setting for our New Year's kiss," he said with a smile and captured Ollie's mouth, kissing him thoroughly, one hand on Ollie's ass and one on the doorknob. "I love you. Happy New Year."

"I love you too. Happy New Year, Matt." Ollie hugged him tightly and kissed him again.

"I'll go out first and you follow after a minute, with our coats." Matt opened the door as Bill was coming around the bottom of the stairs, dressed as a 1920s gangster. He quickly closed the door, his heart racing.

"Hi, Bill," he said cheerily, so Ollie could hear, covering his nervousness. "Happy New Year, sir. You're home early, I hope everything is alright."

Bill looked him over. "Happy New Year, Matt. Diana got a headache, I think it's because she and her girlfriends started drinking the champagne too early." He smiled and rolled his eyes. "What were you doing in there?"

"Oh, I was looking for my coat, I think it's in your study though. I'm gonna go say goodbye to Chuck." He started walking away, willing Bill to follow him. "We'll surprise her together, she's in the family room, follow me."

"Lead the way, son," Bill said, following Matt around the corner to the kitchen. Matt was so concerned about getting Bill away from the hall he didn't feel him pause.

Ollie waited, his stomach like lead after hearing Matt greet Bill. He counted to ten, visualizing escaping the house without notice, and then stepped out of the closet. His heart lurched, and he felt his bowels rumble as he saw Bill standing in the doorway to the kitchen staring at him, his face white. Bill closed his mouth and disappeared into the kitchen.

Ollie looked around anxiously as he stood immobilized in the hallway near the front door, ready to race out into the night when Bill reappeared. He gave Bill a tight smile, his head pounding.

"Ollie," he said simply. "We never had a chance to chat, do you have a minute?"

Ollie flicked his eyes to the kitchen doorway behind him. "Yes, sir, of course," he answered quietly putting the coats down, his stomach in knots, and followed him into his study.

Bill closed the door behind them. "Happy New Year," he said in an odd voice. "Sit please." He gestured to the club chairs in front of the fireplace and ran his eyes over Ollie.

"Happy New Year, sir," Ollie replied nervously as he sat.

"New watch?" Bill nodded at Ollie's wrist.

Ollie nodded and swallowed, pulling his sleeves down.

Something flitted across Bill's face as he looked away briefly. "I thought you were going to New York City after Christmas, Ollie."

"Yes, sir, that is what I told you," Ollie answered carefully.

"But you didn't. You stayed here." Ollie nodded silently, holding Bill's gaze. "With Matt I presume."

Ollie looked away, feeling dirty, and then angry for it. "Yes, sir."

Bill took a deep breath and let it out, looking at the door. "Does Finn know?"

"Know that I stayed with Matt?" Ollie feigned obtuseness.

Bill narrowed his eyes imperceptibly at him and looked again at his wrist. "Know *about* you and Matt."

Ollie began nodding, small movements at first and then more noticeably, as his heart pounded. "Yes, sir. She introduced us."

Bill looked away, visibly confused.

"Mr. Hawthorn, sir, please forgive the deception. None of this was meant to hurt anyone. Matt is very private, and what with the military, and now building his business." He held his hand out to his side. "He will never be out. This cannot leave this room, please."

"I'd say that what you two did a short while ago, was reckless, and if he wants secrets kept, I would highly recommend against doing that again, anywhere," Bill answered coolly.

Ollie nodded, feeling the cut, holding his gaze. "I agree, sir. Please know though that this changes nothing. Matt is still the amazing man you know him to be, and he loves your daughter, and you, and your wife very much."

"Well, actually, Oliver, I'd say it changes quite a bit. It crushes me, and my hopes of ever having Matt as a son-in-law," he said with a sad note in his voice as he stood. "But I love him like the son I never had, so don't worry. I won't say anything. And hopefully the incredible disappointment I feel right now about that will go away, some day." He walked to the door and opened it as Ollie stood.

"Thank you, sir." He crossed the room feeling chastised *and* indignant.

Is he judging me? Judging us? Ollie shook Bill's hand politely.

Matt appeared in the open doorway, and stopped short. He shot a glance at Ollie, and looked at Bill with a tight smile.

"Your coat's not in here, Matt," Bill said in a friendly voice, his eyes landing briefly on Matt's Rolex. "But Ollie is, and you're probably looking for him, so I'll leave you two." He stepped in into the hall. "Happy New Year, son." He wrapped his arms around a speechless Matt who returned the hug with a worried look at Ollie.

"Thank you, Bill. Please tell Diana happy new year for me," Matt said with a smile that didn't reach his eyes as they pulled apart.

Ollie grabbed the coats from where he left them and followed Matt outside.

Matt started the car and looked at Ollie. "What the fuck was that all about?" he asked in a tight voice.

Ollie exhaled. "I waited." He shook his head. "I heard your footsteps disappear, I waited again. I took down our coats and I stepped out into the hallway." He looked at Matt who was watching him with a growing panic. "He was standing there, waiting for me."

Matt closed his eyes and crumpled into himself, covering his face with his hands. "Fuck!" he shouted, and slammed the bottom of the steering wheel with the heel of his fist.

Ollie winced and watched Matt put the car into first, pulling away from the curb with a chirp. "It'll be okay, Matt. He promised to keep your secret. He said he loves you like the son he never had."

Matt squeezed his eyes shut briefly and looked back the road, slowing down to the speed limit. "It's not the secret with him. It's how can I ever look him in the eye again now that he knows what I am?"

"What you are?!" Ollie asked incredulously. "You say that like you're a fucking serial murderer. Christ, Matt, you're just gay. Bill knows all about your other remarkable qualities, that's all he cares about," Ollie said, hoping he was right.

"It matters to me, Ollie. Until I met you, I used to wish every day that I wasn't born with these urges. *I hated myself.* I was so ashamed." He shook his head. "And if I feel that way, think of all the other people who feel that way as well."

"Fuck them!" Ollie said angrily. "They're miserable human beings, and have no right to sit in judgement of anyone, especially not to judge someone for who they love. Besides, there aren't nearly as many of them as you think there are. There are far more kind and accepting people than there are bigots." He touched Matt's shoulder, wincing as Matt flinched away. "And, I promise you that the Hawthorns are kind and accepting people who will continue to love you without judgement. They raised Chuck after all."

Matt nodded once reluctantly, pulling into his garage and turning off the car with a grim face.

The elevator ride was tense and silent, and Matt's body language was indescribable. Ollie knew he was angry, but couldn't tell who that anger was directed toward and that made him angry. He followed Matt into the condo and made his way to the bathroom.

"You're not seriously going for a run right now?" Ollie frowned when he came out to find Matt in his reflective running gear. "There are drunk drivers on the roads, it's slippery and not to mention, pitch dark out there. Please, Matt."

Matt zipped his keys in his pocket and pulled a beanie over his head. "I have my phone. You know I gotta do this. I'll be back."

Ollie looked at the door as it slammed behind Matt, and exhaled, trying to release the anxiety he was feeling. He finally fell asleep on the couch, physically and emotionally drained. He woke to the sound of the door opening and sat up, rubbing his eyes. He looked at his new watch and saw that it was three AM. Matt appeared a moment later in the kitchen, and poured himself a glass of water, drinking it slowly as he glanced at Ollie.

"I'm home now, Ollie. Go to bed." He nodded to the bedroom, as he poured another glass. "I still have to shower, I'm gonna be a while."

Ollie stood and nodded. "Thank you for not dying out there. I was really worried," Ollie approached him for a kiss, and Matt stepped back slightly. "I'm all sweaty, let me shower first."

Ollie frowned and walked away, giving him his space, not knowing what else to do, and not wanting to fight. He brushed his teeth, stripped off his clothes and climbed into bed, falling asleep before Matt came into the room.

30

Remember There's a Lot of Bad, and Beware

OLLIE WOKE AND found Matt's side of the bed untouched. He sat up and looked around, and then at his watch, seeing that it was past nine. He pulled on his underwear and left the room calling for Matt. He found a note taped to the door and pulled a face at its location.

*GONE TO THE GYM AND THEN THE OFFICE.
BACK BY 6P – M*

Ollie frowned and got out his phone.

> I thought today was a holiday. Everything ok?

He waited an hour for Matt's reply.

Just a few work fires
I'll bring pizza

Matt came home at six, carrying a box of pizza and his phone. He was dressed in jeans, a black cashmere sweater, and his leather belt with the large silver buckle.

Ollie caught his breath and stood with a smile, hoping Matt's run and day alone had sorted everything. "Hey. I missed you today."

Matt grinned tightly. "I hope you got some studying done, or went out."

"I did both." He met Matt in the kitchen and grabbed him around the waist. "You're looking quite gorgeous. How was work?" he asked and leaned in for a kiss.

Matt closed his eyes and kissed him distractedly. "Busy, I got a lot done. I feel pretty good about what I accomplished today."

Ollie smiled again, his chest hot with uncertainty, hating that he felt the need to dance around Matt. "I'm glad."

They ate in the living room, Matt putting music on, and checking his phone from time to time.

"So, Chuck will be here tomorrow by four, and I'll take you both to the airport," Matt said, not looking at Ollie.

"I can't believe I'm leaving already. It feels like I only just got here," Ollie said sadly as he watched Matt.

Matt nodded silently, without eye contact, and that was the thing that undid him. Ollie put his pizza down and studied Matt carefully. He looked away, not trusting what he saw on Matt's face, and suddenly felt as though he couldn't breathe.

"I just need some air." Ollie stood and walked out onto the deck, closing the slider behind him.

He took several deep breaths of the cold winter air, the shock of it cooling his burning heart, and looked back at Matt, who was staring down at his feet with a grim expression.

Oh *fuck.*

Ollie looked away again, his throat swelling. He blinked frantically, his stomach sinking as he reviewed the past twenty-four hours, and realized Matt was pulling away, cutting him out. Ollie looked back inside to find Matt gone. He was desperate to find a way to bring Matt back to him, but had a sinking feeling he was already lost.

Ollie packed his things, not knowing what else to do, not knowing what to do about *them*, but hoping that intimacy would make Matt realize what he was apparently giving up. He certainly had no intention of giving Matt the fight he seemingly wanted, everything in his body language was begging for Ollie to call him coward. Ollie stood in the doorway of Matt's office a few hours later, feeling empty, and watched him for a moment before breaking the silence.

"Matt."

"Yeah," Matt answered not looking up from his computer.

Ollie sighed quietly. "I leave tomorrow, and I know you're upset, and I know what's coming," he said swallowing, watching as Matt stilled. "Can we just dim the lights and have one more night. You don't even have to say a word, or feel a thing, if you don't want. But I deserve better from you than just being shut out, my final day here. I love you."

Ollie stared at Matt's profile for several breaths and turned to the bedroom with a frown when he got no response.

Everything was in his suitcase except his toothbrush and a suit for the flight. He shut off the light and got into bed, feeling turned inside out. Thirty minutes later he sensed Matt standing by the bed.

"I'm angry, Ollie," he whispered.

Ollie waited. "I know."

"Okay?" Matt asked expectantly.

Ollie bit his lip, and nodded, swallowing the lump in his throat. "Okay," he replied, knowing it would be easier to say goodbye to him this way. To *hate* him.

"Follow me."

ENDURANCE

31

You Tore Out my Heart, and Threw it Away

OLLIE SLEPT FITFULLY, leaving the bed as soon as he heard the condo door close behind Matt as he left for his dawn run. He was surprised by the pain in his heart, because he could've sworn he was dead, or rather, he wished he were. Nearly his entire body was sore, and his head was pounding like a bass drum. He put on his suit thinking about how Matt hadn't said a word to him once he stepped away from the side of the bed, and Ollie had stayed just as silent, his throat hot with unshed tears through it all. He put on his backpack, careful with his shoulder, and wheeled his bag beside him out the door.

The cold air hit him like a slap as he exited the building onto the empty street. He walked to the curb and waited for his taxi, his internal dialogue strangely (and welcomingly) silent.

Ollie spent the day working his way toward the airport. Starting at a coffee shop across town, then moving to a restaurant for food that he barely ate, before finally hailing a taxi to Logan. He spent the remainder of his time in the first-class lounge, drinking and waiting for his flight to begin boarding. He dreaded seeing Finn, knowing that they were seated next to each other on the flight as he had been unable to switch seats. He waited until the absolute last moment to board, wincing slightly at the concern in her eyes when she looked up at him stepping onto the plane.

"Jesus, Ollie, you had me so worried," she said as he sat down and put his seatbelt on. "Matt said you were gone when he came back from his run. What happened?"

Ollie just shook his head, put his eye mask on and turned to the window. Halfway into the flight, when he awakened from his fitful sleep, he felt Finn's hand on his arm.

"Hey," she said gently.

Ollie reluctantly raised his mask, fumbled in his pocket for his paracetamol, and looked at her with dead eyes.

"Please, don't give up hope," she said with a wince. "It just all happened so fast, and I think my father finding out about your relationship pushed him over the edge, but he will realize how much he misses you. They had a long talk yesterday in my dad's study. I don't know what about, but he seemed really happy when he came out."

Ollie took the cocktail off Finn's tray table, washed his pills down with the contents, and then closed his eyes briefly, his stomach churning again. "He was at your house yesterday?"

"Yeah, he came for lunch and stayed the whole day." She pulled back at his expression. "I thought you knew."

"I don't know a bloody thing anymore," he said in a hard voice. "I know you think him leaving your house happy is a good sign, but it isn't for me." He pulled the mask over his eyes again, blinking back tears. "Forgive me for not being interested."

"Well, you two are meant to be, Ollie, and I certainly won't give up hope," she said quietly. "All I ask is that when, not if, but when he comes back, you listen to what he has to say, please. He's stubborn, and he's as inexperienced as they come with love, but he's worth it. I promise you."

Ollie gave her a wry smile without lifting his eye mask and didn't respond. She got everything right about Matt except the last part. Ollie didn't think Matt was worth it at all anymore, but that didn't make the pain go away.

Ollie took the train to Oxford when they landed, telling Finn he was going to his parents instead of riding in her hired car. He took a seat by the window in an empty row and looked out at the grey skies and ever-present rain. He played the game he'd play when he was a child to pass the time, looking ahead at the countryside rushing toward him quickly, visible and discernable, then turned his head to look straight out at the confusing blur as they sped past, and then turned his head again to look behind him, watching the land recede like one frozen perspective, calling ahead to the train 'come back, come back, come back,' in sync with the sound of the steel wheels clicking over the seams in the tracks.

It was like the future, the present and the past all in one view, and more so now than ever. His present was a confusing, painful blur and he felt unnaturally overwhelmed in a way he had never felt before. Breathing was difficult, and he alternated between gasping for air, and holding his breath in fear. He looked ahead again, at the houses and countryside coming toward him fast and steady like his future, whether he wanted it to or not, stretching ahead endlessly it seemed. He looked back at what they had just passed, the dwindling past, ever there, calling to him, but eventually disappearing from view. He took three more paracetamols and closed his eyes, waiting for the pain to stop, while knowing it never really would.

32

Ghost in the Machine

MATT LEFT BILL'S STUDY on New Year's feeling pretty good. He explained that Ollie took things for more than what they were, that they were drunk, Ollie didn't know what he was he was saying. He assured Bill there was nothing there, and that he was still focused on winning Finn back. Bill seemed relieved (but reservedly so).

"I would love for you and Finn to make a go of it again, especially since she seemed fine with you and. . . . " He looked again at Matt's watch. "It is the twenty-first century after all. A couple of my fraternity brothers screwed around with each other in college and then married women. It's not so unheard of. I just want you to be happy."

"It's not like that, Bill," Matt assured him emphatically, but his stomach churned at the lie.

Matt returned to his condo, with the pizza he'd promised, to find Ollie in grey sweats and a t-shirt so tight that he might as well have been naked. Matt had to turn his gaze away and harden his heart as he'd promised himself he would. When he finally did look at Ollie, and saw the expression, the *realization*, on his face, Matt had gotten so angry. He wanted to lash out at the world, break things, hurt someone.

He was angry at Ollie, for being so irresistible, for making him throw away his years of discipline, but he was furious with himself for giving into those dirty urges.

That final 'I love you,' Ollie had uttered was Matt's undoing. That declaration had filled him with rage, and then he had taken that rage out on Ollie, and Ollie had let him, more than once. He'd been brutal, and worried on his dawn run about facing Ollie and his beautiful, wounded eyes, in the cold light of day. So, when he returned and found Ollie gone, he nearly collapsed with relief.

Matt closed his eyes in shame and pulled on his running shoes.

33

No One Dies From Love

HILARY TERM WAS EXCRUCIATING, and everything Ollie needed as a distraction. He focused all his energy on school, and pushed away thoughts of Matt as best he could, knowing it was the only way to tame the blur and confusion of his emotions. He trudged his way through life feeling half-asleep, emotionally drained, his movements sluggish and angry. He dreamt of Matt nearly every night, waking disoriented and aroused. He tried hooking up with other guys (partly to dim the memory of Matt, and partly to deal with his unwelcome hormones), but it would all fall apart, and he would leave humiliated.

The first guy was all tongue and teeth and spit. Not filling his mouth like Matt's tongue would, slow and teasing, or passionately swirling around his, as though Ollie was his oxygen supply and Matt couldn't breathe without him. No, this guy's tongue was on path of destruction, aiming straight for Ollie's throat, his teeth bringing up the rear assault. Ollie fled without a backwards glance, clothes and dignity intact.

The second guy, three weeks later, was equally disappointing. His hands were wrong, his scent was wrong, his cock was wrong. Ollie touched it and felt himself go soft. He zipped his pants, mumbled an

224

excuse and left. Crying himself to sleep once he got back to his room. He only wanted someone to comfort him, distract him, fill the void in his heart, but it seemed that no one ever could.

Ollie lost weight, and stopped caring about his hair, his skincare routine. He went for long runs and played indoor football whenever his schedule would allow, seeking a respite from the despair and loneliness. He went for drinks with the team, and with Ivan and their friends George and Sahil, going through the motions, laughing on the surface but feeling a blur inside. He avoided any one-on-one social situations, not willing or able to tell anyone what he was going through, because aside from his flatmates, who didn't press him when he shut down, no one had known he had even been dating someone.

He had given up on hearing from Matt, not that he would have responded if he had, but it burned a hole in his chest anyway. Finn texted him periodically, and he saw her occasionally around Oxford, but he mostly avoided her. Thankfully their colleges were separate and their chance encounters were rare. She invited him (repeatedly, doggedly really) to finish their Scorsese marathon, but he begged off, the sight of her, the thought of being at her flat, was too painful to consider.

34

Somebody Else

OLLIE'S PARENTS FINALLY CONVINCED HIM to come home for his mother's birthday in February. It was the first time Ollie had been home since before Christmas and his appearance was shocking. He was a husk of himself, and everything about him screamed neglect (wholly unlike Ollie, whose attention to his appearance was borderline obsessive). David met Maggie's eye with a worried frown.

"Help me in the garden, Ollie," his father coaxed gently, as though Ollie was a skittish horse.

"Sure." Ollie followed David out the door to the shed.

David watched Ollie surreptitiously as they moved through the garden, raking out the leaves, cutting the dead wood, and fertilizing the roses for spring. Ollie's movements were methodical and robotic, and his mind seemed a million miles away. Ollie wasn't himself at all and David struggled to find a way to get Ollie to open up.

"You alright?" David asked skeptically. "School going well?"

"Yeah, Dad. It's all good, great marks, everything," Ollie answered with a closed mouth smile.

David's heart flickered in his chest at his son's reticence. He looked at the house and around the yard as he cleared his throat, knowing there could be only one explanation.

"And with . . . Matt?"

Ollie's jaw ticked as his face shuttered. Ollie raked a bit more, and then leaned the rake against the tree.

"I need water."

David watched sadly as Ollie stalked rigidly to the house. He knew Matt would break Ollie's heart, and wished he could have done something about it before it happened.

Cassie came breezing in for dinner, depositing a present at her mother's place-setting before coming into the kitchen. She pulled up at the sight of Ollie, looking ragged from yard work, drinking water at the sink.

"Cor, you're filthy, and you look like shit." She wrinkled her nose. "You should shower before Mum's dinner."

"Duh, of course I will," Ollie replied irritatedly.

Cassie looked at him, and poured herself a glass of wine from the bottle on the table. "You know I thought for a second, that your hot friend Matt, might've been gay, because he was here with you, you *homo*," she teased, "but I Googled him and he's everywhere with some gorgeous brunette. I thought you said he was single." She pouted.

"What are you talking about?" Ollie straightened and looked at his sister, a cold rush pulsing through his body. She pulled out her phone.

"Google, it's this amazing technology that allows you to type in a name or question and then you get all kinds of information back. You should try it sometime," she said while typing quickly, and turned the phone to Ollie. He scrolled through the pictures, the sound of his heart pounding drowned out by the ringing in his ears. It was Matt with Sam. There were several photos of them, some with other people, Sam in different dresses, different hairstyles, Matt looking heartbreakingly beautiful in a Brioni single-button tuxedo, smiling with her under his arm, in Ollie's spot.

"When were these pictures taken?" he heard himself ask calmly, stunned that Matt would move on so quickly.

"I dunno. Looks like maybe January and Valentine's Day from the balloons in that one. She's gorgeous, probably a model, look at her in that dress, do you think she eats?" Cassie shrugged putting her phone away. "I'm bummed, he was hot." She sighed and left the kitchen.

Ollie covered his mouth with his hand and sobbed.

David walked back into the house after driving Ollie to the train, his head heavy on his neck. He found Maggie in bed and looked at her with a pained expression. He went through his bedtime routine quickly and got into bed.

"Maggie, I'm really worried about him," David whispered, as though he were afraid to say the words aloud.

"Me too." Maggie winced. "He was sobbing in his room before dinner. I've never seen him like that. He thinks he'll never find love again. Did he say anything more to you?"

"He told me they broke up, but that's it, and he's usually so open with me." David shook his head. "This is very worrisome. Do you think we should get him a therapist?"

"Yes, if he'll agree to it, absolutely."

"Okay, I'll speak with him this week, and I want him home for the term break," David said turning out the light.

35

Demolition Man

MATT WAS BACK to living his life of a lie, hating himself for both his urges and for being such a coward as to not to allow himself to be with Ollie. He wanted to dismember whomever it was who said, 'it is better to have loved and lost than to have never loved at all.' He wished he had never met Ollie, but not even a heartbeat after that wish, he ached for him.

He punished himself mercilessly with long runs and harsh workouts whenever he thought of Ollie, and he thought of Ollie every. Damn. Day. He wore the Oxford t-shirt as penance, as a reminder of Ollie's perfection, wishing he could be as comfortable with his sexuality as Ollie was. Instead, he was back with Sam; taking her to charity events for appearances, and feeling dead inside.

* * *

Sam was thrilled to have Matt back in her life, and even more determined to be everything she thought he wanted, so this time he wouldn't leave. She dressed carefully, paid attention to his compliments and catalogued what he liked so she could replicate it painstakingly, noticing what he didn't so she wouldn't make the same mistake twice. He was moody in a way that she had never seen before, even snapped at her once for being too clingy, and then ignored her for weeks. When he did text her again, she made herself available, but with a nonchalant attitude that was hard to maintain.

In addition to being moody, he was less interested in sex; gone was the insatiable Matt from the summer. He was replaced with a more reticent Matt, one who made love with his eyes firmly closed and seemed to prefer when the sex was rough. Sam didn't mind and in fact encouraged it (anything to make him happy), so long as he used that lube he had on his side table.

"When did you start using this?" she asked him the first night he took her out.

Something flickered behind Matt's eyes. "My ex liked it. I got used to it." He shrugged and left the room. She felt a stab of jealousy as she waited for him to return. Who was his ex? Finn?

When he didn't come back, she took off her dress and went looking for him, finding him standing in front of his big sliding glass door, staring out at the night. She pressed her naked body against his tuxedo, the fabric bringing her nipples to taut attention, and slipped her arms under his coat around his waist.

"Do you want to make love out here?" she whispered and felt him shake his head before turning in her arms.

He picked her up like she weighed nothing and carried her back to the bedroom, her legs wrapped around his waist as she kissed his neck. She held him tightly as he made love to her, sensing his indifference and wanting to make him feel something for her, wishing he would make a sound, and wondered again who his ex was that left him like this. He pulled out and rolled her over onto her hands and knees, barely running his hands over her in the process. She touched herself, sensing that he was close, and looked over her shoulder at him, finding his face screwed up like he was in pain. She wondered briefly if his gunshot wound was bothering him, before hearing him groan his release as he slowed. Sam began to orgasm as he pulled out, leaving her to finish alone.

That evening had fueled her to try harder, be better, to cement Matt to her side, and it was working, though he wouldn't let her stay a whole weekend, only nights here and there, always kicking her out without morning sex. Sometimes he stayed at her place but he was always gone before she woke, with no note or text to let her know he wasn't coming back, which irritated her, but she would never say. Instead, she slept lightly, hoping to catch him before he snuck off, falling asleep in his arms but finding him with his back to her on the times when she did wake before he left.

One night she woke to him tossing around next to her, caught in some dream. It sounded like he was crying as his arms floundered around the sheets.

"I'm sorry, Holly," he muttered, his voice full of pain, a pain Sam felt acutely as jealousy stabbed her heart.

Sam pressed herself against him, wanting his dream of this *Holly* to stop. Matt came awake with a start and looked at her with a face full of hope that quickly turned guarded with a wince. He left the bed and disappeared into the bathroom. When he finally came back to bed nearly ten minutes later, he rolled on his side away from her.

"Go to sleep," he ordered, not turning his head. Sam closed her eyes, thinking of solutions until she fell asleep.

36

Encirclement and Incentive

MATT LOST WEIGHT (he had no appetite). He threw himself into work (putting in eighteen-hour days) and people were beginning to walk on eggshells around him (his fuse was short but he didn't care). He chased contracts and sought out companies to absorb, determined to make his business thrive as he wasn't. He screened his calls from Finn and Bill, keeping them both at arm's length. His conversations with Finn (when he would answer) were brief and superficial. The more wounded and frustrated she sounded, the more he withdrew. He couldn't believe he was cutting her loose too.

His assistant buzzed his line, interrupting an already shitty late-February day. "What, Stacey?" he answered brusquely.

"There's a Beth Bertrand on the phone for you."

Matt frowned, trying to place the name before his stomach flipped with realization. "Put her through."

"Hi, Beth. How are you?" he answered lightly.

"Great, Matt. I hope your year has been fantastic so far!"

Matt rolled his eyes. *If you only knew.* "To what do I owe this pleasure, Beth?"

"I found the perfect property for you, I told you it might take a while, but there's a townhouse on Marlborough. It's five stories, two units, and the out-of-state owner, who had been renting both, is looking to sell quickly as it's currently vacant, and would love to do so without having to list," she said with a smile in her voice.

Matt felt the room shrink around him and swallowed. "Tell me more," he heard himself say.

"Great! It's a corner townhouse, with a garden-level unit, and the other unit is the upper three floors, plus a roof deck. There's an elevator and four dedicated exterior parking spaces in the alley behind. It's in the heart of the Back Bay, as you know. Walk to the park, walk to shops of course, and walk to the river. Everything you requested, and more. It needs a little work, but it's a hidden gem, and if you don't scoop it up, it won't last an hour."

Matt looked out his office window at the building next door. Thinking of the future, allowing himself to purposefully think of Ollie again, for the first time in nearly a month. "I'll take it. I want to see it today, but know I want it, and I'll pay cash."

He could hear the smile in Beth's voice. "I can meet you there whenever you're free."

"I'll see you in an hour."

He walked the townhouse with Beth, not listening to her chatter about the features, the potential. He was lost in thought about Ollie's features and potential. He shook her hand on the roof, looking at the three-hundred-and-sixty-degree views, his heart banging against the sides of its cage.

"Send me the paperwork," he called over his shoulder as he walked back into the house.

When Matt got back to his condo, he stood in front of the living room slider, staring at the spot on the deck where he imagined he could still see the splatter of Ollie's emphatic orgasm from that glorious night. He often found himself rooted in front of the glass, staring out, not remembering how he got there or why. He would just blink and become aware. Sometimes he thought he could even still smell it, it was so distinctive. Somehow Ollie's semen smelled like what he imagined heaven smelled like, and it tasted even better.

He turned from the window and swallowed the lump in his throat as he crossed to his bedroom to change for a run. He put his phone in his armband and tucked his key in the zippered pocket of his hoodie and paused. He never ran with music, though Ollie always did.

Ollie always had music playing, bringing his little Bluetooth speaker with him whenever he came to Finn's flat or Boston. Matt didn't care for Ollie's taste in music generally, but there were some songs he liked, particularly that new artist Troye something. Those songs, that guy, and several other popular tunes, would be forever associated with Ollie, which meant Matt never listened to the radio or his music app anymore, for fear of hearing one that would remind him. He opened the junk drawer in his kitchen and fished out his earbuds.

Matt ran along the waterfront and through Charlestown, over the bridge to the Charles River, following Memorial Drive, encountering only a few runners in the cold. The music playing in his ears was a playlist Ollie shared and most of it was unlistenable, until the one with the guy singing in falsetto about 'preying on you tonight' came on, the one he used to chase Ollie around his condo to. Tickling him on the bed as he told him he was going to eat him alive. His heart clenched at the memory of Ollie's laughter when Matt howled over him in sync with the singer.

Matt's whole life had been driven by a need to excel, to conquer, and to obliterate obstacles. One of his greatest skills, the one he spent a tremendous amount of time honing (one he had learned from his father), was his ability to divorce himself from emotion: in the military, in business deals, and even in his personal life. He could look back on things he did in the line of duty without remorse, without regret, same with business, same with women. *The ends always justified the means.*

His only weakness, his *Achilles Heel*, was Ollie. He couldn't overcome his desire for him, how deeply he felt about him, and he couldn't overcome the guilt he felt about hurting him. That Beth had called, and that the townhouse was available (when things like that didn't just pop up on the market), was a sign. From whom or what he didn't know, but he had acted impulsively, and needed to strategize, he needed Ollie back in his life. That was an indisputable fact.

He crossed again over the Charles at the Harvard Bridge and reversed direction following Storrow Drive. Adele came into his ears, singing a heartbreaking song about love lasting and sometimes hurting instead. He hurt Ollie. He had shut all but one of his emotions down that night, and let rage rule him. He winced and stopped running, bending over his knees in shame. He swallowed the urge to vomit and straightened, blowing out a breath and after a few moments resumed his run. How could Ollie ever forgive him?

He thinned his lips. *No Lieutenant, that's an unacceptable line of thinking,* he thought harshly and then nodded to himself. Failure to win him back was not an option. He had to devise a plan, make sure that his apology was ironclad and impossible for Ollie to refuse. No mountain was unclimbable with the right equipment, the right determination, and Matt had both in spades.

Wild came on, by that Troye guy, and Matt felt it too was a sign. 'Too long to the weekend?' Too long until April was more like it, but he had to get his ducks in a row before he could go after Ollie. He was done being a fool, and ready to let Ollie drive him wild again. He crossed Storrow Drive at the Arthur Fiedler Bridge and ran down Marlborough Street, past the beautiful brick townhouse that was soon to be theirs.

37

No, I Haven't Moved on, But Trust me I've Tried

OLLIE HEARD HIS PHONE buzz and ignored it. Term was over, had been for nearly two weeks, and he was laying listlessly on the bed in his flat, staring at nothing, feeling nothing, music playing on low. His mother wanted him home, an increasingly worried note in her voice, but he made an excuse about extra schoolwork.

Her birthday dinner had been a disaster. After seeing the photos on Cassie's phone, he cried in his room, his mother knocking gently on the door and sitting next to him on the bed.

"Ollie, darling. I know there's something going on. I'm guessing you and Matt have split," she said as she rubbed his back. "I want you to know that you can always talk to me, or Dad. It's important for you work through your emotions and know that with time you will heal and love again. I promise."

Ollie rolled over to look at her. "I know, Mum. I could find a thousand Henrys, but I'll never find another Matt," he sobbed.

Maggie made a sympathetic sound and pulled him into her arms, trying to soothe him but failing.

Ollie put on a brave face for them at dinner, a hot lump in his throat that food passed with difficulty, and then kept them at bay by staying in Oxford for the rest of the term, even over his birthday. He couldn't stand their worried faces watching him, especially his dad's.

He quickly found himself a lover, partly out of anger and partly because Ivan had said the best way to get over someone was to get under someone. He sought Calvin out, an easy mark. Calvin had begun sitting next to him in class after that fateful November day, and had finally worked up the nerve to ask him for his number. Ollie remembered laughing to himself about the irony of it.

He reveled in Calvin's eager response, but it was short-lived and wholly unfulfilling. They went to dinner, splitting the tab, and then back to Calvin's flat. The first night had been fine, Calvin's kisses soft, and his body hard. They'd given each other hand jobs and Ollie left before eleven. The next time they went out, Ollie was prepared to go all the way, until just before penetration, when he stopped Calvin. He was unable to stand the thought of anyone other than Matt inside him. So, he prepped and fucked Calvin. Calvin had been so thrilled that Ollie called, he didn't care who fucked whom, so long as they fucked, and he was so eager to please (not unlike how Ollie had been with Matt) that Ollie welcomed the adoration.

Calvin was enthusiastic, complimentary, and caring, but they never even made it through a strip of condoms before Ollie ended things. He discovered he was unable to feel anything for anyone else, not happiness, not irritation, not even sadness. He felt broken and so, he holed up in his flat. He couldn't remember when he last showered, or did laundry. The only good thing in his life were his grades, which were perfect.

The doorbell buzzed, snapping him out of his reverie, and he waited for one of his flatmates to answer it. It buzzed again annoyingly, and Ollie remembered that he was alone for the weekend. With a sigh he got off the bed and went downstairs. He opened the door expecting a delivery person or the religious people that sometimes came through, and instead found himself face to face with Matt.

Gorgeous, delicious Matt, looking thinner under his five o'clock shadow, in a Brioni suit, and the trident collar pin through his tie. Ollie's heart clenched, and with a gasp, he made to slam the door, but Matt was faster, putting his foot in and his forearm up. The door bounced back open and Ollie turned hurriedly from the intense look in Matt's eyes.

"Ollie, wait," Matt called.

Ollie winced at the sound of his husky voice, his beautiful American accent, and continued his retreat.

Matt stepped in and closed the door behind him, calling again for Ollie to stop. Ollie turned and wished he could avert his eyes but they were immobilized by Matt's hungry gaze. Ollie knew how awful he looked with his greasy hair, patchy beard, and crumpled clothes, but for some reason, Matt was looking at him as though he was the sexiest man alive.

"You have some nerve," Ollie said after a time, his voice flinty. "Get the fuck out of my flat."

Matt looked away with a pained expression. "Ollie," he said softly. "I'm . . . I'm so, *so* sorry," he stammered.

"Oh, so your mouth *can* say that word," Ollie scoffed angrily, interrupting him. "I didn't know you had it in you. Question is, do you mean it? Are you even capable of regret, *Lieutenant?*"

Matt flinched. "I am, and I do mean it. I am so sorry, Ollie. I am a horrible human being. I can't . . . I thought I could, but I can't live another day without you. Please. *Please* forgive me."

Ollie shook his head slowly, swallowing back his tears. "No way. I don't trust you anymore. You don't care about anyone but yourself." He tightened his jaw, and straightened. "I may be hurting, but I will heal, and I will forget you," he spat angrily, his eyes flashing. "Get the fuck out."

Matt grimaced. "Ollie, please. We're both so miserable, can you just listen to me? Please give me another chance."

Ollie scoffed. "Why should I? You poor baby. What happened? Did Sam dump you? Couldn't have happened to a nicer guy," he said with a sneer. "Find yourself another fuckboy to have on the side with your women." He turned away. "I am not interested in fucked up, closeted, bisexuals."

Matt rushed forward. "Ollie."

Ollie looked down at Matt's hand encircling his bicep with a scowl. Matt loosened his grip but didn't let go.

Ollie looked at the pin through Matt's tie, and closed his eyes. He leaned slightly forward and took a deep breath through his nose, taking in Matt's intoxicating scent. He opened his eyes. "I hate you," he whispered slowly with a hitch in his voice.

"And I love you, Ollie," Matt murmured, rubbing his thumb lightly on Ollie's arm. "I was an idiot. I'm begging here. I will get on my knees." He held Ollie's gaze earnestly. "Please give me another chance. I promise I will never hurt you again."

Ollie looked at Matt's mouth with that last declaration, and then away, trying to ignore the sensation of Matt's hand on his arm, his thumb tracing a fiery line slowly back and forth. Ignore the memory of that mouth on his, on his body. Ollie closed his eyes with an angry sigh.

"You broke me," he whispered looking back at Matt. "You can't just expect me to let you back in, seriously." He paused, his gaze and resolve faltering under Matt's blue-eyed stare. "Certainly not without discussion, conditions, reparations," he added, hating himself for the weakness he felt in Matt's proximity.

Matt smiled inside, his heart lifting.

Progress

He kept his face carefully blank.

"Of course not. Whatever you want. Fuck, I will do anything." He followed Ollie deeper into the house.

Ollie got two beers from the fridge, popped the caps with the opener on the counter and handed one to Matt.

"You don't have anything stronger?" Matt asked.

Ollie leveled his gaze and glared at him.

"Oh, okay, this is great, thanks." Matt held his bottle up in cheers and watched Ollie carefully as he sipped, continuing his planned siege.

Ollie watched him just as carefully, drinking several swallows as he did. "You're an asshole," he said finally.

"I never said I wasn't," Matt answered matter of factly.

Ollie looked away with a frown. "Why would I want to be with you? You told me back at day one, not to jerk you around, and I swore I never would. I kept my promise. And then you go and not only jerk me around, *again* I might add, but you tore out my heart. *Abused* me. Dumped me. And now come crawling back. Fuck you, Lieutenant."

Matt blew out a breath, worried he had misjudged Ollie's defenses, and put his beer down rubbing his hands over his face. He swallowed and nodded slightly.

"I deserve that. Don't think though, Ollie, that you could even come close to hating me as much as I hate myself for what I did. You were the only one who got me. The only one I ever desired more than air, or the ocean. I was a coward. I was weak. I fucked up."

"Yes, you were a fucking coward, and you did fuck all the way up. And not only did you run at the first *stupid* thing, *you fucking coward*, you ran back to *Sam*. Do you know how that makes me feel?

"Cassie showed me the pictures of you two." Ollie's eyes filled. "You tossed me aside like I was nothing, and raced back to her." He exhaled roughly as tears spilled down his cheeks, hating his vulnerability. "Do you love her?" he whispered.

"No! No, Ollie," Matt shouted emphatically. "I was an idiot, I panicked. I didn't want to be with her. I don't love her. I have *never* loved her. I have never loved anyone but you. *Ever*." He approached Ollie slowly. "You were the only reason I stopped hating myself. You are not only enough for me; you are everything to me. My moon, my universe, and I've been so lost without you.

"Ollie, please, I will make it up to you. I will keep all my promises. With you by my side, in my bed," he said huskily, brushing his hand deliberately across the front of his pants. "I promise I will never leave you again."

Ollie closed his eyes as Matt stopped within reach, feeling himself stir in response to Matt's suggestive hand. Every pleasure those hands, that cock, had brought him once upon a time, came screaming into his brain. He measured Matt's words as they coursed through his blood.

Matt really *had* been miserable. He really *was* begging.

Ollie's eyes stopped on Matt's perfect mouth, and he felt his resolve disappear. "Christ. I *hate* you. You bastard. You sadistic, fucking bastard," he whispered and grabbed the back of Matt's head, pulling him in for a deep kiss.

Matt groaned against Ollie's lips, his tongue crossing the divide to fill Ollie's mouth perfectly. Ollie wasn't at all surprised that his body ignited, *of course it did.* Matt was the flame that scorched every bit of him, and burned all the cold from his limbs. He was delicious and familiar, and his firm lips fitted seamlessly against Ollie's mouth as if they had never been gone.

Ollie felt Matt's body react the same way, in fact, he was already hard against Ollie's hip when he pressed their bodies together. Matt gripped Ollie's ass in his strong hands as Ollie slid his arms around Matt's neck. Ollie was ready to drop to his knees, ready to strip his clothes off for Matt's hands, his tongue, when Matt pulled back with one last kiss.

"I assume you have a shower in this house?" Matt murmured against Ollie's mouth, wrinkling his nose.

Ollie exhaled a laugh. "Bloody hell, I forgot how demanding you are." He looked at the stairs, and briefly at the door. "Get undressed and wait in my bed before I change my mind."

Ollie followed closely as Matt took the stairs two at a time and watched as he pulled up in the doorway of his bedroom. Ollie knew it was a filthy mess and smirked to himself as he disappeared into the bathroom.

I bet you can't resist cleaning my room, Lieutenant, he thought as he turned on the shower. *It's the least you can fucking do.*

Ollie let the hot water course over him as he lathered the soap, washing his body thoroughly, thinking about Matt, his reappearance, and their reunion. His stomach somersaulted repeatedly at the thought of Matt waiting gloriously naked in his room, of what they were going to do to each other.

He hurt you. He's a bona fide sadist, and he ditched you at the first sign of someone finding out, his brain interrupted.

He apologized. He missed you. He loves you. He came all this way to tell you, his heart argued.

He is waiting naked in your bedroom, with his beautiful body, his strong hands, his body interjected, sending another pulse of warmth to his groin.

He went back to Sam. There's something shady between those two. You saw how eagerly he touched her at Mistral. Don't believe him, his brain countered.

No, he said he loves you. Take him back and the pain goes away, his heart said firmly.

He is waiting to fuck you with his magnificent cock, and kiss you and love your body with his perfect mouth and tongue. You have to go to him, he will make you all better, his body ordered, his cock approving with an enthusiastic jump.

Yes, he always makes you feel better. He will keep you safe, his heart agreed.

Don't say I didn't warn you, his brain said with a resigned sigh.

Ollie shaved his beard quickly and carefully in the small mirror suction-cupped to the shower wall. He pondered whether there was time to shave all the other hair he had let grow back before deciding there wasn't. He focused on prepping himself for Matt instead, and then washed his hair and brushed his teeth before turning off the water.

He dried himself as he walked the short distance to his room and wrapped the towel around his waist before closing the door with a small click. He looked briefly around the tidied room, noticing Matt's clothes neatly folded and draped over the back of his desk chair and smiled to himself.

I knew you couldn't resist, you neat freak.

Matt stood from the freshly made bed. He had shaved or waxed his chest and the silver trident over his heart gleamed in the low light. Ollie's mouth went dry as he stared at the line of dark hair that began under Matt's bellybutton and disappeared into his underwear. Ollie wondered, ever so briefly, whether Matt had highlighted that on purpose, knowing how much Ollie loved that little goody trail.

He's playing you.

Ollie dragged his eyes away from Matt's gorgeous chest as he silenced his brain. He focused instead on Matt's tattoos, and his fingertips tingled with anticipation at the promise of tracing them again.

Matt's eyes scanned Ollie's body, his pale skin, his new muscles, noticing he was thinner but still utterly beautiful, even with the sparse chest hair that looked so foreign on him. Ollie's eyes were drawn to the bulge in the front of Matt's underwear, as were Matt's to the front of Ollie's towel. Ollie dropped his clothes in a heap as Matt crossed the room in two strides to take him in his arms.

Both let out an involuntary moan as their skin came into contact. Matt pressed his nose to Ollie's neck as his lips found that sensitive spot where his neck met his shoulder and took a deep breath. *Delicious,* he thought as Ollie's scent delivered a jolt to his groin. He pulled back and met Ollie's lips in a deep and bruising kiss that was barely enough.

Matt pulled off Ollie's towel, tossing it on the bed before cupping Ollie's bottom in his hands and pulling his body tight against his own. He slipped his fingers between Ollie's cheeks and groaned when Ollie pushed back into them.

The scent of Ollie filled his nose and his heart the way sunlight filled a dark room, warming every cold thing it touched. Ollie's clean hair (long and pleasantly shaggy), his soft skin, and his firm, familiar body filled Matt with a heat he hadn't truly realized he needed so desperately.

"I missed this." He squeezed Ollie's ass in emphasis. "I can't wait to taste your perfect hole again."

Ollie reached between them and slipped his hand into Matt's underwear. "I missed *this.*" He gripped him tightly and smiled at Matt's long and low moan.

Matt kissed Ollie's neck with urgency as he steered him to the bed and spun him around. Ollie sighed into the mattress, his body instantly loose the minute Matt pushed his knee up, spread his cheeks and touched him with his tongue.

"Ah, fuck. I missed this," Matt groaned and speared Ollie with his tongue.

Matt was slowly losing his control. His plan had been a lengthy and drawn-out seduction where he envisioned Ollie begging with his knees to his chest, but he realized he was the one who couldn't wait. His fingers joined his tongue and he groaned as Ollie writhed.

"I can't wait, Ollie. Tell me how you want it." He rose to his knees and stared down at Ollie's muscular back.

"I want you, deep inside me, with all your skin touching mine. Don't you dare stop touching me." Ollie rolled on his side to stare up at Matt, his pupils blown wide.

Matt growled and rolled Ollie onto his back, fumbling to get his underwear off with Ollie's help, careful to keep their bodies in contact. Ollie's soft tongue on his body, in his mouth, the feeling of Ollie grinding himself on his stomach, drove all sane thought from Matt's head. He moved with Ollie, his fingers pressing and working Ollie open, before rolling him back over and straddling his thighs.

Matt grabbed the bottle of lube and watched Ollie's back twitch in that way it always did when he heard the snap of the lid, like a racehorse waiting for the gate to spring open. He smoothed his fingers over Ollie's hole and then pressed in, curling his finger against Ollie's sweet spot.

Matt moaned and squeezed his thighs when Ollie lifted his hips. He covered Ollie with his body and filled him slowly as he exhaled. He cupped Ollie's fist with his hand and laced their fingers as he began moving, counting backwards from one hundred to prevent himself from coming too soon.

Ollie felt like crying; the dizzying emotions whirling through him were almost too much to bear. The feeling of Matt inside him again after so many months of heartbreak, how impossibly full he felt. The way Matt's large body molded against his own, the long strokes in and out, and the sounds Matt was making, were driving Ollie mad with desire. He raised his hips instinctively, wanting more of Matt, feeling as though he wanted Matt's entire body inside him to soothe his sudden desperate need, and orgasmed unexpectedly against the friction of the sheets. He heard himself calling out Matt's name as his body tingled with release.

Matt increased his pace, his breathing erratic, and then tensed and cried out loudly, his groans filling the small room and echoing deep in Ollie's soul. Matt pressed impossibly deeper, making Ollie aware of the warm wet spot beneath him, and rested his chest against Ollie's back.

Matt bit Ollie's neck gently before kissing his ear.

"Jesus Christ, Ollie. You came before I could even fuck you properly, and thank god, because I couldn't have done any more than that myself. You feel like *heaven*. I missed you." He squeezed Ollie's hand and continued to pant as he caught his breath against Ollie's neck. Ollie felt Matt's other hand smooth back his hair.

"I love you," Matt whispered in Ollie's ear, his breath raising goosebumps on Ollie's skin, before sitting up. He rolled Ollie onto his side so he could spread the towel he retrieved from the foot of the bed and laid next to him, pulling him close.

Ollie was silent, tucked perfectly in his spot under Matt's shoulder, breathing in Matt's scent, as the world came back to him. The light of the room shifted from warm passion to clear, harsh reality, filling him with doubt as his desire subsided. He should've listened to his brain because he now felt foolish for giving in so quickly. Matt had hurt him, physically and emotionally.

Am I an idiot to forgive him? Ollie took a breath and let it out slowly.

"Don't think this means that everything goes immediately back to hunky dory town," Ollie said. "You fucking hurt me. I shouldn't forgive you. I thought I never would."

Matt looked away with a wince. "I know, and I'm sorry," he whispered. "I've run the equivalent of the globe and back. I've punished myself horribly, and every time I did, my brain came back to you. My heart came back to you. I don't want to go through that again. I don't want to put you through that again." He kissed Ollie firmly. "Jesus, I missed you so much."

Matt's eyes followed his hand down Ollie's thigh. Ollie closed his eyes briefly at the sensation and nodded.

"I missed you so much. You felt so good inside me. I thought I had made up the memory just to torment myself, or that it had only been a dream," he said quietly and looked away, listening to his brain for a moment, as Matt kissed the side of his head. "If I'm taking you back, I need to feel equal with you."

He sat up and looked at Matt. "I liked it when you bossed me around because I trusted you, and you said I could always decide, that I could say no. I even let you . . . " He closed his eyes with a wince remembering New Year's. "Because I wanted to be *everything* to you, like a good little masochist," he said wryly. "I want you to feel the same. To do the same. Because I have wants and needs, and they're just as valid as yours."

"What do you want?" Matt whispered; his eyes dark.

Ollie reached across Matt's chest and opened the drawer of his bedside table. He pulled out a condom and raised his eyebrows at Matt.

Matt narrowed his eyes and shook his head. "No way. I fuck you, not the other way around. And besides, I don't even want to know why you have that in your side table when I have never been in your bed," he added with a jealous note in his voice.

"Oh, don't you dare." Ollie shook his head and glared. "Should I get your phone and dial Sam, see what she has to say about the past three months?"

Matt clenched his teeth and searched Ollie face. Ollie could see the gears whirring inside Matt's head as he considered his options.

Choose wisely, Lieutenant, he thought as he began pulling away.

"I love you, Ollie." He gripped Ollie's arm to hold him in place. "You get one shot at this, don't think it will ever happen again."

Ollie smiled triumphantly and kissed him deeply, rolling Matt onto his back.

"I'm sorry I hurt you those times before," Matt panted, wincing as Ollie pulled out. "I understand now."

Ollie laughed breathlessly. "You're such a baby." He kissed Matt's ankle before lowering his leg from his shoulder. "And this was with lube. Besides, you're *massive*, and I take you happily."

"Yeah, you do," Matt said with a pleased tone as he pulled Ollie down for a kiss. "But seriously, we are never doing that again."

Ollie shook his head with a small smile and ran his fingers through the cum on Matt's stomach. "You didn't hate it, but I understand why it's not for you, and I'm fine with that. Never tromp on my heart again, and we'll be good."

Matt kissed Ollie and then watched as he crossed to the trashcan, the condom hitting the plastic liner inside with a small splat.

"I don't want to know . . . *details*. But, were you with anyone?" Matt asked, his voice quiet, hoping against hope the answer was no.

Ollie wiped himself with the towel and got back into bed. "You don't get to ask me that."

Matt winced. "But you know about me. It's only fair, no?"

Ollie exhaled. "There was one. Only, I couldn't stand the thought of anyone but you inside me," he whispered. "So, I played the top, less than a handful of times and never here."

Matt nodded with a small frown, jealous to his core at the thought of anyone else touching Ollie. "I hope you haven't developed a taste for it, Oliver. Because, as I said, that was your only shot," he said as lightly as he could manage and kissed him, pushing aside the angry thoughts of Ollie being a top or bottom for someone else. "I can't stay here tonight, come back to Chuck's."

Ollie hesitated. "I've been dodging Finn, because of you."

"She went home for the holiday, but it's fine, she knows it's because I've been asshole. I told you, she is one of a kind, and completely out of my league, just like you."

He kissed and licked Ollie's upper lip as he rolled away to go to the bathroom. He came back and began dressing.

"Your hair is long. It makes you look like the hipster college student you are." Matt grinned.

"I'm not a hipster." Ollie wrinkled his nose. "I've just been too busy to get it cut. . . ."

"I like it," Matt clarified, sensing Ollie's mood shift. "Pack a bag, you're staying the weekend," Matt added, pulling on his pants. "We're going to see your parents for Easter dinner on Sunday. I called them, so bring a suit."

Ollie widened his eyes. "What? You're not serious?"

"As a heart attack, Ollie. I have some major bridge repairs to make." He buttoned his shirt and tucked it into his pants. He picked up his tie and began putting it on, pleased with how well his shock-and-awe campaign turned out, despite Ollie's counter-offensive.

"What if you came here and I told you to go fuck yourself?" Ollie frowned. "That's awfully presumptuous of you."

"You did tell me to go fuck myself." Matt looked over his shoulder at Ollie, scanning his naked body slowly and then held his gaze for a few beats before turning back to the mirror. He grinned at him in the reflection; the grin he knew Ollie couldn't resist. "But you didn't mean it. You couldn't possibly, could you?" he asked with a quirked eyebrow. He slowly brushed imaginary lint off the front of his pants, drawing Ollie's eye, before looking at his reflection to put the pin through his collar and tie.

Ollie pulled a face and sighed exasperatedly, flopping back on his pillow. "You cocky bastard."

"Yes, but I'm your cocky bastard, so get dressed." Matt grinned and pulled Ollie's overnight bag from the closet.

$$
\begin{array}{c}
\rule{60pt}{1pt}\\[4pt]
38\\[4pt]
\rule{60pt}{1pt}
\end{array}
$$

Smooth Operator

SUNDAY WAS A MIXTURE of relief and tension. Ollie's parents were relieved by Ollie's returned happiness, and tense because of the months that he had suffered. Matt worked hard to win David and Maggie over with his smooth and charming ways, and for the most part he succeeded, though David kept up his guard. Ollie did his best to play peacekeeper, because though he wasn't ready to dive headfirst in with Matt just yet, he didn't want their relationship rebuilding to be hindered by his parents's hesitation.

"You're in a happy mood," Cassie remarked to Ollie in the kitchen as they were clearing the plates. "Quite a change from the wraith you've been as of late. You have a new boyfriend?"

"I've a job lined up in America when I graduate. I'm ecstatic at the prospect of being an ocean away from my pesky little sister," he teased.

Cassie pulled a face. "You think it's going to be easy to work for someone you so clearly have the hots for? Someone who won't ever reciprocate because he's straight?"

"What makes you think I have the hots for him?" Ollie asked primly.

"Christ, the way you look at him, first of all. Of course, I do it too so that's how I recognize. He is stunning." She laughed and made a dramatic face. "And secondly, you should've seen your face when I showed you those pictures." She shook her head. "Like you thought you had a chance with him but found out it could never be. Weirdly jealous."

"You're right, he is gorgeous," Ollie answered, glad she hadn't speculated closer to the truth. "But as you said, it's unrequited. I'm sure I'll meet some handsome American and fall in love once I'm there."

Cassie laughed and went out to the garden, her phone buzzing in her hand as Ollie's mother came in from the dining room with the last of the dishes.

She looked at Ollie with a soft smile. "It's wonderful to see you smiling again."

"I know, Mum, it's wonderful to want to smile again."

She looked at Cassie on the phone in the garden and then back at the door to the dining room. "I see he's as skinny as you are, he must have had an awful time of it too. Why? If you were both so miserable, what happened?"

Ollie took a deep breath and let it out slowly. "Matt's a complicated person, he's unlike anyone I've ever loved. He needs me. He just got scared. I want to focus on our future, not our past, not our pain, there's no sense in dwelling on it."

"Okay." Maggie nodded in understanding. "Speaking of your future, you're certain you want to go to America?"

"Yes. We want to be together, and I want to see what it would be like to work for him. It's only a six-week internship, and then I can decide."

"Will you live with him?"

Ollie shook his head. "We can't, but I'm sure he'll help me find a decent place, and I'll make sure it's two bedrooms so you and Dad can come visit."

"I just want you to be happy, so I hope it all works out." She kissed his cheek and looked at Cassie coming toward the house. "Matt and your father are in the study," she said with a nod to the doorway.

Ollie found them drinking scotch and ran his eyes over Matt as he stepped into the room.

God, I missed looking at you, Ollie thought as he closed the door.

"Hey," Matt said as he lifted slightly from his seat on the couch.

"Hey," Ollie said with a smile and poured himself two fingers of scotch. He sat next to Matt, close but not touching, smiling as Matt put his arm on the back of the sofa behind him.

"What are you two talking about?" Ollie asked cautiously with a glance at his father.

"Just about your internship plans," David said, his voice guarded. "You're going then?"

"Yes. I love Boston, and Matt's offering me quite the opportunity." Ollie smiled at Matt.

Matt returned the smile and looked back at David. "He's brilliant. I'm thrilled he agreed."

Ollie beamed at the praise and took a sip of scotch for his nerves. There were two opposing energies in the room, and he felt the pressure in his chest like a rugby number eight was standing on him. His father was unhappy, and Matt was euphoric, clearly oblivious to David's reserve, though, Ollie supposed an American could interpret David's reticent behavior as stereotypically British.

David watched Matt carefully, suspiciously, really. He was relieved that Ollie was back to his normal self, and somewhat grateful that Matt was not only back to make things right, but that he was also giving Ollie a remarkable opportunity. David had been following SharkFinn closely, and saw that Ollie could stand to do very well in a job there, provided his new boss didn't take advantage of him, or break his heart again.

"Oliver is brilliant, and *young*," David said pointedly to Matt, while holding his hand up at Ollie's protest. "I hope you've thought everything through."

"I have, Dad. I promise," Ollie placated and finished his scotch in one swallow. "We should go." He looked at Matt as he stood. "It's a long ride back to Oxford."

David watched Ollie usher Matt out the front door to their waiting car after saying their goodbyes, Maggie tucked under his arm as the Range Rover backed out of the driveway. He knew Ollie was just avoiding a confrontation, and David prayed Ollie had really thought things through.

"What did he say?" Maggie asked turning and following David up the stairs after he locked the front door.

"He said he was caught up with work, his company was expanding massively, so I get it, but why at the expense of Oliver?" David puzzled as they got ready for bed. "He's in Oxford, not making demands on Matt's time in Boston."

Maggie recounted her conversation with Ollie in the kitchen and gnawed her lip. "Ollie was like a whole new person tonight, and I just want him to be happy."

David nodded in agreement. "He was his old self, and while I am so happy he's up again, I'm disconcerted that his happiness is so wrapped up in someone else, someone so repressed and secretive," David shook his head. "I told you before, I think it's an awful way to live, and I just don't want Ollie hurt again."

"Me either, darling, but we can't make his decisions for him anymore." She kissed him and got her book off the nightstand.

39

All According to Plan

MATT WAS ABLE TO GET a long run and workout in before having to log into email on Monday. He was in bed next to Ollie, laptop open, his hair damp from the shower when Ollie stirred. Ollie smiled sleepily and kissed Matt's nipple as he rolled toward him.

"There's coffee on your side table, sleepyhead. I swear to god, I have never seen someone who sleeps as much as you do," Matt added with a laugh.

"I earn my sleep with you," Ollie said with a sly smile as he reached for his coffee and took a swallow.

Matt scoffed. "Since I do easily seventy-five percent of the work or more while you just lay there and enjoy yourself, I should be the one sleeping in."

"That is so not true, last night as case in point. You called me cowboy. Suggested getting me a hat and boots as you filled my ass. And no one makes you get up."

Matt poked Ollie in the side and smiled when he shrieked. "Oh right, like I could stay asleep next to you. Do you know you sigh and moan in your sleep? It wakes me every time, and takes all my willpower not to wake you by fucking you into the mattress, for fear of getting yelled at."

Ollie scoffed. "First, when have I ever yelled at you for waking me with your magnificent cock? And second, I most assuredly do not sigh and moan in my sleep."

"Oh yes you do, my love, and your moaning sets me off, such that I have to go for a run to get out my sexual frustration. I never used to run until I met you," he added with a grin.

"Liar!" Ollie laughed and leaned over and bit Matt's nipple.

"Ow," Matt cried with a laugh and put his laptop on the side table. He rolled over on top of Ollie pinning him to the bed. Kissing his mouth, face, and neck, he looked down at him, his heart full to bursting. "I love you, Oliver Turner."

* * *

Ollie gave Matt a quick kiss and headed to the market to pick up food for dinner, and to give them both space to think. He searched for ingredients mindlessly, both thrilled and nervous about how easily they slipped back into their relationship. Now that they'd decided to move forward with his internship, Ollie agonized about the future.

Where will I live? How can I afford to live in Boston without a flatmate? How could Matt and I have a relationship if I did have a flatmate?

He put a whole chicken in his cart and continued to the produce to find veggies for dinner. He put two pints of blueberries in the cart next to the bag of apples, both out of season and likely flavorless, but full of fiber. He shook his head to himself at how quickly he'd begun to think of ways to accommodate Matt again, physically and emotionally. Would it be worth it?

What if someone else finds out and Matt dumps you again? his brain interjected. *You'll be stuck with a lease, and be out of a job, with no visa, no prospects.*

He's not going to dump us again, his heart scoffed. *And we'll be much more careful, besides, I'm not letting him back in until I know for sure.*

He can't keep his hands or eyes, or tongue, off me, his body bragged. *He's not going anywhere.*

Ollie nodded to himself in agreement and headed to the checkout. He let himself back into the flat with his bounty and saw that Matt was exactly how he left him: fully concentrating on his laptop. Ollie quickly assembled a small charcuterie board and put it on the desk next to Matt, kissing his neck, before going back to the kitchen to make dinner.

Ollie lost himself in meal prep, loving the ritual of transforming ingredients into a meal. He rubbed a paste of freshly roasted garlic cloves, olive oil and *herbs d' Provence* on the skin of the chicken he'd cut up and put it in the oven, letting the chicken cook slightly before adding a sheet pan of seasoned baby potatoes. He set the timer, made a quick chimichurri of carrot greens, parsley and dill for the carrots and potatoes, and sat back with his phone.

He felt eyes on him after a time and turned to find Matt watching him hungrily, the snack board empty beside him.

"Jesus, that smells amazing, and now I'm starving. Get over here," Matt commanded with a smile.

Ollie turned off his phone and walked to Matt as he closed his laptop. "Sit."

"I'll crush you in that chair," Ollie scoffed.

Matt pulled him down to sit across his thighs, his arms linked around Ollie's hips. "You're far too skinny now, Ollie. You won't crush me, at least not until I fatten you back up." He pulled Ollie's head down for kiss, smothering his protests about ever having been fat. "I'm moving," Matt said after a moment.

"You're leaving Boston?"

Matt shook his head with a chuckle, "Never. No, I bought a townhouse on Marlborough Street, it's in the heart of the Back Bay."

Ollie made a sound of appreciation. "Nice."

"It's two units, five floors, elevator, roof deck, four parking spots." He reached for a folder on the desk and handed it to Ollie. "I'm selling the first-floor unit."

Ollie opened the folder and saw a purchase and sale agreement with a few post-it flags stuck to the pages indicating where a signature was needed. He scanned the writing and saw his name. He looked up at Matt, fully confused with what he was reading.

"I expect you'll go through that with your fine-tooth comb." Matt smiled gently at him.

Ollie furrowed his brow. "I can't afford a flat in Boston. Christ, I can't afford a flat anywhere."

"Ollie, don't be dumb." Matt raised his eyebrows.

Ollie smiled shyly as realization washed over him. "So, I'll live downstairs and you'll live upstairs?"

Matt shook his head and laughed lightly. "No. You will live with me and sleep in our bed," he answered in his commanding tone. "We will furnish and decorate your condo to seem as though you live there, for appearances. We can use it as guest quarters for when your parents come, or as an office. Heck, we can use it ourselves for a change of scenery if we want. I don't give a fuck what we do with it. The important thing is that you will live with me, and we will be hiding in plain sight." He shrugged happily. "I love you."

Ollie tossed the folder onto the desk and adjusted himself to be astride Matt. He met Matt's urgent and passionate kiss, running his hands through Matt's hair as Matt ran his hands up Ollie's back under his shirt.

Ollie silenced his brain before it could even make a sound, knowing that it was going to say something he didn't want to hear about Matt controlling him, keeping him under his thumb. Instead, he listened to his body and his heart as he savored the taste of Matt's mouth and skin. Matt's hands gripped Ollie's ass beneath his clothes, one finger circling his asshole pleadingly, as he placed open mouthed kisses over every bit of Ollie's exposed skin. They kissed and writhed, Matt's erection growing between Ollie's legs and Ollie's pressing urgently on Matt's taut abdomen. They ignored the world around them until the kitchen timer beeped and Ollie peeled himself off Matt's lap with a disgruntled sigh, adjusting the front of his sweatpants as he walked to the kitchen.

"Be careful you don't slam that beautiful thing in the oven door," Matt teased huskily, his hair in disarray. "I want it in my mouth later."

Ollie grinned at him over his shoulder as he put the carrots in with a shake of his ass.

"Christ," Ollie sighed, Matt breathing heavy in his ear. "That was amazing." He turned his head and kissed him.

Matt made a sound of agreement, and pulled away as Ollie fell forward off his knees and onto the bed with a smile. Matt returned a second later and held something in front of Ollie.

"You left this," he said in a quiet voice. Ollie opened his eyes, and reached out for his Rolex. He held it carefully in his hand. "I want you to put it on, and never take it off again."

Ollie slipped it on his wrist and fastened it. Matt rolled him onto his back and kissed him thoroughly before standing and leaving the room. Ollie stared at the watch on his wrist, and then up at the ceiling, thinking about that wonderful, happy Christmas, and the devastating New Year's that followed. He got up when Matt came back, and went to the bathroom, deep in thought.

Matt was scrolling intently through his phone, still working on east coast time, catching up on the never-ending mountain of emails.

"Do you want me to get your laptop?" Ollie asked from the doorway after studying him briefly.

"Yes please," Matt replied without looking up.

Ollie came back with the laptop and the folder for the condo. He sat up in bed next to Matt and opened the folder. Under the document were pictures of the property. Ollie thought it was beautiful, but dated, and was definitely going to need work. He said as much to Matt.

"I know, it's being renovated now as we speak. Just so happens that Chuck's roommate from college, Naomi, you met her at the New Year's Eve party, is starting her own design business so I thought I'd be her first big client," he answered with a smile.

Ollie winced slightly, he wanted to forget all about that party, and looked down at the document, thinking with a frown.

"When did you buy this townhouse?" he asked quietly, knowing how long these transactions could take, not to mention finding builders to renovate.

Matt looked at Ollie. "March first."

Ollie chewed his lip thinking.

"What's wrong? I thought you'd be happy." Matt put his laptop on the side table.

"Part of me is happy, Matt," Ollie said looking down at his lap, feeling breathless. "But a bigger part of me is feeling very manipulated. That was more than a month ago, and houses aren't sold in a day.

"I feel as though you are orchestrating my life, putting things in motion for me, without my input. I feel like I'm losing my free will, and at breakneck speed." He looked over at Matt who was watching him worriedly. "What would you have done if I had really told you to go fuck yourself, when you came to my flat? If I were happy and had moved on with someone else."

Matt took a breath and let it out. "Ollie, how far do you think I would have gotten in my business if I went into every situation thinking 'what if I fail?' How alive do you think I would be if I thought that on any of my missions? Fuck, even BUD/S." He shook his head. "No, I run through all scenarios beforehand and make sure the one I want to happen does happen. There's always a plan B, but I've come in so prepared, that I've only ever needed it once, and that was not from my mistake." He glanced at his scar. "And I handled that situation, decisively."

Ollie closed his eyes, and tried to imagine living with that level of confidence, and discipline. He could either embrace it and learn from Matt, or listen to his shrieking brain (who was banging the warning bell loudly) and leave.

If you hurt him, what makes you think he won't shoot you in the leg and stab you in the neck? his brain scoffed.

Shut up. You're such a drama queen, his heart chided.

"I love you, and I will move heaven and earth to make you mine," Matt said firmly, interrupting Ollie's inner dialogue. "And in return, I will give you whatever you want, treat you with the highest level of respect, and love you and every inch of your glorious body. I told you from the very beginning that you are a grown man who makes his own decisions. You have free will, you can say no, it's just my job to make sure you don't want to."

Ollie opened his eyes and looked at Matt. A thrill ran through his blood at Matt's words and at the look on his face. He ran his eyes over the length of Matt's magnificent body and then around the room thinking.

"I want to see the building, in person. I want to see the designs, meet with Naomi. I want to have input," Ollie voiced what his brain was insisting.

Matt smiled; his eyes hooded. "You can have whatever you want, my love. I live and breathe for you. Now kiss me."

40

Secrets Spilled

OLLIE RECOGNIZED NAOMI IMMEDIATELY. A stunning, willowy blonde, with clear blue eyes and gorgeous bone structure, who looked like she stepped from the pages of Vogue. She hugged him at the door and he kissed both her cheeks before diving right into the tour of the space. He followed her through the first-floor unit, as she described her ideas and pointed out what she thought should stay and what needed to go, referring to the several design boards she had with her, and the fabric, and tile samples.

"Of course, all these old homes have incredible bones and detail work you just don't see in new construction, so we'll try to keep as much of that as we can. There are gorgeous hardwood floors throughout, even under some of that horrible wall-to-wall carpet, so we will just get them refinished and focus on changing the flooring in the two and a half bathrooms down here," she said.

Ollie nodded along, not changing a thing with her plans; she had impeccable taste, and somehow knew exactly what he liked. Ollie had a strong suspicion that Matt had something to do with that, and didn't mind.

Matt came through the door at that moment and kissed Naomi hello. He shook Ollie's hand firmly. "How's everything?"

"We just finished going over this unit, shall we look upstairs?" Naomi suggested.

"Lead the way," Matt answered, letting Naomi and Ollie go in front of him. He palmed Ollie's ass as he walked past.

"The elevator, which you know is direct access, goes to every level from this unit to the fifth floor with a key. The roof deck is accessed by a staircase on the alley side of the fifth floor. There is also a staircase connecting all the floors." She pointed to a wall. "It was closed in on this level, and the second level, when the property was subdivided, but remains open upstairs between the remaining floors. Would you be interested in opening it up again?" She looked at them both meaning-fully. Ollie held his breath.

Matt paused a moment. "Yes, for the second floor, but keep the first floor enclosed, we plan on using it as a guest-quarters primarily."

"Great!" she answered with a smile.

Ollie stared at Matt, stunned to his toes. *Did he just out us to her?*

"You're catching flies, Ollie," Matt said without looking at him.

Ollie closed his mouth and grinned.

Construction had already begun on the upper four floors, and Naomi walked Ollie through, reviewing the design boards with him as she had downstairs. Matt hung back on his phone, looking up occasionally to watch them walk through the rooms.

"There's a lot of light up here, from the skylights and it's fortu-nate that you have the end townhouse, it's quite a rare thing to come on the market," she was saying. "We've got a lot of privacy planned, curtains, blinds, furniture arrangement, et cetera. You're gonna love it when it's done."

"I know I will, you've got a great eye. Incredible talent."

"Thank you." Naomi smiled and opened her mouth to say something when Matt appeared in the doorway.

"You guys about done? I wanna show you something in the primary bath," he said to Naomi, and looked at Ollie. "We'll be right back."

Ollie nodded, recognizing a dismissal when he heard one, and went down to the kitchen to look at the design boards again.

"Thanks for doing this, everything is perfect, you have a gift." Matt took a breath and held Naomi's gaze. "I'm not sure how you knew, and, I'm hoping it's not that we're giving off a vibe. Because that is the exact opposite of what we are trying to achieve."

Naomi shook her head. "Oh no, Matt. Definitely no vibe, I really just guessed."

"I will pay you double to keep quiet, to *everybody* about this."

"I can't believe I'm turning down extra money, but there's no need." She shook her head. "You're Finn's best friend, and a really great guy. I would never betray your privacy. Besides, I need your referrals." She laughed.

Matt followed her out of the bathroom, glad he took a gamble on Naomi, setting his plan in motion. They joined Ollie in the kitchen, laughing their way down the staircase.

"Thank you, Naomi," Matt said, kissing her on the cheek. "We look forward to watching the project unfold."

"Bye, guys, I'll keep you posted." Naomi kissed Ollie's cheek and got on the elevator.

Matt turned to Ollie. "Well, what do you think?"

Ollie nodded slowly with a big smile. "It's bloody fabulous."

Matt put his arms around him and kissed him with relief. "I think you're bloody fabulous, and I can't wait to live here with you." He reached into his pocket and put a small bottle of Swiss Navy on the kitchen counter, pulling Ollie in tight to his body. "What d'you say we christen the place, gorgeous?"

———

41

———

What Is and What Should Never Be

OLLIE WENT BACK TO OXFORD on the fifteenth to finish his final 'Trinity' term. Matt arrived at his office the day after Ollie left, having worked from home while Ollie was in town.

"Good morning, Stacey," he said with a broad smile.

"Morning, Matt," Stacey replied, a brief look of shock on her face at his happy mood.

"I need you to work with Barbara in HR, and Brad in legal, on bringing in an intern from the UK. I need you to find out what they need from him in order to get a visa, and do whatever we need to on our end to be compliant with employment law."

"Of course. What is his name, and what department will he be interning in?" She uncapped her pen.

"Oliver Turner, legal. He's coming to us as a special request from Finn, he's her hire," Matt answered and turned to his office, ending the conversation.

* * *

Matt made arrangements to fly to the UK the first weekend in May, his first trip back since Easter. Finn was in the final phase of her dissertation on the intertwined lives of humans and gods in ancient Mesopotamia, and spending even more time in Ned's library. She offered up her flat and Matt's body tingled just thinking about being alone with Ollie. The things he was going to do to Ollie, the things Ollie was going to do to him, and felt himself grow hard.

His office phone buzzed, snapping him rudely out of his fantasy. "Yes, Stacey?"

"There's a Samantha Wilcox here to see you, Mr. Dion."

Matt's erection instantly deflated as he looked up through the glass wall of his office and saw Sam standing in front of Stacey's desk, looking at him. His stomach plummeted. He had broken it off with Sam when he bought the townhouse, but she had been reaching out recently and he'd been ignoring her texts and calls.

"Send her in."

He stood as she came through the glass door, and closed it behind her. She looked stunning in a brightly patterned, fitted, V-neck dress with a filmy layered skirt and stilettos, her hair long and loose down her back.

He came around his desk and kissed her cheek. "You look beautiful, Sam."

"So do you, Matt," she replied, her eyes warm as her voice trembled, her hands lingering on his chest. He stepped back and gestured to the chair in front of him, as he leaned his hip on the desk opposite her.

"What can I do for you?"

She sat and tossed her hair lightly. "I'm pregnant."

"What?" Matt frowned and stood; his body instantly tense. "I always used a condom."

"Condoms break."

He narrowed his eyes and turned away thinking, his stomach frozen as he thought only of Ollie.

"You'll get an abortion. I of course will pay for it, and go with you."
He looked back at her.

"What?"

"You're not keeping it. I don't want a child," Matt said simply.

"And if I do?" she asked, her eyes shining wetly.

Matt shook his head, his body going cold. No, no, no, he thought. "You're young, and beautiful, you don't want to be a single mom. It's a hard existence, not to mention limits your prospects for finding the love of your life."

She looked at her lap. "I have found the love of my life." She lifted her head with a wounded expression.

Matt shook his head, incapable of speech.

She winced. "I thought you'd be happy, I thought you wanted kids."

"Not like this. Sam, I'm not ready. Please, get an abortion." He reached for her hand and lifted her out of the chair, hugging her. She put her arms around his neck, and breathed deeply through her nose, kissing his neck and pressing herself against him lightly. Looking out the glass walls of his office, he caught Stacey watching them.

His mind was reeling, and he knew he needed to be careful. If she didn't have an abortion, things were going to get ugly and on so many levels. He quickly ran through the OODA loop, Observe-Orient-Decide-Act, that he learned at Annapolis and honed in the Navy.

"Let's have lunch," he said simply. "We can talk it through."

Sam smiled hopefully, pulling slowly out of his arms. "Okay, I'd like that."

Matt put on his suit coat and his phone in his pocket, following Sam out of his office.

"Cancel my two o'clock, Stacey," he ordered as they walked past her desk, thinking to himself that his next office space would have solid walls, not glass.

*　*　*

"I know I said I could come this weekend, but I've got an important negotiation that has stalled somewhat, and I'm sure you could use the time to study," Matt said to Ollie later on the phone.

Ollie smothered his disappointed sigh, knowing that he had an overwhelming amount of work to get done, but that he would have gladly worked like a maniac either before or after Matt's visit, just so he could see him.

"I understand, and you're right, I've a bit to focus on anyway that I can't ignore. When will I see you?"

"It won't be for another couple of weeks, if I'm lucky, and we have to discuss the J-1 visa for your internship here. Have you gone to the Consulate yet?"

Ollie's stomach tightened with disappointment. "I haven't seen you for weeks, and now you're saying it'll be more than a month?" He grimaced at the neediness in his voice.

"Believe me, Ollie, I miss you more than you could imagine. Sleeping alone, on a futon in a construction-dusty townhouse, is less than ideal. I promise I'll make it up to you. Please get to the Consulate."

Ollie sighed. "I'll make an appointment for next week."

"Okay, I love you."

"Just book your tickets, Lieutenant. I do so hate to be kept waiting."

42

Coercion

"SAM, YOU'RE MAKING THE RIGHT DECISION," Matt murmured against her ear. "We can talk about having kids later. I'm far too busy and you're too young, we're both too young. It would be hard." They were in her bed, Matt spooned behind her. He felt her nod as he stroked her arm, wishing he could be anywhere else.

"I know. You're right. It's terrifying to think about having a baby now." She paused. "I just missed you so much, I thought it would bring us back together, and I'm so glad that it has."

Matt kissed her shoulder and winced at her words. "What time is the appointment tomorrow? I'll come pick you up."

"Ten. You're not spending the night?" she asked incredulously.

"I will, but I have to go for a run and shower in the morning, you know that. I'll come back and get you."

She rolled over and kissed him, running her hands over his skin slowly with a sigh, reaching into his underwear to stroke him. He closed his eyes and caressed her, thinking and not thinking of Ollie. She eased his underwear off as he tore open the condom wrapper with his teeth.

"It's okay, I'm already pregnant," she murmured against his mouth, licking his lip and grinding against him.

Matt rolled it on anyway, ignoring her, focusing on being with her now, so he never had to be with her, *ever*.

He woke early, as usual, pushing the covers back and got out of bed quietly. He looked back at Sam and saw blood on the bed underneath her. He tugged the sheets back more, and shook her gently. She looked up at him sleepily.

"Samantha, doll, you're bleeding."

She sat up suddenly and looked between her legs, lurching out of bed to the bathroom. Matt looked contemplatively at the large stain in the bed before following her.

* * *

"You've had a miscarriage, I'm sorry, Samantha," her doctor said, as Matt sat next to her holding her hand. "There's no reason to believe that you will have any trouble conceiving in the future. Unfortunately, these things just happen."

Sam wept quietly as the doctor continued with a litany of instructions and some prescriptions, Matt nodding on Sam's behalf. The exam room door closed behind the doctor when she was done, and Matt turned to Sam.

"Let me help you get dressed." Matt's body was tingling with relief, and he had to fight to keep that relief off of his face.

43

Blindsided

MATT NEARLY LEAPT out of the car before it finished coming to a stop and waited impatiently at the door for the driver to bring his bag. He pressed a generous tip into his hand and watched as he made his way back to the car before putting his key in Finn's doorknob, only to have it pulled away from him as Ollie appeared.

"Get in here," Ollie said, grabbing Matt's wrist with a huge smile, turning and walking into the flat. "Chuck's gone to Sophie's for a movie night and is staying over," he continued, pulling Matt to him after he shut the door.

Matt wrapped his arms around Ollie and kissed him deeply, not saying a word. He pulled back after several moments to look at him. "You cut your hair."

"We can discuss my hair later." Ollie licked Matt's lip. "I've missed you desperately, so take off your clothes. It's been more than a month and I'm going to die if I don't feel your naked skin on mine in the next thirty seconds."

Matt could only stay the weekend, and they spent every moment of it together, Ollie studying while Matt worked, their bodies always in contact. Matt watched Ollie covertly as he concentrated on his schoolwork, sighing at the beauty of his face, his shorter hair full of sexy waves.

"You seem awfully happy," Ollie remarked in the afternoon as they were sitting on the couch.

"I'm so happy to be here with you. Let's not go so long again between seeing each other."

"I know, that really was too long. But I mean you seem more so than usual. Work is going well? Did you finish that negotiation?"

Matt nodded with a smile, fighting the urge to utterly beam with relief. "Yes, with a perfect outcome. I still have some finessing and follow-up that needs to be done, but I anticipate closing everything by the time you come for the summer. And the townhouse is looking amazing. I can't wait for you to see it, to move in."

"I can't wait to see it, and move in." Ollie kissed him. "The pictures you've been sending look fantastic.

"I went to the Consulate, we should be all set with the J-1, I sent the paperwork to Barbara."

"Outstanding. Everything is really coming together." Matt touched his face and kissed him gently. "Just what, one more month?"

Ollie nodded. "Will you come for graduation?"

"I wouldn't miss it—or Chuck's—for the world, my love." He pressed him back onto the couch, losing himself in Ollie once again.

Matt's phone began buzzing on the coffee table. Ollie listened to the shower running, and looked at the screen, pulling up with a scowl and a flash of jealousy at the name. He narrowed his eyes as he looked around angrily.

Matt opened the bathroom door as he toweled himself off and called out for Ollie, checking the bedroom. He looked for his phone and found it under a note.

Gone for a run — O

He picked up his phone and saw the missed call from Sam. He closed his eyes and blew out a worried breath.

Fuck.

Ollie let himself in, appearing on the steps nearly two hours later, sweaty and carrying a six-pack of beer.

Matt looked up from his laptop, and smiled with relief. "How was it?"

"You're right, it does clear the head when one is troubled." Ollie put the beer in the fridge, leaving one out and poured himself a glass of water.

Matt watched Ollie's back worriedly.

"Why is Sam calling you?" Ollie asked quietly before turning around.

Matt shrugged as nonchalantly as possible. "She calls from time to time. I imagine she's hopeful there's still a chance. Which of course, there isn't. Not a snowball's chance in hell."

"You know she's a particular thorn in my side." Ollie paused. "If it were the bloke I fucked during our time apart, calling me, how would you feel?"

Matt felt a flash of anger, and it must've shown on his face.

"Exactly," Ollie scoffed and opened his beer. "Do you answer?"

"Not usually, no." He shook his head and pushed aside his jealousy. "Ollie, it doesn't matter if she and I talked every day, we are never, *ever* getting back together, and nothing she could ever do would sway me from that. I love you, and only you. She is nothing."

"I don't want you to answer, *not ever*," Ollie said quietly but firmly.

"Okay, babe, I won't." Matt stood, relieved it was settled so easily. "Now, go shower. I've ordered Indian that I'm leaving now to get. We'll have a nice dinner, and then I'm going to fuck you silly."

Ollie smiled. "Okay. But get extra naan, I'm hungry."

"Yes, sir." He kissed him and left the flat with a light heart.

Matt came back from the bathroom and spooned himself around Ollie's naked body. "I love being with you, the feeling of your absurdly smooth skin against mine. I can't wait until after graduation when you come to live with me, and I get to have your glorious body next to mine every night. I love you."

"I can't wait either, Lieutenant."

Matt was silent as he ran through every conversation they'd had since they reunited. "You haven't said I love you," Matt whispered. "Not since New Year's."

Ollie pressed his lips together.

Matt loosened his arms. "What's going on, Ollie? Is your heart in this?"

Ollie continued to be silent and Matt's stomach sank with each passing second.

"You hurt me. I gave you my heart once and you threw it away. It shattered into a million pieces." Ollie's body was still and tense. "You've come back, and I'm so happy, but I'm still putting the pieces back together. I crave being with you. I look forward to living with you and working for you in Boston, but you can't have my heart back. Especially not while *Sam* is still calling you."

Matt felt short of breath. "I promised, I will never hurt you again. I love you, but if this is one-sided? Oh god." Matt sat up, his head spinning.

"That's not what I said." Ollie rolled onto his back and looked up at him. "You have to earn back my trust, and I know once both our feet are on the same continent, at the same time, for longer than a week, we will be right as rain. You're on probation, Lieutenant, and if you want me, and for me to be in your life, you have to accept that, and work hard for those three words, and my heart."

Matt turned his head to look at Ollie, feeling for the first time in their relationship that he didn't have the upper hand, and his stomach clenched with unease. The thought of losing Ollie, or Ollie not reciprocating his love was overwhelming and dizzying. He closed his eyes as his mind raced, searching for solutions.

He laid back, and rolled on his side to face Ollie and began nodding slowly. "I want your heart back because it *belongs* to me. I will stop at nothing until I have it. And when I do get it, I will guard it with my life, Oliver."

Ollie held Matt's gaze and took his hand, lacing their fingers together. He stared at their joined hands for a time before meeting Matt's eye again and leaning forward to kiss him softly.

Matt returned the kiss, opening his mouth to Ollie's tongue and with a sigh he rolled on top of Ollie, burying his fingers in Ollie's hair as he settled between his legs.

"I love you, Ollie," he breathed against his lips.

44

Imminent Retreat

BACK IN BOSTON, Matt began to extricate himself from Sam and her thoughts of a future for them. He had less than a month to pull it off, and after his conversation with Ollie, he was even more determined to get out and focus only on Ollie.

She was needy and upset about the miscarriage, but Matt had a plan he had to stick to. He took her to dinner at Mistral (knowing he would never take Ollie there again), and then back to her place, stopping in the entryway after closing the door.

He kissed her, holding her loosely around the waist, and measured his words carefully. "Sam, doll, there's no sense in being upset about something that we had already decided not to keep." He hugged her and kissed the side of her head. "Everything happens for a reason. This was meant to be, and you will have children someday." He tilted her face up to look at him. "You're gonna be a great mom, especially if you grow stronger from this experience. Take a deep breath and move forward. There's no other direction to go. Trust me."

She smiled up at him, wrapping her arms around his neck and then smoothed her hands down his chest. "You're right. You always know what to say. I love your confidence, your strength." She stood on her tiptoes and kissed him, coaxing his lips open as she began untucking his shirt.

He groaned inwardly and stifled a sigh as he kissed her, letting her tongue touch his. He ran his hands lightly over her body. "Doll, you're still healing, and I can't stay," he said pulling back and re-tucking his shirt. "I have an early flight tomorrow. I'll call you when I get back from the west coast."

She frowned sadly. "You only just got back from the UK."

"I know. This is how my life is, and this is exactly why you didn't need a baby at this point in yours." He kissed her and turned to leave. "Remember that."

Matt waited a week, called her and took her to dinner, his mind elsewhere the entire time. He spent the night at her urging but didn't have any intention of ever sleeping with her again. She wanted to please him, putting her hand down his pants, insisting. He closed his eyes and let her give him a mediocre blow job. Afterward he lay awake discontentedly thinking of Ollie, and prayed he never found out.

$$45$$

Wrecking Ball

"WHAT ARE YOU THINKING ABOUT?" Sam asked him the next morning as he sat at her kitchen table, staring at the bowl of fruit in the middle.

He pulled his eyes away and looked at her, so pretty, so sweet, so undeserving of what he was about to do. He took a breath and let it out, pushing his coffee mug away.

"You are so perfect, in so, *so* many ways. But, Sam, you're not only spinning your wheels with me, you're wasting your time." He looked away from the pained expression on her face. "I care about you, and thought maybe I could find my way to you, but. . . . " He shook his head. "You deserve so much better than me."

"I love you, Matt," she cried, her eyes filling with tears. "I don't want anyone but you, there is no one better."

He sighed and met her eye, holding her gaze for a moment before standing. "I can't do this."

"You're seeing someone else, aren't you? Is it Holly?"

Matt looked at her with a puzzled frown, not sure if he heard her correctly. "What are you talking about?" He felt his stomach go cold.

"You called out for her in your sleep back in February. You said you were sorry. You fucking her again? Your lube slut," she shouted angrily.

Matt blew out a breath. She was so close to the truth, too close. He shook his head emphatically. "There's no Holly, there's no one."

"Then it's Finn. You're back with her, aren't you?" She stood and wiped her face angrily. "I wondered about your trips to the UK, you've been weird ever since you came back. You bastard," she spat.

Matt looked away, wondering if he should let her think that was the reason why. "Sam, the reason why this isn't working has nothing to do with anyone else. I take full responsibility for not being able to give you what you need. I can't be the man you want me to be." He turned and left.

46

Pomp and Circumstance

THE WEEK AFTER the fourth of July, Matt traveled to Oxford with Finn's parents Bill and Diana. Matt had finally been able to relax around Bill after a month or so of awkwardness, but his unease began to resurface during the flight and only escalated once they landed.

Ollie still hasn't told you he loves you. If you reject him in front of Bill, he may walk away, forever.

How could he balance the two, and save face? His mind raced away from him as they waited for their bags.

No, Lieutenant. Stop doubting. You need to focus on winning Ollie's heart. That's all that matters.

He snapped to attention when the luggage belt started moving and grabbed their bags with a determined smile.

* * *

Things were initially awkward after the ceremony. Matt had introduced the two sets of parents before they all sat together in the stands of the Sheldonian Theatre. Outside the building as they stood chatting, he tried to balance his attention between David and Bill, whose pensive gaze he felt on him as he spoke amiably with David.

Matt had to fight the urge to pull back from the conversation, torn between acting like he barely knew Ollie's family, and wanting to gain back David's respect. David had been cooler toward him since his reconciliation with Ollie, and all Matt wanted was for David to smile honestly at him again.

When Ollie and Finn finally joined them, Ollie greeted Finn's parents stiffly, and then his own parents and Cassie warmly, all while trying to avoid staring at Matt like a lovesick puppy.

"We've booked a restaurant near here, for Finn and her friends. Please join us," Diana said to Maggie and David.

Maggie smiled. "We'd love to, thank you." She looked at David and Ollie, who nodded in agreement.

Matt felt Finn's touch on his elbow as he watched things unfold between the parents.

"What if you didn't worry about my dad?" she said quietly and looked up at him with a concerned expression. "What if, you only worried about enjoying yourself, and celebrating me, and Ollie, for our achievements? And, if you put your arm around Ollie, and toasted him and his awards at the party, everyone would applaud, but more importantly Ollie would feel seen and loved. And you could do all of that as a good friend, and none would be the wiser."

Matt looked down at her and took a calming breath. "Jesus Christ, Chuck." He shook his head and kissed her. "Are you even real? I'm growing very tired of you being right all the time."

"That's Doctor Chuck to you now." She grinned.

"And I'm so damn proud of you, you nerd." He lifted her off her feet in a bear hug and swung her around, her squeal drawing attention.

At the celebration Matt toasted not only Finn, but also Ollie, pulling each one under his arm separately as he did. Ollie smiling from ear to ear just as Finn predicted.

"I love you," he whispered seriously in Ollie's ear as he gave him a bro hug. Ollie nodded his head quickly against his neck and pulled away, spinning around to look at his parents and the crowd of friends.

"There's dancing!" Finn announced, and the DJ kicked up the music.

Matt spent time with Ollie's parents, the three of them speaking with pride about Ollie, and briefly about Ollie's move.

"I'm sure he's said, but Ollie has a large condo for you guys to come visit, anytime, and I mean that. We'd love to see you. I'd love to see you," Matt added with a smile.

"We haven't been to Boston since before we had kids," David replied. "We'd love to come visit."

"Say the word, I'll send tickets, my treat."

Maggie beamed and grabbed Matt's face in both hands, kissing him soundly. "You are a prince."

"And you are shut off," David said to her with a teasing smile. He shook Matt's hand firmly, saying nothing, but nodded with polite expression that did nothing to settle Matt's nerves.

Cassie appeared, breaking the tension. "What am I missing out on?"

She looked tipsily at her mother who was already on her way over to Diana.

"Do I get a kiss?" She pulled Matt's head down without waiting for a response.

He smiled against her mouth, careful not to return the kiss as he searched for Ollie. His eyes found him and his smirking face effortlessly.

Oh, I'll spank that look off your face, he thought as he winked at Ollie.

"Go dance," he commanded lightly as he let go of Cassie.

Matt watched Cassie saunter onto the dance floor until his eye was drawn to Bill making his way over to him with a drink in his hand.

"Are you enjoying yourselves?" Bill asked as he scanned his eyes over Matt and David.

"Immensely. Great party," David said as he shook Bill's hand. "Thank you so much for including us. We just adore Finn."

"Our pleasure, glad you could join us. We know how much Finn, and Matt, love Oliver," Bill added, looking at Matt.

Matt shifted his gaze to the ground nervously as his heart raced, wondering what glances with Ollie Bill had witnessed, while David looked sharply at Bill.

"I read the graduation pamphlet and saw Oliver's name quite a few times." Bill looked at David. "Those awards? He's an impressive young man. You should be proud."

Bill shifted his gaze to Matt. "You said in your toast he's coming to work for you?"

"Yes, sir," Matt replied, trying to keep the nervousness out of his voice. "He is, as you say, a very impressive young man. SharkFinn is lucky to have scooped him up."

Bill looked at him for a moment. "As are you, Matt." He smiled and walked away.

Matt studied Bill's retreating form for a moment before looking back at David who was watching him intently.

"Does he know?" David asked quietly.

Matt sighed. "Yes, and no, but now I think yes." He chewed his lip briefly. Matt saw David's frown and immediately snapped into damage control.

"Let's have another drink, sir. Tonight is for celebration, not speculation and worry." He put his arm around David's shoulder and walked with him to the open bar as he fought the urge to flee.

47

Shipping up to Boston

"I PROMISED I WOULDN'T CRY, but, Ollie, you're my baby, and now you'll be so far away," his mother said tearfully as they stood outside the international terminal at Heathrow two days later. "Please call me regularly and come home for holidays or I will worry."

"I love you, Mum." Ollie hugged her tightly. "You'll hear more from me than you did when I was at university, I promise."

"You had better keep your word, son," David admonished, his eyes shining. "Your mother will keep me up with her wailing if you don't." He hugged Ollie tightly.

"I'll make sure he does, sir," Matt said hugging David and then Maggie. "And I'll send you tickets. Let's plan for early fall, if that works for you."

"That sounds lovely," David replied. "I'll look at my work calendar and email you."

"Perfect." Matt looked at Ollie expectantly.

"We've got to go catch our flight. I'll call you when we land. Love you both," Ollie said and turned to follow Matt to the expedited security gate, admiring stares following them both.

They boarded the plane and waited for their champagne. Matt clinked his glass to Ollie's.

"Here's to your bright future, and our happiness," he added quietly. Ollie beamed. "*Slainte.*"

They arrived at the townhouse mid-afternoon. Matt opening the garden-level door under the exterior brick staircase dramatically and showing him around. Ollie couldn't believe it was the same space that he had seen two months prior, gasping over the marble, the details, the furniture, the bathrooms, and the gleaming floors. Naomi's vision had been brought to life, and everything was picture-perfect, and brightly lit to compensate for being below stairs.

Matt put their bags in the primary suite and kissed Ollie deeply with a long look, before leading him to the elevator to check on the renovations upstairs. Matt palmed Ollie's bottom with a grin before the doors opened and looked around to be sure the workers were gone. Ollie followed Matt around with a smile, his own smile nearly splitting his face in two. The townhouse had been completely overhauled, and while there were still at least a few months to go before it would be finished, Ollie could see how beautiful it would be when it was done.

"This looks amazing." He glanced back at him as they stood on the roof deck overlooking the neighborhood and the city beyond, the breeze coming off the river and over the buildings ruffling Ollie's hair lightly, making the streaks of white blonde sparkle. "I can't believe I'm to live here, and with you," he marveled. "Pinch me. This has to be a dream."

"I will do more than pinch you once we get back downstairs," Matt answered waggling his eyebrows.

Ollie looked at him with a solemn expression. "I mean it, Lieutenant," he said softly, shaking his head slightly.

Matt looked at him, his eyes intent. After a moment he nodded. "I know. I can't believe it either," he whispered.

48

Secrets

OLLIE GOT ACCLIMATED at work without Matt's guidance, for appearances. They arrived separately at the office building in Kendall Square on the first day, and every day after that. Ollie completed a brief training and was given a small office in the four-person legal department on the other side of the building from Matt.

He worked hard getting up to speed, and then worked long days, every day, proving himself. He slept less than he ever had in his life due to the workload and Matt's seemingly endless needs between the sheets (and in the shower, and on the floor, and over the back of the couch), but he woke every morning with a smile. School had been grueling, but that had been scholarly work. Working at SharkFinn was real world, making deals, making money, making Matt happy. Ollie had never felt so fulfilled and his heart was back together and so full of love for Matt, he couldn't wait to tell him.

His six-week internship was nearly finished and he'd received his written (and very generous) offer from Barbara that morning. He left the letter open on his desk where he could glance at it from time to time with a smile.

Matt peeked his head into Ollie's small office after lunch. "We're going to dinner tonight to celebrate you becoming an official part of my legal team," he said his eyes twinkling. "Come to my office at six."

"Yes, sir. I can't wait to come." He smiled mischievously.

Matt raised his eyebrows and left, closing the glass door behind him.

Matt brought a portfolio of work with them that legitimately needed to be reviewed, but could have been done at home. Ollie didn't care, he just wanted to be out with Matt, under whatever work guise necessary, and then get him home so he could confess his undying love for him. Ollie grinned happily at the thought.

Matt took him to Yvonne's in Downtown Crossing, Matt wearing his trident collar pin and cuff links for the special occasion. Ollie glanced questioningly at the barbershop chairs next to the hostess stand, before following Matt and the hostess through an industrial looking doorway in the back wall. He gasped lightly as he found himself in a low-lit opulent space with brick walls, wood paneling, and ornate ceiling tiles. They were seated at a table in the corner with four chairs in the library dining area next to the smaller marble bar, Matt having requested something out of the way so they could 'work.'

Ollie sat to Matt's right so they could look over the documents together, but more so that they could have a quiet conversation in the loud space, and so Matt could brush his knee against Ollie's under the tablecloth from time to time. The waiter reappeared with their drinks and Matt ordered dinner, looking Ollie over discreetly as the waiter left and then scanned the room, smiling at some women at the bar.

"So, one more week and then you're officially mine," Matt said with a grin.

"I haven't signed the offer yet." Ollie shrugged dramatically.

Matt furrowed his brow. "Are you holding out for something more?"

"Well, the offer is very generous, but I feel as though I need a little more persuasion, some more convincing," Ollie said and sipped his drink, looking away. "I mean, I was promised naked Fridays, and I've yet to experience one." He sucked his teeth and made a dramatic face.

Matt laughed low in his throat. "Well, I'll make a compelling argument tonight, and spend the rest of the weekend really convincing you. And next Friday will be naked." He looked up as the server appeared with their appetizers, and ordered another round of cocktails.

Ollie made a thoughtful sound as he watched the waiter walk away. "I look forward to you pleading your case, hearing your *oral arguments.*" Ollie raised his eyebrows at Matt.

Matt shook his head and dug into his food with a grin.

Ollie sat back when the meal was finished and looked at Matt. "Thank you," he said quietly, his heart so full it hurt. "This was really spectacular."

Matt smiled; his eyes smoky. He mimed a request for the check to the waiter and looked around. Ollie checked his phone while Matt paid and then followed him from the table, watching Matt's fluid gait admiringly. Suddenly Matt's back went tense and his step faltered. Ollie looked around, instantly alert.

"Matt." Sam's voice was like the screech of a needle across a record and brought everything to a halt. She was wearing a form-fitting black dress and minimal gold jewelry, her hair loose and sexy. She looked stunning and Ollie ground his teeth while his spirits plummeted. Sam gazed at Matt hungrily with a slightly wounded expression.

"Sam. Hi," Matt said with a tight smile. "You remember Oliver."

"Hi, Oliver." Sam smiled sweetly, "Imani was just asking about you the other day and she's on her way. You guys should stay."

Ollie noticed a flicker of hope pass through Sam's eyes as she looked between them.

"We were just leaving," Matt replied.

Sam looked at him for a moment, with an expression like disbelief. "That's a constant state with you." She paused angrily. "I'm so much better now, not that you care. But I am. I'll never be as happy about the loss as you so clearly were, but at least I don't cry about it or you anymore."

Matt slid a glance at Ollie. "Glad to hear it, Sam, goodnight." He started to walk away but turned back when he realized Ollie wasn't behind him.

Ollie had been watching the exchange, trying to follow what Sam was talking about. Clearly, by Matt's reaction, the tension in his body, the tightness around his eyes and mouth, this was something he didn't want him to find out about.

"What loss?" Ollie asked Sam. "If you don't mind me asking."

Sam turned to look at him as if just remembering he was there. "I had a miscarriage." She looked at Matt and put her chin up slightly. "See, I can say it and not break down."

Ollie's dinner churned and he felt his heart lurch. He nodded with a concerned expression, not looking at Matt. "How awful for you." He swallowed roughly. "When?"

"May."

Ollie looked at Matt, who was standing with his eyes closed. Ollie felt the air being sucked out of the restaurant as the crowd suddenly became deafeningly loud.

"Whoa." He held up his hands defensively as his mind raced. "I'm terribly sorry for you, Sam. For you *both*. Forgive my intrusion, I'll leave you two alone now."

Ollie turned and strode out of the restaurant, remaining as calm as possible though his insides were liquifying. He made it outside and halfway up the alley as he took several deep breaths of the hot night air. His heart was splintering painfully, and he fought desperately to hold it together. The stench of the nearby subway entrance was nauseating to his already upset stomach and he loosened his tie as he heard Matt call his name.

"Ollie." Matt grabbed his elbow. "The car is this way," he said quietly and directed Ollie.

Ollie pulled his arm out of Matt's grasp. "Don't touch me," he hissed.

"Ollie, we're going home. I will explain everything, and you will listen." Matt stared at him.

Ollie studied him, as if seeing him for the first time. "No," he said firmly.

Matt's eyes tightened, he looked around, seeing the people walking along the strip outside the alley, some turning in and passing by.

"Ollie, don't do this here," he said in a quiet but firm voice. "Come *home*."

Ollie looked up at the night sky and took a deep breath. "No," he repeated. "I'll be home later, *maybe*. I don't want to hear anything out of your mouth right now."

"Ollie. No," Matt said firmly, in a quiet voice.

Ollie's eyes flashed at Matt's audacity. "Chase me then, Lieutenant. Beg me, *loudly*, to come home now, preferably on your knees. Otherwise, I'll see you when I see you." Ollie turned on his heel and strode out of the alley.

Matt watched helplessly as Ollie turned left at the corner of the building and disappeared from view. He clenched his fists and with a glance back at Yvonne's he strode out of the alley and turned right toward the parking garage.

Matt paced the condo like a caged tiger and sipped his whisky. He had changed into shorts and a t-shirt, waiting hours for Ollie, occasionally stopping to sit at the kitchen island to check his phone. By two in the morning, he was frantic with worry. Ollie's phone eventually just went to voicemail, and he never responded to any of the texts.

Matt laid on the couch, not wanting to leave sight of the door as his heart burned. He was furious with Sam, with the universe, and he fought to gain clarity, to find a solution. He finally fell asleep for a couple of hours, and woke to the faint light of dawn and a still empty condo.

"Fuck!" he shouted, his breath hitching. He was desperate for a run but worried about missing Ollie if he returned. Finally, he couldn't take another minute of sitting still and put on his sneakers. He ran fast but not far, returning home for a shower and to continue to wait, seeing no sign of Ollie. His head started to pound and he realized he hadn't had any food or water since the night before. He drank a glass of water, sat heavily on the couch and closed his eyes.

49

Tipping Point

OLLIE WALKED THE STREETS of Boston, ducking into the bar at the Ritz sometime around eleven. He had three whiskies in a row and then got himself a room, feeling he absolutely had the right to stay somewhere so expensive. He stripped off all his clothes and crawled between the sheets, his body numb, his heart aching, and sobbed himself to sleep.

Ollie woke after nine with a headache and cotton mouth. He brushed his teeth with the toothbrush provided by the hotel and called down for coffee, water, and acetaminophen. He looked at his phone on the nightstand, and decided he didn't want to turn it back on. He had turned it off shortly after leaving Matt, not wanting to hear the buzzing of Matt calling and texting. *What on earth could he possibly say for himself?* Ollie couldn't believe he nearly let his guard down again with him.

I told you so, his brain said in a singsong voice.

You didn't get back together until April, and the miscarriage was in May, he could've gotten her pregnant before they broke up, his heart suggested.

He was probably fucking you both at the same time. How do you know he even broke up with her? Maybe he's still fucking her. You don't check his phone;

she could still be calling him. *He doesn't get home until late some days,* his brain said cruelly.

No way. She acted like she hadn't seen him in ages. He loves you. He told you he never loved her. He can't fake how he is with you, his heart urged.

His body was absolutely silent.

Ollie put his head in his hands and heard a knock at the door. He panicked momentarily, thinking that somehow Matt had found him. He put on the robe and looked through the peep hole and saw room service with a tray. He sighed, relieved and disappointed that it wasn't Matt.

He let the server in and tipped him after he watched him pour the coffee, taking the Tylenol with large swallows of the bottled water after he left.

You can't hide here forever, his heart said gently. *Go home. Listen to what he has to say.*

Don't be ridiculous! You will make plans to go back to the UK. Your internship is over, you should sell your condo, to really fuck with him, his brain commanded.

Ollie went back to bed after extending his checkout time, sleeping through the afternoon. He woke, or rather his body woke him, his erection pressing against the sheets.

Go home, it said.

Oh, fuck off, you horny wanker, his brain said in disgust.

Go home, listen to him, like your heart said, and then have make up sex. It's the best kind. Remember? his body urged, his erection twitching with the summoned memory.

I'm sure he has a good explanation. Go, listen, his heart pleaded. *If not, then we'll listen to the asshole in your head.*

I'm the voice of reason, not an asshole. If he didn't listen to me at least occasionally, you two would have had us all in ruins by now, his brain scoffed.

"Shut up all of you!" Ollie shouted and slammed the bathroom door.

He took a long shower and took his time doing his hair, the ritual soothing him. He put his suit back on and his tie in his pocket, leaving the top two buttons of his shirt undone, his silver chain catching the light. He pocketed his phone, left a tip for housekeeping, and headed back to the bar for a bite to eat.

He picked at a salad and drank two pints, aware of the man at the other end of the bar, watching him. He was at least fifteen years older, and had wavy, dark brown hair with graying temples, and a handsome face. He was dressed in a long-sleeve Henley-type shirt and faded jeans, and looked like a model for Ralph Lauren.

The bartender put another pint in front of him. "This is from that guy down there."

Ollie furrowed his brow, not in the slightest bit interested in being picked up, but couldn't help his polite nature. He held up the pint in cheers to the man.

The man picked up his cocktail and came over. "I'm not trying to pick you up. You just look like you've had a pretty shitty day." He smiled and sat down next to Ollie on the corner, so he could face him. "I've had my fair share of those and am always thankful for the kindness of strangers when I travel."

Up close the man was even more attractive, in a confident, Patrick Dempsey kind of way, with laugh lines around his clear blue eyes. As well as lines between his eyebrows that spoke of stressful days. His only jewelry was a platinum Tag Hauer watch. "Thank you. It's been a fairly trying twenty-four hours for sure," Ollie said with chagrin.

His eyebrows went up at Ollie's accent. "Where are you from?"

"London, but Oxford most recently. Just finishing up an internship here in Cambridge."

"I'm Sebastian." He held his hand out and waited expectantly.

"Oliver." He shook his hand firmly, feeling the slightest of tingles as their palms touched.

"So, Oliver, how do you like it? Working in America. Think you want to stay?" Sebastian asked, his eyes flickering as though he felt the tingle too.

Ollie took a deep breath. "I liked it. It was hard but rewarding. I thought I wanted to stay, but I'm really not sure. I'm keeping my options open. What do you do?"

"I work for a software start-up, great company but it's hectic. Lots of travel. I'm from San Francisco," he replied with nuance. If Ollie had any doubt as to Sebastian's sexual orientation, he just purposefully revealed it like a wink. "What do you do? Who was your internship with?"

"I'm a lawyer, at a cybersecurity company. Just one week to go." "You get your degree at Oxford?" Sebastian asked, taking a sip of his drink.

"Yes. I have my master's in law and finance, and my MBA." He took a long swallow of his beer.

Sebastian's eyes flickered to Ollie's throat before widening with admiration. "Wow, impressive. Did your company offer you a job, or are you looking for one?"

"They offered, but I haven't accepted."

"You're keeping your options open," Sebastian said with a smile. "Smart. You should shop your resume around, I'm betting your international background and degrees would be prized by many companies. I know I'd love to see it."

Ollie laughed inwardly, remaining expressionless. Oh, *to go from fucking one boss, to another,* he thought, because despite what Sebastian said, he was most definitely trying to pick him up.

"I obviously don't have it on me. And I still don't know if I even want to stay in America," Ollie said, hoping to end the conversation as he picked up his glass.

Sebastian reached into his pocket and pulled a business card out of his wallet. "Send it to me if you decide to stay in the states, I mean it. The west coast is beautiful, San Francisco is an amazing city."

Ollie took it with his left hand, the sleeve of his suit riding up, revealing his still shiny-and-new-looking Rolex. He glanced briefly at the card, noting that Sebastian was the CEO and co-founder of that software start-up, before tucking the card into the inside pocket of his coat.

Sebastian's eyes lingered on Ollie's watch. "Must have been a well-paying internship."

Ollie straightened his sleeve. "It was a gift."

Sebastian's eyebrows went up. "From your girlfriend?"

"No," Ollie answered quietly and held Sebastian's gaze briefly before finishing his beer.

"I knew it," Sebastian whispered, just loud enough for Ollie to hear.

Ollie stood and threw some bills down on the bar. "Thank you for the drink. It was nice meeting you."

Sebastian stood and shook Ollie's hand. "I hope I hear from you, Oliver."

Ollie nodded politely and left without a backwards glance.

Ollie took a long walk, thinking of how much his life had changed in such a short period of time. All the things he was once so certain of, now felt like smoke in his hands. His feet were beginning to hurt and he needed clothes, he needed his things and like his heart said, he couldn't hide forever. He turned and headed to Marlborough Street; his feet like lead.

50

About Today

MATT HEARD A KEY in the door after dark and strode over eagerly, before hanging back to give Ollie space. Ollie appeared a moment later in the archway from the foyer.

"Where the hell have you been?" Matt asked in a rush. "I've been out of my mind."

Ollie put his tie and phone on the kitchen island and with a glance at Matt, went to the side bar to pour himself a whisky.

"I've been out. I still don't want to talk to you," he said harshly without looking at Matt. "I'm only home because I need clothes, and I'm sleeping in the other bedroom tonight."

"No, Ollie," Matt said quietly. "Look at me."

Ollie stared at him angrily, and put his drink on the bar. He shook his head slowly.

"I don't even know what I'm doing here. You got her *pregnant*." He covered his face and then dropped his hands. "I'm no mathematician but it had to have been fairly recently. Were you fucking us both at the same time?" He stared at Matt with a look of contempt. "You pig."

Matt winced looking away briefly. He knew he had to make Ollie listen, but he hadn't anticipated just how angry Ollie would be.

"No, Ollie I wasn't. I really need you to listen to me. I know right now, anything I say is going to sound like backpedaling, but please hear me out." He paused. "I was an idiot to have ever left you. We established that. And you know, that I was stupid enough to go out with Sam a few times while you and I were apart." He held Ollie's gaze. "I always used a condom, but somehow—"

"I don't need the visual thank you," Ollie interrupted angrily.

Matt winced again. "She came to me after I broke it off and told me she was pregnant." Matt picked up the whiskey bottle contemplating a drink but put it back down again.

"When did you break it off with her?" Ollie asked angrily.

"Right after I bought this townhouse." He looked earnestly at Ollie. "I never wanted to be with her, and I certainly didn't want to have a baby with her. I told her to get an abortion, and she finally agreed, but it wasn't easy for me to get her to." He looked away. "It ended up not mattering in the end because of the miscarriage, and she's right. I was fucking relieved." He took Ollie's hand and held his gaze. "I kept it from you because it has no bearing on our relationship. She means nothing to me, and she never will."

Ollie took his hand carefully out of Matt's with a scowl. "She was nearly the mother of your child. How can you speak so callously of her? I mean, of course I don't want you to pine for her, but to be so cruel. It's not terribly appealing, Matthew. She seems like a perfectly nice person." He picked up his drink and walked to the kitchen.

"I didn't mean it quite like that." Matt followed him with his eyes, "I just meant that you are the only person I care about, and I will do anything for you. What do you want to hear?"

"I want to hear that you are not so careless with people's feelings. That you won't be careless with mine," he said searching Matt's face. "Again," he whispered and then looked away with a wince.

"That's why you couldn't visit in May. She was your 'negotiation.'" He frowned incredulously. "Christ, the way you were talking about it, that was a human being you were so pleased to be done with. 'Perfect outcome, finessing.' Jesus! The Navy really did a number on you, didn't they? Sometimes you're like a machine, wholly without feeling. Unless you were always this way, in which case. . . ." Ollie shook his head with a frown. "Did you talk about me like that?"

Matt crossed the room and put his arms around Ollie.

"No, Ollie. No. I was just using euphemisms, to hide the truth from you, I didn't actually think like that about her. And I won't hurt you, not ever again." He stroked Ollie's back. "I do have feelings, and the ones I have for you are quite real, and often overwhelming. I love you. You know I love you. I will do anything, please forgive me."

Ollie closed his eyes and remained still. "I wish keeping secrets from me, and lying to me didn't come so easily to you. I wish you had just told me."

Matt stepped back. "While you were still in school?" he scoffed. "There was no way I was going to risk telling you while you were an ocean away. I worried you would convince yourself that you didn't want me anymore." He looked at Ollie with his heart in his throat. "And I didn't tell you when you moved here, because it was done, and never needed mentioning. I didn't want this to happen. Please, Ollie," he whispered. "I've barely slept, I haven't eaten. I can't live without you."

Ollie closed his mouth and studied Matt carefully, shaking his head slightly. "I should walk out that door and never come back. I thought about it. I planned on it." His eyes filled. "I just don't think I can get through the rest of my life, always worrying and wondering if you're going to hop the fence again, leaving me broken on my side of it."

"Ollie," Matt pleaded as a pulse of panic shot through him. "Oh, god. I love you. I don't want anyone but you. Please don't leave me. I never wanted to hop the fence. I was being an idiot."

"The worst part is, I was about to give you my heart last night." Tears spilled over Ollie's lids as he shook his head. "Now I don't think you can ever have it back."

Matt felt everything inside him shut down, and a dull roar began to rise in his ears.

"No, no, no, Ollie, please." He grabbed Ollie and hugged him tightly. "I was wrong to leave you, and I've been here making it up to you, I love you. What happened with Sam happened when we were apart, I never fucked around on you.

"Please give me another chance." He kissed Ollie's neck. "Please. I will cherish your heart."

Matt rubbed Ollie's back and then ran his hands through Ollie's hair. Ollie was his everything and the idea of losing him, *because of Sam*, made Matt sick. He kissed Ollie's lips tentatively, and then again more firmly when he saw Ollie's eyelids flicker.

"Please. I love you," Matt whispered against Ollie's lips as he feathered kisses lightly, fearful of pushing too far, of breaking the spell he was beginning to weave. "You are my moon, my universe, my reason for being. I was a shell and you made me whole. It's you, only you."

Matt felt Ollie respond ever so slightly, and parted his lips in silent invitation, holding his breath as he tightened his fingers in Ollie's hair. Ollie returned the kiss with an open mouth and Matt exhaled as he eased his tongue in cautiously. Ollie's arms came up around his waist and he swirled his tongue around Matt's in response, before suddenly pushing Matt away.

"You're so," Ollie made a disgruntled sound full of irritation, "right now. Kissing my ass, begging me not to leave. But I've yet to hear you say 'sorry' to me." Ollie raised his eyebrows and shook his head. "Fuck you, Matt. It's *me* here," Ollie implored. "You love me 'so much,'" Ollie made air quotes, "but you disrespect me by not expressing your remorse. You fucked up then you covered it up, so the least you can do is say 'sorry.' Though we both know I deserve so much more than that."

Matt swallowed with a harsh click of his throat. Ollie was right, and yet it was so hard for him to say it. His father had hammered into him that expressing regret was a weakness. A sign of failure. An expression to avoid at all costs, and Matt had integrated that notion into his life. It was a hard habit to break, but for Ollie . . . he needed to cave.

"I'm sorry, Ollie. So sorry." Matt shook his head. "I will make it up to you. You deserve the world, and I will continue to give you that, and more, if you'll just forgive me."

Ollie made a thoughtful sound. "See how easy that was? The ground didn't open. The earth didn't shake. The sky didn't fall."

Matt winced and looked away.

Ollie turned and ran his hands through his hair, then picked up his glass, and finished the whisky in one swallow. Ollie took off his suit coat and put it on the back of the island barstool as he kicked off his shoes. Matt watched as Ollie continued to disrobe, the clothing falling to the floor around him as he kept his eyes locked on Matt's. Every bit in a puddle on the floor at his feet until he was left in nothing but his underwear, The sexy style Ollie wore when he had something extra planned for Matt.

Matt groaned.

Ollie looked down at the mess of clothes and then met Matt's eyes with a gleam.

"You don't get any of this tonight." He ran his hands over his pebbled nipples, down his bare chest and then stroked himself briefly over the front of his briefs, deliberately drawing Matt's eye. "Maybe not tomorrow night either."

Ollie picked up his phone and strode out of the room without a backwards glance, his perfect round ass taunting Matt.

Matt found Ollie on top of the bed covers, stroking himself while watching the door. He pulled up and his mouth went dry at the tantalizing sight. Ollie narrowed his eyes and stared back, his hand never slowing. Matt slipped his hand into his lounge pants and adjusted himself before crossing to the side of the bed.

"Let me," Matt whispered and rested his hand on Ollie's firm thigh.

"No, Lieutenant. I'm doing this because I don't want you. Because I don't want to want you," he gritted out and shifted his leg away. "I told you. You can't have me tonight, but I will have you know what you risked losing." He shifted his gaze to what his hand was doing, teasing his thumb over the wet crown of his cock.

Matt made a sound of frustration, his eyes shifting from Ollie's face to Ollie's hand stroking himself. He took off his shirt and held Ollie's gaze.

"Well, then don't mind if I join you. Because I want you, and I *want* to want you."

Matt took the lube off the bed next to Ollie and poured a generous amount into his hand. He began stroking himself in long slow pumps with a small grin that turned serious as his eyes darkened with lust. He studied the lines of Ollie's gorgeous body and listened to the sound of their breathing as their hands moved nearly in sync. He wanted to touch Ollie's hardened nipples, run his fingers between Ollie's muscular thighs, but didn't dare.

Ollie tried to look away, but Matt's beautiful erection, the sight of it in his large hand, the veins standing out on his muscled forearm, were too riveting to ignore. Ollie closed his eyes determinedly and fought a moan. Ollie's hand moved faster of its own accord; he just wanted to come and extinguish the burning need he had for Matt in that moment. He was furious with his body's response, and while he had decided he would stay with Matt, his brain insisted that he torment Matt first.

Ollie's ear perked up at the sound of Matt's aroused breathing coming in short gasps, *the most alluring sound.* He heard the sound of Matt's hand moving slickly over himself, *the second most alluring sound,* and felt himself begin to come undone.

"God, you are so sexy. That fucking body, all tense, your balls so tight. You're close, aren't you?" Matt moaned. "Look at me."

Ollie opened his eyes, and lost himself at what he saw, crying out involuntarily as he came in long hot spurts. Matt followed a second later, his splatters mingling with Ollie's on his chest as he groaned through his release.

Matt leaned briefly against the side of the bed before reaching for his shirt and mopping Ollie's chest and then himself. "That was hot." He smiled at Ollie before disappearing into the bathroom.

Ollie watched Matt leave, feeling simultaneously triumphant at having been able to resist Matt, and frustrated that he hadn't actually been able to completely exclude him from his sexual experience.

But you didn't want to exclude him, his body interjected. *Why else were you watching the door so intently?*

Yeah, you were wondering what was taking him so long, his brain said with disdain. *You know he was just cleaning up after you in the kitchen. I hope he doesn't find that business card. He's so jealous.*

Ollie sat up and swung his feet to the floor. He heard Matt turn on the sink faucet as he pulled a pair of trunks from his dresser and left the bedroom in a hurry.

His shoes were on the mat by the door, and his belt was hanging on the coat rack, but his clothes were missing. He found them in the dry-cleaning hamper in the laundry room, but the pockets were all empty. He looked briefly around the kitchen and then went back to the bedroom, with one ear on the bathroom, and picked up Matt's lounge pants. He found the business card and his wallet in the pocket. He put the card in his wallet and put both in his top dresser drawer.

Ollie grabbed his phone charger, found a shirt, and went to the study to watch TV. He found twenty missed messages from Matt and as many missed calls when he turned his phone back on. There were a handful of voicemails that he deleted after listening to the first two before shutting it off and turning his attention to *Schitt's Creek*.

Matt appeared in the doorway a short while later, an unreadable expression on his beautiful face. He was in one of his US Navy t-shirts and grey sweatpants.

"You coming to bed?"

"Later. I'm not tired just yet," Ollie replied, muting the TV.

"You hungry?"

Ollie shrugged. "Why? Are you making cereal?"

Matt laughed lightly. "I do make a mean bowl of cereal. I meant I could order take-out, if you're hungry."

Ollie looked back at the TV and unmuted it. He wasn't really ready to play nice with Matt, but Matt was making himself hard to resist and Ollie needed to stay strong.

Those fucking sweatpants though. . . .

"Ollie, come here," Matt commanded.

Ollie sighed and put down the remote. He stood and stopped just out of reach, waiting expectantly.

"Ollie," Matt said quietly. "I don't know what else to say or do. Please."

Ollie closed his eyes and sighed after several moments.

Bloody hell, this man.

"Lieutenant, when you said you were going to fuck up, I really wish you had been more clear about just how often you were planning on doing so." He opened his eyes and gave him a wry smile.

Matt sagged slightly and stepped forward to pull Ollie into his arms, kissing his neck.

"I love you."

Ollie thought for a moment and put his hands on Matt's hips. He pressed his thumbs into the flesh above the bone (where Matt often bruised him) and kissed Matt roughly.

Time for head games.

"I'm angry. Okay?" Ollie said expectantly.

Matt pulled back. "What?"

Ollie paused, savoring Matt's shocked expression. "I *am* angry, I don't trust you right now, and I should punish you the way you do me," he added in a whisper. "But I won't."

"Oh, okay." Matt looked away. "I suppose if the situation were reversed, I would be so very, *very* angry with you." He looked back at him, something like a flicker behind his eyes. "Ollie, forgive me, you can trust me."

"Well, I'm glad I didn't have to spell it out for you. But just remember how forgiving I'm being with you, and that it's not weakness. Besides, the shoe won't ever be on the other foot. I will never impregnate someone."

Matt nodded slowly. "I don't think you're weak at all." He paused as though a thought crossed his mind. "Have you ever had sex with a woman?"

"Yes," Ollie answered. "Two. One in secondary and one in college. It was fine." He shrugged. "I could never have done it for ten years though. Their bodies are," he paused wrinkling his nose, "squishy. Don't ever get fat."

Matt ordered sushi and they ate on the loveseat, watching a Marvel movie. Ollie tried to keep his admiring sighs to a minimum when Chris Hemsworth was onscreen, but judging from Matt's irritated insults about Thor, he guessed he wasn't being so subtle. When the movie ended Ollie left the room, leaving Matt to clean up.

Ollie brushed his teeth on autopilot, wondering if he had been too harsh about the whole thing. He and Matt hadn't been together when he got Sam pregnant. He spat in the sink and blew out a breath. Matt had fucked up, and hid it from him, but wouldn't have Ollie done the same in Matt's shoes? He turned off his toothbrush and went into the bedroom, putting his clothes on the bench at the foot of the bed before climbing under the covers.

If they were to move forward, and be solid, Ollie needed to be the mature one, and make sure that Matt never strayed or panicked again. Ollie had a choice: be all in or all out. He could pack up and leave, or stay and nurture their relationship. It was an overwhelming decision, and Ollie did his best to calm the tumult in his mind.

Ollie looked up as Matt came through the bedroom door with a smile and crossed to the bathroom, reappearing a few minutes later. Matt stripped down to his underwear, leaving his clothes on the bench next to Ollie's, and slid into bed next to him.

"Can I touch you?"

Ollie's stomach fluttered at Matt's soft voice. His brain insisted that he stick to his guns for the night. "You can spoon me, but I meant what I said. You punish with violence. I punish with abstinence."

Matt exhaled and wrapped his body around Ollie's, his half-hard dick pressing against Ollie's bottom.

Ollie thought of anything he could to keep himself from growing hard at the feeling of it. He fought it successfully, even though Matt was deliberate in keeping it pressed against Ollie's bottom, especially as it grew fully hard and insistent.

"Lieutenant."

"What?" Matt whispered, his breath warm and minty on Ollie's neck, Matt's lips brushing his ear.

Ollie pulled away and rolled onto his back. "Goodnight," he said firmly, determined to stick to his guns.

Matt let out a heavy, disappointed sigh and rolled onto his back, his erection a bulge under the sheets. Ollie closed his eyes against it.

Ollie was nearly dozing, his breathing finally even and his head clear.

"Why did you have Sebastian Miller's business card?"

Ollie's eyes opened as his stomach fluttered. "Why were you going through my pockets?"

"Don't answer my question with a question. But for your information, I was just getting your stinky suit ready for the dry-cleaners."

"Well, no one asked you to. I was going to do that in the morning." He rolled on his side away from Matt, ending the conversation.

Matt waited for the answer that he sensed he wasn't going to get without prodding. He knew who Sebastian Miller was, had met him once, on a trip to Silicon Valley. He also knew that Sebastian was gay, quite handsome, and had undoubtedly hit on Ollie, just as he had on Matt when they met. He Googled Sebastian while Ollie was watching TV and saw that his latest start-up looked very promising. He was definitely going to keep his eye on it, and his eye on Sebastian.

That Ollie had taken his wallet and the business card from his lounge pants, and then hidden both in his dresser drawer was concerning. Just how much Matt wanted to risk by pressing the issue, when things were so tenuous between them, was another question entirely. He decided to drop it, focusing instead on making sure Ollie wanted to fuck him in the morning.

51

Cape Hope

OLLIE WOKE TO THE SMELL of a freshly showered Matt, pressing himself against his bottom, nuzzling his neck, and kissing the sensitive spot behind his ear. Ollie's morning wood was straining insistently against the front of his underwear desperate for Matt's mouth, or hand, or both, and he surrendered blissfully to Matt's advances, having decided he had punished them both long enough.

"Join me on the roof after your shower," Matt said thirty minutes later as he left the bathroom.

Ollie watched him leave and shampooed his hair, thinking about forgiveness, about Matt's unanswered question about Sebastian, and about the future of their relationship. Ollie had decided to be 'all in' with Matt, while knowing he needed to make Matt work hard for his forgiveness. He knew this time he would stitch his heart together with titanium and Teflon, and he would never be caught vulnerable again.

He turned his thoughts to Sebastian. *Why was I so evasive with Matt about our harmless interaction?*

You wanted Matt on his back foot for a change, where he belongs, his brain responded.

And you felt a spark of attraction, which we are definitely going to ignore, his heart said pointedly to his body. *I'm certain it was because we were feeling so confused.*

Ollie rinsed the shampoo from his hair and ignored his inner dialogue. He was going to throw himself into SharkFinn, and Matt, making sure that they were solid and successful, such that nothing from the past or going forward could ever shake their foundation.

Ollie found Matt basking in the early morning sunlight on the roof deck, dressed in shorts and another tight US Navy t-shirt, looking like a god. Matt stood with a sexy smile and poured more coffee for himself and a mug for Ollie.

"Chuck has invited us to her beach house in Truro," Matt said as he sat on the sectional next to Ollie, the row of arborvitae shielding them from view. "Naomi did the whole house, apparently and, unsurprisingly, it's amazing. Let's get out of the city. We'll scoop Naomi up on our way out."

Ollie smiled. "I've heard a tremendous amount about this Cape Cod of yours. It sounds beautiful and perfect. And we need a reboot," Ollie said with raised eyebrows.

"Excellent. I've rented a boat." Matt grinned knowingly. "You're gonna get to see me on the water. It's where I'm at home."

Ollie made an appreciative sound. "That sounds hot. You in a bathing suit? I can't wait." His eyes skimming Matt's body, his resolve even more solidified.

* * *

They picked Naomi up at her apartment in Brookline after lunch on Friday and headed down Interstate 93 to Route 3. Naomi and Ollie chatting about design ideas and catching up about each other's lives while Matt smiled to himself, thrilled at Ollie's loving behavior all week. Matt had worried about Ollie withholding his affection, or holding on to his anger about Sam, but he had been the opposite. Behind closed doors Ollie had thrown himself wholeheartedly into their relationship, meeting Matt's needs as voraciously, twice during the week waking him out of a deep sleep with his mouth stroking him. Ollie still hadn't told him that he loved him, but Matt understood why, and focused on making sure that he did everything in his power to make Ollie want to.

It was a hot afternoon, but once they crossed the Sagamore Bridge the temperature dropped at least ten degrees. Pulling into Finn's driveway in Truro was like crossing into another world, the crushed stone and seashells crunching under the tires of Matt's Audi signaling their arrival into paradise.

"Wow. I can't wait to see the interior," Ollie said enthusiastically to Naomi, admiring the weathered shingles and large windows as Finn came out the door.

Ollie couldn't believe his eyes as he followed Finn inside, though he knew just how talented Naomi was. Everything was designed around the expansive views of the water, and it felt as though the house went on forever. The main floor was largely an open floorplan with three suites: the large primary suite on one side, and two smaller suites on the other side of the kitchen. There were three more suites upstairs and a large sunny office lined with bookshelves.

"Christ Naomi, this is beautiful." Ollie smiled and kissed her cheek. "You are incredible."

Naomi beamed. "It's my passion. Thank you."

"I got lobsters for dinner," Finn announced. "And I've set up chairs on the beach. Get yourselves changed and, Matt, bring the cooler with you."

Ollie played frisbee on the beach with Matt when Matt became antsy sitting still. Then, while Finn made dinner, they rinsed in the outdoor shower, Matt following Ollie into the stall and getting on his knees.

*　*　*

Ollie woke to the smell of coffee on his side table and Matt's freshly showered skin next to him. He was still full from dinner the night before, and had the slightest bit of a hangover. He took a long sip of his lukewarm coffee and looked at the window, then back at Matt.

"Christ, Lieutenant. I've just realized that your glorious scent, the one that makes my toes curl with pleasure, is the same as the one that is coming in through the window," Ollie said with his nose pressed to Matt's abdomen. "How do you do that? You smell like sun-kissed sand, salty air, and paradise." He pushed the covers down not waiting for an answer.

Matt drove them to the harbor after breakfast, and they loaded their things onto the boat, including the large cooler of food and drinks that Finn and Ollie had packed, and towels and sunscreen. Matt ran through a quick check of the instruments and engine, and then drove out into the bay like he had done it a million times before, though Ollie was guessing he hadn't. Ollie could easily picture him behind the wheel of a military boat, so confident, so calming for the people who served under him. He imagined Matt's SEAL team must have functioned like a well-oiled machine under his command, just like SharkFinn.

Ollie took pictures all day, sending several to his parents, and keeping even more for himself. He must have taken a million of Matt in his short red swim trunks, trunks that reminded him of James Bond's in *Casino Royale*, only Matt managed to look even sexier. He was like a god, especially in the water. Ollie marveled at the way he dove in without a splash (as though the water parted for him in anticipation), how he swam without fear of sharks or currents (or minding the cold), and how his body glistened under the waves like a fish . . . no, like he was Poseidon himself.

After most of the day on the boat and dinner at Mac's in Wellfleet, they dragged the Adirondack chairs to the beach. Matt and Ollie carried the firepit down, smiling at each other, reveling in the moment, Matt holding Ollie's gaze as they walked through the warm sand.

"You're so beautiful," Matt sighed, "and you today, in that little swimsuit of yours." Matt hummed. "Makes me want to move to an island in the Caribbean with you."

"I would move in a heartbeat, for the same reason. You really are something in the water," Ollie replied. "And Christ, your body, I swear I could never get enough of looking at you, touching you."

Matt smiled his flirtatious smile, the one that made Ollie weak in the knees, and lowered the firepit. "I'm gonna touch the hell out of you later." He winked.

Matt filled the cast iron basin with firewood and driftwood and lit it, the sparks rising above the flames and floating away like wishes coming true. They roasted marshmallows and made s'mores as the moon rose over the ocean, Matt sitting back and watching them, drinking his scotch, not wanting the mess of melted marshmallows and chocolate.

The only people they saw was a couple with a large German Shepherd, who stopped to chat and take their picture. Finn was captivated with the dog and watched as they walked away, the well-trained dog on a verbal leash.

"That dog is gorgeous," Finn declared as she pulled out her phone to look up the breeder's information the couple had given her. "I'm definitely getting one!"

"Kodi might have an opinion about that," Matt said sarcastically.

"What an incredible weekend," Ollie said to Matt later, the moonlight shining into the bedroom through the large picture window. "The Cape is magical. You on the Cape are magical. I'm so glad we got out of the city."

Matt smiled. "I agree. I'm gonna get us a place here, but it has to be right on the water. I mean listen to that." He stood next to Ollie near the open side window and listened to the steady sound. He turned and grabbed a towel from the chair. "Come on," he said as he strode out of the bedroom.

They slipped quietly out of the house and to the cabana. Matt spread the beach towel on the bed and untied all the curtains except for the ones facing the ocean.

"Get in there." He smacked Ollie's bottom and smiled when he jumped.

Ollie's eyes shone brightly in the dark as he did as he was told. They undressed each other unhurriedly, Matt murmuring in Italian between kisses. He pulled Ollie into his arms, running a hand down the length of Ollie's body slowly and cupping his bottom firmly with a small sigh. "You look so beautiful in the moonlight."

"So do you. Christ, this is amazing," Ollie breathed against Matt's mouth, reaching between them and taking Matt in his hand. "I can't wait to have you inside me in full view of the ocean."

Matt made a low sound, and kissed Ollie possessively, caressing his tongue as the curtains billowing lightly around them. "Oh, Ollie, I can't wait to *be* inside you in full view of the ocean."

* * *

Matt woke Finn, shaking her shoulder gently. "Come on sleepyhead, suns almost up. Let's run the beach."

Matt laughed as she groaned and rolled out of bed with a sigh.

They ran along the beach, as the sun came up to their right. Matt noticed that Finn's breathing was labored and slowed slightly. His eyes scanned the beach and the waves and the houses sprinkled along the shore. He looked at Finn.

"Something's been on your mind, Chuck. I've sensed it all weekend."

Finn frowned, and then sighed. "I've been offered a job." She smiled. "And I accepted."

"That's great news!"

"It's in Baltimore."

Matt slowed and then stopped. "What? Harvard didn't want you?" He scowled, disappointment welling up inside him.

Finn stopped running and looked away, panting. "Johns Hopkins offered me more freedom, and it's tenure track. I don't want to leave you." She looked out over the water. "Having you and Ollie here together in Boston, is a dream, and the thought of this all the time," she waved back toward her house, "would be bliss. Unless I had a boyfriend of course, in which case you would be a complete ass." She pushed his shoulder lightly as he laughed. "Upside is you could stay with me, have your own room, since you're in DC so much for work. It's maybe an hour drive."

Matt blew out a breath and nodded slowly. "I survived four years of you in Oxford, I suppose I could survive a few more of you in Baltimore. At least we'll be on the same continent, and the best side of said continent," he added with a grin. "Speaking of Baltimore, I'd definitely feel better about you with a German Shepherd at your side."

"Baltimore is beautiful, and perfectly safe, just you wait and see," Finn chastised.

"Can I be selfish and request that it's not forever?" he asked with a soft expression.

Finn looked away and then back with a smile. "If you agree to let me find myself a man, in which case I will force him to come back to Boston."

Matt rolled his eyes. "I would agree to that in a heartbeat, if I thought there was even one man on this planet worthy of you."

Finn put her knuckles to her eyes and turned to run back down the beach. "I just want to get laid, Matt, please, without your voice in the back of my head categorizing the guy's every failing."

He threw his head back and laughed before chasing her down the beach. "Just call me Jiminy."

* * *

The drive back to Boston was quiet, the three of them forlorn about having to go back to work and reality, the sand still in their hair.

"Naomi," Matt said after a long silence as they drove over the Sagamore Bridge. Spending the weekend with her had cemented his plan.

"Yeah?"

"Would you consider doing for Ollie, what Chuck does occasionally for me?" He looked at her in the rearview mirror. "We're coming up on fundraising and holiday seasons, and he could use a gorgeous woman on his arm." He smiled at Ollie.

"Seriously? I'd love to!" she exclaimed happily. "We have so much fun together. What exactly does this entail?"

"Great!" Matt smiled enthusiastically. "Hand holding, a few kisses for appearances, nothing more." He looked at Ollie. "Though he does get pretty handsy when he's been drinking." He gestured with his thumb and winked.

"I do no such thing," Ollie said primly. "That's you!"

Naomi laughed.

"Also, these events are filled with people looking to have their homes, and second homes, and third homes, redecorated. This could be very lucrative for you."

"Great! Ollie can get as handsy as he wants." She patted Ollie's shoulder.

"Thanks, I mean it." Matt looked at her again in the mirror.

52

The Out-of-Towners

OLLIE'S PARENTS CAME at the end of September, and toured the town-house with smiles, marveling over Naomi's design choices, the brightly lit rooms, and the guest suites on the third floor. Matt and David hung back on the tour of the primary suite, checking out the home gym down the hall instead. Matt was pleased with David's approval, not just of the house but of him, and them. It felt like he was finally thawing, and the smile reached his eyes.

* * *

The first few days were a whirlwind of sightseeing, Ollie taking his parents around Boston, showing them all the tourist spots he'd been to with Matt, while Matt worked. Matt rented a Range Rover for a trip to Vermont to see the foliage, and to buy maple syrup, and on the fourth day they toured Newport and the cliff walk, Matt pointing out Finn's ancestors' summer home.

"I got you a reservation at Selene's. It's right next to the State House and the food is amazing. You guys will love it." Matt announced on the drive home. He reached into his coat pocket and withdrew a billfold containing several hundred-dollar bills.

"Won't you be joining us?" David asked from the back seat.

Matt shook his head once as he changed lanes. "I have a meeting."

Ollie looked out the window at Matt's lie and suppressed a sigh.

Ollie and his parents were seated next to the bar, in front of the large window overlooking the Boston Common, so his parents could enjoy the view and people watch. Ollie ordered a pint for himself and a bottle of white for the table, scanning the room, like Matt would.

He turned to his parents with a smile. "What's been your favorite place so far?"

"I loved Newport. Those houses, the architecture, some of them so similar to the country estates of England," David answered, taking a sip of his wine.

"Me too," Maggie replied. "But I especially love the waterfront here, the brick sidewalks, the Custom House, all those condos right on the harbor walk. Just beautiful."

"I agree, I really fell in love with this city. Wait until you see Finn's place on the beach. It's spectacular and beautifully decorated. Her friend Naomi did the design there too."

"We can't wait, sounds wonderful," Maggie said.

"Yes, it certainly does," David agreed, sipping his wine thoughtfully. "How are you, Ollie? Things going well here?"

Ollie nodded with a broad smile. "Oh yes, it's been perfect. I love my job. I've joined a football club. It's been a dream."

"We see that, and it makes us so happy for, and proud of, you," David began. "I just wish Matt could be here, I guess."

"Yes, darling. What your father is trying to say is we hope that you're truly happy, and we do like Matt," she stressed. "We just hope it's not too stifling. Too compartmentalized."

Ollie shook his head with a smile. "No, Mum, Dad, it's perfect. You know I was never swanning around, kissing guys in public. He's really great to me. I'm so happy."

"You must be. You accepted his job offer," David said as the waiter brought the bottle of wine and poured. "People at work still don't know? Don't suspect?"

Ollie sipped his pint and shook his head. "No. I barely see him at work, and when I do it's so busy there's no looks being exchanged or anything. We don't travel together to or from work either. It's not far from the house, I walk, or bike."

David nodded. "Well, that's good. It's apparent there would be difficulty if anyone found out," he said with a glance at Maggie.

"No one is going to find out, Dad. We're very careful," Ollie said emphatically, remembering the disaster that happened with Bill.

The food arrived and they chatted between bites about Cassie, and the family, and Lyon. As they were finishing, Ollie looked up to see two women pulling out barstools towards their end of the bar. His stomach sank, and as he was watched, the woman closest to him turned and met his eye. He saw recognition on her face as she broke into an uncertain smile.

"Oliver?" Imani asked.

Ollie stood, putting his napkin on the table.

"Imani, how nice to see you." He stepped forward stiffly to meet her kiss. "Sam." He smiled tightly over Imani's shoulder.

Sam nodded with a smile, and looked behind him to see who he was with. Her face fell slightly.

"Imani, Sam, these are my parents, David and Maggie."

David half stood. "Nice to meet you." Maggie turned in her chair and smiled politely.

Imani touched his arm, "I hear you live here now." She smiled seductively. "We should have dinner."

"I do, and . . . that would be nice," Ollie replied politely with a nod.

"Is Matt here?" Sam asked hopefully, looking at all the plates on the table.

"No," Ollie scoffed with a small laugh. "My *boss* isn't out to dinner with me and my parents." He pulled a face while wishing he could tell her to fuck all the way off with her pining.

By the way, Sam, Matt sucks cock like a kid eats ice cream, he thought spitefully.

Sam smiled tightly. "No, of course not. Well, when you see him, tell that bastard I said hello." She turned on her heel and took her seat with a toss of her head.

Imani looked at Sam's back and handed Ollie her business card with her eyebrows raised.

"Call me." She smiled and kissed his cheek before joining Sam at the bar.

Ollie turned back to his parents, who were staring at him with their mouths open. He looked for the server and signaled for the check, sitting down warily, finishing his wine in one swallow.

"Who are those women?" his mother asked quietly.

Ollie looked away and rubbed his eye with his fingertips, wishing desperately that he didn't have to explain.

"Sam, is Matt's ex-girlfriend." He winced at his parents' expressions. "And Imani, she thinks, well, that I'm straight," he whispered the last word. "Now you see the main reason why he doesn't join us for dinner." Ollie shrugged unhappily.

His father nodded quietly, and then shook his head with a sigh.

The server appeared with the check and Ollie pulled out the cash and paid, noticing two men greeting Sam and Imani as he and his parents left.

"Join me for a scotch before you go up, please," David said pointedly as they went in the entrance under the front stairs.

Ollie nodded, his feet leaden, knowing his dad wanted the whole story and he couldn't give it to him.

Maggie went to the bedroom as David went to the bar, poured two glasses, and joined Ollie on the couch.

"*Slainte.*"

"So, what's really going on, Oliver?" David asked after a moment of savoring the scotch. "You seemed pretty upset to see those women. And that Sam, didn't seem to be too pleased with Matt."

Ollie took a small sip of scotch. "I'm not a tremendous fan of Sam's past relationship with Matt. She's a particular bone of contention between us," Ollie began, choosing his words carefully. "They were together when I met him, and," he paused, "again when we split this winter."

David frowned and tilted his head. "What? Does he have feelings for her?"

"No, Dad. It's complicated. See, Matt was 'straight' when we met, but obviously not. Not truly," Ollie laughed humorlessly. "She was in love with him. That's why she's cross, she doesn't know about Matt. Nobody here knows. I mean, until me, there was nothing to know, but. . . ." He shrugged.

David looked away with a slightly shocked expression. "I guess that explains how he hides it so well. You do too, even more so now your mother and I have noticed." He swirled his glass, watching the liquid for a moment. "Why did he get back together with her if he doesn't have feelings for her?"

Ollie closed his eyes and blew out a breath. "Matt got scared. Someone saw us come out of a closet, separately, but it was pretty clear we had been up to something. Straight guys don't hang out in the closet together." He exhaled a short laugh and made a face. "It was just a New Year's kiss.

"He got back with her for appearances. Of course, I didn't know that at the time."

David studied him with a look of concern. "Jesus Christ, Oliver. That's what that was all about?"

"Yeah, Dad, but please don't be upset. We're past that and he's better now."

David exhaled a skeptical sound. "Are you sure he won't panic again, or have a change of heart, like he did with her?"

Ollie nodded with certainty. "I'm positive. This winter was a blip because it was all so new for him, and he discovered he couldn't live without me," Ollie smiled lightly. "We're so much more careful now, and we've been through the worst of it, we're stronger than ever. He loves me."

"Well, I'm very glad to hear that," David said and looked at his drink and back at Ollie. "But I think it's awful that you have to be 'careful' with your relationship. I wish he could accept himself, for your sake."

"Me too, but baby steps. Rome wasn't built in a day."

The elevator whirred to life behind them.

"Dad, please don't say anything about Sam, or our conversation. It will upset him tremendously," Ollie said urgently.

"Right. I won't say a word," David answered with a furrowed brow.

Ollie stood as Matt came into the room wearing jeans and a cream-colored t-shirt, his SEAL tattoo peeking out from beneath the bottom of the sleeve.

"You're having scotch without me?" he asked in his gravelly voice, with a sexy grin as he walked to the bar and poured one finger of MacCallum in a glass. He sat in the chair next to Ollie and clinked glasses. "Cheers."

"*Slainte*," David and Ollie said in unison.

"How was dinner?"

"Delicious, wonderful ambiance. Really superb location, lots of history," David answered, watching Matt with speculative eyes.

"Yes, the old parts of Boston have a distinctly British feel to them, for obvious reasons." Matt smiled.

"I have to laugh at what you Americans call old over here."

"Right?"

"What time are we getting on the road tomorrow?" Ollie asked, mindful of his father's scrutiny of Matt. "Mum was asking."

"I have back-to-back meetings until three, two of which you're going to be in, and then we can get on the road," Matt answered, standing up with his glass. "We'll go to Mac's for dinner."

David and Ollie stood, Ollie following Matt to the elevator. "Tell Mum goodnight."

"Goodnight, guys," David called.

Maggie looked up as David came in and paused the TV.

"Well, what happened? What did Ollie say?"

David blew out a breath and began undressing. He went into the bathroom without a word, leaving Maggie waiting impatiently.

David got into bed and recounted the conversation with Ollie, unable to hide his anger at times.

"Some bad-ass Navy SEAL," David scoffed derisively. "It was over nothing, and, Maggie, you saw Oliver this winter. I honestly thought he was going kill himself," David whispered. "He's so happy now, and I respect Matt, and what he has done in his short life, but I can't forget what he did to our boy, and I can't help but worry that he might do it again."

"Jesus." Maggie frowned. "I agree. That seems like an awfully extreme reaction, and this winter was dreadful. I worried for him too, but Matt loves Oliver. Whatever they went through made them stronger. They're fine; we have to believe that." She kissed David's shoulder.

* * *

Ollie emptied his pockets on his dresser and plugged his phone in, watching Matt brush his teeth through the open bathroom door. He joined him at the second sink and began brushing his own, thinking how things were back to how he wanted them, back to how Matt wanted them: Matt in charge, and Ollie with agency.

"Where are we sleeping at Chuck's?" Ollie asked around the toothbrush. "Please don't say the room next to my parents," he added with a dirty grin.

Matt raised his eyebrows, spitting in the sink and rinsing his mouth. "No, Ollie, you make far too much noise for that."

Ollie laughed. "Actually, you're the screamer."

Matt grinned. "We'll put your parents upstairs." He disappeared into the bedroom. Ollie continued brushing his teeth and then turned his toothbrush off and spat in the sink.

"Get in here, Ollie. I want you to make me scream," Matt called.

53

Home by the Sea

OLLIE WOKE TO MATT'S USUAL NOTE. This one saying that he would see him at the HR meeting at noon. He looked at his side table and smiled at the mug of coffee waiting for him. He drank his coffee while scrolling through his phone, answering an email from Stacey about hiring an assistant for him. He got out of bed and saw his bag packed next to Matt's and smiled again.

Matt was so organized and efficient and knew exactly what Ollie would need at the beach, and what he wanted Ollie to wear while they were there. Ollie took a quick shower and put his cleansers, lotions, balm, and hair products and toothbrush in his toiletry bag after blow drying his hair. He donned his navy Tom Ford suit, with a white shirt and a pink and white polka dot tie, and went downstairs in search of his parents.

"I'm just off to work, but Matt and I will be back around three and then we'll go straight to the beach after he and I change."

"Sounds wonderful. Your father and I are going to pop over to the Trident bookstore on Newbury grab a bite and a book. I think there's an author reading too that we're going to try to catch," Maggie answered, kissing Ollie's cheek. "You look so handsome," she added with a proud smile as she patted his chest.

"Thanks, Mum. Matt bought me this suit." He looked down at himself. "It's really the tailoring that makes it. Matt has the best. Said Tony worked for his mother."

"You look very smart," David chimed in.

"Oh, is Matt's mother a seamstress?"

"She was. He said she made all their clothes for years, until his sisters wanted store-bought." Ollie laughed lightly. "Matt takes care of her now so she doesn't have to work. I think she just makes things for the grandkids and such. You should meet her next time you come. She's lovely."

"I would love to meet her," Maggie said enthusiastically. "Wait, does she know?"

"Yes, I met her at Christmas, and somehow, she just knew. Mother's intuition." Ollie shrugged. "None of his sisters know." A shadow flitted across Ollie's face. "Finn's dad knows."

"I wondered," David remarked.

"Oh?" Ollie stopped zipping his folio case and looked at his dad. Unease burbling in his belly.

"He said some cryptic stuff to Matt at the graduation party. He also said some very kind and flattering things about you," his father added with a smile.

"Really?" Ollie felt a small glow of happiness. *Maybe Bill didn't hate him after all.* "Well, I'm off. See you around three."

Ollie watched his parents have the same reaction to Finn's beach house he had as they pulled into her driveway. He gave them a quick tour, listening as they praised the space and gasped at the view from their bedroom, before they headed to Mac's Shack in Wellfleet. Matt parked in the back of the lot and led them to the outside bar, ordering a round before going into the dining room to eat.

The restaurant was crowded, the food delicious, and Matt was relaxed, leaning back in the banquette with a satisfied smile as he listened to Ollie's parents. Ollie noticed again that there was something about Matt being close to the ocean that instantly changed him, relaxed him. Ollie looked around the dining room with a pleasant feeling in his belly before bringing his gaze back to Matt, who was watching him with inquisitive eyes. Matt tilted his head with a soft look and continued his conversation with Maggie. Ollie just smiled broadly and drank his beer.

Their meals came and conversation turned to Matt's time on the Cape as a teen, and accompanying his sister Lisa on her trips to Finn's parents' house on Nantucket.

"Oh, your poor sister. You as her chaperone." Ollie made a face and rolled his eyes.

Matt laughed and gave Ollie a look that said he was going to pay for that eye roll later.

"Well, I can see how you fell in love with it. It's beautiful," Maggie said. "We never went to the beach when the kids were young. We always go to David's brother Lloyd's in Lyon, near the river."

"Ollie told me a little bit about the chateau." Matt nodded. "Sounds beautiful."

"It is." David looked at Maggie in agreement. "You should come with us some time."

Ollie glanced at Matt and then shook his head. "I don't think so, Dad, but thank you."

"Oh right," David looked at Matt and sighed quietly.

Matt shrugged. "Maybe." Ollie's eyes widened in disbelief. "If we're there for work, and they'd be interested in meeting Ollie's boss."

"I think they'd love to meet you. And you know, the French are very open," David said pointedly.

Matt looked away and flagged the waiter for the dessert menu.

They said their goodnights to Ollie's parents in the living room and Ollie watched Matt's back as he followed him into the bedroom, feeling as though he could never get tired of looking at him and his beautiful body. He closed the door and leaned back against it.

"Matt."

Matt turned expectantly as he pulled his sweater over his head. "Yeah?"

Ollie looked at the trident tattoo over Matt's heart, positioned as if it were guarding it. He knew he was the one person that trident was ever lowered for.

"I love you," he breathed, and held Matt's gaze.

He watched Matt's face soften with something like relief as he exhaled with a small smile.

"Oh god, Ollie. I love you *so* much. Come here." He gestured with his arms open and Ollie stepped into his embrace, melding his body against Matt's with a whole-body sigh.

* * *

Ollie woke to an empty bed and a note as usual. He sighed happily at Matt's sweet compulsion, and from the passionate memories of the previous night. Their chemistry had always been off the charts, but the way Matt had loved every inch of him after he finally said those three words took Ollie to new heights and solidified his resolve.

Matt was the only man for him; they were made for each other.

He brushed his teeth and went in search of coffee knowing his parents would be up soon. Matt had programmed the machine and the coffee was just finishing brewing as Ollie pulled out the things he brought to make for breakfast. He filled the electric kettle with water for tea and turned on the oven.

His parents came into the kitchen as he was taking the bacon out of the oven.

"Morning. There's tea and coffee, and breakfast will be ready soon." Ollie gestured to the counter where he had set out mugs and tea bags. "Did you sleep well?"

"Like a dream," Maggie answered and smiled at David. "We had the window open a bit and the ocean was just magical to listen to."

They all looked up at the slider as Matt came in from the outdoor shower, carrying his running clothes and sneakers against his thigh, with a towel slung low around his waist. His hair was still wet and tousled, and his torso and tattoos glistened with water droplets.

God he's a vision, Ollie thought and wiped his chin reflexively.

"Morning," Matt said with an upnod and walked past them down the hall to the bedroom.

Ollie tore his eyes away and found his mother staring after Matt with her mouth open. Maggie caught Ollie's eye and blushed.

"Maybe I should get a tattoo," David interjected irritatedly.

Maggie laughed and kissed his cheek. "If a tattoo would make you look like that, I will drive you to the parlor right now."

Ollie threw his head back and laughed.

And that gorgeous fucking man is all mine, he thought as he turned back to breakfast.

"Does he run every morning?" David asked, pouring hot water into a mug.

"Yes, I think ten or twelve kilometers," Ollie answered, scraping the melon he had diced into the big bowl with the other cut fruit.

Matt appeared a moment later, dressed in jeans and a t-shirt, his hair still damp and tousled, his feet bare and sexy.

He popped a piece of bacon in his mouth. "What was so funny?"

Ollie looked at his mother and snickered. "Nothing."

Matt shrugged. "Where's the rest of breakfast, I'm starving."

Ollie gave him an empty bowl and pushed the large bowl of fruit his way with a spoon. He poured a mug of coffee and put it in front of Matt.

"The frittatas are almost done. You want water?"

"Yes, please."

Ollie poured a big glass of water and handed it to Matt who took it and drank deeply, handing it back to him to refill when it was empty. Ollie glanced at his father who was watching them with a judgey twist to his mouth. He turned away and filled the glass, refusing to feel bad about taking care of the man he loved.

Matt took his bowl of fruit and mug of coffee to the long farm-house table in front of the windows that overlooked the sand and ocean beyond. David joined him, sitting across, while Maggie helped Ollie get breakfast and juice set on the table. Ollie put the glass of water in front of Matt before sitting down next to him and making a plate.

Matt covered Ollie's bare foot with his under the table while holding a conversation with David. His warm arch cupping the hump of Ollie's foot protectively. Ollie smiled at Matt's profile, and took a bite of fruit while his heart beat madly in his chest.

I love you, Ollie thought and then stared down at his plate. *I never stopped loving you, you bastard.*

Matt had two full plates of food and sat back with his hands laced on top of his head. "Delicious as always, Ollie. Thank you." He smiled with a wink.

Ollie returned his gaze with a warm feeling in his chest as Matt's phone buzzed on the kitchen island. Matt squeezed Ollie's thigh tightly before jumping up.

"Hey, Chuck, we're just enjoying your view." He smiled at the three of them, the phone to his ear. "No, but I can be," he said and walked to the slider, closing it behind him.

Ollie and his parents watched as he looked right and then left, and headed toward the water. Matt stopped halfway down the wooden boardwalk and turned to look back at the house, an incredulous expression on his face that morphed into a giant smile as he looked to his right. He held up his finger to say 'back in a minute,' and then continued at a light jog to the beach, turned left, and disappeared.

"I wonder what that was all about?" David mused.

Ollie was beginning to get a little antsy, when forty-five minutes later, he finally saw Matt walking back up to the house, grinning from ear to ear.

"What is it?" Ollie stood as his parents looked up from the couch.

Matt picked him up without a word and swung him around, taking his face in both hands and kissing him soundly on the mouth when he put him back down. Ollie's eyes nearly popped out of his head as he looked at his parents and blushed; their eyes nearly as wide.

"Chuck," Matt laughed, his blue eyes shining happily. "Put a deposit down on the house next door for me. I pass papers in a month." He bit his lip and held Ollie's gaze intently. "We're gonna have a beach house."

"Here? Oh my god, that's fantastic!" Ollie cried and looked happily at his parents who stood and hugged them both at the news.

"We'll celebrate over lunch, in P-Town," Matt announced. "Let's leave in thirty minutes or so," he added with a nod, and left the room.

"Sounds perfect," Maggie answered.

"Ollie," Matt called expectantly from the bedroom.

Ollie stepped through the door and closed it behind him. Matt was still grinning but his eyes were hot.

"I need you."

Ollie looked over his shoulder, and back at Matt. "They're in the living room, and you're not quiet."

"I don't fucking care. Jesus, I just kissed you in front of them. I must be going insane." He pulled Ollie to him and kissed him, his tongue eager and insistent as he steered Ollie to the massive window. "I will be insane if I can't have you right now. Christ, I'm so happy, I'm horny," he said against Ollie's lips and pushed down his sweats as Ollie undid the button and zipper on Matt's jeans.

He reached behind his head and pulled his shirt off as Ollie did the same. He drew Ollie into his arms, savoring his smooth, warm skin.

"God, you smell like heaven," Matt said between kisses, holding his head between his hands and coaxed his mouth open, sweeping his tongue slowly through Ollie's mouth. "Grab the sill," Matt commanded, as he turned Ollie to face the ocean, running the palm of his hand slowly down Ollie's spine before lowering to his knees. "By this time next year, I'm gonna be fucking you with this view every damn day."

Thirty-five minutes later they departed for the tip of the Cape. It was a gorgeous fall day and the streets were swarming with pedestrians, many walking arm-in-arm or holding hands. Matt suspected that Ollie wanted them to do the same, but as much as he wanted to claim Ollie for the world to see, he would never risk it.

Someone might recognize me.

You're on the verge of great things, Bill's words echoed.

Matt steered them into a few art studios, hoping to get some inspiration for the new house. He'd been soaring internally, his heart so full and happy with how things had gone all weekend, it took him a moment to realize he was surrounded by paintings of naked men and Ollie and Maggie were oohing and aahing over the images.

"We're not hanging any of these at the house," Matt said with a frown. He looked around at the other customers in the shop to be sure he wasn't overheard.

"Oh, I dunno that you should give an outright no." Ollie shrugged and swept his arm at the wall in front of him. "I think one of these might be of you. That one in particular." He pointed. "Look at the muscular dimples above the ass cheeks. Thumbprints of god, just like yours."

Matt felt himself blush as he looked at Maggie who was chuckling as she turned away.

"You're ridiculous, Oliver. That's not me, and we're not buying that." He leaned in close to Ollie's ear. "I'm gonna give you some thumbprints from god later. I'll make sure they stay all week."

Matt quirked his eyebrow and turned away at Ollie's quiet gasp. Ollie was so easy to rile, and Matt had to subtly adjust his dick as he left the shop.

They shopped for souvenirs after lunch, and stopped at Mac's seafood market on the way out of town to pick up lobsters for dinner. Matt sent Ollie down to the ocean to get water for the big lobster pot.

Finn's cabana was covered in heavy canvas for the winter, but the lounge chairs were still on the deck. They sat and soaked up the afternoon sun before dinner, Maggie reading a novel and David dozing. Ollie turned his head to find Matt staring at him with an inscrutable expression. He smiled in return and held his gaze. Matt reached out and laced his fingers through Ollie's, then turned his face back to the sky. Ollie's stomach did a little somersault and he closed his eyes contentedly, wishing the day would never end.

* * *

David brushed his teeth, lost in thought and looking in the mirror, but not seeing himself. He joined Maggie in the bed which was so much bigger than their bed at home; super-sized, like everything in America. He settled under the covers and listened to the ocean through the open window.

Maggie put her book down. "Everything okay?"

"What?" David turned his head to look at her. "Oh, yes, fine." He let out a big breath.

Maggie waited.

"I just can't help but think that someone's going to figure out about them, and he's going to panic again, or that he's so in denial that he can't ever be truly happy, can he? Can't go anywhere alone with the person he loves? Will come to Lyon but as his boyfriend's *boss*?" David shook his head. "What a bloody way to live. God, and Ollie's completely fine with it."

"Oh, darling. Still worried about that? Matt loves him. He had his crisis, but realized he couldn't live without him. It won't happen again. Lots of people are private about their romantic lives." Maggie touched David's arm. "They're fine, don't worry."

"How can I not worry? Ollie's like a 1950s housewife around him. He watches him like he's a god, and I can't imagine what Ollie's like at work. And Christ, work?" David said emphatically. "If Matt decides he's done, Ollie can't keep working there. So, it'll be a broken heart *and* a broken career. I just worry. I mean, he has all his eggs in one basket here, and Matt dropped him like a hot potato once already."

Maggie winced. "Believe me, I wish I could wave a magic wand and protect my children, I know you do too. But Ollie's a grown man. We can't make his decisions for him, or tell him what to do anymore, and if we try, he'll just shut us out. He's got a great life here, and you know I never wanted him to leave the UK.

"I think what you're missing is that Matt watches Ollie like *he's* a god. As he should, because we both know what an amazing man our son is. He's just like you." She smiled. "Matt is Mr. Man around you, so I can see how you would miss it. But when you're not looking, or especially when you're not around, Matt can't take his eyes off Ollie. He's changed his life for him, he bought that beautiful row house, *gave* Ollie the flat on the first-floor. He called that beach house theirs. He loves him; he's not going back to being the unhappy man he was. He tried that, and barely lasted three months." Maggie smiled and crossed the bed to David. "Don't worry. I think they're going to be as happy as we have been." She kissed him gently.

David pulled back after a moment. "Oh god. Are they going to bicker over the dishwasher and fight over which show to watch?" He mock frowned.

"You asshole." Maggie leaned her head back and laughed. David kissed her exposed throat and rolled her onto her back.

*   *   *

On Sunday they packed the car and headed back to Boston for Ollie's afternoon soccer game and his parents' flight back to London at eight. It was hard to leave the paradise of Truro, but the ride home was filled with happy discussions about the new house, which they had all toured, and the planned renovations, and all the things Maggie and David loved about their visit.

Matt dropped Ollie and his parents at Logan after Ollie's soccer game, waiting in the cell phone lot with jumbled thoughts until Ollie called for him.

"That was a fantastic visit. Thank you," Ollie said with a smile as he got back in the car. "My parents really love you."

"They're great people. I enjoyed having them." Matt smiled tightly as he navigated traffic back to Marlborough Street. "Your dad though. He was giving off a strange vibe to me on the Cape. Said some cryptic shit. What was that about?"

Shit. Ollie looked worriedly at Matt's profile. "No, he wasn't," he lied. He knew exactly what his father was on about, and it cut because it meant David didn't trust Matt, and Matt was picking up on it. Matt frowned and glanced briefly at Ollie. "Are you telling me I was imagining things?"

Ollie was silent for several beats. *You'll have to do better than that, Lieutenant, if you want to trap a lawyer.*

"How am I supposed to answer that?" Ollie scoffed. "Just get us home so I can shower off the mud and enjoy having you all to myself again."

PART THREE

EVENTING

54

Papercut

OLLIE WAS IN HIS HOME OFFICE, getting caught up with work emails after his parents' visit, when Matt appeared in his doorway just after lunch.

"Where'd this come from?" Matt asked. Ollie looked up from his computer to see Matt holding a business card in his hand.

"I don't know, what is it?"

"Imani's business card." He raised his eyebrows.

Ollie looked away. *Fuck, I thought I threw that away.*

"We ran into them at Selene's."

"Them?" Matt asked in a strangled voice.

Ollie nodded. Matt closed his eyes.

"Ollie, please tell me she didn't say anything. Oh god, why didn't you tell me?"

Ollie exhaled a mirthless laugh through his nose. "She called you a bastard. But that's it. And it wasn't worth making you upset over."

Matt wiped his hand over his face. "In front of your parents."

Ollie nodded again.

"What did you tell them?"

"Just that she was an ex, and that she was still upset over the break-up. That's all," he added meaningfully.

"I knew I wasn't fucking imagining things," Matt said angrily and ripped the card in half, throwing it in the trash. He left the room, his body rigid.

Ollie closed his eyes and sat back in his chair. *What will the punishment be this time,* he wondered.

Ollie was making dinner when he heard the elevator go up to the fourth floor. Matt came down the stairs thirty minutes later. He was freshly showered and dressed in lounge pants and a t-shirt, having worked out in the home gym after his run. He filled his empty Hydroflask from the fridge dispenser and kissed Ollie's neck.

"I'm starving, how long till dinner."

"I bet you are. You've been gone all afternoon."

Ollie pushed the bowl of crackers and charcuterie board of cheese, apple slices, and meats that he had assembled in anticipation of Matt's hunger, toward him.

"This will tide you over. Dinner will be ready in less than ten minutes." He paused with a sigh. "Now you're going to be up all-night working, aren't you?"

Matt shrugged stuffing a hunk of cheese, soppressata, and several apple slices in his mouth and turned away with a handful of crackers. He got the cocktail shaker, shoveled the crackers into his mouth and filled the shaker with ice. Ollie watched as he made himself a martini and cringed slightly.

"You want to talk about it?" Ollie asked. "You save your martinis for two occasions, and I don't think this is the celebratory one."

"It's not. And no, I don't particularly want to talk about it right now."

Ollie turned with a sigh and took the sizzling chicken, shrimp, peppers, and onions, out of the oven. He set out the shredded cheese, sour cream, guacamole and salsa, and unwrapped the tortillas from the tinfoil.

"Smells amazing, what are we having?"

Matt came to stand behind him, a strange vibe emanating from him. The hairs on the back of Ollie's neck raised slightly.

"Chicken and shrimp fajitas."

"Yum." Matt made four and began eating them standing at the island, drinking his martini between bites. Ollie made one and sat in a barstool opposite him.

"You should sit, I'd like the company." Ollie looked at him with raised eyebrows. "I would think a margarita would taste better with these. I could make you one."

"Tequila makes me angry. You don't want me drinking that tonight."

Ollie widened his eyes and looked away with a sinking feeling. "I guess that answers my question as to why you don't drink it."

Matt sat in the stool next to him and continued to eat.

Ollie chewed slowly as he measured his words. "They were joined by two blokes as we were leaving, if that's any consolation."

Matt looked at him. "Some." He finished his drink and made himself another, returning to the island after skewering a few more olives. "I just fucking wish she didn't have a homing beacon on us. This is my city. I don't want to live in fear of seeing her everywhere." He walked agitatedly to the pan and stuffed a few pieces of chicken in his mouth, his muscles flexing with the motion. He chewed and held Ollie's gaze. "But . . . that's not the only thing I'm upset about."

Ollie looked down at his plate, uncomfortable with Matt's probing gaze. "What else has made you angry, Lieutenant?" He glanced back up to find Matt still staring at him.

"What exactly did you say to your father?" He raised his eyebrows expectantly.

"I told you. That she was an ex, and still upset about the break-up." Ollie finished his fajita.

Matt narrowed his eyes. "I thought about it on my run. He was watching me funny when I joined you for scotch, and on the Cape. He was perfectly pleasant but there was a vibe, some comments. So, I'm gonna ask you again. What *exactly* did you tell your father?"

Ollie frowned at Matt's tone. "That you were with Sam when we met, and again in the winter when you *dumped* me, because you got scared," he said pointedly. "And that it was complicated, that you were straight when we met and no one here knows about you because there was nothing to know until me."

Matt looked away. He popped another piece of chicken into his mouth, picked up his drink and left the kitchen.

Ollie was in the home theater on the third floor, avoiding Matt and his dark mood, when he saw motion in the doorway. He muted the telly expectantly.

"I'm furious with myself for having done this to you, *to us*. I'm furious with her, and her popping up all over the place," Matt said angrily from the doorway, his eyes dark. "What I did with Sam this winter was poorly planned, poorly executed, and completely unlike me. And I am angry about the consequences of my horrible judgement."

"People make mistakes, Matt. You're human for Christ's sake, and I've forgiven you. It's done," Ollie said firmly.

"I'm so angry with her for being a constant reminder of how I hurt you, and for your father to see that, and know about it too, is such an embarrassment." Matt looked down and then back up at Ollie, his eyes still dark. "I'm angry you told him anything."

"Matt, he's my father. We're close, he was worried," Ollie said defensively.

"What happens with us, is just for us. I don't want you saying anything to anyone," Matt said firmly.

Ollie looked away, feeling as though he had betrayed the sanctity of their relationship, but resenting being chastised. "I'm sorry, it's just . . . I'm used to being open with my dad when he asks me questions. He was worried, and I didn't go into detail. I was vague, I swear."

"Okay. Just remember, I like and guard my privacy, and I expect you to as well," Matt said, his eyes fidgety. He brought his gaze back to Ollie and sighed. "I hate that I hurt you, and you being confronted by my mistake continually." He shook his head. "You don't deserve that. I feel like . . . it feels like I failed you."

"You haven't failed me. I don't care if we run into her. I don't love it, but I'm no longer worried that you'll leave me for her. You've explained.

"Unless there is something more you're not telling me, and you're worried that she'll blurt it out." Ollie studied Matt carefully. "I know you've implied that there's something you did, in order to get her to agree." Ollie felt the familiar clench of jealousy and anger at the memory. "I *never* want to know what that was, because I have accepted it, and it's done and in the past. And you did it for us. I pray she doesn't blurt it out, but please know that while I will hate hearing what happened with you two, I have already forgiven you, and I don't want to speak of it ever again, *Matteo*." He looked down and took a breath. "Is there something more than that?"

Ollie met Matt's eye, and sat silently, waiting, willing Matt to say no.

Matt shook his head. "No. No, there is nothing more."

Ollie blew out his breath. "Good. Shall I get you a hair shirt, or will I be your hair shirt tonight?" he whispered feeling a twinge of relief and a twinge at the thought of Matt being rough.

You really are a bloody masochist, his brain scolded.

Matt's eyes flared as he adjusted himself in his pants, and the twinge in Ollie's sweats became a raging hard on.

Proudly so, his body responded.

"Do you want to be? I'll go easy on you. You're not the one I'm truly angry with," Matt said quietly, his deep raspy voice raising the hairs on Ollie's arms.

Ollie licked his lips as he stared at the front of Matt's lounge pants, and then back up at his face. "I told you before, I wouldn't dream of asking you to take it easy on me, Lieutenant."

Matt made a small sound of pleasure that Ollie felt in his soul.

"Follow me."

* * *

Ollie startled when Matt ducked into his office at work and closed the door. It had been two days since he had followed Matt willingly into the shower, and he looked up at him expectantly.

"I had Stacey make you an appointment with Tony. It's in your calendar. I bought you a tux; it's a Tom Ford of course. You look magnificent in his clothes, and his underwear. Though I prefer you out of both," he added with a smile.

"Well, thank you. When's the appointment?" He leaned back in his chair and crossed his arms.

"Tomorrow morning. I'll drop you and wait. Shouldn't take long."

Ollie laughed in disbelief. "You want me to disrobe in front of someone so soon? Marks and all." He looked down at himself. "You gave me hickeys this time, Lieutenant. He's going to think I was with a teenager."

Matt exhaled a laugh. "Those are for my eyes only." He gave Ollie a burning look. "You'll keep your t-shirt on."

Matt left as suddenly as he had appeared, leaving Ollie to stare after him with a happy sigh.

55

Tuxes and Tumult

MATT'S PHONE BUZZED and he smiled at the name on the screen.

"Hey, Chuck. Welcome back to the land of cool people."

"Fuck off." Finn laughed. "I was calling to find out when the first party Naomi and I are joining you for will be, but now I'm thinking she and I are gonna head to Cabo, and you fuckers can find someone else to cover for you."

Matt grinned. "As if it's not already in your calendar circled a million times in red. And, Chuck, you can threaten all you want, but you know there's nowhere you'd rather be than by my side. You miss me, admit it."

"Your fucking ego." Finn laughed. "Can we stay downstairs? It'll be easier."

"Of course. You guys can come anytime and stay however long you want. You know that. That's why I gave you a key."

"I don't have a key to Ollie's place."

"Well, I will remedy that. See you Thursday."

* * *

Matt and Ollie arrived home after work to find Finn and Naomi having wine and getting ready to go out, blasting music through the Bluetooth speakers.

Ollie raised his eyebrows.

Matt shrugged with a grin. "It's Chuck. And I'm giving her a key to your flat, unless you want them staying up here?" he trailed off.

Ollie smiled. "Please, give her the key."

Matt pulled a key on a keychain that said Chuck, out of his pocket and handed it to Finn.

"You ladies finish getting ready downstairs. We leave in an hour."

Finn took the key with a kiss on Matt's cheek, grabbed her garment bag and wine glass, and followed Naomi to the elevator.

An hour later, Matt and Ollie took the elevator to the first floor, dressed in their tuxedos. Matt kissed Ollie swiftly before the doors opened.

"You look so fucking fine. Tonight's gonna be hard."

"*Hard?*" Ollie asked with a salacious chuckle, cupping the front of Matt's pants.

Matt groaned and nodded emphatically. "Yes."

The doors opened to reveal Finn and Naomi waiting for them. Finn in a knee length red silk halter dress that dipped between her breasts and tied with a long bow over her bare back. Naomi was wearing a strappy grey velvet floor-length gown with a plunging neckline and slit up to her mid-thigh.

Matt widened his eyes. "Jesus Christ, ladies. We wanted to have fun tonight, not have to fight every man in the room." He pulled Finn in for a light kiss, making sure to not muss her red lipstick.

Ollie did the same to Naomi. "Christ, you look beautiful," he said with a flirty grin.

She blushed, pleased. "Holy shit your accent, in that tux . . . Mr. Bond."

Matt grinned. "Right? You should hear him speak French." He waggled his eyebrows. "Let's get to the ball."

The photographers were in full force for the event, and one of them, a society photographer, recognized Finn. They posed for pictures together and then as couples before moving into the ballroom. Ollie thought briefly of the pictures of Matt with Sam, wishing he could've been in his spot under Matt's arm instead of posing with Naomi, and twisted his mouth before pushing those thoughts aside.

Matt and Ollie headed straight to one of the several bars for drinks, while Finn and Naomi figured out where their table was. Matt had bought two tables for work; all of his VPs were there with their dates or spouses. Finn and Naomi made their rounds at the two tables, Naomi being introduced as Ollie's girlfriend, and everyone greeting Finn familiarly, knowing her as Matt's silent partner and on-again-off-again girlfriend. Matt and Ollie watched Finn and Naomi as they headed to the silent auction items, their blonde heads close to each other before separating and browsing the descriptions.

Matt scanned the room briefly, finding too many eyes on Finn and glanced at Ollie with a scowl before striding off in Finn's direction.

Ollie watched Matt, with his natural fluid ease, working the room, making his way to Finn, and decided to go in search of Naomi, coming up behind her as Matt had done to Finn. "See anything you like?" he murmured against her neck.

She reached up and cupped his chin. "Just you," she said with a smile and kissed him over her shoulder.

Ollie squeezed her slim waist and stood to her left, his hand resting low on her hip as he watched Matt and Finn take their seats. He scanned the ballroom, his eyes screeching to a halt as they landed on Sam, sitting at a table by the window, watching Matt and Finn with wounded and angry eyes. He looked back at Matt in panic at the same moment Matt noticed Sam, and saw a cloud pass over Matt's face as he turned away quickly.

Ollie shifted his attention to Naomi who was moving down the auction table and thought of how awful it would be to be Sam, witnessing Matt and Finn cuddling. As much as he didn't like Sam (and he *really* didn't like her), he knew exactly how she was feeling. It had been devastating to see photos of Matt and Sam together.

How does anyone move on from that man?

Ollie couldn't and hadn't.

He was fully in Matt's orbit, and his heart sang knowing that Matt wanted and needed him there.

Matt pulled Finn into his lap and wrapped his arms around her waist as she draped hers around his shoulders. "I hope you enjoy these things with me as much as I do with you. I'm really grateful for you, I hope you know that," he said quietly against Finn's throat. "I know someday you're gonna find a guy and then I'll really be heartbroken."

Finn searched his face, with a soft expression. "You will always be my number one. He will have to understand that. It's a requirement." She kissed him softly as he squeezed her waist. "I'll find myself an Ollie, if I'm lucky," she added with a smile and moved to her chair.

Matt looked around the crowded room, recognizing a few faces, until his eyes landed on Sam, watching him from a few tables away. He shifted his gaze quickly, cursing to himself, and worrying about Ollie as he finished his drink. He looked for Ollie as he made his way to the bar with Finn's drink order, refusing to be flustered. He ordered a bourbon, two white wines, and a beer, and put a twenty in the tip jar.

Ollie appeared at his elbow, wearing a guarded expression and took his and Naomi's drinks. Matt noticed Ollie's step falter when he turned and sighed quietly after picking up his drink and Finn's when he found himself (unsurprisingly) face to face with Sam.

She was wearing a backless, form-fitting, silver dress, that cut straight like a blade across her collar bone and fell well above her knee. Her hair was twisted into a French knot with loose tendrils framing her face. Matt glanced at Ollie's back and hoped he really meant what he said about not caring if they bumped into her again.

"Hello, Sam. You look beautiful," he said with a polite smile as his gut churned.

"Hi, Matt," she replied with a tilt to her head, her dress catching the light as she moved. "I thought you might be here."

Matt laughed humorlessly through his nose, remembering this was the event where they had met two years ago.

"You are back with her then," Sam said simply, a wounded look passing over her features. "I knew it."

"Sam," he said quietly. "You are a wonderful, beautiful person. I never wanted to hurt you. Chuck is the only woman I have ever loved." He gave her a conciliatory look, speaking the truth.

Sam moved her jaw, and swallowed. "Yeah, her pictures all over your condo should have been my first warning. That she had a key to your place should've been my second." She shook her head. "I should've known better," she whispered and turned to the bartender, dismissing Matt.

Matt caught Ollie's expectant look as he returned to the table and gave him a small shrug. Ollie nodded once and turned to put his arm on the back of Naomi's chair, kissing her bare shoulder as she spoke to the woman on her other side.

I'm so lucky, Matt thought and then turned his attention to Finn.

"Cheers." Matt clinked his glass to Finn's.

"Sam's here I see," she said quietly. "Is that going to be a problem?" She shifted her eye to Ollie briefly.

"No, but I gotta tell you something, and I don't want the shock to register on your face, okay?"

Finn gave him a wide smile. "Okay, how's this?"

"A little too bright, Chuck, but you're on the right track." He grinned briefly and then drew back his smile. "I got Sam pregnant."

Finn's eyes widened briefly but she kept her smile. "What the fuck? When?"

"Yeah. Not my proudest moment in the history of Ollie and me." He gave her the pertinent details, studying her eyes for judgment. "Ollie knows."

"Whoa," Finn breathed through her smile, "that is some big-time shit." She touched his face gently. "I wish you had told me."

"Like I said, it wasn't my proudest moment." He gave her a wry smile. "I did not want to have a baby with her." He blew out a breath, happy she hadn't judged him. "I feel awful for saying it, but I dodged a bullet there. In a perfect world, you would be the mother of my children." He kissed her shoulder.

"You keep cock-blocking me and you'll get that wish, you jerk."

Matt threw his head back and laughed. "All part of my master plan. I remember that pact we made. I only have to make sure you stay single for less than a decade now. I've done harder things in the same amount of time, as you know." He shrugged and wiped his hands against each other. "This will be easy peasy."

After dinner, Naomi headed to the bathroom and Finn went to bid on some auction items while Ollie grabbed another beer at the bar.

"See anything good?" Ollie asked Finn as he sidled up to her.

Finn smiled, her eyes even with his in her stilettos. "A few fun things. Not many for four though." She leaned her shoulder against his.

He touched her waist and felt her stiffen as someone appeared on her other side. He gripped her hip tightly when he saw who it was.

"Hi, Sam," Finn said brightly. "Love your dress."

Sam smiled at Ollie. "Hello, Oliver. You look very handsome."

He gave her a tight smile. "Hello, Sam. You're looking well."

"Thanks." Sam shifted her gaze to Finn and tilted her head. "You're all finished with school then?"

"Yes, I'm teaching at Johns Hopkins."

Sam studied her intently, and flicked a glance toward Matt's table. "Oh, so you don't live here, but you two are back together? How's that working?"

Finn smiled tightly and flicked a glance at Ollie. "He's in DC quite a bit, and I'm here. We make it work."

"When did you guys get back together?"

"Why do you ask?"

"Did he tell you about us? About our *baby*," she said harshly. A wounded expression flitted across her face as she swayed ever so slightly in her stilettos.

Ollie let out a breath. Sam was clearly drunk and he wondered if he should step in.

Finn nodded. "Yes, Matt tells me everything," she replied calmly. "I'm sorry for your loss, but I know you weren't planning on keeping it. Who are you here with?"

"A guy I've been seeing since this summer. Toby. He treats me like a queen," Sam replied haughtily.

"That's wonderful," Finn said sweetly. "Matt only wants you to be happy. We both do. Toby is probably wondering where you are." She met Ollie's eye and made to move away.

"You stole him from me," Sam said angrily, and Ollie felt Finn cringe alongside him. "We were back together. We talked about having kids, and then you crooked your little finger and he went running to the UK. I knew when he got back that you had sunk your teeth into him again. You couldn't stand the thought of him happy with someone else. For fuck's sake, you don't even live here," she scoffed. "I would move anywhere he was. Doesn't seem like he's much of a priority for you.

"I honestly don't know what he sees in you. I think you're a bitch and you just string him along. You should shit or get off the pot." Sam finished her diatribe, her face flushed with anger.

Ollie's body went cold as he felt his own face flush. He searched the room for Matt and found him talking with Naomi, looking at them with barely concealed worry. Naomi nodded at Matt before heading over.

Ollie looked back at Sam. He winced at the anger and hurt on her face, and wondered at the type of person who could crush someone like that, and do it without feeling. Matt had broken both their hearts, but he had been cruel to Sam in a way that Ollie couldn't fathom. He blew out a breath as Naomi's overly bright voice cut in.

"There you are!" she exclaimed looping her arm through Finn's. "Come see this auction item you won't believe it. Excuse us," Naomi said without looking at Sam. "You too, Ollie." She grabbed his arm and pulled them away.

"Who the hell was that?" Naomi looked at Finn once they were out of earshot.

"Matt's ex, I'll fill you in later," Finn replied, visibly shaken.

"Oh," Naomi looked at Ollie with concern.

"It's okay," Ollie said with a twist to his mouth, thinking it was anything but.

Ollie's eyes found Matt again as they made their way toward him. He had made a promise to Matt that he had forgiven him, sin unseen, but seriously doubted his ability to do so now that he knew the details. Never, in his wildest dreams, had he considered that Matt would be so devious as to make her think they had a future. One with *children*. He didn't even want to think about how far Matt had taken his game of playing house with her.

Matt didn't talk much about his time in the service, but he spoke quite a bit about the OODA loop, strategy, and outcomes. How he used them in business, and how he'd even applied the practice to win Ollie back. It was unsettling to think that the Matt he knew could behave in such a cold and calculating way. He needed to believe that Matt, the soft vulnerable one that he saw behind closed doors, was the *real* Matt, and that the machine he showed the world was just a façade, otherwise Ollie's heart would disintegrate, and he would have to question all his choices.

The band started playing as Ollie, Finn and Naomi made their way back to the table, Matt watching Ollie carefully.

"Everything okay?" Matt asked cautiously, glancing at Finn.

Finn made a sound and pulled a face. "I'll tell you later. She's very angry and on her way to Drunk Town."

Ollie searched Finn's face for disgust, or judgement as she looked at Matt, and found none. He turned his attention back to Matt as he reacted to her news.

"Fuck," Matt muttered. "Do you know who she's here with?"

"Some guy named Toby. I think he's the guy with light brown hair sitting over at the table by the window." She gestured with her chin discreetly. "He had his arm around her earlier."

"Thanks." He took a deep breath and, with a guarded glance at Ollie, strode away.

Ollie watched his broad back as he weaved through the crowd and knew he couldn't do anything but love that flawed man.

Matt made his way over to where Finn indicated, looking for Sam along the way.

"Toby?"

Toby turned from talking to the person to his right, and stood when he saw Matt.

"Yeah?" He was several inches shorter than Matt, just shy of six feet, and handsome, but not in a way that would last.

Matt shook Toby's hand. "Matt Dion. You don't know me, but I've come to recommend that you take Samantha home."

"What do you mean?"

"I mean she's had too much to drink and is beginning to act upset."

Toby frowned at him and looked away thinking. "Oh, I know who you are," he scoffed and rolled his eyes. "If she's acting upset, I think it's you who should be leaving. I'm not going anywhere."

Matt took a deep breath, noticing that Toby seemed slightly intoxicated. He shook his head lightly.

"Jesus. Sam deserves better than you."

He turned, and Toby shoved his shoulder as he walked away. Matt, anticipating such a move, absorbed the shove entirely in his shoulder.

"What the fuck did you just say to me?" Toby said angrily to Matt's back.

Matt turned and noticed Toby was off balance ever so slightly and shoved him just hard enough to knock him off his feet and back into his chair. Matt made to leave again and heard the chair fall back as Toby launched himself out of it. He felt Toby's hand grab his shoulder and pivoted to face him, leaning well back from his expected, drunken, and amateurish, swing. He heard commotion behind him as people began to gather.

"You have short arms," Matt scoffed without flinching.

Toby's face turned red with rage, and he lunged again, punching straight at Matt's face. Matt leaned left, and as Toby's arm came past his shoulder he used Toby's momentum against him, grabbing his wrist and spinning him around in one smooth motion. He tucked Toby's arm up behind his back in a police hold. Toby cried out in pain.

"One small push and it breaks, or dislocates. I can't remember which. Shall we see?" Matt said calmly and quietly against the side of Toby's head, applying slight pressure to his twisted arm for emphasis.

Toby grunted through his heavy breathing.

"You need to leave with Sam, for her sake," Matt ordered quietly. He looked to his right and saw Sam watching with a mixture of desire and embarrassment.

"You must be a complete imbecile to pick a fight with a former Navy SEAL," SharkFinn's CFO Fred scoffed to Toby as he appeared next to Matt.

"Mr. Dion." A large man in a black suit appeared from within the crowd. "What's going on, sir?"

"Toby here, was just leaving with his date." He nodded to where Sam was standing. "Perhaps you could help them find their way out of the building," Matt answered, loosening his hold on Toby's arm.

"Certainly, sir."

Matt let go completely, pushing Toby slightly away from him and turned to see Ollie staring at him, his eyes wide and dark. He grinned, happy to see heat in Ollie's eyes instead of what he saw earlier.

"Did someone say dessert?" he asked as Finn appeared, shaking her head.

He put his arm around her, kissing the side of her head as they walked back to the table, Ollie on his right.

"What was that all about?" Ollie asked when they sat down, the table abuzz. "Are you okay?"

"Of course. He barely touched me," Matt scoffed. "That was Sam's date. I politely asked him to take her home because she's drunk, and he took offense to the suggestion." Matt shrugged and searched Ollie's face.

Ollie held his gaze. "Well, now they're being escorted out, and we can move on," he said pointedly.

Matt exhaled with relief, and counted his lucky stars, again, as he shifted his gaze away from Ollie with a nod.

It was close to midnight when they got home, saying their goodnights in Ollie's condo on the garden level before getting in the elevator.

"Thank you, Naomi. Tonight was amazing, and I look forward to our next fancy party." Ollie leaned in for a kiss.

Naomi returned the kiss happily. "Tonight was wonderful. I will work very hard to not actually fall in love with you, Ollie," she teased. "You're one lucky dude, Matt."

"I know." Matt grinned, feeling his luck all the way down to his toes. "Goodnight, ladies."

Matt and Ollie continued to the fourth floor in silence, stepping out into the hallway and walking toward their suite.

"I shouldn't say this, because I certainly don't want to encourage the behavior, but that was hot, Lieutenant. I got hard watching you handle that man. You really know how to move. It happened so fast, your reaction time and all. Very stimulating."

"You really got hard at the party tonight? Watching me?" he asked huskily with a grin.

Ollie nodded, licking his lips. Matt hummed low in his throat as he took his tuxedo jacket off when they reached the bedroom.

"I'm going to visit all your erogenous zones tonight," Matt said and closed the door behind them.

Ollie kissed Matt softly and rolled off him with a smile. "I love you." He turned his head and studied Matt's profile, wondering again at what burned beneath the surface. "You used that arm hold on me," Ollie said after several moments, his voice just above a whisper. "Quite painful."

Matt winced, and turned his head to look at Ollie. "Every part of me is sorry for that night, Ollie."

Ollie made a small sound, appreciative of Matt's remorse.

"Honestly, it was only the reason you did it that hurt me, Lieutenant. My body healed just fine, my heart nearly didn't." He turned on his side to kiss Matt's shoulder, and pressed himself against him. "I love you so much. I've never been happier."

Matt came up on his elbow to face Ollie. "I am the luckiest man on the planet," he said huskily. "I don't deserve you, and I'm so glad that hasn't registered in your brain." He grinned and kissed him until he was dizzy.

56

Fire and Rain

THE NEW YEAR WAS HECTIC, prepping for SharkFinn's year-end in February, flying to Baltimore with Naomi to help Finn move into her new house, and overseeing the construction of their beach house. They managed to sneak away for a brief weekend on the Cape and walked through the shell of their house after the workers left.

It was quiet as they made their way through the framed rooms in the frigid cold. Matt laced his fingers through Ollie's as they tried to imagine the finished space.

"This is amazing. I can't believe it." Ollie stopped in front of the giant window in their upstairs bedroom.

Matt let go of Ollie's hand and stood behind him, wrapping his arms around Ollie's waist. He nuzzled his cold cheek against Ollie's neck and laughed when Ollie shivered.

"Right here, this view. It's where we're gonna christen the house." He dropped a hand to the front of Ollie's pants and squeezed lightly.

"When it's finished, you mean?" Ollie turned his head for a kiss.

Matt bit Ollie's neck and then licked the bruised spot as he reached into his jacket pocket.

"No, I mean right now." Matt popped the button on Ollie's jeans and kissed Ollie's complaints about the cold away as he stood a small bottle of lube on the window sill. "I'll have you hot in no time."

* * *

They were back to work the following Monday, Matt daydreaming about Ollie's frigid ass and cries of ecstasy as he fucked him against the glass when his phone buzzed quietly in his pocket. He glanced around the conference room at his VPs and then looked at the screen.

He stood with a small frown as Bryan, his VP of sales, stopped talking.

"I gotta take this. I'll just be a minute." He put the phone to his ear and left the room without looking at Ollie.

"Hey, Chuck, everything alright?" Matt asked with concern as he closed the door. She never called during work hours. He waited for her to speak but all he heard was sobbing.

"Chuck! What's wrong? Are you okay?" he asked in as calm a tone as he could manage, panic in his gut. He strode quickly into his office and closed the door. "Take a deep breath."

He could hear her trying to speak through the tears. "My mom, she d-, she's. . . ." Finn choked, unable to say the dreadful word, before bursting into tears again.

Matt's stomach sank as he made sense of her unfinished words. "Oh no. No." He closed his eyes tightly. "I'll be on the next flight to Baltimore. Or do you want me to send a driver for you, and I'll meet you at Logan. Just tell me what you want me to do."

"Come," she whimpered.

"I'll be there ASAP. I love you." He pocketed his phone and left his office.

"Book me on the next flight to Baltimore, I don't care which airline," he said to Stacey as he walked by her desk on his way to Ollie's office.

Matt walked past the glass of the conference room without looking in, slowing his stride a beat before continuing on, knowing Ollie would follow. He hoped, belatedly, that no one would think it was odd.

Ollie appeared a moment later, his face full of worry.

"Chuck's mom died," he said as Ollie closed the office door behind him. He held up his hand. "She was a wreck. I have no details, but I'm leaving now for the airport. I'll be home tomorrow or the next day."

"Oh, Christ. I'm so sorry. Jesus, she was so young. Shall I come with you?"

Matt shook his head. "No, we can't." He gestured outside the glass office wall. "And I'll be right back. I love you," he added quietly, staring at Ollie, wishing he could take Ollie in his arms.

"I love you too," Ollie whispered with an understanding nod.

Matt went back to his office to get his keys, and an update from Stacey. "You're on the noon JetBlue. I've already called Trey for a pick-up when you arrive."

"Thank you, Stacey. You're the best," he replied, grateful for her and for Trey, the former Marine he found in Baltimore who had just started a car service and always made Matt's travel needs a priority. He cleared his throat. "Diana Hawthorn died. I'll be working remotely the next couple of days. I'll email you details for flowers, et cetera. Please make sure my office is locked up."

"Absolutely, Matt. I'm so sorry."

* * *

Matt arrived back at the brownstone late the following night, and hugged Ollie tightly with a kiss.

"I took her home, but she didn't want to be alone, so she's downstairs. I'm sleeping down there tonight. I hope that's okay?"

Ollie nodded. "Of course. What happened?"

Matt shook his head and exhaled. "They were skiing in Colorado. She fell, hit her head, and seemed fine. They checked her out, sent her back to the condo or wherever, and she . . . " He winced and squeezed his eyes shut. "She was a spectacular woman." His voice caught.

Ollie hugged him and kissed his neck. "Oh, darling, I'm so, so sorry."

Matt squeezed him and let out a sob. Ollie stroked the back of his head as Matt's arms came up around him, his shoulders shaking. Ollie held him, soothing him as best he could until Matt finally pulled back wiping his eyes.

"I love you." Ollie kissed him softly. "Now go back downstairs. She needs you."

* * *

Finn stayed until her father returned from Colorado. Naomi coming the second day to stay with her. The funeral was a somber event, attended by hundreds of people, her mother having been a fixture in the community and a scion of one of America's most well-known dynasties. Finn and her father were shell-shocked. Matt stayed the night in Wellesley with her, Ollie encouraging him to.

It was well after midnight by the time Matt climbed under the covers behind Finn. He kissed her shoulder and held her loosely.

"I don't know what I would do without you." Finn shook her head slightly and gripped his forearm. "As much as I pine for a boyfriend, no one could ever hold me and soothe me without an ulterior motive like you do." She drew a shaky breath. "I don't know how people can want to have sex at a time like this, while I just want to mourn my mom."

She rolled on her back to look at him in the dark, her eyes shining with unshed tears. "You said you were blessed to find me, but I was far more blessed to find you. And we're both blessed with Ollie, who allows you be here with me. He gets us."

Matt closed his eyes and exhaled through his nose. "Ollie is a treasure, as are you. Go to sleep. I'm right here with you."

He kissed her cheek. She rolled back in his arms and soon her breathing was slow and even. Matt lay awake a few moments longer, reveling in his luck to have two such perfect people in his life, when he was so flawed himself.

* * *

Matt let himself back in Finn's house just before seven after his ten-mile run. Sweating under his zip-hoodie he stopped short at the sight of Bill making coffee. He wiped his face and took a glass from the cabinet, filling it from the fridge dispenser.

"Morning," he said before drinking deeply. He filled the glass again.

"Morning, Matt. Not too icy out there?"

"No, sir, I run in the road. Not any traffic here at this hour." He paused and cleared his throat. "I'm sorry, Bill. How you holding up?"

Bill looked away, getting two mugs down from the cabinet. "It fucking sucks. I'm not gonna sugar coat it. She was the love of my life." He looked back at Matt. "I'm so grateful for you, and how you're caring for Finn." He shook his head slightly, watching the coffee maker. "You two clearly love each other. I only wish. . . ." He stopped, closing his eyes, and waited for the coffee to finish brewing. He poured two mugs and passed one to Matt.

"Life is short." Bill frowned emotionally. "You need to embrace who you love, because they could be taken from you." He snapped his fingers and Matt flinched reflexively. "And as much as I wish, with all my being, that that person for you is Finn, I know it's not." He looked away. "What keeps me from screaming about that," he paused with a small smile, looking back at Matt, "is that you do love her and are there for her one hundred percent. And, that the person you do love seems like a great guy who not only loves my daughter as well, but also understands you the two of you. That is rare."

Matt shifted on his feet awkwardly and wondered if he'd ever feel comfortable about his relationship with Ollie around Bill.

"I love her, and will always be there for her, for you both." Matt nodded and squeezed Bill's shoulder before making a hasty exit with his mug of coffee.

57

A Sorta Fairytale

FINN THREW HERSELF INTO WORK. Matt and Ollie took turns going to visit her and sometimes went together, staying in Matt's east-facing suite at Finn's. Matt decided he needed a company jet, and began looking at options, after speaking with his CFO Fred about feasibility and tax write-offs.

"If I'm to make this trip regularly, for Chuck and for work, as well as have my sales team travel, I think it's a worthwhile investment," he said to Ollie as they were getting ready for bed.

"I think it's a worthwhile investment for membership in the Mile-High Club alone," Ollie said salaciously.

Matt looked up and smiled, with an appreciative sound. "I didn't even think of that. Fly without a flight attendant, and get a plane with separate compartments, one with a locking door. Oh my god, Ollie, get over here. Little Matt just woke up and he *needs* you."

* * *

Matt was driven to start the new fiscal year strong, making up for the time he spent with Finn, and he left it to Ollie and Naomi to work together on the beach house when he could spare him.

The house was coming together in a way that filled Ollie with excitement and wonder and a tiny bit of anxiety. He had grown wary of their good fortune when it always seemed tempered with calamity. But reminded himself that with each catastrophe, he and Matt had only grown stronger and more determined in their love for each other. So, he focused on making sure the house was perfect and enjoying himself with Naomi, which was easy to do. They passed the hours getting to know each other, talking about things he would never tell Matt, and listening to her stories of Matt from before Ollie knew him. Unsurprisingly, he had been an enigma (still was) but a tense one, who smiled but never laughed much.

"I never found him approachable, not like now. I always wondered how Finn ever got close to him. I asked her about it, thinking maybe it was the war that made him that way, but she said he was always closed off," Naomi said as she sat on the couch next to Ollie with her wine.

"You changed him. I think that's what I picked up on at the townhouse. I mean, it could've been that he was doing you a favor and helping find you a place to live, but the way he came into the room." She shook her head lightly. "It was like his whole body was smiling, and not at me." Ollie looked at the foam on his pint, his belly warm. "And you," she elbowed him with a laugh, "how could he not smile with his whole body at you? You are such an amazing guy, and I love how in love the two of you are."

Ollie beamed with pleasure. "I've never had this. He's changed me too." He took a sip of his beer. "My last long-term boyfriend, Henry, I thought *that* was love, but no way. When I broke up with him, I thought there was something wrong with me, and all our gay friends agreed." Ollie looked at Naomi, raised his brows and twisted his mouth. "He got them all in the 'divorce,'" he said making air quotes.

"They sided with him?" Naomi frowned. "What did you do?"

Ollie winced. "Nothing bad. I mean, not abrupt and heart-breaking like Matt did to me. But I—you know you can't help when you stop loving someone or help that they don't stop loving you." He finished his beer. "I don't blame our friends really, for siding with Henry. He needed them more than I did, and I had my mates. I've told you about them. God, they would go gaga for you." Ollie laughed and stood. "You can never meet them. They're wankers and you would judge me forever."

Naomi let Ollie pull her to her feet as she laughed. "I'm sure they're great guys. Goodnight." She kissed him lightly and took his empty glass. "We have to be up early for the flooring."

*   *   *

The builders promised the house would be ready by the end of July and Matt's plan was that he and Ollie would move to Truro for the remainder of the summer and work remotely on their separate servers, like they had at the townhouse. Aside from a few business trips, and a couple of in-person staff meetings, Matt was looking forward to working with his toes in the sand.

"I want you to see how it's coming together, but I also want you to be surprised," Ollie said shyly to Matt one night, as they sat in the home theater watching a show. "Naomi is just amazing. I love her like you love Chuck."

Matt tilted his head to the side. "Probably not as much as I love Chuck, but I get the sentiment. I can't wait to see it too. I trust you implicitly and love your taste, if not your messiness."

Ollie gasped. "I am not messy anymore," he said primly.

"Oh yes you are. And late for everything, always." Matt laughed shaking his head, as Ollie threw a pillow at him. He tackled him on the couch and tickled him, Ollie squirming and laughing.

"Stop, stop. I can't breathe!" Ollie cried.

Matt kissed his laughing mouth. "I would have you clean or messy, on time or hours late, Ollie, just so long as I have you," he said with a grin and kissed him soundly.

58

Somebody That I Used to Know

THE SHARKFINN COMPANY PICNIC took place the week after the Fourth of July on the east roof deck of the MIT Pavilion, right on the Charles River with expansive views of Boston and Cambridge. The weather was perfect: sunny and not too hot, with a breeze off the river. Matt chose to spend most of his time leaning against the railing overlooking the water, holding court.

He and Ollie were both in Tom Ford linen suits, Matt's white, with a light brown shirt underneath, the cuffs slightly longer than the jacket, and Ollie's beige, with a light blue shirt, both without ties, their silver necklaces gleaming in the sunlight between the open necks of their shirts.

"Let's ditch the party and rent a sailboat," Matt said, only half-jokingly.

Ollie laughed. "We should definitely do that another time. I used to sail with Ivan. I love it."

"Really? Captain Ollie." Matt ran his eyes discreetly over him and looked away as Fred approached them, dressed casually and oozing the confidence of a successful and self-assured financier.

"Thinking about a swim, Matt?" Fred asked with a smile.

"It crossed my mind," Matt answered easily with a grin and nodded at Ollie. "Our GC here talked me out of it, apparently, it's against the law. How was the west coast?" he asked Fred, changing the subject to business as their VP of marketing, Sydney, joined them.

Ollie looked for a waiter and ordered a pint. He was standing on the periphery of Matt's little group, and tilted his face to the sky as he closed his eyes and absorbed the warm sun.

"Bloody hell, Oliver Turner!" someone exclaimed in a Geordie accent.

He turned his head sharply at the voice, and saw a tall, handsome waiter with neatly styled black hair and warm brown eyes holding a tray with his pint.

"Hello, Andy," he replied startled, looking around briefly, shocked to see Andy *the asshole*, standing next to him on a roof deck in Cambridge. "Haven't seen you in years."

"Cor, you're looking more gorgeous than ever. Nice suit," Andy said appreciatively as he shook his hand and pulled him in for a tight, one-armed hug, tucking the drink tray under his arm as he pressed his cheek into Ollie's neck. "What are you doing here? This your company party?"

Ollie nodded. "What are you doing here? I mean are you living in Boston now?"

"Just here for the summer so far. Hard to get a work permit." He smiled. "I'm working as a waiter, and doing some house painting. You know, keeping busy, enjoying America." He looked Ollie up and down appreciatively. "I'm living in Somerville. We should totally go out. I've missed you." He made a flirty sound and looked at Ollie's mouth. "Were you this beautiful when we dated?"

Ollie snuck a glance at Matt and saw him watching them. Shit.

"Ah, I'm not like *that* anymore," he said quietly to Andy.

Andy looked at him skeptically. "You're a bottom, Ollie, you don't drop out of the game. I mean, maybe you've crossed over but no, you liked it too much to stop," he added suggestively and waggled his eyebrows.

Ollie had been easing away from the group while talking with Andy and he cringed when Andy said that, praying that no one overheard.

"No one here knows about my past." He frowned at Andy. "Christ, these are my co-workers, please," he added quietly with a smile for cover.

Andy shrugged. "Fine, sorry," he apologized. "Still, I'd sure fancy a tup with you, for old time's sake." He touched Ollie's bicep and then hummed appreciatively as he squeezed. "Give me your number." He pulled out his phone and swiped into his contacts expectantly.

Ollie shook his head, cringing at the sight of the phone in Andy's hand. "No, sorry. I'm in a relationship."

"Oh, that's too bad." He looked over Ollie's shoulder as he pocketed his phone. "Who's that man staring at me? He's gorgeous, but he looks bloody *radge*."

Ollie closed his eyes and took a deep breath, his stomach clenching.

"Oh, that's most assuredly my boss. He asked me to go speak with the tech team about something important. I've gotta run. Sorry, Andy." He smiled politely. "Nice to see you."

"Nice seeing you too. You're looking really fit, Ol." He swept his eyes over Ollie's body. "I hope I see you and your beautiful ass again."

Ollie's stomach was in knots. He definitely did not want to have a conversation with Matt at that moment. He hurried across the deck and with a forced smile he joined the developers, a group of men and women closer to his age, nearly all graduates of MIT. He felt Matt's eyes on him as he finished his beer. He flagged another waiter and asked for tequila over ice with a lime.

Andy delivered it with a wink and a smile, and turned to the group, taking drink orders before heading back to the bar.

Ollie sensed Matt before he appeared at his elbow.

"Hey, guys," Matt said fluidly to the group, all of whom straightened noticeably in his presence. "Enjoying yourselves?"

They nodded and praised the event, conversation bantering back and forth, all while Ollie avoided Matt's eye.

"Ollie, can I borrow you for a minute?" Matt asked.

Ollie nodded. "Of course." He looked at Matt and then quickly away at what he saw behind Matt's eyes.

There was no place they could have a private conversation, and Ollie wasn't sure why Matt wanted to risk it. He led Ollie down the stairs to the dock, and stood among the sailboats with their backs to the pavilion.

"Who is that waiter?" Matt asked, his voice tight.

"He's nobody. Please, let's talk about this at home."

Matt laughed mirthlessly and Ollie felt a shiver down his spine.

"That was not nobody, and now your answer makes me feel like punching something."

Ollie shook his head and swallowed. "Honestly, Matt, we should rejoin the party." Ollie turned to leave.

"Stop," Matt commanded harshly under his breath. "I can't touch you here but imagine that my hand is gripping your arm right now."

A thrill went through Ollie's body, part fear, part desire as he came to a stop.

"This time I really need to hear that it was nothing. And know that I won't believe you if you try to tell me that he wanted a book recommendation," Matt added angrily.

Ollie turned back to look at Matt. "No, he wanted my number." Ollie winced at the expression on Matt's face. "But I didn't give it to him! Christ, Matt. Please, let's talk about this at home." He looked up at the deck and saw Fred looking at them over the railing.

Matt nodded his head slowly, his jaw ticking. "That man better not come anywhere near me." He stalked angrily away.

Ollie worried slightly for Andy's safety as he followed Matt back into the party, hanging back briefly to compose himself.

Matt was among his VPs when Ollie returned to the deck. He was chatting casually but Ollie knew his body language (hadn't he studied his mercurial man for nearly two years?). Matt was coiled like a viper ready to strike, and while the martini in his hand was worrisome, it thankfully wasn't tequila. He looked around nervously for Andy and saw him behind the bar. Ollie's only consolation was that Matt would never cause a scene at his own party, former lover of Ollie's or not.

Ollie rejoined the group, and stood in Matt's eyeline, smiling and chatting with Sydney, hoping to set Matt's mind at ease, prove to him his worry was for naught. The food was laid out on the buffet and people were peeling off to fill their plates. Ollie wasn't hungry but he went for food anyway, putting some on a plate and not eating any of it, always warily looking for Andy, and keeping a close eye on Matt, who also wasn't eating.

He saw Matt order another drink and cringed when he saw Andy appear with it on a tray a short while later.

"I'll take that." Ollie intercepted him with a tight smile.

"I really should deliver it." Andy stopped, moving the tray slightly away from Ollie's reach. "It's for your boss. Maybe he's hiring," he added with a flick of his eyebrows.

Ollie shook his head and spoke firmly. "Trust me, he's just got some bad news recently, so he's in a foul mood. I'll bring it to him."

Andy shrugged. "Suit yourself. But put in a good word for me." He winked and swooped the tray closer.

Ollie nodded stiffly, and took the martini, waiting for Andy to walk away before turning to Matt.

"Here you are."

Matt took it with barely a glance at Ollie. Ollie looked around the circle and saw everyone digging into their barbecue without notice, except for Fred, who was watching him with interest.

After everyone had eaten, Matt called attention and made a toast, praising his top executives and his VPs and their teams, individually, starting with the developers and ending with Bryan and his sales team. Cheers were said all around and glasses clinked. It didn't escape Ollie's attention that Matt acknowledged only 'his legal team,' and sighed, turning away to hide his disappointment.

"Feel free to stay, the bar's open until sunset," Matt called, and with a pointed look at Ollie he turned and left.

Ollie waited a beat and made to follow him out when Fred stopped him.

"Matt seemed pretty mad at you. What'd you do?"

Ollie scrambled for an excuse, looking around before meeting Fred's intent gaze. "He asked me about a UK competitor, and I didn't give him the information he wanted. Now I'm afraid I have to go back to work, and put out some fires." He gave Fred a wry grin.

Fred nodded. "Oh yeah, he'll expect that on his desk by morning. Good luck. I noticed he glossed over all your hard work in his speech, so you might want to be really thorough in your follow-up with him," Fred added, somewhat cryptically.

Ollie's phone began to buzz in his pocket. He looked over the railing and saw Matt standing rigidly on the path along the river, looking back at the building, searching for him. "Thanks, Fred. I've got to take this call. Enjoy the rest of the day." Ollie smiled calmly (feeling anything but) and pulled out his phone. "Hello, this is Oliver," he answered formally for Fred's benefit as he walked away.

"Why the fuck aren't you right behind me?" Matt asked angrily. "Who you talking to?"

Ollie went quickly down the stairs and turned left outside the pavilion, headed for the Mass Ave. Bridge.

"Fred stopped me and now I'm walking toward you, *lunatic*."

Matt shot him a look as he put his phone away and began walking ahead, clearly visible in his white suit. Ollie caught up with his long stride at the bridge. They walked back to the townhouse in silence and rode the elevator to the fourth floor. Matt began stripping off his suit and changed into his running clothes.

"What did Fred want?" Matt asked suspiciously, his movements jerky.

"He wanted to know why you were so angry with me." Ollie shook his head. "People saw us on the dock. You're making a big deal out of nothing."

"I hardly think you letting some guy grope and eye-fuck you is nothing," Matt said angrily. "What did you tell Fred?"

"I didn't let him grope me!" Ollie answered indignantly. "And I told Fred you asked about a UK competitor and I didn't have the information you wanted."

Matt laughed humorlessly. "You got that fucking right. I don't know if I want to run first, or hear all about it first, So, you tell me."

"There's nothing to tell." Ollie shook his head. "It was years ago during undergrad. I didn't torment myself with questions about you and Sam, I suggest you do the same. Go for your run."

Matt pressed his lips together. "So, he *was* your lover." He grimaced, clenching his fists, and looked away. "I'd say it's quite a bit different than Sam. He's a man. A handsome one at that. I can't help it, Ollie; it infuriates me."

"What do you want me to say? I'm sorry I ever had a life before you?" Ollie frowned. "I can't change my past. What I can do, is tell you that I love you, and only you, and nothing from before I met you has any meaning to me. In my opinion, my life didn't start until I met you."

He touched Matt's arm. "Look at me." Matt met his eye, and Ollie saw the worry and the anger in them. "I love you so much. Seeing him was just embarrassing, and nothing else. You have no reason to be jealous, of anyone. I want you to go for your run, think about all that is good and perfect in our life, and then come home and fuck me silly. Or, if you're still angry. . . ."

Matt smiled and exhaled through his nose. "I love you. Sometimes I just wish I could put my arms around you in public, and declare my love, let the world know you are *mine*," he said forcefully. "It made me so angry to see that he was hitting on you, and that you couldn't point to me and say, 'I'm with him.' And I knew that's exactly what he was doing, the way he was looking at you. It was all over his smug face. I wanted to punch him. A lot," he said wryly. "Does that bastard live here? Because if I see him again, I will punch him." He frowned and kissed Ollie lightly.

"Just for the summer it sounds like, and in Somerville." He kissed Matt lingeringly. "Why don't you fuck me however you need to, and then go for your run, hm? I do so hate to be kept waiting."

Ollie smiled as Matt's grip on his body turned painful.

Ollie heard the distant whir of the elevator a few hours later, well after dark. It stopped on the floor above, Matt having a shower before coming in search of Ollie. He waited with a slight smile, and ten minutes later Matt appeared in the doorway of the TV room. Ollie beamed and paused the show, scanning his eyes over a damp-haired Matt, looking like a dream in a t-shirt and grey sweatpants.

"Hello gorgeous," Ollie murmured with an appreciative sound. "You truly are magnificent. I can't believe you're mine."

Matt smiled and made a small sound.

Ollie sat up and swallowed nervously at the look in Matt's eyes. "What?"

Matt stepped into the room and dropped to his knee in front of him, taking his hand. "I love you, Oliver Turner. I want to commit myself to you, forever. And I want to do it in front of our loved ones who know. It's not a marriage proposal, but it's what I got."

Ollie's mouth dropped open as he searched Matt's face. Finally, he found his voice.

"Whoa, you're serious? Oh my god. Yes, a thousand times yes!"

Matt beamed and kissed Ollie, his tongue warm and insistent against Ollie's. He pulled back and looked at the TV, the screen frozen on a handsome, dark-haired man running with a gun in his hand.

"Whatcha watching?"

"*Hawaii Five-O*," Ollie answered with a grin, his heart hammering in his ears. "You look just like him you know. And he strides around all gorgeous and half-cocked just like you."

Matt shook his head with a laugh. "Speaking of half-cocked." He looked at Ollie's lap. "He do that to you?"

"No, that is one hundred percent courtesy of you, Lieutenant." Ollie kissed him softly, his eyes burning.

"Good," Matt answered against Ollie's lips.

59

Dream On

MATT MADE PHONE CALLS the following day, letting everyone know it was a special occasion, and to bring dress clothes. He emailed Ollie's parents their plane tickets after they confirmed their availability and reached out to a couple of clambake companies on the Cape. Then he called Naomi to brainstorm design and lighting ideas for the event and swore her to secrecy. He wanted Ollie to be surprised.

* * *

August came in a rush, and Matt was leaving to pick his mother up at her house on his way to the Cape.

"I'll see you tomorrow." Matt kissed Ollie gently as he squeezed his ass. "I'm picking you guys up at the pier, what time?"

"I think we'll be able to make the five thirty, which puts us in P-town around seven," Ollie answered, running his fingers through Matt's short, soft hair. "I really can't wait for Sunday," he whispered and touched Matt's neck, where his necklace should have been, before fingering his own bare neck.

Matt made a soft sound. "Me neither. You better make that ferry. It's the last one of the day, and it's bad enough that I have to go one night without you. I won't tolerate two if it's not a business trip." He smiled against Ollie's lips.

Ollie watched Matt pull his new Range Rover out of the parking spot next to the Audi S4 Matt had given him for Christmas. The taillights disappeared down the alley leaving the townhouse suddenly huge and silent. He went back into his office and tied up the week's loose ends, wanting to be able to shut work off for the weekend and focus only on the upcoming commitment ceremony.

Ollie turned off his computer after a few hours and went upstairs to change and hit the treadmill. He turned on his playlist and started to run, losing himself in his exercise and thoughts of Matt.

They'd been together two years, and so much had happened. There had been so much growth on both their parts, but he never imagined he would be on the verge of a ceremony that felt like a wedding—

BUT ISN'T, his brain interrupted firmly and brashly.

Ollie scowled. *I don't want a wedding.*

Yes, you do, his heart countered. You have always been a romantic. You've wanted a wedding since you were little, and now you desperately want to be Mr. Oliver Dion.

That's never going to happen, Oliver, his brain said pragmatically. This ceremony is secret. No one other than the eight of you will ever know. There's no officiator, there's no certificate, there's no photographer, there's no band, and most importantly, there's no ring, his brain added cruelly.

Matt's doing something with the necklaces, his heart defended loudly. It's just as good as a ring.

But it's not a ring, and no one ever looks at your necklaces, his brain scoffed.

Ollie turned up the music with a frown and tuned out his inner dialogue, choosing instead to let his body think of Matt, which brought heat to his groin and a smile to his face.

* * *

Ollie took a cab to the airport and waited for his parents, his stomach full of butterflies. The doors from the airport terminal opened and a sea of people came pouring through, Ollie's parents near the front, looking tanned and relaxed from their two weeks in Lyon.

He hugged them warmly and took his mother's bags and his father's carry-on. He led them to the shuttle bus that would take them to the water taxi as his parents chatted about the flight and the weather in London.

"There's a water taxi?" David puzzled.

"Yes, Matt says it's the best way to get to the ferry, and the harbor is beautiful. I've never actually been on it yet, so I'm as eager as you to see what it's all about."

They boarded the small MBTA ferry boat bound for Long Wharf, where they would wait for the catamaran to Provincetown. Ollie looked at his Rolex and saw they had an hour, and smiled with relief. He didn't want to miss the ferry either.

Ollie bought their tickets at the wharf while his parents watched the harbor seals outside the Aquarium. They had a drink on the ferry and watched the city disappear from view as they sped to the Cape.

"So, how have you been, Ollie?" his father asked, an odd edge to his tone. "We missed you for your birthday, and at Easter and in Lyon. I can't believe we haven't seen you since Christmas." He shook his head, looking at Maggie.

"I know, it's the longest I've ever gone without seeing you, but thankfully we've been able to talk and use FaceTime," he said, feeling chastised.

"It's just not the same, you know that," David said quietly. "Your mother really missed you. I really missed you."

"I'm sorry, Dad, but with Chuck's mother passing, and work being really busy, and traveling a ton, and working on the beach house, which you're going to love, trust me," he interjected with a smile, "I've just been too busy to get away. I've chatted with Guy—I always do—but how was Lyon?"

"Wonderful as always. They had a great year last year for grapes, and things look equally well for the Cotes du Rhone this year, so spirits were high. Guy complained quite a bit about you blowing him off again. You had better be planning to go next year, Oliver," David said firmly.

"Okay, I get it. I'm sorry. Can you stop making me feel bad? This is going to be a great weekend, and I don't want it spoiled." Ollie stood and went inside to get another drink. The butterflies were gone and replaced with a sour feeling. He shook his head as he waited in line. He felt his mother next to him and looked at her.

"I'm sorry, darling. Your father really just had a hard time not seeing you for so long; we both did. And he doesn't mean to make you feel bad. We worry about you and about your happiness, and it's easy to fake that over the phone." She put her arms around his waist as he put his arm on her shoulder, pulling her to his side. "Dad worries because of last year."

"Oh, Mum, there's nothing to worry about. Matt and I are so solid, so happy." Ollie beamed and ordered two beers and a wine. He handed the wine to his mother and carried the beer back outside, handing one to his father and clinked their cans.

"Mum, Dad, things are perfect with me, and I'm so happy you're here. Matt can't wait to see you either," he added quietly, mindful of the people around them. "We have a big dinner planned, and the house is just gorgeous. We're going to have a grand weekend. And I will be home for Christmas, I promise, and Easter, with Matt hopefully." He smiled. "And I will talk to Guy about Lyon next summer."

"Great." David smiled with relief.

Matt left the fragrant smelling house, his mother and Finn prepping a feast for the evening, to get Ollie and his parents from the ferry. He wasn't sure if it was the magnitude of the weekend, or just another realization about his relationship with Ollie, but he felt as though he couldn't breathe as freely without Ollie in his proximity. It was disconcerting, but strangely freeing to finally allow himself to admit just how much he depended on Ollie and how much he loved him.

It was a short drive up Route 6, and fifteen minutes later he was turning onto Commercial Street and then into the MacMillan Pier parking lot, searching for Ollie's familiar frame in the low-light among the crowd. He smiled with relief when he saw him and his smooth stride. Ollie's body was so strong and beautiful, and Matt admired him openly from the privacy of his car, knowing he wasn't the only male admirer to do so, but that he was the only one that mattered. Ollie was carrying and wheeling all of his parents' bags except for the one David was wheeling next to him.

Matt got out of the car with a broad smile for Ollie as he took the bags, greeting Maggie and David warmly, before loading their bags into the back of his Range Rover. Matt was determined to win David over and prove to him that his love for Ollie was solid and genuine. He also hoped his new truck would be recognized as a nod to Ollie's (and David's) heritage.

"Did you have a good trip? You found your way alright, obviously." Matt smiled at Ollie.

"Yes, the water taxi was amazing. Being on the harbor was lovely," Maggie replied.

Ollie met Matt's eye in the rearview. "It really is the most beautiful city. You're right."

"You're damn right it is." Matt beamed.

"So, what's the occasion?" David asked.

"It's a surprise, sir." Matt smiled and looked again at Ollie in the mirror.

"Sounds intriguing," David replied looking at Maggie in the backseat.

The seashells and crushed stone crunched under the tires as Matt pulled up to the house. Every light was on, the glass on the driveway side not as expansive as the front facing the water, but no less stunning. Matt and Ollie carried the bags in, Matt putting them in the first-floor suite while Ollie brought his parents into the house for introductions and a tour.

Matt's mother, Antonia, came around the large kitchen island to shake David and Maggie's hands with a big smile as Ollie introduced them. After his parents hugged Finn warmly, Ollie pulled Naomi to his side, introducing her, and smiling as they praised her talents. He gave his parents the tour, showing them the upstairs and then to their suite off the foyer, before returning to the dining room for dinner.

"This *cioppino* is delicious," Maggie praised Antonia, disposing of her clam shell in one of the big bowls on the table.

"*Grazie*. It is my grandmother's recipe; I tweak it depending on what's in season and who's eating." She smiled at Matt. "This one likes extra everything; he's always had a taste for the sea, like his grandfather."

Ollie smiled at Matt who was gazing at his mother lovingly.

"No one can make seafood taste as good as you do, Ma. Except maybe Ollie." He winked at Ollie.

"And he loves being in the sea," Antonia continued, before turning her gaze to Ollie. "You should've seen him as a boy, Oliver. He was a mess on land, but put him in the water, whether it was a pool or the ocean, and he was the most graceful body you have ever seen, *molto bello*. He has since found his land legs, magnificently I might add. But I probably don't have to tell you that." She grinned mischievously.

Matt blushed. "Ma," he admonished sneaking a glance at Ollie' parents.

Ollie smiled. "He does stride about quite confidently, *molto bello*." He caught Matt's eye. "*Il est l'homme le plus magnifique de tous les temps.*"

Matt returned his gaze, not knowing what Ollie said, but understanding the tone.

Ollie met his father's eye with a light blush.

"You weren't kidding about the French." Naomi pointed her fork at Matt with a smile.

Matt flicked his eyebrows up at her.

"I agree with you wholeheartedly, Ollie," Finn added with a grin.

Ollie wiped the counters down as the dishwasher hummed quietly and stopped to sip his wine, startling slightly when he felt Matt come up behind him. Matt wrapped both arms around Ollie's middle and rested his chin on Ollie's shoulder as he squeezed.

"I love you so much," Matt whispered in Ollie's ear and pressed himself lightly against him, the front of his thighs molding perfectly to the back of Ollie's.

Ollie closed his eyes, goosebumps covering his skin from Matt's voice and breath against his neck. "I love you too," Ollie breathed, thrilled and shocked that Matt was holding him in front of everyone sitting in the living room.

Ollie caught Antonia's eye briefly before she looked over his shoulder at Matt with a soft smile. He felt Matt's lips on his temple before he pulled away with one last squeeze of his waist.

"I've got some work. I'll see you upstairs," Matt said softly before turning down the hall to his office.

David yawned as he closed the bedroom door behind him, following Maggie into the large beautifully decorated suite. He lifted their suitcases onto the matching wood luggage stands on either side of the low dresser, and changed for bed, lost in thought.

"Well, do you see now you were worried for nothing," Maggie said as she emerged from the bathroom dressed in her summer pajamas. "Ollie and Matt are very much in love."

David nodded with a small smile. "Yes, Matt was uncharacteristically loving toward Ollie. I think that was the first time I'd actually ever seen him touch Oliver."

"Oh, stop it. They've hugged in front of us. You're so cynical about him," Maggie admonished. "What is it?"

"Those hugs are the same bro-hugs he gives me," David scoffed. "He shows more affection to Finn that he ever has to Ollie. He kisses her all the time, I mean, she lives next door, does he have to slobber all over her every time she shows up or leaves?"

Maggie laughed. "You're being ridiculous. He does no such thing, but of course he loves her. Ollie told me she's responsible for everything, his company, co-signing their townhouse, securing this beach house, as you know, and for introducing them. Obviously, he's grateful."

"I know. I guess it's not just that." David folded his clothes and put them in the chair under the window. "He's so flashy, and bossy, and American," he said derisively. "I miss Henry. I mean, Henry was kind, and fawned all over Ollie, and wasn't afraid to hold his hand in public," he added as he worried again for his son. "Do you think Matt makes Ollie walk on the other side of the road when they're alone?"

Maggie rolled her eyes. "You're absurd. I liked Henry too, but he was a little boring, and you remember how he just couldn't let Ollie go. Matt isn't flashy, he's confident, and he's head and shoulders above Henry. You said so yourself."

"That was *before* he broke Ollie's heart, and before I knew about that woman, Sam." Even saying her name was distasteful.

"They've put that past them, and so should you," Maggie said firmly. "There's something going on this weekend, so focus on that. Maybe they're getting married," Maggie said excitedly and bit her lip.

David scoffed a laugh. "No way. You're high if you believe that. No, it's more likely that it's Finn's birthday or something and he's hired elephants and skywriters and cannons that shoot glitter everywhere."

Maggie smacked David's shoulder with the back of her hand. "Stop it. They really could be. We were told to bring dress clothes, and it's a surprise, and Ollie said it was going to be a grand weekend."

David held her gaze as his mind whirred. "If that's so, and Cassie isn't here, then I'm going to be very angry, and I will say something."

Ollie scanned work emails in his office overlooking what would soon be the rose garden, before shutting down his computer and heading upstairs. He saw Matt cleaning the kitchen and unloading the dishwasher as he passed. He made quick work of stripping down to his briefs for bed and went to the bathroom to brush his teeth.

"Your parents liked the house?"

Ollie startled with a cry at Matt's silent appearance. "You sneaky bastard!" He grinned and rinsed his toothbrush as Matt kissed his naked shoulder. "They love the house, I mean of course. What's not to love?" he said and closed his eyes at the sensation of Matt's scruff on his sensitive skin. "Naomi has worked her magic yet again, and I think it's her best yet. I still can't believe this is the same house we toured last fall, and that it's ours," he added with emphasis.

Matt took Ollie's hand with a smile. "Tomorrow is a big day," he said quietly looking intently at Ollie.

Ollie's stomach began fluttering.

"But tonight is for us," Matt continued, his blue eyes dark and fathomless. "Put on something nice. Not tomorrow's suit, but something. And meet me on the beach in five minutes." He kissed Ollie gently.

Ollie searched his face for a moment and then nodded while his stomach flipped like a gymnast at the Olympics. He turned to the walk-in closet and went inside as he heard Matt take his bag and leave.

Ollie searched through his limited wardrobe and finally pulled on a pair of linen pants and a soft V-neck t-shirt that Matt bought him. He smoothed his hair in front of the large mirror opposite the bed then made his way to the deserted beach. There were no lights beyond their house and the air was still; only the sound of the waves kissing the shore could be heard. He saw Matt at the water line, illuminated by the soft moonlight. He stopped in his tracks, and stared.

"Christ, Lieutenant, what have you got on?" Ollie breathed and nearly stumbled from the weakness in his knees. *Christ, that was really a thing, and not some stupid romance trope.*

Matt's smile widened as he straightened from cuffing his pants, his summer-white Naval uniform glowing in the moonlight. "Cuff your pants, Ollie, and join me," he said as he stepped into the water.

Ollie hurriedly cuffed his pants below his knees and walked to Matt, his feet sinking in the wet sand, the cool water encircling his calves like hugs.

"My god, Lieutenant." Ollie gasped quietly. "You are positively magnificent in that uniform. You are keeping that on when we get back inside." Ollie grinned and smoothed his hands over Matt's chest.

Matt nodded and gripped Ollie's waist tightly, his fingers digging in his flesh. He focused on Ollie's lips before pulling him in for a brief but deep kiss.

"Tomorrow is for them, but tonight is for us, as I said." He searched Ollie's face. "I need to make this commitment to you in the water, where I am at peace.

"I love you." He looked down at the water swirling around their feet. "The pull and push we feel now, from the ocean, it's us. It's me, pushing away because I'm stubborn, and it's you pulling me back to us. And it's you pushing away from my nonsense, and me pulling you back into my arms." He saw Ollie's eyes shining in the moonlight. "Us. The way you love me, your patience with me, the way you get me. . . ." He swallowed. "I would die for you. I would kill for you. I would do anything you wanted me to. You have no idea the power you have over me, like the power of the moon over the oceans." He kissed Ollie softly.

Ollie shook his head, trying to clear the cobwebs of disbelief. "Seriously?" He blew out a breath and tried to collect his thoughts. "I would do anything for you. You have taught me things about life, about myself, that I never knew possible. It hasn't always been easy for us, or pleasant, or something others would understand, but I wouldn't trade it for the world. I was such a naïve little boy. You've opened my eyes and given me the world.

"You are a gift, who doesn't know how precious he is. How is it that you stride around so confident, so self-assured, and yet you don't truly see your own worth?" Ollie held Matt's gaze, his eyes shining. "I love you, more than life itself. I know this because, I wanted to die when you left me. And look at where we are now. You on the verge of admitting to our family and friends, *out loud*, that you love me." He smiled and shook his head in disbelief. "And we have a life together. A beautiful life together. Our home in Boston, our beach house, the opportunities that you have given me." He furrowed his brow. "I would have been a cog in a wheel in the UK."

Matt's eyes were dark. "And I would have driven myself into the ground by now."

Matt cupped Ollie's face in his hands and pressed his lips gently against Ollie's, teasing with his tongue. Matt carded his fingers through Ollie's hair as Ollie opened his mouth wider with a moan.

Oh, this man, he will be the death of you, his brain whispered.

"God, I love you, Ollie. You are one in a billion." Matt panted against Ollie's mouth, interrupting his intrusive thoughts.

Matt ran his hands down Ollie's body and around to the front, undoing the button and zipper of his pants. Ollie stopped him, shaking his head as he remembered where they were. He looked around.

"You are in your uniform, Lieutenant. Let's go inside."

Matt nodded against Ollie's neck. "After I get on my knees in the ocean for you," he whispered.

"Christ, Matt," Ollie exhaled and looked up at the moon as Matt knelt in the surf, taking him in his mouth, sending shivers down Ollie's legs and into his toes.

60

Cold Feet

FINN AND BILL arrived in time for a light lunch at Matt and Ollie's. Bill strode in with his unique confidence and looked around, hugging Matt tightly as he congratulated him on the house.

"This is spectacular, son." He patted Matt's bicep.

"Thank you, sir." Matt beamed. "Finn made this happen, like everything else that's wonderful in my life. I don't know what I'd do without her."

Bill smiled. "Me either. I look forward to the tour later. Let me say my hellos to your surprising guests," he said and walked away.

David took Bill's outstretched hand and held his shock. He met Maggie's equally confused gaze over Bill's shoulder as they hugged.

"Does he know?" David mouthed with a furrowed brow.

Maggie responded with a slight shrug as Bill greeted Antonia.

"Wasn't expecting to see you all here," Bill said, interrupting their silent exchange. He looked at Antonia. "Your daughters coming with their families as well?"

Antonia shook her head and glanced at Matt opening bottles of wine in the kitchen. "My daughters don't know about them."

Bill raised his eyebrows. "Ah," he said simply and looked at David and Maggie. "But you know, and Naomi?"

Maggie nodded.

"How do you know?" David puzzled.

Bill took a breath and looked between Matt and Ollie, who had appeared from the back of the house. "I caught them coming out of the closet at my house, literally, one New Year's."

Maggie and David exchanged a glance.

"Oh," Maggie said eventually.

Bill sighed awkwardly. "Well, are we drinking with lunch?" he asked no one in particular and caught Ollie's eye as he came forward hesitantly.

"Hi Bill," Ollie said, extending his hand. "Wonderful to see you again, sir."

"Nice to see you too, Ollie," Bill said with a smile. "You're a bit more tan than you were at the last board meeting."

"Yes, well, uh, so are you, you look good." He cleared his throat nervously. "Can I get you something to drink?"

"I see Matt opening wine. I'll have a glass of white. Thank you."

"Antonia?"

"I'll have red, please, dear." She smiled.

Maggie followed Ollie into the kitchen. "I'll help pour and serve."

"Thanks, Mum."

Ollie stood next to Matt, who stepped away with a look at Bill. Ollie made a small harrumph sound.

"Bill would like a glass of white," Ollie said and watched as his mother poured two glasses of red wine and left the kitchen. "Are we shouting our vows at each other later from a safe, hetero distance, Lieutenant?" He raised his eyebrows.

Matt glanced again at Bill before looking back at Ollie. "He's freaking me out. I shouldn't have invited him." He shook his head and poured the wine, his hand shaking ever so slightly.

Ollie put his hand on Matt's arm when he put the bottle down. "Bill loves you. He knows about us. He's here, in our house. He knows we're together. You can do this," Ollie said firmly. "I'm not asking for you to grope me, but I am asking that you don't jump away when I stand close to you around the people who know about us." He smiled at Matt. "I love you. I can't wait to say so in front of them out there later." He nodded to the deck beyond the slider.

Matt nodded slowly, a secret smile on his face. "You're right, Ollie. I love you," he whispered and picked up the glass of white.

"No, let me bring it to him. You bring me a pint," Ollie said, taking the glass from Matt's hand, brushing his fingers as he did so.

"Here you are, sir." Ollie delivered the glass to Bill with a smile, standing next to his father who was mid-conversation with Bill.

"Thank you." Bill took the glass and raised it slightly before taking a large sip.

Matt appeared at his side with two pint glasses and handed one to Ollie. He clinked the glass around the circle of parents.

"Cheers," he said smoothly.

Ollie noticed Matt's right eyelid jumping ever so slightly. He wanted to run his hand down Matt's back soothingly, but knew if he did, both eyelids would jump, so he refrained.

"Your father was telling me you two play tennis and squash." Bill said to Ollie.

"Yes, I played varsity all through secondary and bit at Oxford, but haven't played either one here, so I'm quite rusty."

Bill smiled broadly. "I played varsity too, and belong to several tennis clubs, including the Tennis and Racquet Club in Boston not far from you two." He glanced between Matt and Ollie. "I'm always looking for new partners. You bring your racquets across the pond?"

Ollie smiled as his heart leapt at finding a bond with Bill, someone who Matt held in such high esteem that he had been willing to throw away his own happiness for fear of Bill's negative judgement.

"I did, and I would be honored to play with you, and thrilled for the opportunity. I miss it."

"Fantastic," Bill nodded. "I'll email you when I close up the house in Nantucket. We'll schedule a match."

"Can't wait." Ollie clinked his glass to Bill's and glanced at his parents with a smile. "Where did you grow up and play your varsity tennis and squash?"

Bill sipped his wine. "In Beverly, it's a town on the north of Boston if you don't know," he added for David and Maggie's sake, "in a house on the ocean. My brother owns the house now, but that's neither here nor there." Bill smiled. "I went to Exeter. It's a private school in New Hampshire, and then I went to Yale."

"Impressive. Yale is quite acclaimed, for a new school that is," David teased.

Bill laughed. "Yes, I suppose compared to Oxford everything is new. Our oldest university is what, six hundred years younger, and Yale is a hundred years younger than that, but who's counting?" David chuckled and raised his glass. "Did you go to Oxford like Ollie here?" Bill asked David.

"I did, as did my older brother, my father, my grandfather, et cetera, et cetera," David nodded.

"What about Eton?" Bill asked, watching Finn carrying plates of sandwiches out to the deck.

"Went there too, as did my brother, my father, my grandfather, et cetera." He laughed.

Bill looked at Ollie. "Did you go to Eton?"

Ollie shrugged. "Of course."

Bill swept his eyes over Ollie speculatively. "Play polo?"

"Yes," Ollie replied and looked at Matt, just in time to catch the most peculiar expression cross his features before disappearing.

"What position?" Bill asked offhandedly but seemingly holding his breath.

"Usually three, sometimes one," Ollie answered quietly, shifting his eyes to Matt.

"Wow. I was going to ask if you were any good, but if you played three then. . . ." He raised his eyebrows impressed.

"Ollie was phenomenal," David said with pride. "He gave it up though, for football."

Ollie blushed under the scrutiny, wary of Matt's strange reaction. "It's a lot of work and expense, keeping polo ponies. All I need for football are boots and shin guards." He looked at Bill. "Did you play?"

"I did. I started as number one, but switched to two before college, because I was good at covering the other team's three," he said with a grin. "I played at the North Shore Polo Club, and then for Yale." He looked at his glass of wine. "I played a little after I got married, but then turned my attention to racquet sports and cars. I haven't played in a few years, but I have a couple of polo ponies that a player at the club in Dover rides. We should play. I still ride when I can, but haven't held a mallet in a few years." Bill grinned.

Ollie looked at David who had his brows raised encouragingly. "Sure, I'd give it a shot. I'd have to ride for a bit first. We'll just tack it onto our growing list of activities." He chuckled. "I hope I still have time for work."

"Sounds like a plan, Ollie. I'll talk to your boss and make sure you get the time off." Bill looked at Matt and winked.

Matt made a gesture as if to say, 'by all means.'

"Let's eat," Finn called, drawing their attention as she finished setting out the sandwiches.

After lunch, during which Bill and David discussed golf, Matt gave Bill the tour of the house, skipping his and Ollie's room, and ending back out on the empty deck.

"So, why are we really here, Matt?" Bill asked, turning to face him.

Matt shrugged and looked out at the ocean; his stomach suddenly unsettled. "Can't we just want to have our family together?"

Matt squirmed slightly under Bill's scrutiny and shifted his gaze. His eyes paused on Ollie laughing with Finn and Naomi inside the house and his nerves intensified.

"You two getting married?" Bill asked quietly.

Matt turned his head sharply. "No!" Matt shook his head. "Bill, no, *never*," he scoffed.

Bill held his hands up. "There's nothing wrong with that. As I told you last year, I just want you to be happy, and the more time I spend with Ollie, the more I like him. He seems like a fairly remarkable young man. Quite the athlete," Bill said with an impressed chuckle, smiling as Matt relaxed. "And he reminds me of Finn in many ways. Very engaging, intelligent."

"I can't tell you how happy it makes me to hear your approval," Matt said quietly. "You, of all people, Bill, I care the most about what you think of me. I would sooner die than disappoint you."

"I am so proud of you, son," Bill said earnestly. "You have done great things, overcome so much, and are destined for even greater things."

Bill pulled Matt into a brief hug.

Matt sighed with relief. "Thank you. I owe so much of it to you, sir."

Finn, Naomi, and Bill left for Finn's house with the promise they'd be back for cocktails before dinner while Ollie and his mother and Antonia left for the farmer's market to get eggs and things for brunch in the morning.

David grabbed a book and parked himself on the large sectional on the deck. He'd just finished a chapter when he heard the slider open and looked up to see Matt in swim trunks with a pair of swim goggles on his head. He scanned his eyes down Matt's body, stopping briefly on the scar just above the waist band of his trunks.

"I'm going for a quick swim, I'll be back."

"That's a big a scar for an appendix."

Matt looked down. "I was shot. In the Middle East." He pulled his swimsuit up over the scar.

"Whoa." David felt his eyes widen. "I take it the bullet missed your appendix or you wouldn't be standing here."

"I had it out when I was seven."

"Well, that's lucky, I guess. Hit anything else?"

"Nah, I got lucky as you say." He gave David a wry grin. "But if I were really lucky, I wouldn't have gotten shot in the first place."

Matt left the deck with a nod and headed to the water.

David watched him pensively. He couldn't imagine going to war, never mind surviving a gunshot. Perhaps he'd been judging Matt too harshly after all.

Matt dropped his towel near the dune grass and bushes, lowered his goggles, and waded into the water, diving in once it was over his knees. He swam out a ways, and then followed the shoreline, doing a medium-paced crawl, quickly losing himself in the repetition. His mother was right: he loved being in the water, particularly the ocean. He felt alive and strangely soothed, as though it were a large womb and nothing bad could ever happen to him when he was immersed in it.

He was one of those people who always encountered ocean life and had discovered, when he was young, that not only was he always followed by fish and other marine life, but he could actually catch fish with his hands. A trick he used to impress many a friend, his SEAL teammates, and his father.

My father.

Matt didn't know why he popped into his head, and he wished he hadn't. He definitely wouldn't be wishing his father was looking down from heaven later on tonight, like everyone always says about their deceased loved ones at times like these. Dominic Diontangelo would most assuredly *not* want to see his only son commit himself to a man. He had made his thoughts on gay people, gay men in particular, very clear. It wasn't until Matt was ten that he began to pay attention to his father's disdain.

"Elton John is such a fag. Why would they let him perform at her funeral? Of all people."

Matt's father loved Princess Diana and was watching her funeral before work while Antonia was pinning the hem of Matt's new school pants as he stood on a stepstool.

"Dominic. Watch your language," his mother scolded in Italian.

"What? It's the truth." He shrugged with a scowl.

Matt looked between his parents as his father muted the TV. "What's a fag?"

"Something you don't never wanna be," Dominic said firmly, his eyes flashing.

Matt stared at the TV wondering. He made up his mind to never play the piano and sing, because that seemed to be this Elton John's crime.

A year later on the way home from school he found out what the word meant when Billy Wagner was harassing John Lyons on the way home from school, calling him a fag as the three of them followed John from the bus stop.

"I am not!" John yelled over his shoulder.

Matt looked at John who he'd known since kindergarten and then at Billy. "He doesn't play the piano."

Billy gave him a strange look and turned his attention back to John. "Are too. Peter and Dylan said you looked at their dicks at the urinal. That's a pretty faggy thing to do. You want to suck their dicks, don't you?"

Matt frowned trying to understand what Billy was saying. John turned down his street, and Billy kept harassing him, until he disappeared from view as they kept walking.

"What's a fag?"

Billy looked at him. "You don't know?"

"No, you idiot, why else would I ask?" Matt had straightened, towering over Billy who teased people because he was shorter than everyone else in the grade.

"It's a guy who likes to suck dick. A homo," Billy shrugged, cowed by Matt.

"Oh, gross," Matt replied, and meant it at the time.

Matt lifted his head and looked at the shoreline and then at his watch. He somersaulted under the water and swam back toward the house two miles away, noticing the fish that scattered from his wake when he turned.

He saw Ollie scanning the waves from the beach as he approached, and felt guilty for making him worry. He kicked his legs powerfully to cause a splash and saw Ollie sag with relief and begin walking toward him along the shore carrying his towel.

"Jesus Christ, Lieutenant! My dad said you went for a quick swim and it's been over two hours," he chastised with a shake of his head.

"Ollie, you should never worry about me in the water," he said with a smile, lifting his goggles, and took the towel from Ollie's hand, looking both ways down the beach before kissing him briefly.

"Of course I worry. There are sharks, and currents, and boats, and you've never been gone that long before. I would die if anything happened to you," Ollie said, looking him over and keeping up easily with Matt's long stride.

"You're all pruny, and I hope your goggle marks go away in time for the ceremony or I'm not going to want any pictures with you," Ollie added.

Matt poked Ollie's tickle spot, causing Ollie to shriek and step away. "Now I'm definitely wearing them for the ceremony." Matt flashed a smile and continued walking to the house as Ollie's laughter followed him.

"The clambake caterers are going to be here in about thirty minutes," Ollie said as they approached the house.

Matt's nerves began percolating as he nodded a distracted 'hello' to David.

"You certainly had Ollie in a panic," David remarked with a smile as they passed.

"I know." Matt continued around the deck to the outdoor shower on the side of the house, Ollie following him.

Matt stopped at the wooden door and looked at Ollie. "What are you doing?" he asked incredulously.

"I thought I'd watch." He gave a light shrug, a twinkle of mischief in his eye.

Matt shook his head and gestured with his thumb. "Scram."

Ollie hesitated. "Okay." He turned and left, wondering at Matt's sudden mood.

Ollie walked past his father into the house. No one was in the living area and Ollie figured his mother and Antonia were off taking naps. He climbed the stairs wanting a nap himself after the exhaustion of the day, but there was no time. He closed the bedroom door behind him and looked around the large sunny room. The bed was made, the covers so taut you could bounce a quarter on them, and the closet and bathroom doors were shut. Matt never liked anything left open or messy, even Ollie's side table was tidy though he knew he left a pile of papers and books on it.

Ollie crossed to the closet and opened the door to retrieve his blue and white seersucker suit. He hung it on the back of the closet door and stood back to admire it with a sigh before stripping off his clothes for a quick shower. He was tucking his bunched-up towel on the rack as Matt appeared to hang his own towel.

Matt straightened Ollie's towel by habit, and scanned his eyes over Ollie's naked body, as Ollie did the same to him, before leaving the bathroom without a word.

Ollie followed him out, his eyes locked on Matt's muscular ass. A beautiful ass highlighted by the tan lines his short swim trunks left.

"You are so gorgeous. I could never get sick of looking at you," Ollie said, watching Matt pull on his underwear. "Everything alright, Lieutenant?" Ollie puzzled at Matt's broody silence.

"You never told me you played polo. And I asked you."

"It didn't seem like a serious question. In fact, it felt more like you were mocking me, and not in a nice way," Ollie replied with a scowl. "Besides, I thought you *Googled* me." Ollie emphasized the word.

"I was only looking at social media. It wasn't a background check."

"Sorry, though I'm not sure why I'm apologizing. I played polo," he said as if he were announcing it, and watched Matt walk into the closet. "Somehow I feel as though that's not what this is about."

"This what?" Matt asked as he hung his white linen suit in front of Ollie's.

"Your strange attitude and behavior. Are you having second thoughts?" Ollie asked quietly as Matt paused. His heart sank and he swallowed roughly. "Because if so, that's fine. No one knows, except for Chuck and Naomi, and we can cancel the ceremony. It's not really a ceremony anyway, I don't know why I keep calling it that." He shook his head, feeling awkward. "We can just say we wanted to get everyone together for a clambake at your new house," Ollie said in a calm voice, keeping his emotions in careful check. "The girls would understand."

Matt turned to face Ollie. "I swim, I run, I play basketball. I did all those things as a kid because they require little to no equipment. You saw where I grew up. I guess I liked it better when I thought we weren't so far apart."

"Oh my god. That's what this is about?" Ollie stepped forward. "Matt, don't be ridiculous. We aren't far apart at all, and I don't care about any of that. I love you." He put his arms around Matt's neck. "Besides, you have everything now. You can do whatever you want."

"But I'd never be as good as someone who's done it their whole life," Matt said, his eyes guarded.

"Who cares?" Ollie scoffed with a smile.

"I care." Matt pulled out of Ollie's arms.

"Well, that tells me that your belief is wrong. Matt, you're a born athlete, you could pick up any sport and master it in half the time as anyone else by gift and sheer will."

Matt made a disgruntled sound and walked away.

"Stop running from me!" Ollie barked.

Matt whirled around with a surprised scowl.

"I'm not sure where any of this is coming from, but I'm guessing it has to do with Bill. And maybe you're just picking a fight because you're still worried about him. Matt, you know I love you with all my heart, and I care fuck-all for where you grew up or how much money you had or didn't have. I don't care how much money you have now. That's not why I fell in love with you."

Ollie took Matt's hand. "I fell in love with you because you have an inner strength and drive that I find intoxicating, and you are so smart, and loving, and you're fucking beautiful," Ollie added with a small laugh. "Not to mention that you love me, in a way I have *never* been loved before or ever will be again." He held Matt's gaze. "Now, if you're having doubts, that's normal. I don't want to do this tonight though if so. There is no rush. I don't want it to happen if you're not one hundred percent. Because even though it's not official to the world, it is to me."

He lowered his gaze to Matt's mouth as it descended on his. Matt let go of Ollie's hand and buried his fingers in Ollie's hair, deepening the kiss, filling Ollie's mouth perfectly with his tongue, kissing him as though his life depended on it. Ollie matched him breath for breath, running his hands up Matt's naked back and digging in with his hungry fingers.

Matt pulled his head back and stared into Ollie's eyes, his pupils so dilated his eyes looked black.

"I love you, and there's no canceling tonight. I guess I was just suffering from a momentary lapse of reason." He sighed. "I really wish I could love every inch of your glorious body right now, but the catering trucks are rumbling into the driveway as we speak, and we need to get dressed." He kissed him again. "I'll fuck you silly later."

"I can't wait to savor every minute of the rest of the day. I love you, you fool." Ollie grinned and turned to his suit on the door.

61

Committed

OLLIE TOOK HIS TIME with his hair, blowing it smooth again because of the humidity, wanting it to be perfect and not poofy, though Matt liked it au natural. He watched the caterers through the windows taking over the dining side of the deck and the sandy spot just beyond and wondered briefly where he and Matt were to exchange their commitment vows.

Matt was talking to Bill in the living room when Ollie finally made his way downstairs. Bill was dressed in a tan linen suit, a white button-down open at the throat underneath, and looked every inch the well-bred man he was. The kind of man who aged like a fine wine, growing more handsome ever year.

Ollie felt a pang of sadness, thinking about Finn's mother. He and Matt had only been together a short time compared to Bill and Diana, and yet the fear Ollie had felt earlier when he couldn't find Matt had been crippling. He blew out a breath and stopped when he heard his mother's voice from hallway.

"Ollie, you look marvelous!" Maggie cried. "I adore seersucker."

"Mum. You look stunning," Ollie said emphatically, admiring the brown and white polka dot dress she was wearing that made her look like an older, blonde version of Julia Roberts from *Pretty Woman*. Ollie kissed her cheek. "Very flirty and beachy."

He smiled and met his father's eye as he took the pint David was handing him.

"You're looking quite dapper, Dad. That suit reminds me of Lyon. You two are a handsome couple." Ollie winked at his mother.

David clinked his glass to Ollie's and glanced at Matt. "So are you two," he countered with a grin and a nod at Matt.

Ollie blushed lightly. "Thank you." He looked over his shoulder at the bustling workers outside. "We're so glad you guys could come to our housewarming, and it really was long past time for you to meet Matt's mum. She's so wonderful, right?"

"Oh, she's lovely, and she had the most complimentary things to say about you."

Ollie blushed lightly, so happy to have won Antonia's heart. He glanced at Matt and led his parents out to the deck to enjoy the evening. A light breeze was coming off the water and the sky was a stunning deep blue as the sun began her journey to bed. Antonia came out to join them, dressed in a simple, mint green, but high quality, linen dress, and colorfully patterned light jacket, her short hair styled in waves. She had on emerald jewelry that was understated but clearly high-quality and Ollie flicked another glance at Matt through the glass.

"Antonia, you look beautiful," Ollie stated with a broad smile and kissed her cheek.

"*Grazie*," she replied, squeezing his shoulder. She sat on the sectional next to him with her glass of wine and looked at David and Maggie. "He's such a charmer." She nodded her head at Ollie.

"He gets that from his father," Maggie said with a coy smile at David, as Matt and Bill came out the slider at the same time Finn and Naomi came up the beach, dressed in matching maxi dresses, Finn's a deep blue and Naomi's the color of the Mediterranean Sea.

They look like bridesmaids, Ollie thought.

But they're not, his brain replied curtly.

Ollie slammed the door on his inner dialogue and focused on Matt as he towered over the sectional in front of him. Matt gestured with his head at Antonia for her to move over and sat down with his thigh pressed against Ollie's. Ollie's stomach fluttered happily when he felt Matt's thumb caress the back of his neck as Matt slid his arm across the back of the couch behind him.

The scent of sandalwood, and beach, and ocean, enveloped him as the heat from Matt's armpit warmed him. It took all of Ollie's willpower to not tuck himself into that spot, his spot, the safe, possessive spot that he never wanted to leave. His fingers itched to span themselves across Matt's impossibly hard stomach, and then dip below his belt.

Ollie turned his attention to the caterers who were pouring wine and serving tiny appetizers on trays until it was time for them to move to the long dining table that Naomi had custom made. There were string lights on the open umbrellas and votive candles on the table around the blue and white hydrangea arrangements. The ambiance couldn't have been more perfect, and Ollie took a breath, listening to his heart sing so loud he couldn't hear his brain.

Matt held court from his spot on the end, Ollie to his right (as always) and smiled over their guests as they feasted on clam chowder, lobster, chicken, potatoes, and corn. He sat back in his chair and looked at Ollie whose blonde hair caught the candlelight as the sky turned into a gorgeous kaleidoscope of colors. He wished he could take Ollie's hand and kiss each fingertip but the caterers were hovering.

The sun was setting but extending her reach across the ocean toward the house, all pink and golden melding with blue and purple. Over the house the sky was a deep, brilliant blue and the moon was visible, not quite full, and not yet bright, because the sun wasn't done showing off. Matt turned his gaze back to the table and found Ollie looking at him. He smiled and straightened in his chair, turning his attention to the table.

"We're having dessert at Chuck's. If you will all follow me." Matt stood.

The sound of chairs pushing back from the table and light chatter filled the air.

"Ollie, you stay and be sure the caterers get out okay. Give them this." He pulled an envelope out of his inside suit coat pocket. "When they're gone, take off your shoes and come up the beach." He squeezed Ollie's hand briefly.

"Okay." Ollie hesitated at the change of plans.

Ollie watched everyone leave through the house, headed for the lighted path Matt had landscapers cut into the tree line off the driveway. The caterers packed the dirty dishes and all their equipment quickly and efficiently into the small truck parked on the grass next to the house. He gave the chef the envelope and took his shoes and socks off on the deck as the truck pulled away.

He headed down the beach, the sky still light, though now mostly blue and purple as the sun had all but disappeared into the horizon. The moon was bright, and becoming brighter with every step Ollie took, it seemed. He stopped at the gap in the bushes and dune grass in front of Finn's house and stared in shock before turning and walking up the wooden boardwalk. There was an eight-by-ten-foot pergola over the sand in front of Finn's deck.

String lights twinkled in the growing darkness among the fresh flowers and vines wrapped around the temporary structure. Ollie's feet sank into the soft sand as he stepped off the end of the walkway and approached Matt who was flanked on either side by Finn and Naomi.

"You little schemer," he said with a small smile. Matt grinned his knee-buckling grin and winked. Ollie looked at Naomi. "I take it you had a hand in this?"

Naomi nodded with a broad smile.

Ollie looked at his parents on the deck with Bill and Antonia and returned their happy smiles, lost in the moment. He then turned his gaze to Matt, whose eyes were flitting between the moon and the unnaturally still bay.

"I'm so glad you all could be here today with us." Matt snapped out of his stupor to look at the faces watching them. "I'm so grateful that you all understand just how much I value my privacy, our privacy." He looked at Ollie. "As I said a moment ago, it's not a wedding, but it means just as much to me, to us.

"I think you all know how hard this is for me." Matt glanced at his mother and briefly at Bill. "It's one of the hardest things I've ever done, and I've served countless tours overseas. I've been *shot*," Matt added dramatically. "But, it's important to me, and more importantly, to Ollie, that we do this in front of you, our insular and exclusive pod of people who know about us." He turned and faced Ollie who was watching him with a smile. "Oliver, I'll let you start, while I work up the courage to say my part." He winked.

Ollie glanced nervously at his parents, and then back at Matt. "The happiest day of my life was the day I met you, Matthew. And I thank god, and Finn," he glanced at her standing to Matt's left with a smile, "every day for bringing you to me. Never in a thousand years could I ever have imagined being with someone like you, someone so perfect for me. Christ, an *American*." He held Matt's gaze with shining eyes. "It hasn't always been easy, but nothing worth having ever is.

"It was a leap of faith for me to move here, to be with you, to work with you. I recognize that you've given me everything, and more than I could ever have wanted or dreamed of for myself. The love you have given me, the world you have shared with me, know no equal. You hold my heart and my soul in your hands. I plan on spending the rest of my life making you as happy as you make me." He grinned softly. "Your turn."

He felt Naomi's hand on his elbow and looked questioningly at her. She handed him a necklace with a small pendant.

"For Matt," she whispered.

He took it from her and looked at what Matt had added. It was a silver, dime-sized replica of the moon, complete with laser etchings of the craters and shadows. Ollie gasped lightly and looked up at Matt who was staring at him with soft eyes. Ollie undid the clasp and put it around Matt's neck, their bodies nearly touching.

"I love it," Ollie whispered. "I love you." He touched the moon that hung just below the hollow of Matt's throat and stepped back.

Matt exhaled quietly and took Ollie's hand, brushing his thumb over Ollie's knuckles. "For so long, I was living a lie. I told myself I was happy, but I was just going through the motions of life. I had a huge hole in my heart. It felt like I didn't even have a heart. And then Chuck introduced me to you. Perfect, beautiful you. And it was like someone woke me up from a terrible dream, and I could breathe again. Move again. Feel again." Matt watched as Ollie's eyes began to fill. "And then, because of my crushing stupidity, my misguided self-importance, my *cowardice*, I nearly lost you." He shook his head and squeezed Ollie's hand lightly. "It was then that I realized the hole in my heart was Ollie-sized and Ollie-shaped, and the only way that I could ever live or be happy, was to beg you to take me back. Which you did, you fool." He smiled. "Now you're stuck with me.

"I plan on spending the rest of my life making you as happy as you make me."

He turned slightly, letting go of Ollie's hand to take Ollie's necklace from Finn. There was a tiny trident top, a perfect replica of Matt's tattoo, hanging from the longer middle tine. He clasped the necklace behind Ollie's neck and smoothed the small pendant at the base of his throat before wiping the tear that spilled down Ollie's cheek with his thumb. He held Ollie's jaw gently between his thumb and forefinger and tilted his face up.

"I love you, Oliver David Turner," Matt said huskily.

"And I love you, Matthew Dominic Dion," Ollie whispered.

Matt leaned forward and brushed a chaste kiss across Ollie's lips and held his gaze. He turned to their guests. "Now let's have some champagne!"

ACKNOWLEDGMENTS

First and foremost, thank you to Julie Gallagher, a woman who wears many hats, and is responsible for my book design and production. I couldn't have published my debut novel or any of my books without her expert guidance and patience.

Thanks to Kim Bertrand, who was one of the first people to read this book back when it was nearly complete shite. *Appearances* was only the second book I had ever written, and as such has gone through many, many edits. I hope this final version is one you will all love.

Thanks to my dear friend John Stella, who as I have mentioned before has read everything I've written and still likes me. He gave me great feedback and helped with some of the more intimate details of Matt and Ollie's relationship. We have some of the best lunch dates, and probably should start a podcast with our discussions.

Thanks to Bob Barlow, who read a VERY early excerpt and didn't mince words when it came to his hatred of Matt, and his disdain for Ollie for putting up with him. When I asked why he didn't like Matt, Bob said, "first of all, he answered the door barefoot." (I didn't get a second of all). Then he said Ollie was stunted and problematic. Which, he was at first. So, thank you Bob for helping me give Ollie a backbone.

Thank you to Hally, my silver sister, who let me read this to her while she cleaned her house, recovered from neck surgery, and on long walks during COVID. She knows how much Matt & Ollie mean to me, and may love them both as much as I do. She asks about them as though they're real (spoiler alert: in my head they are) so, thank you for indulging me, babe!

Thank you to Duney Roberts, my former work-husband, now gym buddy, and part-time marketing consultant, who went through this book with a fine-tooth comb and gave me many comments to laugh over. His insight and edits helped focus my narrative on many things, including not naming real places, advising against using real products, and begging me to 'free the bush!'

Thanks to my fabulous interns, Pilar Gomes, Grant Riley, and Molly Brooks, for their hard work on marketing and handling my social media. I wish I could keep you forever.

Thanks to my BookTok friends/influencers, Angharad Davies, and Bernice, who have given me nothing but support and incredible amplification on TikTok. I don't know how I got so lucky as to have you respond to my DMs but thank you!!

Thank you to Kevin Groppe. A man I am so pleased to call friend. He was my English teacher in high school, and such a great influence that I took every class he taught—even the ones I wasn't so interested in. He read this, and book 2 (that will be coming soon!), and said, "I love how much you love these characters." (God, I love that soft critique so much). And then said, "these books are looong." I cut A LOT because of Kevin (he was right of course), and will make those scenes available to anyone who wants more of Matt & Ollie—sign up for my newsletter and bonus content on my website (www.thforestauthor.com).

Thank you to Kristin Brothers, who has not only been a dedicated friend for almost two decades, but who has also taken it upon herself to pimp me and my books out wherever she goes. We bonded one night in the early 2000s over a discussion about Brazilian waxes, and I've been hooked ever since. (You know I'm a slut for people with no filter). I am so grateful for your friendship!

Thanks to Miranda Simon, who listened to, and read this book as it evolved and helped with Matt's character development. Her insight as a social worker who specializes in trauma was invaluable.

And finally, thank you to my husband, the saint. He listened to Matt & Ollie first (before Robby and his men, and before Kelly and his loves), and never had anything but encouragement for me, despite not being a purveyor of MM romance. He also indulges me when I point out where Matt and Ollie live, the things Matt does or says, and when I cook meals for him that Ollie makes for Matt as though Ollie himself sent me the recipes. Every time my hub counts out his push-ups, I'm quick to say, "Matt does a hundred of those, and then a hundred more...."

PLAYLIST *

Don't Get me Wrong – The Pretenders

Heaven's Only Wishful (Extended Version) – MorMor

We Found Love – Rihanna & Calvin Harris

It's No Good – Depeche Mode

She's Not Me – Madonna

Flesh for Fantasy – Billy Idol

One Step Forward Three Steps Back – Olivia Rodrigo

Dreaming (Feat. Bruno Major) – SG Lewis

Paper & Glue – Vandelux

Bite – Troye Sivan

Only Fools – Troye Sivan

Master & Servant – Depeche Mode

Wait For Me – Kings of Leon

Shake the Disease – Depeche Mode

Animals – Maroon 5

Just Can't Get Enough – Depeche Mode

All My Love – Elderbrook

Should I Stay or Should I Go? – The Clash

The Scientist – Coldplay

I Miss You – Blink 182

Crush – Cigarettes After Sex

Assassin – Sultan + Shepard

Walking on a Dream – Empire of the Sun

Trustfall – P!nk

Running up That Hill – Kate Bush

Thank You – Dido

When the Party's Over – Billie Eilish

Erotica – Madonna

Last Christmas – Wham!

Evergreen (You Didn't Deserve Me at All) – Omar Apollo

Wild World – Cat Stevens

Walls – Kings of Leon

Another Love (Zwette Edit) – Tom Odell

No One Dies From Love – Tove Lo

Somebody Else – The 1975

Demolition Man – The Police

Wild – Troye Sivan

You – Troye Sivan

Smooth Operator – Sade

Be Real – Rasmus Faber & Metaxas

Wildest Dreams (Taylor's Version) – Taylor Swift

What is and What Should Never Be – Led Zeppelin

When Am I Gonna Lose You – Local Natives

This is the Last Time – The National

Munich – Editors

Wrecking Ball – Miley Cyrus

Pomp & Circumstance – Edward Elger

Shipping up to Boston – Dropkick Murphys

Secrets – Regard

Take a Bow – Madonna

About Today – The National

Hate That I Love You – Rihanna & Ne-Yo

Don't You Worry Child – Swedish House Mafia

Naama (Feat. Nathan Nicholson) – Sultan + Shepard

Papercut – Troye Sivan

Love Like That (Feat. Dani Poppitt) – Kaskade

Fire and Rain – James Taylor

A Sorta Fairytale – Tori Amos

Somebody That I Used to Know – Goyte

You and Me – Shallou

Run Away (Extended Mix) – Ben Böhmer & Tinlicker

What a Heavenly Way to Die – Troye Sivan

*Link available on my Website